D0502653

Jerusalem Beach

Jerusalem Beach

Stories

Iddo Gefen

TRANSLATED BY DANIELLA ZAMIR

ASTRA HOUSE | NEW YORK

Originally published in the Hebrew language as
Chof HaYam Shel Yerushalayim by Iddo Gefen.

Astra House
A Division of Astra Publishing House
astrahouse.com
Printed in the United States of America

Publisher's Cataloging-in-Publication Data
Names: Gefen, Iddo, author. | Zamir, Daniella, translator.
Title: Jerusalem Beach : stories / Iddo Gefen; translated by Daniella Zamir.
Description: New York, NY: Astra House, 2021.
Identifiers: LCCN: 2021909404 | ISBN: 978-1-6626-0043-2 (hardcover) |
978-1-6626-0044-9 (ebook)
Subjects: LCSH Israel—Fiction. | Jews—Fiction. | Short stories. |
BISAC FICTION / Short Stories (single author) |
FICTION / World Literature / Middle East / Israel | FICTION / Jewish
Classification: LCC PJ5054.G44 J47 2021 | DDC 892.437—dc23

First edition

10 9 8 7 6 5 4 3 2 1

Design by Richard Oriolo
The text is set in Fairfield LTD.
The titles are set in Concept Sans Bold.

To my parents

Contents

Jerusalem Beach

The Geriatric Platoon

1.

GRANDPA ENLISTED IN the Golani infantry brigade at the age of eighty. This was six months ago, a little after Grandma Miriam had suffered a stroke in the shower and died on the spot. A month and a half later, he packed a bag, stuffing it with four undershirts, five pairs of underwear, a flashlight, two cans of sardines, a biography of Moshe Sharett, and anti-chafing cream. He also added a sweater. Not because he thought he might be cold, but because he continued to fear the woman he had loved even after she had passed away. Then he canceled his subscription to the Lev Cinema, paid his debt to the butcher and called Frankel to tell him he was quitting the Friday morning gang, and they should invite Yoske Cohen to take his place.

Dad thought Grandpa had lost his marbles, told him that's not how normal people cope. "Go on a cruise to the Caribbean or something," he grumbled at him the night before the draft. "You don't have to help death along."

Grandpa said it was the other way 'round, that he was trying to outrun death, but Dad wouldn't listen. He took a black notebook and pen out of his pocket, and started jotting down numbers. "Eighty-year-old soldier. One thousand ninety-five days in the military. A monthly salary of 893 shekels." Then he mumbled to himself a series of convoluted formulas only he understood. Dad had worked his whole life as a life insurance actuary, or as he once explained to me, "someone who determines how much a person's life is worth." It wasn't merely a profession to him. It was a worldview, almost a religion. Every component of his life was configured into charts and numbers. Alma always joked that he probably had an equation that determined the value of their love.

Dad finished scribbling in his illegible handwriting and looked at Grandpa. "According to the average life span, your hereditary background and health, you have another four years to live, maybe a little less," he determined with stifling indifference. "Wasting those years cleaning toilets and on guard duty is simply flawed logic, there's no other way to put it."

Grandpa didn't have the tools to counter his son's complex formulas. He owned a grocery store, and even then Grandma Miriam was the one who handled the money. He tried explaining that many his age were reenlisting, that the situation down south was more precarious than ever, that someone had to defend this country instead of all those deadbeat dodgers crowding the cafés in Tel Aviv. He also said we had absolutely nothing to worry about. That he'd go to general boot camp like Yehuda from the doctor's office and then pursue a desk job at the army headquarters.

"The paycheck isn't too great, but even a few shekels is something. That way I can also help you out, Yermi," Grandpa said, and immediately realized he'd gone too far.

"Obviously it's just a suggestion," he said, shifting into damage control. "You don't have to . . ."

"I won't take a single shekel from you," Dad declared, shutting down any further discussion of the debts. "If Mom were alive, you wouldn't dare enlist."

"True," Grandpa admitted. "But she isn't."

Dad left the room, and Grandpa went back to packing his bag. He tried zipping it up, but his hands were trembling and the bag fell off the bed, photos of Grandma Miriam scattering across the floor. I helped him put everything back into the bag only to see him empty it out onto the bed again a moment later.

He wouldn't stop saying something was missing, but he didn't know what.

2.

alman1964@gmail.com
July 16, 2009, 04:45:02
Subject: Hi Yuli
How are you?
Get back to me when you read this.
Best,
Alma Rosenblum,
Emissary for the Jewish Agency for Israel in New Delhi

3.

THE FOLLOWING DAY, on the way to the Reception and Sorting Base, Grandpa and I listened to Kol Yisrael. The broadcaster was interviewing some guy who had hiked the Israel National Trail with nothing but a hundred shekels in his pocket and two pairs of socks.

"I should add that to my list," Grandpa said and cleared his throat.

"You know what I regret not having done?" he said when he realized I wasn't going to ask.

"What?" I asked reluctantly, and he started listing the items slowly in a monotonous voice:

Hiking the Israel National Trail.
Eating Mom's gefilte fish again.
Visiting the Arad Visitors' Center.
Finding the old grocery store's sign. Maybe in the Jaffa flea market.
Tracking down Tamar Weitzman, my first high school girlfriend who went to America and disappeared.
Smoking a Cuban cigar.
Telling Golda that on second thought, she wasn't to blame for the war.

He fell silent, waiting for my reaction, but I continued to look out at the road quietly. I wasn't in the mood to talk about the list again, which I already knew by heart, the list of all the things he never did and now never would do. Because my grandpa, ever since I could remember him, never stopped talking about the day he'd die. He let everyone know he'd be out of here in no time, and he also liked telling people exactly when and how it would happen, including a detailed arrangement of the eulogizers at his funeral. Grandma Miriam refused to listen. She always said that if he dared bring his death into their home, she'd kill him herself, either with a frying pan or a rolling pin, whichever was closer. So he kept quiet in her presence. But when I was a kid, whenever Grandpa took me to the movies on a Saturday morning, he would start up again. He said I was the only one he could trust, and I listened silently, letting him go on and on until I could recite by heart his last day on earth like I could the whole team of Hapoel Kfar Saba F.C., or entire dialogues from my favorite movie, *Giv'at Halfon*. Carrying the burden, keeping my grandpa alive.

4.

A CORPORAL WITH round-rimmed glasses stood at the entrance of the reception base. "You've got your call-up papers?" he asked me. With a trembling hand, barely able to see a thing with his bucket hat covering half his face, Grandpa handed him his draft notice before I could get a word out. The soldier considered the draft slip and turned his gaze back to Grandpa. "No shit. You da man!" He slapped Grandpa's shoulder. "It's thanks to dudes like you that the people of Israel are still kicking ass. Yochai, come see this," he yelled to a soldier next to him. "Another one joining the oldies. I'm telling you, these men are the real motherfuckers!"

Everyone around us started looking at Grandpa, who was awkwardly shrinking into himself. Then came a round of applause. I pulled him into the square inside the base and we sat down on a bench, waiting for his name to be called. I bought him a Diet Coke but he didn't want to drink. He looked a little lost, as if in some state of pretrauma. An elderly man who had arrived with what seemed like his entire extended family stood beside us. Grandpa looked at the man's children and grandchildren and wife, who was literally crying on his shoulder. I wanted him to stop looking at them, so I told him to check his bag to see that nothing was missing. He seemed happy that someone was giving him orders and promptly began rummaging through the bag, until finally he announced he had forgotten to pack a towel.

"Don't worry, cozy up to the CSM and he'll fix you up with a towel in no time."

Grandpa nodded and then asked: "What's a CSM?" I told him it was short for "company sergeant major," to which he replied they had just called them "sarge" when he served in the science corps sixty years ago. After a moment he added, "I haven't slept outside the house in years."

"You can still change your mind. Just say the word, and we'll drive back to Ramat Gan and have a falafel at the Georgian's."

He feigned a smile. Five minutes later, the name Zvi Neuerman flashed on the big electronic board. A soldier with a green beret appeared from within the crowd, picked up Grandpa's bag, and requested that he follow him. Grandpa put his hand on my shoulder, turned around, and started walking toward the bus. He didn't even say goodbye. He wasn't fond of goodbyes and didn't really know how to go about them. When the doctor at the hospital had told him to say a final goodbye to

Grandma Miriam, he stared at her for a few minutes and said he was just popping out for a moment to buy a pretzel. He didn't come back.

I followed him to the bus. He struggled up the stairs, lumbering slowly all the way to the back seat. I waved to him with both hands. He glanced at me, then quickly averted his gaze.

"They get old so fast, huh?" a woman standing next to me said. She had a high-pitched, slightly irritating voice, pretty curls, a blue dress, and black rubber boots.

"Totally," I answered.

"What's your excuse?" she asked. "Why did you make him enlist?"

"We didn't make him, he wanted to." On the bus, an elderly man sat by the window, obstructing my view of Grandpa.

"Why did he want to?"

"He said there were too many draft dodgers in Tel Aviv," I said, wishing she'd just go away.

"You're fucking with me," she replied.

"Excuse me?" I looked at her. She was smirking, satisfied that she'd finally managed to catch my attention.

"Old men don't sign up for the army because of draft dodgers in Tel Aviv." She fished a pack of gum out of her bag and offered me a piece.

"I hate gum."

The bus started crawling along, all the old fogies waving at their families. All except for my grandpa, who was hiding among them. The bus left the terminal and was instantly replaced by another one. I was beginning to feel hemmed in. Everyone was standing too close to one another. Too close to me.

"Say," the woman started up again. Wouldn't give me a moment's peace. "Why did you guys even let him enlist? Got fed up taking care of him?"

"Are you one of those Checkpoint Watch women? What do you want from me?" I asked. My throat was dry. The air rebelled, refusing to enter my body.

"I'm from Checkpoint Watch and the Mizrahi Coalition Against the Conscription of the Elderly," she said and snickered. "Just kidding, sweetheart, honestly. Why so serious? Just say you can't be bothered to look after your grandfather. It's fine, really. Between you and me, we're all a bunch of assholes here."

I took a deep breath.

"Hey, are you okay?" Her tone lost its sarcastic edge. "You look really pale."

"I'm fine," I answered with a stifled voice. "Just a touch of asthma."

"You don't have an inhaler?" she asked. I searched my pockets. It took me a few moments to realize I actually didn't.

"I have to get out of here," I announced, and started scurrying toward to the exit. She yelled something, but I couldn't hear. I was already outside the reception base. The way to the parking lot was longer than I had remembered. I made it to my car and found a bottle of sun-scorched water lying on the back seat. I downed it in one gulp. Then I turned on the air conditioner to full blast. A soldier who was passing by knocked on my window, miming if everything was okay. I gestured yes and released the hand brake. I just wanted to get out of there. I rolled out of the parking lot and pulled over at the first bus stop. It was empty. It took me a few moments to catch my breath. Once I managed to pull myself together, I headed to the call center downtown. The shift manager, a guy who had been two grades below me in high school, said it would be the last time I showed up late without notifying him.

5.

alman1964@gmail.com
July 17, 2009, 02:12:35
Subject: Re: Hi Yuli
An Israeli traveler stopping by our office left behind a two-month-old copy of *Yedioth Ahronoth*. I have no idea why he had carried it around with him for so long. In any case, I saw Miriam's name

in the obituaries. I'm so sorry. She was a lovely woman. It's true we didn't always get along, but she really was a wonderful woman.
I hope you and your father are okay. Did you change your number? I called but it said the number was disconnected. Honestly, I'm not even sure this is the right email address.
Best,
Alma Rosenblum,
Emissary for the Jewish Agency for Israel in New Delhi

6.

alman1964@gmail.com
July 17, 2009, 11:56:20
Subject: Re: Hi Yuli
Delivery to the following recipient failed permanently:
yuli.neuerman@gmail.com
Technical details of permanent failure:
Google tried to deliver your message, but it was rejected by the server for the recipient domain gmail.com by gmail-smtp-in.l .google.com. [2607:f8b0:4001:c1b::1a].
The error that the other server returned was:
550-5.1.1 The email account that you tried to reach does not exist. Please try
550-5.1.1 double-checking the recipient's email address for typos or
550-5.1.1 unnecessary spaces. Learn more at
550 5.1.1 http://support.google.com/mail/bin/answer.py?answer=6596 q18si1996584ico.33—gsmtp

7.

alman1964@gmail.com
July 17, 2009, 11:56:20
Subject: Re: Hi Yuli
Why didn't it send??? I need to talk to you.

Best,
Alma Rosenblum,
Emissary for the Jewish Agency for Israel in New Delhi

8.

alman1964@gmail.com
July 17, 2009, 12:16:34
Subject: Re: Hi Yuli
Delivery to the following recipient failed permanently:
yuli.neuerman@gmail.com
Technical details of permanent failure:
Google tried to deliver your message, but it was rejected by the server for the recipient domain gmail.com by gmail-smtp-in.l .google.com. [2607:f8b0:4001:c1b::1a].
The error that the other server returned was:
550-5.1.1 The email account that you tried to reach does not exist. Please try
550-5.1.1 double-checking the recipient's email address for typos or
550-5.1.1 unnecessary spaces. Learn more at
550 5.1.1 http://support.google.com/mail/bin/answer.py?answer=6596 q18si1996584ico.33—gsmtp

9.

GRANDPA CAME HOME for the weekend. When Dad and I went to visit him, we found him sitting alone on the roof. Stripped down to his underwear and white T-shirt, he had placed his black army boots near the entrance to the balcony and hung his uniforms on the clothesline. He held an IWI Tavor rifle in one hand and a cup of black coffee in the other.

"I see they were generous with the equipment," I said to Grandpa, who turned his head to me, nodding contentedly. Dad pulled up a chair and sat down beside him silently.

"Well," I asked, "how was it?"

"Grueling," he replied. "Especially in the reception base. They're worse than the Social Security office, believe me. Just filling out the forms at the sorting officer's took me four hours."

"What forms?" Dad asked, to which Grandpa smiled. "I assumed you'd want copies," he said, taking out a few folded papers from his pocket. "Don't worry, the sorting officer said it was routine protocol. To make sure you didn't send me off to the army just because you didn't feel like forking up the money for a retirement home."

Dad skimmed through the forms. "Congrats, looks like you signed a terrific contract."

"I actually didn't even read it."

"I can tell," Dad said. "Just so you know, if you happen to be dying as we speak, or get Alzheimer's, the army won't have to pay you a single shekel. That's one upstanding organization, your IDF," he said to me, and sighed. Even two years after my discharge, to him I was still the commander in chief's official representative. Dad unzipped his black fanny pack and fished out a few papers. "Like I thought," he said, "we're going to have to get private health insurance." He handed Grandpa a pen and a few folded forms.

"Your son is tougher than the squad commanders at boot camp, huh?" I said to Grandpa, after which Dad shoved a few forms into my hand as well.

"What, I'm being drafted again too? Last time I checked I already served my stint in Golani," I said.

"Employment and bank forms," he explained. "I'm guessing you haven't noticed that you've been working for two months without getting paid."

"What do you mean?"

"Your salary hasn't been transferred to your bank account. You've been volunteering at the call center, which is nice of you, but not what I'd call financially sound. Go ahead, what do you care, it's always good to fill out forms," he said, and meant it. Dad was the one person in the world who liked bureaucracy. I don't mean he learned to live with it. He liked bureaucracy the way he liked pistachio ice cream and organized tours of Kibbutz Kfar Blum. Something about the meticulous order, the unambiguous questions, soothed him. I filled everything out in a few seconds, but Grandpa took Dad's rebuke to heart and carefully considered each and every sentence.

"Does this form also cover injuries sustained under operational circumstances?" Grandpa asked. "War, covert missions, etc."

"I'm not sure a rusty stapler falls under the category of operational circumstances," Dad said with a smile.

"What stapler?" Grandpa puzzled, turning his gaze to me. "Golani is no joke. You more than anyone should know!"

Dad and I laughed. Grandpa didn't understand why.

"Who'd recruit you to Golani?"

"They already did. They've opened a new training course," he replied, and went back to the forms.

"What are you talking about?" I asked him, hoping he'd give some reasonable explanation before Dad lost it. Grandpa told us that once he finished signing all the forms, the sorting officer patted him on the back and said that a man like him could make an even more significant contribution. That it wasn't every day a veteran in such great shape reenlisted.

"And you're telling me you said yes?" Dad asked.

"Of course. If I'm called upon to serve my country, who am I to say no? The nice fellow said I was born to be an infantryman. Even said I had the makings of an officer. Can you believe it, Yuli? We could both end up platoon commanders!"

"You're actually talking to me about Bahad 1? Officers school??" Dad cut him off and shifted his gaze to me. "Could you please explain to me how senior citizens are enlisting to Golani and I'm the only one who thinks the world's gone mad?"

Grandpa took a sip of his coffee. He tried to divert the conversation by mentioning there was some of Grandma Miriam's soup left in the freezer, and that we were welcome to stay for dinner.

"Pea soup won't help you here," Dad said. His face flushed red. Truth be told, at that moment, I agreed with him. I was also starting to feel that this whole enlisting business had gone too far, but I didn't want to leave Grandpa to fend for himself.

"It's not as if they're going to deploy him to Lebanon tomorrow," I said, trying to calm things down. "They'll probably set him up with a suitable position, it's a special unit for people his age, isn't it?"

Grandpa nodded.

"How exactly is enlisting to Golani suitable for an eighty-year-old man, in any scenario?"

"They know what they're doing. I bet they adjusted the whole training course for them, I'm telling you. Old people are doing crazy things nowadays. Just yesterday I read about a ninety-year-old Japanese man who ran a full marathon. Compared to him, Grandpa's still a baby."

"You truly don't grasp the difference between a marathon and boot camp?" Dad yelled. "The army isn't supposed to provide employment for bored widowers. How could you, who fought a war, not understand that?"

"Because you, who served as a student-soldier in the Tel Aviv headquarters, *do* understand?" I barked at him. "What's the big deal? So he'll pull a little guard duty. It's better than lying in bed all day waiting for a stroke."

Grandpa coughed. I could see by his expression that he was trying to hide the insult; with a few brief sentences, we'd practically buried him alive.

"I don't know about you guys," he said, "but I'm going to enjoy a nice bowl of soup." Grandpa got up, took a few steps toward the stairs, and stumbled on a loose tile. His cup almost fell, and the remainder of his coffee spilled over his white shirt, staining it with black, moist grains. Dad rushed toward him. He picked him up gently, cleaned his hands with a torn tissue he fished out of his pocket. Then he went downstairs to fetch a wet kitchen towel. I offered Grandpa to help him down the stairs.

"Don't. At eighty, a man should start learning to manage by himself," he announced and descended the entire staircase, only to come back up because he had forgotten his rifle on the roof.

10.

alman1964@gmail.com
July 27, 2009, 03:52:48
Subject: Re: Hi Yuli
You're not getting my emails. I know. I got one of those automatic notices. But I'm going to keep writing you anyway. Okay? I can't really explain it. I feel I need to, even if you won't read it. Actually, maybe *because* you won't read it. I know it's silly. Trust me, I know, but since I saw Miriam's obituary, I've been having all these thoughts but no one to share them with. It's pathetic, I know, but what can I say, it's the truth. Who am I going to tell? The Indians? The twenty-year-old backpackers? The Chabad rabbi who visits our offices every Monday and Thursday and still doesn't understand how a mother can leave everything behind and move to India on her own?

So I'll write you. Just a little. That's my biggest flaw anyway, right? That I always put myself first. You said it yourself the last time we spoke on the phone. You said that the day I boarded the plane you realized I'd always put myself first. That you had always suspected it, but that my going to India proved it once and for all. Believe me, had I known that three months later you would stop answering my calls, I would never even have considered hanging up.

I tried calling you, as I'm sure you know. Five times this past week alone. You didn't answer. Not assigning blame, just stating a fact. Surprisingly, your father did pick up. Actually, it's not surprising at all. Pretending everything's fine is practically his expertise. He told me Miriam fell in the shower. Strange, isn't it? How a person can fall in the shower, and in a split second it's all over. Just like that. He also told me your grandpa enlisted in that old people's combat unit (is it actually called the geriatric platoon?? Has to be a joke.). Listen, I'm the last person who can criticize the country, but this sounds a bit wacky . . . What exactly are they going to do with them? Who are they going to fight? Hamas? Hezbollah? Your father didn't explain. He never does. He wouldn't talk about the debts either. I tried talking to him, believe me I tried. He probably doesn't talk to you about it either. Or maybe he even told you it had been resolved. Sounds like him. What can I tell you, Yuli, I wish he'd confide in you, just a little. Not for your sake, but for his. Secrets rot the soul, it isn't healthy to live like that.

This is so ridiculous. Writing to no one.

I'm going to stop now.

Best,
Alma Rosenblum,
Emissary for the Jewish Agency for Israel in New Delhi

11.

GRANDPA DIDN'T COME home the following Friday, nor did he answer his phone. I made a few calls to people I knew from the army and finally reached a welfare NCO at the Golani training base. After looking into the matter, she told me that Grandpa had been granted a lone soldier status. Having informed them he couldn't live alone, he was being housed at the Senior Citizens' Center in Rehovot. According to the NCO, he said he was being neglected by his family, and she subtly inquired whether social services were involved.

I couldn't believe he had lied like that. Badmouthed the only two people in the world who looked after him. The day Grandma Miriam died, I quit my job at the restaurant I'd been working at before the call center, and Dad took a month's leave from work even though he couldn't really afford it. And despite the fact that for the past thirty years he and Grandpa had only been pretending to talk to each other. I don't know why. Maybe it's because of Alma, or maybe there are other reasons. Actually, I'm not even sure they know, but it was hard not to notice the distance between them; how they always settled for a hesitant handshake, like businessmen in a useless meeting. Dad tried laughing it off, said it was just the way of Ashkenazi families, and left it at that.

I walked into Dad's study. He was sitting at his desk in front of piles of papers. The moment I entered, he folded the letter he was reading. I couldn't see what was written in it, but I spotted the logo of a law firm. I preferred not to ask.

"Listen, you were right," I admitted, not without frustration, and told him everything. "I'm going to call his platoon commander right now and tell him they have to send Grandpa home."

Dad opened one of the drawers and took out a pill sheet. "Headache," he said and swallowed two pills without water. "You're going to do no such thing."

"Have you lost it? Any second now they're going to charge us with abusing the elderly!"

"Don't be dramatic."

"Listen, I've talked to people in the brigade, you have no idea what he's telling them about us."

"I know," he answered. "The NCO called me."

"What?"

"Someone called me last night. Some soldier. She said Grandpa wants to move to one of those homes for elderly soldiers, but that they only accept soldiers who don't have a supportive family."

"Well, did you set things straight?"

"Yes. I told her we didn't look after him at all."

"You're joking, right?"

"Absolutely not," Dad said. "I told them we'd be happy if the home could take him off our hands."

"What? How could you even say something like that?"

"Easily. If he wants to move in with his friends, who am I to stop him?" he explained calmly, and I couldn't understand how the most rational man I knew could actually think that way.

"You gave him hell when he wanted to enlist, and now it's not driving you crazy that everyone thinks he's some abused old man?"

"No. That's not it at all."

"Then what is it?"

"The thing is, old people aren't supposed to be protecting us . . ."

Dad fell silent. He noticed I was staring at a repossession notice that lay on his desk. He folded it in two and quickly shoved it back into the envelope.

"What's that?" I asked.

"None of your business," he answered adamantly. "As with Grandpa. Simply none of your business."

"Don't you think it's time you explained to me what's going on?" I asked, but he didn't answer. He stacked a few papers into a neat pile, switched off the light, and walked out.

12.

SATURDAY MORNING I went to see Grandpa. First, to tell him off, and second, to check that he was okay. The Senior Citizens' Center in Rehovot wasn't the miserable sight I'd expected. It was a three-story building with a large aquarium at the entrance. A few old people sat in black leather armchairs in the first-floor foyer, talking about shooting range practice. Other than the topic of conversation, the place pretty much resembled an old age home. The receptionist said that Zvi Neuerman was in room 306, third floor. The door was open. I walked in without knocking. Grandpa was sitting on the bed with two other old men, in the middle of a round of backgammon. He didn't know how to play backgammon, but neither he nor the old man next to him seemed to mind.

"I'm glad to see they're not neglecting you here," I said to him. He smiled in reply, deliberately ignoring my sarcastic tone.

"Well, look what the cat dragged in! Lovely to see you," Grandpa said. He was wearing fatigues and a T-shirt, and a dog tag with his name on it around his neck. "Meet Nathaniel Shapiro, fellow platoon member, and Yossi Buzaglo, history NCO in the education corps," he said, pointing at his friends.

"Who's this youngin'?" Shapiro asked. Grandpa laughed and slapped me on the shoulder.

"You heard I got top marks on my CPR test?"

"You're being serious? You're talking to me about some CPR test? Where did you get the nerve to tell that welfare NCO that we're—"

"The only one in the whole platoon, ain't that something?" he cut me off, and started rhapsodizing about the AN/PRC 77 Radio Set training and target practice. Grandpa said he got a little nervous at first but then started to enjoy himself, and that even Waxman, the platoon commander, had praised his steady grip.

"Is 4cm grouping considered good?" he asked.

"That's not the issue," I growled. "I can't believe you said—"

"So it's not good," he said, lowering his gaze.

"It just has nothing to do with it. And 4cm is great for your first target practice. But listen, what you told them doesn't make any sense."

"You're just trying to make me feel better."

"No, seriously, for your first try it's great. Really."

"Hear that, Buzaglo? My grandson here was in Golani, and he says it's a great score! Ain't that something?"

I gave up. I realized I wasn't going to get through to him.

"Neuerman, stop being such a newbie," Shapiro said, standing by the door. "And quit wearing your weapon like that, strapped across your chest. No one does that."

Grandpa got upset and announced there was no such thing as too cautious when it came to safety, at which Shapiro smiled and said he was just gung-ho because he was dying to be admitted to the squad commanders' course.

Afterward, Grandpa quietly asked me what "gung-ho" meant and whether it was good or bad.

I lied and said it depended on how you looked at it.

Grandpa stared at a photo of Grandma Miriam that lay on his bedside table. It had been taken during their trip to Niagara Falls six years earlier. Grandma was cocooned in a red raincoat, her face barely visible. The white sheets on Grandpa's bed boasted the logo of the Association for the Elderly, and hanging on the wall above it was a frayed poster of Barbra Streisand.

"Buzaglo heard I like her so he set me up with the poster."

I told him it looked like a real warrior's bed, and he gave a satisfied smile. He glanced at Grandma's photo again. "If she could only see me now," he said. "She would never have believed it."

He suggested I stay a bit longer and join them for lunch in the dining hall, announcing proudly that it was goulash day, but I told him I had to get going. He thanked me for coming and hugged me so tightly that for a moment I felt bad for rushing to leave. Grandpa went back to his backgammon game and tossed the dice.

"Oooh, a triple win! You bastard," Shapiro said. Grandpa had no idea what a triple win meant, but he couldn't stop smiling.

13.

alman1964@gmail.com
August 8, 2009, 01:31:24
Subject: Re: Hi Yuli
Once a month, Yuli. I promise not to write more than one email a month, but I can't not write you at all. I've tried. I even bought a journal. One of those fancy ones with a brown cover. I wrote you there a few times, but it just doesn't do the trick. This whole thing is moronic, I know. Believe me, I know. After all, what's the difference, right? It's not as if these emails are actually reaching you. It's like writing to a brick wall, but what can I do. The journal didn't provide any solace, while an email that doesn't even reach its recipient does. And I've already decided that wherever I manage to find solace, I won't go looking for the reason. So I'm going to keep writing you. Only once a month. No more than that. Okay, Yuli?

Oh, how I love that name. You know I have a calendar in my office that I keep open to the month of July? I keep thinking to myself how lucky I am that your father insisted on naming you Yuli and not Nadav, like I wanted. Just imagine, I'd be stuck in this stinking office in Delhi without anything to remind me of you. The thought alone is unbearable.

You know, I had planned on hanging up in the middle of our conversation. This isn't easy to admit even to myself, but my hanging up—right after you told me I'd always put myself first—was planned. It's hard to explain, but from the day I decided to divorce your father, I knew that conversation was coming. I had played it out in my head thousands of times. How you were going to yell at me, vent your anger. It scared me so much I even rehearsed the scene in front of the mirror, tried to figure out how I'd answer. What I could say to mollify you. Like when you were little, remember? When Dad broke your Game Boy and you threw a tantrum, and I hugged you so tightly and said I wouldn't stop until I popped you like a balloon and deflated all the anger? And you started to laugh.

Every parent who gets divorced eats themselves up about it, scared they messed up their kids' lives. But a mom who gives up custody like that, without putting up a fight? And not only that, but leaves her ex all alone with debts that are basically her fault? I cannot begin to describe the amount of self-hatred I had to deal with, Yuli. I really can't. And trust me, I know perfectly well I'm the last person who deserves pity in this whole story. I keep hearing Miriam's voice in my head, reminding me of that. I don't want to speak evil of her, she was still your grandmother. Let's just say she couldn't stand me from the moment we met. And I can't blame her, you know? She was right all along. What business did a thirty-year-old actuary have with an eighteen-year-old soldier? A man so cautious he never even jaywalked. She couldn't understand how her son came back one day from reserve duty at the army headquarters with an orphaned clerk. A girl from a kibbutz without a shekel to her name. What can I tell you, Yuli? I understand her. It was an odd choice. But your father was an odd man. I knew that from the moment I saw him. A guy walking around with a fanny pack and a calculator in his shirt pocket because he never knew when he might need it, cannot be described as normal.

But neither could I. That's why we were such a good match. How does that Yehuda Amichai poem go? People use each other. And we definitely used each other. With our hands. Mouths. Eyes. With our loneliness. We were one of those couples people see on the street and feel a little sorry for, because you can tell neither of them is much of a catch. Everybody is so sure love is two people who chose to be together. But I always knew it was the other way around. It's when two people feel that this is their one and only chance at love, so they hold on tightly and don't let go. Hold on to each other until their knuckles are white. Because they know that in this world there's only one person they'll get the chance to love, so they better not screw it up.

You know when I realized your dad and I were one of those couples? The day he took me to Shalom Meir Tower. That weekend you left for your first summer camp with the scouts. Remember? Your dad wouldn't explain why he was dragging me on a Friday night to the eighteenth floor of a closed office building. Would you believe that your dad, that dork, would do such a thing? I remember he opened the door and I thought he had gone mad. I was sure he had actually broken into the place! He pulled me into the most beautiful room in the office, a giant room overlooking Jaffa, with a gorgeous parquet floor. He stood me in front of the window and announced: "We're going for it." And before I even realized what he was talking about, that klutz tried to kiss me but tripped and took me down with him. It was only in the hospital, when they put a cast on my leg, that he whispered in my ear that he had rented the place. The entire office. And that very morning had quit his job at the insurance agency. And that he and I were going to set up the travel agency I had always dreamed of.

Believe me, I thought he was crazy. I'm not joking, Yuli. I told him it was hardly the right time to talk about it, that it was simply nonsense. And right then and there in front of the nurse, I started yelling at him that we'd need to take out a second mortgage to rent an office like that, and that he didn't even know anything about international travel, that I myself had barely been in the industry for four years. And that we needed to save money, like adults, so you could go to college like everyone else. And while I was busy yelling at him, your father put his finger on my lips and said that worst case scenario we'd fall on each other's asses, which we had already proven we were pretty good at.

Oh, what can I tell you, Yuli? It was the kitschiest, most romantic thing an utterly unromantic man had ever said to me (you know that on our very first date he declared he wouldn't be celebrating any anniversaries? Said he found them a waste of time and money). And at that moment I realized the lengths he'd go for me. I also realized that what we had between us wasn't exactly love but something even stronger, something miserable but at the same time more binding, which I can't even attempt to define.

But why am I telling you all this, Yuli? Parents aren't supposed to share romantic anecdotes with their children. And besides, unlike us, you turned out to be beautiful. You can choose any woman you want.

Good thing these words aren't reaching anyone.

I hope I'll be able to wait another month, Yuli. I sincerely hope.

Best,

Alma Rosenblum,

Emissary for the Jewish Agency for Israel in New Delhi

14.

I SAW GRANDPA changing before my eyes with every visit to the Senior Citizens' Center. His potbelly gradually shrank and his back slightly straightened. He claimed that years of Grandma Miriam's gefilte fish and tzimmes had turned him into a real warrior, he just hadn't known it at the time. While most soldiers in his platoon enjoyed a variety of exemptions (like Moshe Levy, who didn't have to pull guard duty for more than an hour at a stretch, or Alex Lieberman, stationed within three hundred meters from a bathroom), Grandpa finished his first foot drill without requiring any sick leave the following day. Even the hazings by the young commanders didn't bother him. When they assigned him the worst guard duty shifts, late at night, or sent him to fetch "electricity powder" from the company supply room, he did it with a smile. He had even stopped talking about his death, the elaborate morbidities now replaced by anecdotes about Company Commander Waxman's operational experience, and the surprise of smoked tuna during urban warfare week. Which made me understand that maybe you're never too old to turn over a new leaf.

Not once did Dad ask me to tell him about Grandpa, but when I did anyway, he listened attentively; he let out a small smile when he heard they picked Grandpa to be the signaler on the company march, and couldn't suppress his anger when I told him they took away Grandpa's Shabbat leave because he didn't shave. And he even came to the induction ceremony, at which Grandpa took his oath; showed up with a white wide-brimmed hat and a pair of Alma's old sunglasses and videotaped the whole thing, his hand trembling when Grandpa received his Golani badge. Grandpa himself didn't seem too excited when he placed his hand on the Bible and pledged allegiance to the State of Israel. It was only on the way home, when we stopped for a falafel from Georgian's, that Grandpa told me he was tired because he couldn't fall asleep last night.

"Well, it makes sense, the induction is a pretty exciting thing," I told him, to which he announced it had nothing to do with that. "Today's our anniversary," he said, and didn't elaborate.

15.

THE FIRST TIME I heard Grandpa swearing was when he called to tell me they were being sent to secure one of the settlements in the Valley, near the Jordanian border. They were just going to sit there, without even doing patrol duty. To me it was obvious they'd be assigned to one of those meaningless missions, that no one actually expected them to do anything serious. But Grandpa was shocked, didn't see it coming. He dismissed Waxman's explanations about how they didn't have enough experience for an active mission on the Gaza front line, that in any case half the platoon had hearing aids so they couldn't be anywhere near whistling mortar bombs. He told me over the phone that his entire platoon was a bunch of cowards that wanted nothing more than to go home to their Filipino caregivers on the weekends, and that tomorrow he was going to get his release form signed, leave the Geriatric Platoon and join a unit with real combat soldiers. Said he'd give anything to go down to Gaza and bump a terrorist or two, show that goddamn army what he was worth.

"Believe me when I say you have no idea what you're talking about," I told him.

"I know perfectly well what I'm talking about, and don't you treat me like a child."

"But you sound like one," I replied. "You think the army is a game?"

"You think you can teach me something because you fought in Lebanon?" Grandpa said. "Because you saw a few bullets fly past your head? I was here in '48, I know more about war than you ever will," he announced, and hung up.

I tried calling him back twice but he wouldn't pick up. That night, Dad told me he had called him. Grandpa said they were already in Ro'i, a small moshav on the Jordanian border, a two-hour drive from anywhere that mattered. That they had unloaded their equipment and he had already been dispatched to guard duty, when he got caught reading Moshe Shamir's *He Walked Through the Fields*, and Waxman took away his Shabbat leave once again.

"We've got no choice," Dad said. "We're going to have to visit the wayward soldier."

From that point on, Dad was completely consumed with the preparations around the trip. He had bought three cookbooks, and each night I'd come home to find him at the stove. He used to cook quite often, but ever since Alma had left, Dad tried to avoid spending time in the kitchen, which remained Alma's territory even after she was gone. He'd have lunch in a restaurant or café, and at night grab a yogurt from the fridge or a few almonds from the pantry, quickly darting out of the kitchen for any other room.

Spending such long stretches of time in the spot that had once been hers made Dad start talking about her again. Not explicitly, but with offhand remarks that brought her back into the house ("Did you know we bought this blender in France?" "She never liked garlic sauce." "I still have to fix her coffeemaker.").

During that entire week, when I came home from work, he'd ask me to taste his daily concoction and rate it from one to ten. The spicy *chraime* fish got a five, the honey-glazed chicken a six, and the pasta with mushroom sauce a three. I suggested we just bring him takeout from a nice restaurant, explaining that it was commonly done nowadays, but Dad took offense and continued cooking. I'm not sure what he based his final decision on, but we ended up making our way to the outpost with two pots of Vietnamese chicken mixed with caramelized rice and stuffed grape leaves. The original recipe had called for Swiss chard, but neither of us knew exactly what that was. Dad drove and I held the pots tightly on my lap, having wrapped them first in plaid kitchen towels like he had asked me to. Every now and then, when we hit a red light, Dad lifted one of the lids and inhaled the fragrant steam with the earnestness of a child taking in the scent of the ocean.

16.

alman1964@gmail.com
September 19, 2009, 01:54:09
Subject: Re: Hi Yuli

I visited the Taj Mahal yesterday. Can you believe I've been here three years and only yesterday saw it for the first time? So why didn't I visit it before, you ask (not really)? I'm not sure. After all, planning trips to India was my favorite thing to do when I was a travel agent, and almost everyone who visits makes a beeline for the Taj. I knew everything there is to know about that place. And I mean everything. From the phone number of the best taxi driver in Agra to how to get into the compound for the local price. And suddenly yesterday, two Israelis walked into my office, mistaking it for a Chabad house. David and Tamar, a retired couple, incredibly sweet people. They only wanted to ask if I knew a decent restaurant in the area, and ended up staying for two hours. What did we talk about, you ask (but not really)? What didn't we talk about! How best to get around India, my three years here, David's service in the air force (he was a pilot!). At some point he mentioned they were both from Kibbutz Be'eri, and they were so delighted to hear that I was originally from Kibbutz Nahal Oz that they invited me to come with them to the Taj Mahal. At first I turned their invitation down, thinking they were just being polite, but then Tamar said there was no point arguing because they wouldn't take no for an answer. And that they'd pick me up at 7:00 A.M. I can't explain it, Yuli, but something about her tone, and that adamant hand gesture, suddenly reminded me of my mother. And I said yes, without even thinking. The kind of yes that leaves no room for a change of heart. They picked me up the following day (yesterday), and four hours later we were standing in front of the Taj Mahal. And the funniest thing is that I ended up giving them a three-hour tour, even though I'd never been there before! Crazy, huh? It was all from memory!

On our way back, I saw in the rearview mirror that David was holding Tamar's hand. They asked me if I'd always dreamed about living abroad, and I don't know exactly why, but I found myself telling them about the fourth day of the Yom Kippur War, after they had told me my father was killed. How I ran up and down the entire kibbutz yelling that I was going to get away from this stinking country the first opportunity I got and move to Scandinavia. That in Scandinavia people didn't die because the cold kept them safe like an icebox. Which is odd, Yuli, because I hadn't thought about that day in years. I had completely forgotten about it. Forgotten all my promises. Because kids make a lot of promises that they don't make good on. But during that ride from Agra to Delhi, all those memories suddenly resurfaced. And as I'm writing you this, I'm realizing that maybe my trip to India really did begin there, the day my father got killed. And that maybe, when I think about it, India is the closest I've ever been to a teenage rebellion. Because I never actually rebelled, you know? By the time I was ready to rebel against someone, both my parents were already dead. My rebellions were unsuccessful and short-lived. The day after I rebelled against the kibbutz and moved to Tel Aviv, I became a soldier; and a moment after I decided to rebel against the army, I met your father. Three weeks after my discharge I was already his wife, and nine months later, your mother. And once I became a mother, I knew my chance to rebel against the world was over. Because mothers aren't allowed to rebel, right? At least that's what I used to think. Today I'm not so sure anymore. Maybe because we tend to do things backward in our family. Look at your grandfather. He's finally free of Miriam, and he goes and enlists in the army. And you, such a golden child, for the past two years you're suddenly stuck with no direction in life. Actually, there's only one person I know who'll never rebel, and that's your father. Because unlike people like us, who are a bit weaker, he's always there. He'd never run off to India or enlist in Golani. I bet psychologists would say he's coping with the situation better than all of us, but I think that's bullshit. It's not healthy for a person to just resign himself to the role the world has fated him with.

I wanted to write you the moment I came back from the Taj. Because I needed to share all this with someone before I forgot. But you know, Yuli, now, writing about my trip to Agra, everything feels a bit strange. Not that you're actually receiving these emails, and yet, it feels like you are supposed to be the one writing them. As if we have somehow traded places. As if I stole your trip. Which is silly, I know, but sometimes it feels as if there was only one seat left on that plane to India, and I stole it from you.

I hope that thought never crossed your mind. I really do.

Best,
Alma Rosenblum,
Emissary for the Jewish Agency for Israel in New Delhi

17.

AT THE ENTRANCE to the Ro'i settlement, we saw Shapiro next to the security booth in a bulletproof vest and a dinky old helmet. He was sitting on a white plastic chair, his eyes closed, basking in the last moments of shade. I honked at him. He almost fell off his chair. Then he yawned, stretched and got up (not without considerable effort), shuffled toward the car and stuck his head through the window.

"You guys are allowed to sit during guard duty?" I asked.

"What do you think? Almost everyone in the platoon has an exemption from standing," he replied with a smile.

"So shouldn't you at least . . . like, be awake?"

He took a crinkled piece of paper out of his pocket. "Authorization to nap," he said, waving it proudly. "Ten minutes every hour. I'm the only one in the whole platoon who has it!"

"What are you reading?" he asked and pointed at the book resting on the back seat.

"*The Myth of Sisyphus*," I replied. "Albert Camus."

"God, awfully boring, that one. Only a French fatty can turn a story worth a sentence and a half into a whole book."

Shapiro informed us that Grandpa had just finished guard duty on the tower, opened the gate, and suggested we wait for him in the parking spot in front of the administrative office. He glanced at the pots and added, "You should know you've got some serious competition. My granddaughter brought over some of her delicacies."

Right after Dad parked the car, we heard a shout.

"Gourevitch!" a man hollered. "If you're not here in thirty seconds I'm shooting you myself."

I recognized Grandpa's voice immediately.

The tower wasn't a watchtower, but a water tower with "Let IDF kick ass and bust heads!" sprayed across its tank in black graffiti, next to "Eitan Tayeb is innocent!"

When I got there, Gourevitch was just climbing up the stairs with his bulletproof vest in his hand. He almost slipped off every stair, and Grandpa kept yelling at him from above that he had better move his ass if he didn't want to end up like Kastner. Once Gourevitch made it all the way up, almost unconscious from the effort, Grandpa nimbly bounded down the stairs. He hugged me and said that Gourevitch was such a newbie.

We sat down on the grass near the parking lot, under the shade of a tree. Grandpa removed the rifle strapped across his chest and gave Dad a slap on the back. "What happened that you decided to cook?" he asked, to which Dad quickly replied, "What happened that you decided to enlist?"

They both smiled. Producing a black pepper mill and a bottle of chili powder, Dad said the recipe called for seasoning right before serving. He ladled a spoonful of the dish into a blue plastic bowl he had bought especially for the occasion.

"What's this?" Grandpa asked.

"Vietnamese Chicken," I replied.

He sniffed it. "Say, they eat their chicken cold in Vietnam?"

"We didn't think that one through," I replied, and Dad lowered his gaze.

"Don't worry," Grandpa quickly blurted, "believe me, I'm so hungry I wouldn't know the difference, but why don't you serve the kid first, he still has some growing up to do."

I took a bite and immediately knew the chili's punch was more than Grandpa's palate could bear. But before I could warn him, he had shoveled a forkful into his mouth. He could barely chew. His face contorted and his grip tightened around his weapon from the exertion of swallowing. At the end of the brief skirmish between Grandpa and the Far East, Grandpa came out on top, but just barely.

"Hey, this isn't half bad," he said, nearly gagging.

Dad quickly tasted the dish. "I don't get it," he mumbled, "it was supposed to be sweet."

"It's a real delicacy," Grandpa insisted. "Here, I'll take another bite just to prove it to you." His face a bright red, Grandpa looked so miserable that the offer alone had made Dad burst into laughter, and Grandpa let out a sigh of relief once he realized he wouldn't have to face the challenge again. They agreed that next time Dad would bring falafel from the Georgian, and all I could think about was how fragile the moment was.

"I have to admit you let us down a little," Dad said, and Grandpa raised a baffled eyebrow. "I was sure you'd be hating every moment here. That we'd find you halfway to defecting to the Jordanian army."

Grandpa shrugged and said he'd rather be serving in the special forces unit, but he decided to give his platoon another chance. "Most of the men here are deadbeats, but a few aren't too bad."

On our way back to the car we saw Shapiro and a few other elderlies from the platoon sitting on a bench. Grandpa introduced them to us with such pride, it was easy to forget that only a few days ago he had expressed a sincere willingness to smash their heads in with the butt of his rifle.

"You should know your grandpa is a real warrior," one of them told me, pointing his walking stick at him. "God have mercy on the poor terrorist who comes up against him."

"Come on, guys, that's enough," Grandpa said, but I could see on his face how much he wanted them to continue. To carry on with the same admiring tone that highlighted the difference between them, and made it clear he stood apart.

"I have a granddaughter here to show off too," Shapiro mentioned proudly, and pointed at a girl in a turquoise sweater. She looked familiar, but her black sunglasses made it difficult to say from where.

"Avigail, meet Yuli."

"We've already met once," Avigail said.

"Really?" Shapiro asked.

I said "No" and she said "Yes" the exact same moment.

"Don't try to deny it," she said. That cheeky smile. It was the girl I had met at the Reception and Sorting Base.

"Okay, I don't want to know," Shapiro said and then turned to Grandpa. "If they end up getting married, you're paying for the wedding hall."

Grandpa smiled and put his hand on my shoulder. "We'll see about that. My grandson is one hell of a catch." Then he added in a serious tone, "Did you know kiddo here fought in the Second Lebanon War?"

Their smiles turned into curious glances.

"Really?" Shapiro asked. "What brigade?"

"Golani," I replied.

"An elite unit! Egoz," Grandpa added.

Admiring gazes were showered upon me. One of them even started clapping. "So you were in the Battle of Bint Jbeil? With Roi Klein, rest in peace?" one of them asked.

"No."

"So where were you?"

"Maroun al-Ras."

"What did you do there?"

"We fought."

"And kicked some Hezbollah ass?"

"Yes," I replied.

"Why are you so blasé about it?" Avigail asked.

"Because it's not such a big deal," I replied.

"Or maybe because it fucked you up a little," she said.

For a while, no one said a word.

"Say, how come I didn't know all this?" Grandpa wondered, pleased with the attention I was getting from his platoonmates. "Guys, I propose my grandson share some battle stories. Yuli, tell us exactly what happened over there. We could use a few tips from a real pro."

"We have to get going," Dad cut him off, and started pushing me toward the car. "I still have to go over a few reports today."

"Wait a minute, Yermi," Grandpa said, trying to catch my hand. "Give us a few more minutes with the kid. They all want to hear what he has to say."

"Some other time," Dad announced in a tone that left little room for negotiation. "We have to go," he said, and Grandpa had no choice but to accept it with the same nervous silence that hung between me and Dad the entire way home.

"It's been a long time since you talked about what happened over there," Dad said as he parked the car near our house. "I think you should reconsider therapy or something." He was struggling to get the words out. "You should see someone," he continued. "The things you went through in Lebanon. It isn't normal."

"I'm not the only one who went through it."

"That doesn't mean it's normal," he replied. "You talk about it like you saw it in a movie, like it wasn't even you there."

"I get that you're worried, but everything's okay, really."

"What are you talking about, Yuli?" he said with what sounded like anger that had been accumulating for some time. "You've been stuck for the past two years, Yuli. Two years. You can't keep wasting your life."

"Why not?"

"Because you're better than that."

"Maybe I'm not," I said.

It pained him to hear it like that, unfiltered. He was still sure it was just a phase. That soon I'd get my act together and enroll at Harvard or something, like I had promised him long ago.

We were both quiet, I'm not sure for how long.

"The pill you saw me take . . . ," he said hesitantly, lingering on every syllable. "Those aren't for headaches. Since your mother left, with everything that's been going on with the debts, with your grandpa . . . It hasn't been easy. I mean, I'm trying to take care of it, but it's not easy," he said with a sigh. "It helps me. You understand? That's why I said what I said. Maybe, just maybe, you should at least consider treatment."

He waited a little until he realized I wasn't going to respond.

"We're too much alike," he said, and got out of the car, leaving me alone with the cold pot.

18.

alman1964@gmail.com
October 26, 2009, 04:32:58
Subject: Re: Hi Yuli
Come on, Yuli. Why don't you pack a bag and fly to South America or Lapland or wherever you feel like going? To disprove everything I wrote in my last email. What's stopping you, my child? I really don't think you understand how much the thought troubles me. So much so that I've even made up a theory to try to explain it. I'm serious. It's been on my mind for a long time. I call it the spots theory. It seems to me that every person has one spot in the world he's connected to. It sounds obvious, I know. After all, everyone

has a country and city they're connected to. But I'm starting to think it isn't the country that keeps us rooted. Nor our education, friends, or family. It's something a lot more specific, much more precise. A spot in the world that pulls us in like a magnet. Your dad is a good example. His spot was the office. Fifteen years he worked his ass off there, and in that tiny spot, a square meter of an office, he was happier than I'll ever be able to understand. Today I can't believe how arrogant I had been, but back then I truly didn't believe a person could be happy calculating formulas all day, and that even if he believed he was happy—he was just fooling himself. That's why I wanted him to help me set up the travel agency. True, it was my dream and not his, but I wasn't going to let the facts get in my way. What can I tell you, Yuli? I was a well-intentioned idiot. Your grandpa's spot is obvious. His roof in Ramat Gan. I remember how he used to change whenever we went up there. I mean it. Watch him the next time he walks up the stairs to the roof. You'll see how something in his soul is set free. How he walks differently, talks differently. As if the roof is his escape from reality. I can't explain exactly what comes over him there, but with your grandpa you can really see what a good spot can do for a person.

Are you starting to understand what I'm talking about? I doubt it. Not only because it doesn't make a whole lot of sense, but also because neither of us has spots. I mean, I assume we do, but we just haven't found them yet. I honestly can't say where your spot is, but I'm sure it's in Israel. Maybe it's right under your nose. Maybe even somewhere in our house. Because that would explain everything, you know? Why you're so stuck in place. Remember you once told me about dark energy? You told me scientists are now saying 70 percent of the universe is comprised of something completely unknown. And that something affects our every movement in space, and we can't even explain how. And I didn't understand a single word you were saying, I never do when you talk about those things, but I haven't stopped thinking about it ever since. That there's a hidden force affecting our lives. And the spots are exactly the same. Pushing and pulling us while we delude ourselves into believing we have complete control over our lives. But it's all just make-believe. Even moving to India didn't change anything. I'm still spending my days in an office, still stuck, just on a different continent.

You're a little stuck too, huh? More like a lot stuck. I've heard from your father that the subject of university is not to be broached. And that your friends have all moved on with their lives and that you've fallen out of touch with them (don't be mad, he didn't want to rat you out, he only told me after I yelled at him that you were my son too). I'm trying not to ask myself how much of this is my fault. Clearly I'm guilty, it's just a question of how much. I'm sure the war is also to blame. Yes, the war. The one we haven't talked about. You know I've been bracing myself for this question for two years now? How could I not come? How could I not board the first flight to Israel the moment it all began? For two years I've been rehearsing the lousy answer I'd give you. But you never asked. I remember when we talked on the phone after you got back, and you said there's nothing to tell, and I kept insisting, but you said there was no point because I could never understand *Lebanon*, and I felt as if we were back in your high school days, after your dad and I divorced. When you would come over to my place once every two weeks and not say so much as a word. And I so wanted you to talk to me. That's why I was thrilled when your teacher called to tell me you wrote that civics paper about the Spartan approach. Brilliant as always, but also a little troubling; she suggested we talk to you, make sure everything was okay, and I instantly knew that phone call was a chance to peek into your world. I knew you wouldn't show me the paper if I came out and asked for it, so I went into your room and searched every drawer until I found it. You're probably still angry about that, but try to understand me. You wouldn't talk to me back then. You never really talked to me. Neither before the war, nor after. You wouldn't say anything other than "it was fine," as if it was just another boring day at school. How I yearned to get another phone call like the one I got from your teacher, for someone to give me a clue into what was going on in that head of yours. But no commander called. And whenever we spoke I kept begging you to share your feelings with me, to share anything. And I told you it was true I might not be so great at it, but I was still your mother. Oh, my Yuli, remember what you said? I'm sure you don't. It came out so naturally I don't think you even noticed. But I'll never forget it. Believe me.

"I guess not every woman is meant to be a mother." That's what you said. With some kind of excruciatingly sober rationality you must have gotten from your dad, not from me. My heart went up in flames, Yuli. Burned to dust. But I didn't say a word. And we've never discussed those words. As if they never even left your mouth. But they continued to gnaw at me. I think it was after that conversation that you started calling me Alma. I mean, every now and then you would do that, that's why I didn't notice at first, but with time I realized the word *Mom* had completely disappeared from your vocabulary. To this day I don't know if it was a conscious decision you made or something that just happened on its own. It's a paradox, you know? Because if we were a little closer I'd work up the nerve to ask you about it, but if we were a little closer, you'd probably still be calling me Mom. Right?

So much is missing between us, Yuli.

Best,

Alma Rosenblum,

Emissary for the Jewish Agency for Israel in New Delhi

19.

AT 6:00 A.M. the following day, I got a phone call from Shapiro. He said Grandpa had been admitted to HaEmek hospital, that he couldn't talk about it over the phone and would explain everything once I got there. I leaped out of bed, left a note for Dad, and sped up north. I couldn't imagine what had happened. How could he be in the hospital? Just yesterday he had looked like a Chuck Norris action figure. Hospitalization? He must be unconscious. Grandpa would never willingly set foot in a hospital. Even when Grandma Miriam was diagnosed with pneumonia and was admitted for three days, he refused to visit. He claimed they made those places so miserable on purpose, so that people would start thinking death wasn't the worst option, and he had no intention of falling for that ruse.

Dad called as I drove past Hadera. "I didn't understand your note. Where are you going this early?"

"Grandpa is in the hospital," I replied.

"Your grandpa? Who managed to pull that off?"

"That's what I'm going to find out."

"I see," he said, and fell silent.

"I hope it's nothing serious," I said.

"Yes. Yes. So do I. Okay, keep me updated."

"I will."

"Good, so we'll talk later. I have to go over a case file."

"What case file?" I asked.

"Since when do you care?" Dad scoffed.

"I don't," I replied. "But I have a long drive ahead of me."

He said it was an interesting case. Some guy who had taken out a three-million-dollar life insurance policy and killed himself less than an hour after signing the paperwork.

"What you call a man with a plan . . ."

"Yes," Dad said, "only his family won't be getting the money. There are laws against such cases, so people won't start jumping off roofs whenever they're a few shekels short. That's why I always say how important it is to read the . . ."

"Fine print," I completed his sentence.

"Speaking of fine print, you have to sort out your bank account forms. How many times do I have to tell you that it's money going down the drain?"

"I already did," I replied.

"What? When?"

"Last night, after we got back from the Valley."

"How? Online?"

"Yup."

"Okay, good."

I was waiting for more, but he said he had to hang up.

They had put him in the medical corps ward, room 213. He was lying in the bed closest to the window, his head slouching to the left and his right hand slumped across the bedrail. His eyes were closed. Shapiro sat to his left, his leg in bandages; he tried scratching it with the butt of his rifle, without much success. I put my hand on Grandpa's shoulder and gave him a gentle shake. He didn't wake up.

"Don't worry, your old man's fine," Shapiro immediately said. "A little neck pain from the fall, probably nothing serious. Trust me, they only brought him in because he's an old fart."

"How the hell did you guys end up in the hospital?"

"Operational activity," Shapiro announced.

"Please, who are you kidding?" I said in a huff. "What's this operational activity nonsense? I saw you guys yesterday, no one said a word about operational activity."

"Of course no one said a word," Shapiro said, waving dismissively. "We're talking covert mission. Your grandpa explicitly forbade us from disclosing any details."

"My grandfather forbade you? What the fuck? You guys are commandos now? Who exactly would send you on a covert mission?"

"No one. Your grandfather decided we should send ourselves."

Oh god, what had he talked them into? I considered Grandpa again, lying there in his field pants and an undershirt reeking of sweat, patches of white stubble on his cheek.

"He wouldn't put on the hospital gown," Shapiro said. I straightened the pillow behind Grandpa's neck, then sat back down on my chair and looked at Shapiro. "Okay, tell me what mess he has gotten the two of you into, and don't give me any bullshit about how you're not allowed to talk about it."

He looked at Grandpa, closed his eyes, opened them and turned his gaze back to me. "He'd been planning it for the past two weeks," he said, sighing. Grandpa had pulled him aside in the dining hall for a discreet conversation, saying he couldn't understand why they weren't sending them on real missions, arguing that even scarecrows could secure a sleepy settlement in the Valley. "I tried calming him down, but he announced it was time we thought outside the box, just like Ariel Sharon when he established Unit 101. To show the top dogs what we're worth."

They set off on their mission last night. Yossi Gourevitch and Alex Lieberman, the platoon driver, showed up too. They took the quartermaster's Renault Kangoo and patrolled the area, wanting to show everyone they shouldn't be messed with.

"Within three hours we had already canvassed the area twice, like champs," Shapiro said. "Even your grandpa was proud of us. But the moment we started heading back, he noticed someone running behind us."

"What? Who?"

"A very suspicious man!" Shapiro exclaimed. "Your grandpa tried to get out of the car, but he was so nervous his hands shook, so it took him a few moments to get out. He finally managed, but the thing is, Gourevitch, that useless bugger, also fumbled. Hit my knee with his weapon and tripped right over your grandpa."

He said that by the time the three of them had gotten back on their feet, the man was already two hundred meters ahead of them, and kept running. "Your grandpa was so upset he tossed his weapon to the ground and started cursing us. Said some very unpleasant things. I can't blame Gourevitch."

"Blame him for what?"

"Shooting."

"Shooting?" I asked, thinking I must have misheard.

"Yes, yes, fired his weapon, shot the guy. Seconds later we heard the guy screaming, and saw him collapse to the ground."

"You didn't just say that, Shapiro."

"It's the truth, I'm afraid. We shot the guy."

I got up and checked that no one was standing in the hallway. Then I shut the door and sat back down in front of Shapiro, who was trying to avoid eye contact.

"Now tell me exactly, and I mean exactly, what you did from that moment on," I said. He told me that they walked over to the injured man and found him lying on the ground. "The guy was squirming in pain like you wouldn't believe," Shapiro said. "His knee was covered in blood. I told your grandpa this whole thing has gone too far. That it was supposed to be a nice evening, a morale-boosting activity, not a murder attempt, to which he said he always knew that a leftist who voted Mapam his entire life could not be trusted. Believe me, we could have kept arguing for hours, but Gourevitch started shouting that the guy had passed out. To tell you the truth, Yuli, I think that if it had been up to your grandpa, the poor guy would be buried under a basil bush right now, but Alex and I insisted on calling an ambulance. Eventually the medics also evacuated all three of us—me on account of my bruised knee, your grandpa because of the pain in his neck, and Gourevitch due to a panic attack. I'm not exactly sure what they gave your grandpa, but he's been sleeping like a baby for the past three hours."

"Did you report it to anyone?"

"No," Shapiro said, "but an hour after it happened I got a phone call from Waxman that he was on his way over, and one of the nurses told me the guy we shot was lying on the third floor, being interrogated by soldiers."

I was so angry I grabbed Shapiro's chair, startling him. "No, really, you guys are truly a bunch of dimwits, Shapiro. Morons."

Shapiro remained silent.

"You realize the four of you shot some poor Thai worker?"

"I don't think he looked very Asian . . ."

"No, you really don't get it, huh? Wake up, Shapiro. You're going to spend the rest of your life in prison. You understand? Not military prison, real prison. Honestly, Shapiro, I don't know what to tell you. Shooting a man like that? It's not something the army can just sweep under the rug." I got up and stood next to Grandpa. "Come on, you can stop pretending, I've had enough," I yelled at him. "Wake up. Come on already, wake up!" I gave him a good shake, but he didn't wake up.

"Let him sleep, Yuli, it's not nice what you're doing to him."

"Such an idiot," I hissed at him.

I sat back down in my chair, put my hands on my head, and stared at the floor.

We sat in front of each other in silence. Grandpa coughed every now and then, but with his remarkable stubbornness refused to wake up. I can't say how long we sat there like that before I heard the door open.

An officer with lieutenant's stripes stepped into the room; he looked more or less my age. A tall, balding guy with a buzz cut and a red beret, standing straight with his shoulders back like only officers do. "The Geriatric Platoon" was written on the strap of his M16, which was mounted with a scope and a laser sight—a ridiculously kitted-out weapon, especially for someone commanding elderly soldiers in the Jordan Valley. He considered me in silence, then shot his soldier an indifferent look.

"I'm sorry, Waxman," Shapiro said. "I don't know what came over us, I really—"

"Don't worry," he cut him off. "You'll have enough time to think about it. Can you stand? Walk?"

"Not so much."

Waxman took out his MIRS two-way radio, pressed a button, and grunted something unintelligible. "Someone will help you downstairs in a minute. There's a driver waiting to take you to your interrogation."

Shapiro lowered his gaze. "Will you be there?"

"No. The commander of the regional brigade will be, maybe the general of the central command too."

A few moments later, a soldier walked in with a wheelchair. He helped Shapiro up and eased him into it. "After the interrogation they'll bring you back for hip replacement surgery," Waxman said.

"Out of the frying pan and into the fire," Shapiro replied, shaking his head in frustration as the soldier wheeled him out of the room.

Waxman sat down and pulled a pack of Marlboros out of his pocket. "You're Shapiro's grandkid?" he asked, offering me a cigarette.

I turned it down and pointed at Grandpa.

"His," I said.

Waxman opened the window, took out a lighter and lit up. "Mind if I smoke?" he asked.

"Not personally, but this is a hospital. Maybe not a good idea."

"You're right, bro. When you're right, you're right." He took two long drags, stubbed out the cigarette against the windowpane, and threw it away. "My girlfriend's dying for me to quit anyway." He unbuckled his belt and yanked his shirt out of his pants. Then he looked at Grandpa. "Has a few loose screws, your grandpa, huh? Did Shapiro tell you about the mission your grandpa planned?"

"Nope," I said. "He just complained about his hip."

"Listen, your grandpa planned something straight out of an action movie. I'm talking Hollywood."

"All on his own?" I asked, trying to sound surprised.

"Kept a tight lip," Waxman replied. "Did it all right under my nose."

"So, does this mean he's going to get another Shabbat detention?"

Waxman laughed. "He should be getting a lot more than Shabbat detention, believe me," he said. "But as it stands, it looks like the four of them might be getting a commendation for it."

"What? What are you talking about? Shapiro told me that . . ." I fell silent.

Waxman leaned in. "What did Shapiro tell you?"

I remained silent.

"I know Gourevitch tried to shoot the guy. Don't worry, I know everything."

"What do you mean, 'tried'?" I replied. I couldn't help myself.

"I mean just that, he tried to shoot the guy."

"So how did the guy end up with a bullet in his leg if Gourevitch only *tried*?"

"What bullet in his leg, bro?" Waxman said. He looked at Grandpa, then turned his gaze back to me. "Wait, you want to tell me they actually think Gourevitch got him?" he said, and burst into roaring laughter. "Oh man, that's one of the funniest things I've ever heard. You think Gourevitch could hit a mark from two hundred meters away? At the shooting range that old geezer couldn't hit a target from five centimeters away. The guy stumbled on a rock or something. You think I'd be sitting here smoking a cigarette if they had actually shot that drug mule?"

"Drug mule?"

"Wow, you're really out of it, huh? You haven't heard the news today? The medics found four kilos of cocaine on the dude. In his underwear. Some real fucked-up shit."

He went on about all these senior officers who might attend the commendation ceremony, but I wasn't listening. I was looking at Grandpa, trying to imagine Grandma Miriam sitting there next to him. If it were up to her, she would probably have thrown his ass in jail just for causing her such heartache.

20.

WAXMAN AND I waited there for another hour to see if Grandpa would wake up, and he wouldn't stop rambling the whole time, apparently thrilled by the chance to talk to someone under the age of seventy-five. He told me he had originally served in the paratroopers, said he was the only officer in the IDF willing to take on the role, which was only because he had gotten himself entangled in a blunder in his previous company. Something about a soldier who went missing, probably killed himself. He had to choose between a dishonorable discharge and this shitty role. He said that at the end of the day, being a commander was the same everywhere, the only difference was that the exemptions in the Geriatric Platoon were legit. That there wasn't a single day when he didn't learn of a new disease, and that at this rate he'd end up a specialist in Tel HaShomer Hospital. I asked him how long he planned to stay in the platoon and he said that the moment he finished a year in his current role, he'd see if they'd give him back his old post in the paratroopers. If not, he'd call it quits. "In which case, next year it's law school at Tel Aviv University for me."

"You a student, bro?"

"No," I replied.

"Hm. So what do you do?"

"I'm a recently discharged soldier."

"Where did you serve?"

"Golani."

"No shit, I thought you were some puny desk jockey. Nice, bro. Grandpa following in grandson's footsteps. Like one of those feel-good newspaper articles. So, when were you discharged? July '09?"

"November 2007."

He laughed again. "You're hilarious, dude, you're still calling yourself *recently* discharged? I'm going to use that on myself one day. So you're probably a pothead, backpacked through India and shit?"

"Actually, no," I said.

"South America?"

I shook my head. Waxman gave me a puzzled look.

"So, like, what have you been doing all this time?"

"A bunch of odd jobs, nothing serious."

My answers clearly flustered him. "So what are you saying, bro, don't you want to, like, study something? Get ahead in life?"

"Not right now," I said.

"Okay, now I get you," he said. "I have a friend like you. Sort of a beach bum. Believe me, bro, I'd love to be like you guys, just going with the flow. You probably smoke weed all day, huh?"

"Never even tried it."

"Ever?" he asked incredulously.

"Not even cigarettes," I said. It was a lie. I had smoked one cigarette, the night we left Lebanon. But I had no intention of sharing that with him. I can't even begin to describe my disdain for people like Waxman, who can't complete a sentence without the words "bro" or "dude." Who are sure they have an explanation for just about everything. "Yup, bro, you totally get me. Going with the flow is my middle name."

"Yup, I've got a nose for people," he replied, pleased with himself.

I asked him who would replace him if he returned to the paratroopers. "To be honest, bro, just between you and me, I couldn't give less of a shit. This whole unit is a fucking joke anyway. I give it two years, tops, before they dismantle it."

"What are you talking about? You guys just caught a drug mule, you're at the top of your game."

"A fluke, dude, it was totally a fluke. The fact is this isn't even an operational unit, and I doubt this event is going to change that."

"What do you mean it isn't operational—they were trained as rifleman 07, weren't they?"

"Not really. It's just something I gave them to boost morale. They're barely 01."

I knew they were cutting corners over there, but I never thought it had gone that far. "But they're securing a settlement close to the border, how can that be?"

"I wouldn't call it *securing*, more like sitting around on their asses," Waxman said. "The settlements in the Jordan Valley started whining that the army wasn't protecting them, even though there's nothing to fight over here but sand. Anyway, about two years ago, that Rafi Eitan, the minister of pensioner affairs, offered the chief of staff an insane budget if they established a unit for the elderly, mainly for show. He wanted something for a photo op on TV, you know? To prove he did something with the seven seats he got in the Knesset. But bottom line, bro, no one has any illusions about us. Not the IDF and not the government. On the border itself they've got reserve soldiers, and if anything actually goes down there, which practically never happens, they won't think twice before deploying some real infantrymen. It's just a game everyone's playing. The old geezers are getting something to do, the guys in the settlements know it's better than nothing, and the IDF is getting funding for the whole project plus some extra spending money."

"And your soldiers don't know it's all a sham?" I asked angrily. "That the army is making money off their backs?"

"Please, bro, you think they don't know? They figured it out all by themselves. Your grandpa is the only person in the IDF who's still taking this whole business seriously. I've run out of ways to explain to him that he has to learn to let go a little. Maybe you can have a word with him about it, it might help."

Waxman's MIRS rang.

"It's the division commander," he said proudly, and stepped outside. I stayed with Grandpa for a few more minutes. I couldn't tell whether his expression was placid or perturbed.

The media began reporting the story about the old combat soldiers who caught the drug mule. The entire country was abuzz about it. Grandpa, who woke up the following day, was described as the commander of the operation and hailed a hero. A few journalists tried to swoop down on the hospital to land the first interview with Grandpa, but I made sure no one got in. The only person granted special permission to visit was the minister of the development of the Negev and Galilee, who told Grandpa he represented all that was good and right about Israel. Grandpa tried to appear indifferent to the commotion around him, but I knew all too well that he was loving the attention. That he felt he was finally getting the respect he was due.

A week later, Grandpa returned to the base. Around the same time, the chief of staff announced that the unit had proven its operational value, and that he would explore the possibility of establishing elderly platoons in the Nahal Brigade and the paratroopers. Two days later, while I was attending an open day at the Hebrew University of Jerusalem, I got a phone call from the chambers of the president of Israel. They told me the president wanted to invite the four elderly heroes and their families to receive a special appreciation certificate.

I told Grandpa that I had fought a war and was never awarded that kind of honor, and he replied with a smile that if I asked nicely, he'd give me a few tips.

"Do you believe he got a commendation?" I asked Dad, but he noted it wasn't a commendation, just a letter of appreciation. Ever since Dad had heard about the entire affair, he didn't say a word. Didn't even go to visit Grandpa at the hospital. He said he was terribly busy, that he had all these work things going on, but I knew he just couldn't accept the fact he had been wrong about his father the whole time.

21.

alman1964@gmail.com
November 1, 2009, 02:18:43
Subject: Re: Hi Yuli
I found your civics paper! It was in a shoebox under my bed. It was lying there in a pile of souvenirs I had brought over from my old apartment in Petah Tikva. Remember that apartment? What a dump, huh? I spent three years of my life there. To tell you the truth, I regret every moment. Wasted years. I should have gone to India the day after your Dad and I split up. What little still remained between you and me somehow got ruined

in that apartment. You'd come over once every two weeks, and wouldn't say a word to me. I know you think I didn't try hard enough, but let's face it, Yuli, you didn't give me much of a chance. Maybe I wasn't the perfect mother, but it's not like you were the perfect son. I'd never come out and say it, but I think you know it too.

And then came the phone call from that teacher of yours. What was her name? Dalia? I think it was Dalia. As I already wrote you, at that moment I thought it was a sign from above. I know it sounds like twisted logic to you, but I genuinely believed that even if you caught me going through your things, you wouldn't be angry with me. That you'd even appreciate it, that I'd go to such lengths to be part of your life. You know how much I wanted my mother to go through my things? As a kid I used to write letters containing my most intimate secrets and scatter them around the house, hoping she'd read them, but she never so much as touched them. She just didn't care, Yuli. So when I found your paper on the bed, I truly believed you had left it there for me to find.

"We Were Sparta," you called it, like the title of some highbrow book. I sat there for two hours and three cups of coffee, and what can I tell you, Yuli, my child? I couldn't understand it. Not really. The terms were completely foreign to me, your whole world view undecipherable. I never knew much about Athens or Sparta, so how could I understand what they were supposed to represent? I called your dad and asked him to explain it to me, but he refused to read something of yours that he didn't get directly from you, and once again I felt as though he had defeated me. So I told him he was absolutely right and that I'd overreached, and then I hung up and read it all over again, from the beginning. And a third time. And I started reading about ancient Greece, hoping that if I understood your paper, maybe I'd begin to understand you. Like it was some key card into your mind. And you know what? I daresay maybe I did understand some of it. You wrote that there are two types of power in this world, a moderate power, like Athens was, and a violent one like Sparta. You said it was like the Haganah and the Lehi, or Martin Luther King and Malcolm X, that duos like those existed throughout human history. And if I'm not mistaken, you argued there was one major difference between them—that the moderate power sanctifies the quality of life, while the violent power sanctifies life itself. Meaning, Athens dealt primarily with improving the quality of its citizens' lives, while Sparta was in constant battle over the mere right to live. You also wrote that as human beings, we want to believe the dominant power is the moderate one. That Martin Luther King made a greater impact on the world than Malcolm X, but that we're just deluding ourselves, because we can't handle the truth. Which is that human history is driven by its violent actors. "Like dark energy," you wrote. And after that, you wrote the weirdest thing, which I don't even know if I agree with, but you claimed that the violent force is also the moral one, because life itself should always come first. You wrote that Israel is the Sparta of the twenty-first century, and that that was a good thing. "Because where there is violence, there is life." I'll never forget that sentence. You wrote that people don't even remember history. That Athenian culture might have contributed more to the world, to democracy, but it makes no difference. Because the great war between Athens and Sparta was won by the Spartans, and *that*, we mustn't forget. What can I tell you, my child? All those words, all that violence, seemed so unrelated to you, to that inner peace of yours. I spent days on end trying to figure out where all those theories came from. The need to survive? To fight at all costs? Was it because of the divorce? The debts? I truly don't know, Yuli. To this day, I can't understand it. And it's only now that I'm realizing it was with all those thoughts and convictions that you went off to war. God, that's what you took with you into Lebanon?

I remember when I told you I had read the paper. It was during Friday night dinner. Just the two of us. I couldn't keep it in any longer, so I told you your teacher called. And that I read your paper. And I started telling you how proud I was of you, and that if you wanted, you could become a wonderful university lecturer. And you didn't say a word, Yuli. I tried to read your expression, searching for some clue into your thoughts, but you finished eating and went to your room, and it took me a few days to realize you were angry at me, even though I couldn't understand why. It's not like I read a secret love letter, it was a civics paper. And about such an academic subject, so impersonal. But you must have understood even then what I only learned two years ago, when you were deployed to Lebanon. That wars are not a national issue. It was always a personal matter, perhaps more personal than anything else in this world.

Sometimes I tell myself that's when I lost you—the moment I read your paper. But that isn't the case. It isn't that simple. I wish there was a single moment in time I could point to and say—there, that's when I lost my child. But there is no such moment to cling to. You wouldn't even give me that.

Best,
Alma Rosenblum,
Emissary for the Jewish Agency for Israel in New Delhi

22.

alman1964@gmail.com
November 1, 2009, 02:59:49
Subject: Re: Hi Yuli
Did you know I once bought a ticket home? The day Goldwasser and Regev, may they rest in peace, were abducted, before anyone

knew that war was a war. I bought a ticket. Even packed a bag and drove to the airport. I honestly don't know why I didn't board the plane. Maybe I was afraid I wouldn't be able to handle seeing with my own eyes that you were no longer mine. Because as long as I couldn't see your face, I could at least keep pretending you're mine, you know? It's not much of an excuse, I know. Maybe you were right all along. Maybe some women were never meant to be mothers.

Best,

Alma Rosenblum,

Emissary for the Jewish Agency for Israel in New Delhi

23.

WE NEVER MADE it to the President's Residence in Jerusalem.

I woke up early that morning, put on a white dress shirt, and gave myself a meticulous shave. After I finished getting ready, I went to check on Dad. He was lying in bed, curled under the blanket. He was still asleep. I woke him up and said we had to leave in fifteen minutes. He mumbled an apology, said he must have forgotten to set his alarm clock.

"Maybe you should go without me," he suggested wearily, but I wasn't about to let him get away with not coming.

"Enough. You can at least give him the respect of showing up at the ceremony."

He heaved himself up in bed and stared at the floor.

"You're right," he said. He washed his face and put on his shoes, but persisted in his silent rebellion by refusing to wear anything elegant, settling for a simple gray T-shirt.

"I don't get it. Aren't you proud of him?" I asked as we walked out of the house. "Why are you being so oppositional?"

"It's not that," he said with a sigh. "Sometimes it's just a bit too much, this whole thing."

My phone rang. An unregistered number. "What's up, bro?" asked a voice I couldn't recognize. I put him on speakerphone.

"I'm fine, just, remind me, who is this?"

"Man, I forgot you're such a pothead. It's Waxman," he said, and Dad grimaced.

"Listen, there's a small hitch."

"What kind of hitch?" I asked. Dad leaned into the phone.

"Look, there's no good way to say this, but it looks like Neuerman . . . I mean, your grandpa, has Parkinson's."

Waxman said that when Grandpa had been admitted to the hospital, they ran a few routine tests. Four days ago some troubling results came back, so they brought him in again. He said Grandpa wasn't being very cooperative. "I'm really no expert, but it doesn't sound good." He explained that in hindsight, the doctors thought the neck pain wasn't brought on by Gourevitch falling on him, but were symptoms of the disease. Said it also explained the instances when Grandpa's hands started trembling. That even he had noticed it himself, but thought it was just nerves.

Dad's expression didn't betray the slightest shred of emotion; it remained with the same frozen gaze fixed on the road, and I didn't even know how to begin processing the news. Waxman further explained that according to the doctor he probably still had at least two good years ahead of him, but that we would need to meet with him to receive all the information.

"We could find him a new position in the unit for a few months," he said, "maybe a quartermaster clerk or something. We'll give him the option of an honorable discharge, but I assume you understand he can't keep serving as a combat soldier in the platoon."

"How did Grandpa react to this?" I asked, trying to imagine the look on his face when they gave him the news, but couldn't.

Waxman didn't reply.

"Well, how did he react?"

"Not great, that's why I called you. I mean, at first he seemed pretty blasé about it. Said it was a bunch of baloney. I was sure he didn't really care all that much, but the moment I told him we'd have to consider moving him to a new position . . . well, he disappeared."

"Disappeared?" Dad asked.

"Disappeared."

"What do you mean disappeared?" I asked, wondering how much worse this story could get.

Waxman had no idea where Grandpa was. He said no one knew. The only thing they knew for sure was that the Renault Kangoo had disappeared along with him, and that one of the Thai workers saw the car exiting the settlement at dawn.

"What about the soldier at the gate?"

"On a bathroom break," Waxman relied.

"I don't get it. You can't head a unit without having a soldier go missing on you?" I asked. I wasn't actually expecting an answer.

"Listen, bro, I know it sounds bad, but everything's under control, really. We've got half the command on their feet right now, everyone's looking for him," he said, trying to sound reassuring, talking in that regimental commander's tone. "He's not the first soldier to go AWOL. I'm sure they'll find him in a couple of hours, by threatening Gourevitch or something," he said and laughed.

We didn't.

"Really, you've got nothing to worry about. The moment the ceremony ends, I'll be joining the search efforts myself."

"You'll be joining after the ceremony?"

"Yup, five minutes after it ends, I'm out of there. After all, he's my soldier."

"Are you fucking kidding me?" I yelled at him. "*Your* soldier has gone AWOL. How can you even think of going to the ceremony?"

"Listen, man, it's just going to be a couple of hours," he said defensively. "Hundreds of soldiers are looking for him as we speak, another one won't make a difference," Waxman said, and added in a condescending tone, "It's the president, bro, I can't just bail on him."

"Are you for real? What's up with you? I—" I said, and before I could finish the sentence, Dad took the phone and hung up.

"I've had enough of that moron," he said.

I nodded in agreement. "I'm taking the next exit, we're going to find him."

I'm not even sure I said where I was taking us. We both knew where we should be searching.

"What a mess," Dad mumbled. He shrank into himself, as if Waxman's news had hit him belatedly. "God, what a mess."

"We'll work it out," I told him. "We managed to survive Golani, we'll survive this too."

Dad cracked the window open, struggling to take in a little air. "I'm not so sure," he said, "I'm really not so sure anymore."

24.

THE DOOR WAS OPEN. A trail of army bootprints led us up the staircase. He was there, right where we thought he would be. Standing on the roof with his back to us, approaching the ledge, his rifle slung over his shoulder and his shirt untucked. His brown beret lay unclaimed on the floor. He turned to us for a moment, then went back to studying the cars driving along Jabotinsky Street. Slowly, I stepped forward. Dad remained by the door to the roof, holding on to the handrail.

"Parkinson's, they tell me," he spoke with a tired voice. "Can you believe it? One moment you're getting a commendation, and the next they're telling you you should start thinking of one of those Filipino caregivers."

"Waxman said they need to run a few more tests," I said.

"Oh please," he grumbled, turning to face me. "I may be old, but I'm no idiot. Can you believe this? I make this unit famous, and a moment later they want to get rid of me!" He laughed feebly. "It's like discharging

Ehud Barak right after the '73 raid on Lebanon, or Kahalani after the Yom Kippur War. Can you imagine?"

I didn't know what to say.

"Well, can you?" he barked at me.

"No, actually I can't."

"Of course you can't!" he yelled in an explosion of anger. "If it weren't for me, Waxman and his miserable old schmucks would still be stuck in the Valley guarding mosquitoes. Unthinkable!" he exclaimed, his voice strangled with emotion. "To kick someone to the curb like that? So my hands shake a little, so what? Schneider doesn't have scoliosis? Pinchas doesn't have a catheter? Just like that, to toss someone away like a piece of trash? It's unheard of!"

I wanted to say something soothing, comforting, but the words got stuck in my throat like a jammed M16. I looked at Dad, hoping he'd whip out his calculator or say something logical that would make sense of the situation. But Dad didn't say a word. He just kept standing by the staircase, clutching the handrail, fighting for every breath of air, unable to hide his helplessness.

We stood there, the three Neuerman men, facing each other, not knowing what to do.

"Gourevitch told me he knows of a nice old folks' home," Grandpa said, lowering his voice just to raise it back up. "I'll go to my grave before I move into an old folks' home!" he yelled. "No way, forget it. Fat chance!"

"No one said anything about a retirement home," I tried to clarify, but Grandpa was no longer listening.

"I'll just go on another mission. Yes, that's what I'll do. I'll march into Gaza alone if that's what it takes."

"It won't help," I hissed.

"It would help a great deal. Put that idiot Waxman in his place once and for all."

"Enough already. Enough with that Waxman of yours," I yelled at him. "Enough with going on a mission whenever something in your life goes wrong."

"You don't get to tell me how to live, you hear? No one does."

"Go conquer China for all I care," I said. "You're burning through these years trying to escape them."

"You have no idea—" he yelled and waved his weapon, then tripped, swayed unsteadily for a few moments and fell to his knees. I leaped forward and caught him with both hands a moment before his face hit the floor.

"Bring a chair!" I yelled to Dad who was hesitantly pacing toward us. "Come on, hurry up," I called out and slid the weapon strap off Grandpa's shoulder. Dad brought over a dirty plastic chair from across the roof.

"Hold his back," I told Dad, who still seemed confused. We heaved him up onto the chair. Grandpa's neck tilted sideward and his hands went limp. He could barely keep his eyes open.

"I've had enough," he mumbled between garbled words.

"You can't just give up," I told him, supporting his neck so he wouldn't hit his head against the backrest.

"An eighty-year-old man can do whatever he wants," he declared with a feeble voice.

"You really can't," I replied. "You're not allowed. Gourevitch would miss you too much."

I think I saw a flicker of a smile, but I can't say for sure.

We barely managed to get him down the stairs. His legs kept giving way. He was heavy, a lot heavier than he looked. I put him into bed, peeled off his uniform, and yanked off his boots. I covered him with a blanket while Dad looked at us from the corner of the room. Then I stood beside the bed, my gaze fixed on his chest, making sure he was breathing. Only after he started snoring did I allow myself a deep breath.

Dad and I pulled shifts looking after Grandpa, switching every three hours. One of us was always at his bedside, making sure he wouldn't try to make a run for it or work himself into a heart attack. I don't think we exchanged a single word that entire day. Grandpa didn't get up even once, and seemed pretty relaxed for an old man who only a few hours ago had threatened a ground invasion into Gaza.

At about ten P.M. I finished my shift and came out into the living room. Dad was sitting in the white armchair, staring at the dark TV screen.

I took a glass of water from the kitchen and sat down beside him. Grandpa's weapon lay on the table.

"I'm sorry," he said, "I couldn't, I mean, that moment, I just . . ."

"I didn't know what to do either," I said.

"You did, you were great," he sighed. "This shouldn't be your responsibility, Yuli." He started rummaging through his pants pockets.

"What are you looking for?"

"Pills," he replied. "I probably forgot them at home."

"You? Mr. Organized?"

"I know, right?" he replied, still going through his pockets.

"Go get some sleep," I told him.

"It's my shift. You go sleep."

"It's okay, I'll stay on a bit longer with Grandpa. I'm not tired."

"Okay, so maybe just a short nap," he conceded. "But wake me up in an hour, okay? I'll come switch with you."

"Sure," I lied to him. "No problem."

He slipped off his shoes, kicking them into the middle of the living room instead of placing them neatly side by side like he always did. Then he leaned back in the armchair, struggling to find a comfortable position. I wanted to suggest he move to the couch or something, but I kept quiet.

I went back to Grandpa's room and sat down beside him. I leaned in and took a close look at all the wrinkles and spots webbing his face. I gently smoothed his white hair, with the furtive hope that a neat appearance would keep him safe. It didn't really help. He no longer looked like an eighty-year-old Golanchik. He just looked like an old man. A very old man.

I leaned back and stared at the ceiling. I can't say for sure whether I fell asleep or not.

What I can say is that I heard the gunshot.

25.

yulineuerman@gmail.com
November 6, 2009, 08:57:44
Subject: Update
Hey,
Dad passed away four days ago. The funeral was in Kfar Saba. The shivah is being held at Grandpa's house.

I've moved into Grandpa's for the time being, until things settle down.
You're welcome to call,
Yuli

26.

alman1964@gmail.com
November 6, 2009, 09:52:37
Subject: Re: Update
You're not picking up. I bought a ticket, I'll be there tomorrow evening.
Best,
Alma Rosenblum,
Emissary for the Jewish Agency for Israel in New Delhi

27.

yulineuerman@gmail.com
November 6, 2009, 10:03:04
Subject: Re: Update

You don't have to come.
Yuli

28.

alman1964@gmail.com
November 6, 2009, 10:06:21
Subject: Re: Update
I'm not asking you.
Best,
Alma Rosenblum,
Emissary for the Jewish Agency for Israel in New Delhi

29.

I WASN'T ACTUALLY reading *The Myth of Sisyphus* that day when we visited Grandpa in the Jordan Valley. I mean, I'd read it once, before I enlisted, but when I tried reading it again that evening, I just couldn't. To be honest, since my army days I haven't been reading much. Or at all, really. I try sometimes, but I just can't seem to concentrate. After a few lines, the words start bouncing and blurring on the page and I get a headache and have to stop.

But it doesn't matter, because you don't really have to read the whole book to get it. Shapiro was right. Camus turned a story worth a sentence and a half into a whole book, and let's face it, he gets his point across in the very first line. The rest of the book, like Shapiro put it, is just the babbling of a French fatty.

"There is only one really serious philosophical question," he writes, "and that is suicide."

That's it. That's the gist of it.

I think any normal person thinks about suicide at least once in his life. Not necessarily seriously, but at least superficially considers what would happen if he decided to end his life. The only person I know who never even thought about it once is Grandpa. Even though he never stopped talking about death, I am certain the idea of ending his own life never crossed his mind. He clung to life the way he had clung to Grandma Miriam, as if he never even knew that leaving of his own free will was an option.

Dad, on the other hand, had considered the matter carefully. Apparently, like with everything else in his life, he thought it through, weighing the pros and cons, factoring in the various considerations and implications. Eventually, the last thing he ever did on this planet was depart from it the only way he knew how—not as an impulsive decision, but in a premeditated, carefully planned move.

He had begun taking out life insurance policies a year and a half ago. As of now, I know of at least four different ones. I'm guessing a few more will pop up soon. I don't know if back then he had already decided he was going to go through with it, or whether he just wanted to keep suicide as an option.

It was only a few days after the funeral, as I was tidying up his study, that I started learning new things about him, all these little bits of information I never knew. It's crazy how much you can learn about a person from a few forms. Especially about a person like Dad. Maybe that's why he didn't bother leaving a note. He probably knew there was enough information to explain everything.

There were receipts from all the psychiatric treatments he had undergone. Dozens of prescriptions for the pills he'd taken over the years. According to the dates on the receipts, most of the treatments had taken place after Mom left, but not all. And some of the prescriptions for antidepressants were issued before I was even born. I also found insurance policies he had signed. I even saw my own signature on some of them, although I had no memory of signing them. Maybe it was when he made Grandpa sign those private health insurance forms before he enlisted. He knew I wouldn't read them.

He also kept meticulous records of his debts. Not that I hadn't been aware of this, but I didn't want to get too involved. He owed far more than I had imagined. A few million. Some to the banks, some to friends. The police investigator said there was also a good chance he had gotten entangled with loan sharks. That there were all these calculations that didn't add up. Sums that appeared in one ledger but not in another. He said it was highly unlikely a person like Dad would suddenly be careless with his records, and that he probably settled his debts on the black market before he killed himself, so we'll never really know what happened there.

When the investigator told me that one of the motives behind his suicide was the insurance money, I told him there was no way. That Dad had told me himself life insurance companies wouldn't pay death benefits if the person who took out the policy committed suicide. The investigator said that was only partially correct. The truth, like always, was in the fine print. Your family isn't entitled to the funds if you take out insurance and kill yourself the very next day. The person has to be insured for at least a year for the money to be payable. But once that year is up, the family of the deceased is legally entitled to that money. Dad knew that. Of course he knew.

"So that's why he told me about it? So I wouldn't suspect?" I asked the investigator, but he didn't have the answer to that one.

I like to think he had chosen that day—the day we dragged Grandpa off the roof—for a reason. That it, too, was a well-planned move. That there was a good enough reason behind his decision to leave us on such a shitty day. Grandpa thought it was because of the Tavor rifle. That he saw the opportunity and took it. But I think he's wrong. Dad had enough ways and pills to end his life whenever he wanted. Maybe he had just tried holding on for as long as he could, but knew Grandpa's illness was more than he could deal with. I guess that in his analytical mind, choosing suicide at that particular moment in time was simply the responsible thing to do. His way of ensuring he wouldn't become a burden.

And maybe there is no logical explanation. Maybe plans get messed up even for people like him.

30.

I WAS AWAKENED by a knock on the door. It was the fourth night of the shivah, almost midnight. Another knock. I got up and went to open the door. Shapiro was standing there in his crumpled service dress and a brown beret on his head. He saluted with his left hand and apologized for not coming earlier, said it was all because of that schmuck Waxman, who had taken away his Shabbat leave. He walked into the apartment, leaning on his cane, dragging his army boots across the floor. Avigail was standing behind him. Shapiro dropped his bag at the entrance to the living room and plopped himself onto the worn leather couch. "Oy gevalt," he sighed and took a deep breath. "Listen to me, don't ever get hip replacement surgery."

I made them coffee and the three of us sat down in the living room.

"How are you?" Avigail asked me, placing her hand on top of mine. I imparted a few clichés, about how hard it was and how we were trying to pull through, and withdrew my hand.

"You don't have to say all that tired bullshit," she said. "It's okay if you're not up to talking about it."

"Actually, I'm not."

Shapiro took a sip of his coffee.

"This doesn't have any sugar!" he croaked.

"You're not allowed any," Avigail replied peacefully. "Say, did you even take your pills?"

Shapiro didn't answer.

"Grandpa!" She said he was behaving like a child, then got up and went over to his duffel bag, took out a pillbox and a big plastic baggie. She handed him a few pills and a glass of water, took out rolling paper from her pocket, opened the baggie, and started rolling a joint.

"What gives?" I asked in a huff. "This is totally inappropriate."

"It's for me," Shapiro said. "Medicinal. Top-notch stuff," he announced proudly. "Honey, would you be so kind as to roll one for Yuli as well? He's had a tough week."

"Absolutely not," I said, waving my hands in anger to make it clear there was no way they were going to smoke pot in Grandpa's house.

"Come on, what do you care?" she said. "You've got every excuse."

"How are you even allowed to smoke pot?" I asked Shapiro. "You're a soldier. In the army."

"Right," he replied. "The first IDF soldier with a permit for medicinal weed!"

"The family is awfully proud," Avigail added with a smile.

"Listen, this is not cool," I said. "If Grandpa finds out you smoked in his house . . ."

Avigail stopped rolling and looked somewhere past my shoulder. Shapiro turned his gaze to the same spot, his smile turning hesitant. For a moment, it seemed as if he was struggling to recognize the man in front of him. Grandpa was standing there in a white undershirt, long black pants and slippers, looking at us with a tired gaze.

"You're up?"

He nodded, rooted to his spot. There were a few moments of silence.

"What are you doing?" he asked.

"We came to visit your grandson," Avigail replied. Shapiro kept studying Grandpa with a worried look.

"I mean, what are you doing with that?" he said, pointing at the baggie.

"Oh, that's for my back pain," Shapiro mumbled. "Can't fall asleep without it. Want some?"

"No," he said. "And don't smoke in here."

"Sorry," Avigail said and quickly shoved it all back into her bag. Grandpa considered me for a moment, then looked at Shapiro. "You can do it upstairs," he announced. "Where it won't stink up the house."

Grandpa shuffled back to his room, and two minutes later reappeared with a plaid jacket. Without saying a word, he started up the stairs to the roof, the three of us promptly following him.

We sat there in oppressive silence. Shapiro and Grandpa no longer looked like close friends, more like a couple of old fogies who happened to bump into each other in line at the Social Security office.

"Got a light?" Shapiro asked. Avigail handed him a lighter and he lit the joint and took a deep drag. "Oy," he said. "Oy, this is good."

"Give me the light," Grandpa said and took a cigar out of his jacket pocket. He stared at it for a few moments, drew it to his nose and sniffed. Finally, he lit it, took a few deep drags, and surprisingly, didn't cough even once.

"What's this about, Neuerman? A few days into civilian life and you're already a hedonist? The politicians would be proud of you," Shapiro said quietly, still unsure whether he was allowed to joke.

"I was a hedonist in the army too," Grandpa said. He told us that the day he had escaped from the base he not only stole the unit vehicle but also the cigars, the ones Waxman had bought in Cuba and wouldn't stop bragging about.

"I wanted something to remind me of the little shit," he said.

While Shapiro kept a straight face, Avigail couldn't keep herself from laughing. Eventually Grandpa let out a smile too.

"Neuerman, what do you say, don't you think your grandson should try a little puff?"

"He's a big boy, he can do whatever he wants."

"I've never smoked anything in my life, and I'm not about to start now. You're welcome to offer to your granddaughter instead."

"I don't smoke either," she said. "But it's a shame you won't give it a try. You should know it really helps people with post-trauma."

"And what does that have anything to do with me?" I asked, tensing.

"Oh please, stop kidding yourself. You're fucked up, Yuli. You know that perfectly well. Even now, it's like you're sitting here at someone else's shivah."

"What are you talking about?" I asked her. I looked at Grandpa and Shapiro, but they kept their eyes on the floor, avoiding me.

"Don't take it hard. Happens to the best of us," she said, and once again put her hand on mine.

"I have no idea what you're talking about," I said, riled. But I kept my hand beneath hers.

"You should listen to her," Shapiro said. "Girlie here is a med student."

I was starting to feel light-headed.

"Drink some water and rest your head," she said before I managed to figure out what I was feeling. She leaned my head on her shoulder and started brushing her fingers through my hair. I was hoping she wouldn't stop.

Shapiro told Grandpa they had a new game in the unit. Whenever Gourevitch fell asleep during guard duty, someone would sneak up on him from behind and rasp in his ear, "Neuerman's coming!" He said Gourevitch jolted in fear every time. Grandpa laughed.

After half an hour or so, Avigail announced it was time to get going, and I had to part with her soft body. Shapiro promised to get a few sick days and come visit again. Avigail just smiled without saying a word.

Grandpa and I stayed alone on the roof. He gazed at the high-rises of the diamond district, and I looked up at the sky, waiting for the dizziness to pass.

"Nice girl, Shapiro's granddaughter," he said.

"Yup," I replied. "Nice."

"You know, once upon a time this roof had a full view of the sea."

A sinking heaviness took over me, slowly spreading throughout my body. My every muscle. Had Dad been there, he would have whispered in my ear that Grandpa was talking nonsense again. I just wanted to go back to sleep. Back to a place where I didn't need to face reality.

"Mom sent me an email saying she was on her way over," I said.

"When do you think she'll be here?"

"I'm guessing she's already on the plane."

"You must be happy about it."

"If coming here for five minutes is what helps her feel like she's being a decent human being, then whatever floats her boat."

"Come on, Yuli, enough. Give her a chance."

"You can't give a chance to someone who's never been there," I said.

Grandpa sighed. "Maybe there are things you don't know," he replied. "Things I don't know either. You can't judge her like that."

"So who can?" I asked. "Who's allowed to judge her?"

"I don't know, Yuli, I honestly don't."

We sat there silently for a few moments.

"Are you angry at him?" I asked.

"No," he said. "Are you?"

"Very."

His eyes became red. He turned his gaze back to the high-rises.

"Well, I guess I'm a little angry too," he said, grimacing. "I mean, how, how can a person go kaput just like that? Decide all of a sudden to end his life?" he protested weakly. "I don't even know if I'm angry. I just don't understand."

"It's pretty obvious to me."

"I know the debts weighed heavy on him, but . . ."

"The debts were just an excuse."

"What are you talking about?"

"The debts weren't the reason."

Grandpa hesitated, as if wondering whether he really wanted to ask.

"So why, Yuli? Why would a person do such a thing?"

"Because he had enough," I replied. "He was sick of it all. Tired of living. He was like Mom, thinking only of himself."

I saw how my words physically pained him. He regretted having asked.

"Tell me, you actually believe that nonsense?"

"What can I do," I said. "It's the truth."

"Enough, Yuli. Enough. How can you even say such a thing?" he said in a stifled voice. "Your dad had debts. He needed—"

"We would have managed. You know perfectly well we would have. It was just the easy way out."

Grandpa put his hand on his forehead and shook his head. "You don't understand, Yuli. You're a smart boy, but there are things you just don't understand."

My dizziness only got worse. I tried closing my eyes, but it didn't help.

"You did smoke a cigarette once," Grandpa said, "I know you did."

"Do I look like a smoker?" I asked him. "The smell alone gives me a headache."

"You tried it at least once, I know that much."

"You caught me," I said. "Lucky guess."

Grandpa leaned in closer.

"It's no guess," he said. "Your dad told me."

I looked out at the sky. The noise of the cars down on the street was driving me crazy.

"How could he have told you, he didn't even know about it. It was in the army."

"I'm telling you he knew, Yuli." His words were strained. "He saw it with his own eyes."

Two cars started honking down below. The noise was unbearable.

"Grandpa, cut the crap, okay? It's not cool."

"It was the night you came back from Lebanon, Yuli. I know."

I jumped up from my chair. I thought I was becoming paranoid. That I was starting to hear things.

"He was there. He drove up north two days after the war broke out. He rented a room at some kibbutz there."

"You've really lost your marbles, huh?" I growled. "Enough, I don't want to hear any more of this bullshit. And it isn't like you to pull stupid pranks on me. Leave me alone now."

"It's the God's honest truth, Yuli. He was up north the entire time," he said, his voice strangled. "I'm telling you. I talked to him on the phone every day." He asked me if I remembered how a group of civilians was waiting to cheer us in the assembly area the day we came out of Lebanon.

"No," I said, even though that wasn't entirely true. I did have a vague memory of a few people showing up there with small charcoal grills and Israeli flags. They threw a big barbecue for the whole unit.

"There were a lot of civilians there, Yuli. Your dad was one of them."

"No way," I said. "There's just no way."

"I'm telling you," Grandpa stuttered with a choked-up voice. "He told me everything, said he stood at a distance, but he spotted you, all right. He saw you sitting there alone, far from the rest of your unit, smoking a cigarette. He said it pained him to see you like that."

"Enough already!" I yelled at him. "Enough with the lies. Enough!"

Grandpa's last sentence was more than I could bear. I kept screaming at him that it couldn't be true, that it just made no sense. I sat back down in the chair, my legs shaking. The dizziness was driving me crazy. I couldn't think straight. I felt how everything was crashing into me. Grandpa got up and approached me, putting his hand on my shoulder.

"Then why didn't he tell me about it?" I asked. "Even in passing? He had two years to tell me."

"I don't know," Grandpa replied. "To tell you the truth, I've asked myself the same question more than once."

I let out a bitter laugh. "Driving the entire way there without telling me," I hissed. "It's so like him."

We started dragging ourselves down the stairs, holding on to each other, saying that maybe the two of us ought to consider a career in nursing. I collapsed onto the couch.

Grandpa went to his room, brought a blanket, and covered me up. "So maybe only I should consider a career in nursing," he said, and put his hand on my head. "My Yulinka."

I opened my eyes and saw him looking at me, his eyes full of pity.

"It was on your bucket list," I told him.

"What?" he asked.

"The cigar," I said. "It was on your list."

He smiled. Then he got up and turned off the light.

I closed my eyes and remembered. How I sat there on a rock. How I smoked the cigarette the deputy company sergeant major had brought me. He knew I didn't smoke, but said that at times like these, it didn't really count. I remembered looking at the civilians standing outside the assembly area. At Dad, who stood there with his fanny pack like some sad weirdo, right behind the guy fanning the grill. It looked like he was trying to help him, but he knocked over a plateful of kebabs, doing more harm than good. I remember seeing his face, blurring in the white smoke.

I knew it wasn't a real memory. But at that moment, it made do.

Exit

NEXT TO A RED HILL in the desert, our only daughter wandered and disappeared into the thicket of her dreams, leaving us blind—as we heard the thud of her fall without knowing in which direction to turn.

1.

NELLY WAS THE first to pick up on it. One night, after Shira had fallen asleep, she whispered to me in the kitchen that something was going on with our little girl. Something bad. Not just your everyday blues. Something in her eyes had changed since we moved south. "I'm not speaking metaphorically," she stressed. "There's something in their grayness that doesn't look right. I don't know."

Nelly believed in the body, believed it spoke louder than words. She claimed that's how she could almost always tell when something was about to happen to Shira. I thought there was a simpler explanation.

That she always suspected something was going on with our daughter, so sometimes she also happened to be right. I'm not saying this as criticism. Quite the opposite. Nelly was the better parent. Neither of us doubted that. When Shira was five, even she noted in a passing remark made on Tel Baruch beach that "Mommy loves me more." Nelly quickly denied it, signaled to me to go get the girl an ice cream, and like an idiot I ran a kilometer and a half for a cracked Cornetto, only to run back and discover that a week earlier, Shira had sworn off dairy because her kindergarten teacher said milk was stolen from cows. I don't know whether Nelly forgot to warn me, or if she just wanted to remind me of the power dynamic. I, for my part, tried to come out ahead at least in the more banal areas—parent-teacher conferences, school plays, and sports competitions—where I enjoyed a slight lead. This included the fourth-grade soccer league's final match of the season, when ASA Ramat Aviv beat Beitar Kfar Shalem two to one thanks to Shira blocking a last-minute penalty kick.

A brief hug at the end of the game. That's all I managed to get from her.

"The girl's doing fine," I announced. I told Nelly that I had actually been worried the first two weeks, when she acted as if nothing had changed. No sane girl moves from Tel Aviv to a desert homestead without having some kind of temporary crisis, and it's good for her to finally experience it.

Nelly said I was missing the point and lowered the jar of herbal tea onto the table with a thud. Other than her clothes, it was the only thing she brought with her from our old house, claiming that without it she would go back to smoking in two days. I wasn't as successful at asceticism; I set out south with two bookcases, a telescope, and my framed certificate of excellence from the Technion, which I still haven't found the time to hang. It was the one condition I made when Nelly insisted we move, to take whatever I wanted with me, and to her credit she never gave me any trouble over it.

"It's a little more serious than that, Ofer," she said, adding my name to convey the gravity of the matter.

"You're just getting yourself worked up for no reason," I threw in before she could say anything else. "Give it a couple of weeks, the girl will get used to it."

"That's what I'm trying to explain, I don't think it's just the move," she said, and added in a confiding tone, "Maybe you could talk to her? I've tried but it's not working."

I wanted to say that I'd tried as well, that I'd been trying for some time now and getting nowhere. And that also, I'd lately come to realize that Shira had always belonged more to her than to me. That maybe it was time we considered having another kid. And that we would agree that I get dibs on this one. We'd sign an agreement before he's even born, two kids for two parents. But I didn't really want to bring up the subject, to deal with her adamant assertion that it was all in my head, and her not-so-subtle insinuations that even if it wasn't, a father doesn't talk about his child like that.

"Sure thing," I replied, got up, and went to our bedroom. "I'll talk to her."

2.

I WOKE UP to an empty room. Nelly had left for work early and dropped off Shira at school on her way. She was supposed to start work every day at nine, but insisted on being at the office at eight. To set an example. "To help these people realize their potential, because potential is not something they're short of here in the south," she'd repeat her worn mantra, as if the people of the south were another moisturizer she had taken upon herself to market to the masses. I have to admit I was skeptical at first. When out of nowhere Nelly suggested we move to a remote farm in the south, I didn't buy her sudden Zionist urge to settle and develop the Negev. But after two months here, I'm not so sure anymore. You never know with Nelly. Most of the time she can't stand the world, but every so often she gets these bursts of compassion, which she herself can't explain. She once called me from the car, and sounding rather distraught said she had picked up a homeless Russian she found on the street. She ordered me to switch on the water heater and clear my wet clothes from the bathroom. Only after I said that if Shira caught AIDS it was on her did she come to her senses, dropping the guy off on the Namir highway with two hundred shekels in his pocket.

And yet, Nelly wasn't one to move to the south out of purely altruistic motives. It's tempting to believe we moved because she wanted the promotion, but that wasn't the only reason either. Even though we never discuss it, I know we moved because of me. Because I didn't deliver. Didn't make good on the promise I made on our first date in that dive bar in downtown Haifa.

During our twelve years of marriage, how many times have we discussed that promise? Three? Four? Hard to say exactly. But I do remember what she told me a few months after that first date, when we went on our first vacation together—a bed-and-breakfast in the Galilee. She lay on the bed in a white bathrobe, half naked, ran her fingers through my hair and said that was what had won her over. The promise that by forty, I'd make my first million. She explained it wasn't my desire to get rich that attracted her. It wasn't the money, it was the drive. It was how I said it—not as an aspiration, but a cold fact. "That's what makes you so special," she said, and quickly added, "makes *us* special. The drive to push forward. To succeed unapologetically."

I immediately told her she couldn't be more right. And not because I actually knew she was right like I was hoping she was. I don't know whether I was truly planning on making a million bucks, or just wanted to impress a girl. But with time, I found out I liked playing the guy she wanted me to be. The one who goes once a week to a fusion restaurant without knowing what fusion cuisine means; who surprises his girlfriend with a trip to London on a Wednesday morning for no special reason, just because he feels like it. Nelly says a man is measured by his most ambitious dream, and mine started the day I met her.

There was only one problem with our dreams—she realized them, and I didn't. She beat me four years ago, whizzed past me leaving a trail of dust when she was appointed VP at Segal & Zuzovsky, while I was still stuck in career limbo as a development manager in a series of mediocre start-ups whose idea of a company fun day was an egg-and-spoon race at the Yarkon Park. At first she teased me that I couldn't keep up. But with time the banter died down and was replaced by tedious exchanges such as whose turn it was to take out the trash and which form to fetch from the bank. Petty requests that only reinforced my fear that all the expectations she had of me at the beginning had disappeared along the way, as if she had resigned to spending her life with a lesser man.

I honestly thought the start-up I had joined two years ago, Lucid Memo, was going to change everything. The whole business was based on a Jewish professor of neuroscience from Harvard who immigrated to Israel after reading the book *Start-up Nation*. She moved here and hooked up with an Israeli hi-tech entrepreneur, some guy called Amichai Miner; they decided to devise a technology that would enable people to share memories. Today I can't believe I thought it stood a chance; I guess I just didn't think it through at the time. I even gave up part of my salary in exchange for options in the company. All I wanted was to make good on my promise. To score a knockout against life itself. I worked my ass off, anywhere between fourteen and sixteen hours a day, including weekends. Including holidays. More than I wanted the money, I wanted to get to the moment I could tell Nelly I made an exit, that the company was sold to some Chinese investment fund. To see how she would smile despite herself, exposing that small gap between her two front teeth she always tried to hide.

But that didn't happen. Development stalled and the money started to run out. I was forced to recruit mediocre talent because we couldn't compete with the salaries other companies were offering. Six months later I was fired from my position as head of development, and one of those unremarkable employees took over my role for half the pay. His name was Nicolai, a strange bird who had graduated from college only three years ago; one of those people who thinks that anyone who doesn't vacation abroad at least once a year is living below the poverty line. He still calls me once a month to bitch about his problems at work, failing to comprehend that I have no interest in helping him, even though I've been laying on pretty thick hints about it.

Anyway, instead of celebrating my fortieth birthday on a yacht bound for the Canary Islands like we've always talked about, Nelly and I settled for Eyal Shani's new joint. Rockstar Shlomi Shaban and his actress wife, Yuval Scharf, sat at the table to our right. It was there, shortly before our dessert arrived—chocolate cake sprinkled with sea salt—that Nelly brought up the idea of moving south. "For half a year tops." She said Zuzovsky had asked her to set up the new offices in Mitzpe Ramon. She talked about the unexploited potential of the residents of the Negev. She said that if she did a good job, she'd climb another rung on the ladder to CEO. And that the timing couldn't be better because her parents would be staying in LA for at least another year, so we could live on their farm on Highway 40, a fifteen-minute drive to Mitzpe. Then she launched into a ten-minute monologue about why living at the end of the earth was actually a good thing. That the clean air would do wonders for Shira's asthma. That we always said we wanted to check the living-outside-a-major-city box. And besides, it would be significantly cheaper living on the farm because her parents were even paying the electricity and water, so instead of looking for a new job I could work on developing that app I'd been talking about for over a year now. And what she really wanted to say but chose not to was that it had been two months since I'd been let go and I still hadn't gotten off the couch. That if I wanted to continue being unemployed and depressed, at least I could do it in rent-free shitsville.

I didn't actually need much convincing. Back then, all I wanted was to take a breather. To stop for a moment and figure out what my next step should be after failing to accomplish my one goal.

"No chance," I replied. I argued the move wouldn't be good for Shira. That I couldn't see myself living outside Tel Aviv. I was afraid of telling Nelly the truth because I had the feeling she might be testing me. That she was thinking of leaving me and checking where I stood. So I said there was nothing to talk about, and only after two weeks, when I realized she was serious, did I say I'd do it, just for her.

Shira was psyched about the idea, said living in the desert sounded like a dream. She thought and talked about the world in Disney terms, and meeting her expectations wasn't always easy. She once declared hysterically that she had to find the star closest to the sun otherwise she'd die, forcing Nelly to take her to the observatory in Givatayim that very same evening. When she was eight, she reached the conclusion that she was a secret princess and we were her adoptive parents, thinking the word "adoptive" meant evil. Her first attempt to run away from home soon followed. We found her seven minutes after she walked out the front door, fifty meters from our building. She told us she hadn't dared go any farther because she knew she wasn't allowed to cross the street alone.

We didn't always know how to handle that distant dreaminess of hers, and she certainly didn't know how to handle our sarcasm. She kept saying she'd never be like us when she grew up. On her most recent birthday, when she turned eleven, she even tried hiding the *Encyclopedia of Fairies* she got from her friend, fearing we'd tell her fairies weren't real.

Nelly worried Shira wouldn't fit in at the school in Mitzpe. She claimed that if Shira couldn't even handle us, she wouldn't stand a chance with the children there. They'd eat her alive. I was also afraid the hooligans of Mitzpe would crush her delicate soul, but I thought it was a good opportunity to force her out of her little bubble. Luckily, she landed a good teacher, who even assigned her a "big brother," a year ahead of her. When Shira got home from her first day at her new school, we were on the edge of our seats as if she was returning from the front lines and had lived to tell the tale. Straight off the bat she said we had lied to her, that the kids in Mitzpe listened to exactly the same music as the kids in Tel Aviv, and we both laughed with relief.

Unlike for Shira and Nelly, no one was waiting for me in the south. To be honest, it was a comforting realization. I thought that at first I'd spend most of my time herding sheep, connecting to nature or something like that. But after two days I realized that Nabil, the Bedouin worker who tended to the farm, did everything much better than I ever could. I only got in his way with my silly questions. So after a week of dragging my feet, I decided Nelly was right, that it actually was a good opportunity to start working on my app. I had gotten the idea for it when I was still working for the last start-up; one of the employees at the office had said his dream was to buy a Ferrari, but he had no idea how to even start saving up for it. It got me thinking there could be an app that helped people realize their dreams. You'd type in the thing you wanted most—a Ferrari, a house in Petah Tikva, a monthlong trip to Japan—and the software would calculate your odds of fulfilling that dream based on data such as the price, your salary, and current expenses. And not only would it evaluate the odds, it would also provide an estimated time frame and suggest the necessary steps toward getting that Jet Ski you had always wanted. It would recommend small changes to your spending habits, such as canceling your gym membership that was just a waste of money, or skipping a vacation in Greece. Every so often, the app would even recommend more significant life changes. For example, weighing the possibility of quitting your job as a high school teacher against cashing in on your charisma as a real estate agent. Because values are nice, but then you have only a 4 percent chance of being the proud owner of a Ferrari.

I started spending a few hours a day working on my idea, running market research to see if a similar product already existed, making phone calls to people who could help me get started, trying to write a rudimentary code for the software. I can't say exactly what I did, but I can say it took up most of my time. When I think back on that period, it feels like a faded, dragged-out dream devoid of clear actions. The only thing I remember clearly is that other than working on the app, once a day, a little before sunset, I'd climb up the hill behind the farm and look at the lights coming on across the Mitzpe below.

The official name was "Tel Ahmar"—the Red Hill. But it wasn't really red, just a sandy hill in faded shades of brown. And it wasn't even a hill but a cliff someone had probably fallen off once. No one sets out to visit Tel Ahmar. Most people stumble upon it on their way to Eilat. They climb up the hill and come back sweaty and tired, asking me where the red sand was, to which I reply with the same tired joke that it just ran out an hour ago.

3.

THE DAY AFTER my conversation with Nelly, Shira came home in the afternoon like always. She shut the door behind her, holding a small hoop with colorful threads and beads.

"What's that?" I asked.

"An Indian dream catcher," she replied. I asked who gave it to her, and she said her big brother.

"Nice of him," I said. "Sounds like he likes you."

She blushed, but didn't answer. Didn't even smile. I immediately wanted to change the subject, feeling bad for embarrassing her. I asked if she wanted me to make her something to eat. She said she didn't, which was a relief because there wasn't enough food in the fridge to whip up something nice. I knew I had to talk to her, but didn't know how to begin, and before I could find a way she was already in her room. I stood by her closed door for several moments, then reached out to knock, but the fear that she wouldn't open got the better of me.

I had already come up with the alibi I'd give Nelly, that I hadn't talked to Shira yet because I had to help Nabil tend to an injured sheep. But luckily, I didn't have to lie. Nelly had had a long day at the office and only came back to the B&B around midnight. That's what Nelly and I called the place we lived in, simply because we were unable to call it home. Nelly collapsed onto the mattress without brushing her teeth. Her parents were short, thin people who made do with a narrow double bed. Like every night, we embarked on a long session of awkward fumbling and shoving in an attempt to find a semi-comfortable sleeping position. And I, even though I never told her, liked the small shoves that sometimes turned into brief caresses, intimations of the obscure distance between us.

In hindsight I can say the dream catcher was the first sign, but as with the others that followed, I failed to take notice. That bus she missed, the bleary eyes, that morning I woke her up and for a moment she didn't recognize me. A litany of supposedly random events that only revealed their full meaning with time.

4.

"A TIP FOR LIFE." That was the headline of the newspaper article I had been reading the day it all began. It was about a waitress in the States who received a ten-thousand-dollar check from an old customer, who then killed himself by jumping off a bridge and into the Mississippi River. I hope that before I die someone will solve the mystery of why our minds remember such useless information. Every evening I'd wait for Nelly to bring a copy of *Yedioth Ahronoth* from Mitzpe. I used to wrap it in a blue plastic bag and put it on the table, saving it for the next morning. Nelly reminded me that I was already reading it after everyone else and didn't see the point of putting it off even longer, but I had started to like the idea of living in a different time zone from the rest of the world, a day after everyone else. I liked thinking that when time took a right onto the dirt trail by Highway 40, it came for a little R&R. That here it stopped moving forward at a steady pace, knowing that it was allowed to slow down, even move a few minutes backward, sag, or spill sideways.

I don't remember seeing her walk in. When I raised my head, Shira was already inside the B&B, hanging her black backpack on the hook by the front door.

"Hey, you're back," I said.

"Yup."

"How was school?"

"Fine."

"Good. Did you learn anything interesting?"

"Not really."

We were silent for a few moments.

"Want something to eat?"

"No."

"Are you sure? I can make you a sandwich."

"I'm sure. Thanks."

"Okay. Do you have homework?"

"A little."

"A little is good," I said. "Time to do it?"

"In a minute."

"Good, good."

I went back to the newspaper. Out of the corner of my eye I saw she was still standing there. I looked up and smiled, asked if everything was all right, thinking it might be a good moment to try talking to her. She said everything was fine and even smiled. A small, brief smile. She turned toward her room and I let her go, keeping my eyes on the newspaper even though I couldn't really concentrate. Five, maybe ten minutes later, I heard the keys rattling in the lock. Nelly had a dinner meeting with a potential client, so she had come home early to get ready. She opened the door and took two steps into the B&B. She dropped her bag and crouched down. For a moment I thought she had fallen, but then I realized—Shira had been there the whole time. Sitting in the corner, by the door, and I hadn't noticed. Sitting with her back against the wall, her arms slumped to her sides. Her gaze was fixed to the floor, to a nondescript point in space.

"Shirale, what are you doing here?"

"Nothing," she said.

"How long have you been sitting here like this?"

"I don't know."

Nelly looked at me, waiting for an answer.

"Five minutos," I said in our made-up hybrid of English and Spanish, a secret language Nelly and I tried to invent to replace the Yiddish and Moroccan our grandparents spoke between themselves.

"What's going on, Shira, tell me," Nelly said to her.

Shira didn't reply, and I was getting anxious, my mind racing with a thousand and one frightening scenarios.

"Come on, Shira, explain it to us," I said.

"We need to understand what happened," Nelly added.

"I'm fine, really," she replied with a feeble voice.

"Shira, up, come on. This is no good, sitting on the floor like this." I took two steps toward her.

"Let's move you to a chair, Shirush?"

Shira shrugged her shoulders with reluctance.

"So maybe you and I should go for a little walk?" Nelly suggested.

"Maybe," Shira replied.

"Good, that's a great idea," I said. "We'll go out, get some fresh air."

I bent down to lift her, reaching out both my hands. Shira averted her gaze, and Nelly grabbed my hand. There was something rigid about her touch.

"I forgot to tell you, Nabir wanted you to go help him."

"What?"

"Nabir said he needed you, that there's a problem with the sheep's water tank. Do me a favor, go to him."

"You mean Nabil?"

"Yes, yes. He said it was urgent. Would you go already?"

"But, la niña," I protested.

"Don't worry, I'll stay with her."

I froze.

"Well?" she urged me, her tone slightly raised, just enough so I'd get the hint but Shira wouldn't. I don't know why I agreed, but I went outside. Nabil was sitting by the sheep shed, wearing a hat with the logo of an insurance agency and smoking a Noblesse. He was a big guy who could barely squeeze himself into the white plastic chair. I walked up to him and sputtered, "What's this business with the water tank?" He had no idea what I was talking about. I explained that Nelly said he was looking for me. He still didn't know. I told him it made no sense, because we were just in the middle of something with the girl.

The worst thing was that Nabil figured it out before I did. He understood Nelly had wanted me out of the way.

"Okay, a miscommunication, I guess," I said in a pitiful attempt to save face. "I'll head back."

"Wait," Nabil said. "Your Nelly is a smart woman. That one knows what she's doing." He removed the bag resting on the chair next to him. "Sit, habibi, sit," he said and took another cigarette out of the green pack.

I hesitated for a moment, but sat down.

"Trouble with the girl?" he asked, and I nodded. Nabil took a drag and looked out at the red hill. "There's nothing worse than a man standing helplessly in front of his children," he announced. "Wallah, there really is nothing worse." He turned his gaze to the B&B, watching Nelly opening the front door, folding her arms and looking out at the road. I heaved myself up. "Good luck," Nabil said and smiled. "Or like they say, break a leg."

She apologized before I even reached the doorstep. "I don't know, I was hoping that if just one of us was there it would lower her resistance threshold," she said, quoting yet another term she had picked up from the child psychology books she liked to read. "I couldn't get anything out of her," she sighed. "I don't understand what's going on with her, I really don't." She leaned her head against my chest, instantly dissipating my anger. "We're in over our heads, Ofer. She needs to see a professional."

"What do you mean a professional? A doctor?" I asked.

"A psychologist, an art therapist, I don't know," she said. "Someone who can figure out what's troubling her."

At "psychologist," I thought Tel Aviv. An opportunity for a visit on the grounds that psychoanalysis had yet to find its way south.

"I'll text Sagi, he sees a psychologist on Dizengoff Street, says he's excellent."

Nelly laughed. She said Dizengoff was a three-hour drive, but she could compromise on Beersheba. She said that since I was already going to be there, it might not be such a bad idea to get some therapy myself. "Having an intimate relationship with a city that boasts over seventy percent humidity is not normal," she said, and I laughed. She was like that, could placate me with just a few words after days of estrangement.

5.

THE PSYCHOLOGIST STOPPED the session after half an hour. She came out into the waiting room, caught me napping with an eye half open, and asked if my child was on the autism spectrum.

"Of course not," I replied before even processing the question, and quickly straightened my back.

"I think you need to take her to the hospital," she said, explaining that there was no point completing the session since the child was barely responsive. That it wasn't a psychological matter but a physical one. Neurological, in her opinion. "You haven't taken her to a doctor yet?" she asked with subtle reproach.

I tried defending myself. I said Shira was pretty much a happy girl, but the psychologist opened the clinic door and said, "See for yourself." I approached Shira and put my hand on her back. I asked her how the session was going, but I could already see she wasn't the same girl. Sitting cross-legged, her head drooped like a rag doll's, her brown hair veiling her face. She wouldn't look me in the eye, replied curtly, three words at a time.

I waited with her for two hours in the ER until they took her for a diagnosis. A young intern asked her a series of questions, but she wasn't cooperating. He checked her pupils with a flashlight, then her reflexes. He didn't detect any abnormalities. He called over a doctor who also didn't find anything unusual, and whispered to the intern that something didn't add up. They decided to admit her for further tests.

Nelly freaked out when I told her. She left the office at once, took a car from one of the employees, and raced over at 130 kph. She arrived after Shira had already fallen asleep, sat down on the chair next to me, and rested her head on my shoulder as I gave her a detailed report.

"What have we gotten ourselves into, Ofer?" she whispered, and I recalled another night, a few years back, when she had leaned her head on my shoulder like that. It was after she had gotten drunk on half a bottle of cava and admitted for the first time that she had changed her name from Nili to Nelly because Nili was an old woman's name and Nelly sounded like a Canadian supermodel. I remembered laughing my head off while she dug her face into my shoulder with childish embarrassment.

In the morning Shira underwent a neurological examination that came out normal. Additional tests over the next few days also failed to provide any answers as to what had happened to our daughter. Nelly went back to the farm that first night and I slept on a chair, but once we realized Shira was going to stay in the hospital a little longer, we decided to pull shifts. Nelly took the evening ones, straight from work, and I took the rest. It was clear to us both that I was suspending all work on my app until things cleared up. The doctors told us the symptoms weren't caused by trauma, but the facts didn't interest us. We were consumed by our fears, dedicating our few moments together at the hospital between shifts to our ever-expanding list of suspects without knowing what the indictment was. That "big brother" of hers from school. The bus driver who picked her up every morning. Her teacher. Even Nicolai, my former coworker, had become questionable. Names were added, others temporarily removed, but one always remained, hovering at the top of the list.

Say, is it possible that we left him alone with Shira on the farm? Why is he always working so late? And what's he always fiddling around with behind the B&B? Yeah, and how can he even afford that pickup of his? And why won't he stop asking how Shira is doing? What business is it of his?

I didn't actually think Nabil had done anything to Shira, but there was something comforting in the thought of having an address to direct our pain.

Together, Nelly and I had come to the conclusion that something about his big body was a threat. She wouldn't stop saying that we were smart never to have asked him in for coffee. At first she stated repeatedly that our suspicions had nothing to do with him being a Bedouin, but then she stopped. Said that the whole situation with Shira left her too tired to deal with it, but if she had any energy she would have told him long ago to leave. That living with all the question marks surrounding him was simply impossible. Nelly didn't ask for anything explicitly. Didn't even hint, but I understood it fell to me to take care of it.

Three or four days after Shira was hospitalized, after snatching a few hours of sleep on the farm, I headed back to the hospital so Nelly could go to work. On my way out of the B&B I saw Nabil. He was sitting by his pickup, pouring himself coffee from his orange thermos. He took out half a pita with hummus wrapped in tinfoil and waved at me. I thought I'd put off the conversation for another day, but he gestured me over, leaving me little choice.

"Sabah al khair," he said, and quickly poured coffee into another small glass. "Tafaddal, ya Ofer, tafaddal."

I told him I didn't want any. "Haven't started working yet?" I asked, trying to mimic the psychologist's disapproving tone.

"Two hours ago," he replied. "Sugar?"

Again, I said I didn't want coffee.

"That's a shame, it's good for the soul," he said. "Tell me, how's your little girl?"

I informed him there was no improvement. The doctors couldn't figure out what was wrong with her. Nabil put his hand on his wide chest, his eyes welling up.

"Wallah, what a tragedy," he said in a strangled voice. "Why did this happen to us, why?" he exclaimed, trying to comfort me, which only drove me crazy. With a single word—*us*—he had appropriated my only child. I couldn't stand the thought that just like that, from a few physical gestures and even fewer words, he had expressed everything I wanted to feel but couldn't.

"If you want me to come to the hospital at night to help out, just say the—"

"How about keeping your nose out of it?" Nabil quickly apologized, said I was right and the offer was inappropriate. He took a last sip of his coffee, got up, and announced he was going back to the sheep.

"Listen, Nabil, since we're already talking," I said, "Nelly and I have given it a lot of thought lately. We realized we don't need that much help with the farm."

Nabil washed out the glasses with a squished water bottle. He smiled.

"Obviously, I need help, not you," he said, and burst into laughter.

"I mean, we don't need your help." I saw the lines on his face tensing. It wasn't the first time I had fired someone. The face always does that. People walk around their entire life trying to be unique, but the moment they lose control, the body takes over and they all react the same way. Nabil put down the bottle and glasses on the chair, rubbed his hands on his jeans, and looked at me.

"You don't need help?"

"That's right," I answered.

"Wallah," he said. He clenched his right fist and took a deep breath.

"What is this? Where is this coming from, huh?" he said, raising his voice. "Did Nelly's father say you could do this? I work for him, not for you."

"Yes, we've talked to him, it's all been approved," I lied. Nelly could deal with that one later. His wide frame froze. The possibility that Nabil was innocent evaded me at that moment, making way for the thought of Nelly's smile once I told her I'd dealt with it.

"You know that soon it'll be seven years that I've been working here? Back when the Bezalels were here, before Nelly's father bought the place," he said, and what he meant was long before some retired bank CEO bought himself a farm in the south because he didn't know what to do with all that money.

"Seven years is a long time."

"A *very* long time," he replied, his voice stifled with insult.

"You'll get your full compensation, don't worry. You can leave with a clear mind."

"Oh, I'm not worried, believe me," he said, twirling the water bottle with both his hands. "Just tell me, Ofer, who's going to take care of them now?" he asked, pointing the bottle in the direction of the sheep. Tiny beads of water spilled onto his black rubber boots. "You?"

"Yes," I said. "Me."

"You?"

"Aywa," I replied in Arabic. Nabil laughed again.

"Wallah? What can I say, habibi," he said, and placed his sweaty palm on my shoulder. "Good luck with that. Really, good luck."

Nabil collected the thermos and glasses, turned, and placed everything in the passenger seat of his pickup. I quickly got into my car and saw in the rearview mirror Nabil trailing along the dirt road in the direction of the highway, laughing to himself.

I made it to the hospital an hour and a half later. "You don't need to worry about Nabil anymore," I told Nelly, explaining that I had fired him. She smiled and caressed my cheek, reminding me how gentle hands could be. I spent the entire day with Shira in the presence of that smile, toying with the idea of a start-up that would develop the technology to preserve touch the way you save a photo, so that whenever I wanted, my brain could re-create the exact sensation of her hands at the click of a button. I asked Shira what she thought of my idea, but she didn't even answer. When Nelly arrived in the evening Shira had already fallen asleep, and she said we might as well both sleep at the farm tonight. It wasn't as if the girl was in any real danger, and in any case she always slept through the night.

"She won't even know we weren't here. We could put up a scarecrow with a picture of my head and it would be enough," she said. "Actually, it would probably be enough even when she's awake." For a moment we hesitated about whether we were allowed to laugh. We decided we were, but only a little.

That night Nelly and I had sex like we hadn't had for a long time. The narrow bed continued to close in on us, but also pushed our bodies into each other. Hands to face, lips to neck, feet to knees, eyes to stomach, with no room for unnecessary distance. And everything with swift, precise movements, because the mattress wouldn't allow otherwise.

"We look like a Picasso painting," Nelly said, to which I replied, "Totally," and we smiled at each other because we both knew I had no idea what that meant. Afterward, with her head resting on my chest, it occurred to me that maybe it was better this way—better the girl suffered a bit longer if that meant I would get my Nelly back. But I immediately told myself I was just being foolish, and that the most important thing was that the girl got better. So if one day they invented a machine that read minds, no one would know I had wanted my girl to suffer.

6.

THE DOCTORS DISCHARGED Shira from the hospital after a week, saying that maybe being at home would help her find her way back to herself. The only problem was that the B&B wasn't a home. Not to us, and certainly not to Shira.

"Maybe we should move back to Tel Aviv?" Nelly suggested in the corridor, next to the vending machine. She said she'd probably have to quit her job but maybe that wasn't such a bad thing, that it shouldn't take her more than a month or two to find a new firm. She was surprised I was the one who insisted on staying.

"Another move is hardly what the girl needs right now," I said. "And if I go back to work, who exactly is going to take care of her?"

Nelly nodded, finding my reply reassuring, happy she didn't have to feel like a career-crazed woman. Shira spent the entire ride home sitting in the back seat staring out the window. When we arrived, she unbuckled her seat belt and opened the car door even before I'd switched off the engine. She got out of the car and started running toward the red hill. We were so excited by that sudden display of animation that we left the keys in the ignition and ran after her. She was moving with incredible speed while we panted behind her, laughing that we could barely keep up, then arguing who she had gotten her athletic genes from. And I started thinking that maybe it had all just been a bad, absurd dream, that by tomorrow the girl would be back in school, maybe even cashing in on her classmates' empathy to win the election for student council.

My hopes were dashed once she made it to the top and immediately collapsed onto the ground. She lay on the sand, arms splayed, staring at the sky. We called out: Shira, Shirale, Shirush. We tried everything, but she didn't answer. It took us an hour until she agreed to get up—or more like didn't refuse. On the way down, we held her on either side so she wouldn't fall. We led her to her room and laid her on her bed, quickly tucking the blanket around her, as if it was a straitjacket that would protect her from herself. That evening, Nelly told me she didn't know what she would have done without me. That she didn't know any other man who would take upon himself running a farm with forty sheep and one fading child. She admitted it was hard on her, too hard. That she couldn't bear to see her little girl falling apart before her very eyes. And just like that, with one brief sentence, she shifted the responsibility for our daughter's care over to me.

It began with the typical tasks, putting her to bed at night and making her three hearty meals a day, but very soon it became clear it wasn't enough. Because the girl was barely functional, the circumstances demanded more: help with brushing her teeth, changing her clothes, and taking her on daily walks to the hilltop became an integral part of the job description. And I, who thought I had already missed out on Shira, had gotten a second chance to raise her.

Only tending to the sheep turned out to be a much more complicated task than I had imagined. The one time I tried leading them to the nearby meadow it took me the whole day and I lost two sheep along the way. After that little incident, I decided I ought to keep them within the perimeters of the farm, convincing myself they didn't actually need anything other than food and water. And even if they did, they'd manage. Nabil had left his white plastic chair on the farm, and Shira liked sitting on it and looking at me while I fed the sheep. Sometimes she'd start laughing when she saw what a miserable mess I was making of it, and I'd look at her, hoping she'd never stop. I was the only one who got to see those bursts of life. Those few brief moments, once or twice a day, when the girl smiled or even spoke, emerging from her burned-out soul. One morning, on the hilltop, she said she liked breathing in the desert. And one evening, she asked for another omelet. Said she liked it best when I made it with onions. Nelly didn't believe me, said she needed to see it with her own eyes. I told her that's what drove me crazy; it was one thing if the girl had disappeared completely, but it was clear that beneath it all, Shira was still there.

Two weeks later, Nelly took the girl for a checkup in Beersheba. She offered to drop me off in Mitzpe, so I could take a break for a few hours, get some fresh air. I didn't want to, but Nelly insisted and while she didn't come out and say it, what she meant was that she needed me to take a break so she'd know she was allowed to as well. Because the conference in Tel Aviv was in two weeks' time, and she needed to know it was okay for her to go away for three days.

I gave in, and a moment after she dropped me off at a café, I crossed the street and sat down on a bench as an act of protest. So no one could say I was having a cappuccino while my little girl was having an MRI. But soon enough the Mitzpe sun bested me, forcing me to get up and embark on a quest for the last remnants of shade. Passing by the public library, I negotiated a compromise with myself—I'd sit in the air-conditioned space only if I spent that time trying to figure out what was going on with Shira. It was a small library with a frayed green carpet running the length of the floor, gray steel bookcases lining the walls, and a librarian wearing sunglasses and holding a white cane pacing back and forth by the front door. I wanted to go on the internet, but a few kids who had skipped school were sitting at the only computer station. The kids ignored my presence completely, and I found it rather pleasant thinking I was both there and not there. I spent three hours skimming through all the medical books stacked on the shelf beside the reflexology and shiatzu books. My mind was spinning with the countless illnesses that could have attacked Shira; the various ways in which a person can simply cease to exist were truly unfathomable. Nicolai called me while I was standing with a book in my hand, but the librarian's stern shushing solved my dilemma as to whether I should answer.

When Nelly texted me that they were heading back from Beersheba, I quickly took myself to the café, ordered two cappuccinos, and even drank one so I could tell her they didn't know how to make a proper coffee.

"How was it?" Nelly asked when I got into the car.

"Life altering," I replied, and Nelly laughed. So did Shira. We both swerved our heads toward the back seat.

"See? See?" I told Nelly, who covered her mouth in shock.

"Dad's funny, right?" she said, just to make the girl talk.

"The funniest," Shira said and smiled. Nelly and I looked at each other as if our daughter had just uttered her first word.

"We have to get this on tape," Nelly said and took her phone out of her bag, but her hands were trembling so badly she couldn't unlock the screen. The girl leaned forward into the radio that was playing "Dreamer" by theAngelcy and looked at it intently, as if the song itself was appearing right before her eyes, a defined shape and volume in space.

"I can't take it anymore," she said and leaned her head back. She closed her eyes, the gap between her words and her indifferent gaze unbridgeable.

"Can't take what?" I asked, but the girl was gone. We sat there in silence, the three of us, until Nelly released the handbrake and started driving.

I couldn't fall asleep that night. That sentence, "I can't take it anymore," kept haunting me. It drove me crazy thinking that maybe there were moments in which Shira was aware of her condition. That her consciousness was trapped in a locked-up body. My mind started racing with all the illnesses I had read about in the library. Meningitis and all kinds of tumors and ALS and epilepsy. I counted them one by one like sheep, and at some point I leaped out of bed in a panic and ran to her room. The dream catcher was hung over her bed and her closet was open. The light from the kitchen illuminated her face with a dull yellow glow. Only after watching her chest rise and fall for an entire minute did I allow myself to calm down. I was thinking of stroking her hair and tried to pinpoint when exactly this had happened—when touch stopped being an instinctive action and became one that demanded an explanation and rationale. And before I could find a reason, I saw it before me. I kept studying her from every angle to make sure I didn't get it wrong, and realized Nelly had been right from the very beginning. The clue was there, in her eyes.

A sketch from one of the dozens of library books popped into my head. An illustration that demonstrated how pupils move during a dream, from side to side, back and forth. But beneath her thin eyelids I saw Shira's pupils move differently. In circles, and fast. Too fast.

7.

SHIRA LAY IN bed at the sleep lab, hooked up to all kinds of electrodes and wires.

"You look like a captive alien," I said. Shira didn't laugh. I covered her with the blanket up to her waist because I couldn't tell whether she was actually cold. She fell asleep after a few moments. When she was seven years old, there was a period in which she struggled with sleep but felt bad waking us up, so we didn't know about it until one day Nelly woke up in the middle of the night and found her sitting in the living room staring at the ceiling. It turned out it had been going on for five days. Ever since, every night at bedtime, Nelly would sit on Shira's bed and try to get her to confess, as if Nelly was some Irish priest. She wouldn't let go until Shira spilled her heart out, telling her about the teacher who had yelled at her at school and the boy who whispered to her in the hallway that he loved her. Nelly said she had to know everything. It drove her crazy thinking there might be thoughts buzzing through her daughter's mind that she wasn't privy to. I looked at Shira again and wondered whether her silence was a conscious choice. Maybe she knew exactly what was troubling her, but didn't want to burden us.

I went out into the hallway and sat in one of the chairs. I decided to wait out the night there in the unlikely event that Shira woke up looking for me. An older woman with short red hair sat in front of me, and an agitated old man stood not far from us yelling at one of the technicians.

"Why isn't anyone getting her a pillow? I don't get it," he grumbled. "I just don't get it!"

The technician tried to calm him down, asking what his wife's name was. "Lilian, her name is Lilian," he said and in a huff took to the chair to my left, noticing I was staring at him.

"What are you looking at, huh?"

"Nothing, nothing," I said, and quickly closed my eyes in a conciliatory gesture. I don't know if I'd slightly nodded off before I heard the doctor rushing into the technician's room. The old man, the woman with the red hair, and I all stretched out simultaneously.

"Looks like something serious happened," the woman said.

I got up and stood by the door.

"Can you hear anything?" the old man asked.

I said I couldn't.

A few moments later, the door opened and the doctor darted out into the hallway. He tried sidestepping me without making eye contact, but I leaned slightly to the left, bumping into his shoulder. He looked at me and apologized.

"Is there a problem with one of the patients?" I asked.

He glanced at the two others waiting in the hallway, then looked back at me.

"Are you Shira's father?" he asked.

"Yes," I replied, and felt in the back of my neck two twinges of relief.

"I can't say anything for sure yet. We've discovered a few abnormal findings, but we have to run more tests," he said, and apologized for having to rush off. If Nelly knew I didn't try to stop him, she would have divorced me then and there.

Shira spent the three following nights at the sleep lab. Not that she even noticed. With every night the number of doctors pacing the hallways grew. They didn't try to hide the fact that it had to do with Shira. Unlike with other patients, who got their wake-up call at 6:00 A.M. and were promptly discharged, a doctor came to examine Shira every morning for a whole hour. All the technicians and doctors I tried talking to said more tests had to be run before they could say anything with any certainty, but sometimes they were willing to drop a few hints. Her REM was three times the normal average. Her brain wave activity was abnormal and her breathing erratic. A collection of symptoms that refused to form a definitive diagnosis. On the fourth night, Nelly insisted on coming. She showed up without notice at midnight with a box of cookies and a small pillow, resting her head on my shoulder and commenting that we were already used to sleeping together in uncomfortable places. She set her alarm clock for seven, but one of the technicians woke us up half an hour before it was to go off, asking that we go see the director of the institute for an update on the situation.

I instantly shot up. Nelly remained seated. "Maybe it's better not knowing," she said. I was afraid she was right. We walked into the director's office and sat down. Nelly yawned and stretched her arms while I scanned the room, as if the answer to what had befallen Shira was somewhere within those four walls. A few diplomas boasting Dr. Mendelson's name were hung on the wall behind the desk. The desk itself was rather bare, with nothing on it but a large keyboard, green reading lamp, and a wooden-framed photo of what seemed to be her two blond children. They were wearing buttoned-up shirts and jeans, smiling against the white background of the photography studio.

"Straight out of a Gap catalog," I whispered to Nelly, who then glanced at the photo.

She snorted. "More like a propaganda poster for the Aryan race. Who shot that photo, Goebbels?" she asked just as the director of the institute walked into the room. I covered my mouth, trying not to laugh, doing my best to look like a concerned parent.

The director sat down in front of us, lowering a few thick black notebooks onto the desk. Then she placed her elbows on the desk and crossed her arms, looking at us with a solemn expression and asking how we were holding up.

"Not too great," Nelly said. She gave me a side-glance, saw that I was still trying to suppress my laughter. Dr. Mendelson's German looks didn't help.

"What can I say, Doctor. It's been . . . ," Nelly said with a thin smile only I could see, "a real holocaust."

I cracked up. No matter how hard I tried to get my act together, I just couldn't stop laughing. Which made Nelly laugh, even louder than me. She didn't even try to fight it. I saw the doctor's stern gaze, all the thoughts running through her head about the two wacko parents sitting in front of her. Maybe she got it right, but at that moment, it didn't matter. Dr. Mendelson nudged the stack of notebooks in our direction and opened the top one.

"What's that?" I stuttered between fits of laughter, trying to settle my breathing without much success.

"Shira's dreams," she announced. "We asked her every morning to write down what she could remember from her dreams."

We stopped laughing. We peeked at the pages. There were thousands of misshapen, illegible words, like the doodling of a little girl. "As you know more than anyone, Shira's fine motor skills have suffered a serious deterioration, which is why her handwriting is basically indecipherable," Dr. Mendelson said. She told us one of the technicians tried letting her type her dreams onto a computer, but the result was a nonsensical sequence of letters. She took out a yellow marker from the front pocket of her lab coat. "In the notebook, however, we did find a few words we could make out. Mostly single words, here and there a few short sentences. I'd appreciate it if you could go over it. Maybe there are things you could identify better than us."

We were silent. Dr. Mendelson said she'd give us some time alone and left the room. We stared at the jumbled words in fearful awe. Nelly reached out to the open notebook and pulled it closer to us, then started leafing through the pages slowly. At first she didn't dare look, and once she did, she couldn't understand. The handwriting was crabbed and minuscule, a mishmash of letters bumping into each other as if Shira had wanted to make sure no one could read it. I picked up the marker, and we started going over the text, digging for clues. Slowly, very slowly, the words started to surface—mostly unconnected, but sometimes fragmented, illogical sentences.

No Winnie-the-Pooh

I want!

The dog big love

He came Robert picked me up

Taxi to the beach I couldn't stop crying!!

Because I didn't do my homework Tomer is the most

I was thinking about Yaeli Tarzan

14/4/2002

Too far

Like Bob Dylan The boy wanted a Popsicle

Being a goalkeeper in America Pita with pickles

5/11/2020

We got married by the sea   So I kicked it back

Bamba   I was late for the meeting

I waited some more   for rain

Alone   we met   Netta Lifschitz made fun of me

A girl. I was so happy

Not small   Come?   8/1/2018

Don't want to go to school   we met next to

Who is Netta Lifschitz? Who did she marry? Who's going to come? A girl? How did she know Bob Dylan? Robert? Who the hell is Robert?

Fragments of Shira flashed before us, and we pored over every word, slowly, sifting through traces of the girl's consciousness. And every few moments we backtracked, afraid we might have missed a word and disappointed to find out we hadn't. Her words trampled over each other on the page until they had lost all meaning, contracting and spilling onto the back cover.

"How can someone dream so much, Ofer?" Nelly asked. Like always, she got what this was about before I did. When Dr. Mendelson returned, she started talking about the brain, using all these terms Nelly and I didn't understand, like sleep cycles and EEG. She explained that when we sleep, we cycle through several stages, one of them being REM sleep—a stage characterized by rapid eye movement, when most dreams occur. She further explained that Shira's dreams in each cycle were longer than those of other children her age, but it was a negligible difference, a few minutes at most. "It isn't the actual duration of her dreams, but her subjective experience of that duration. It seems she experiences it as a very long period of time." The doctor believed that was the root of the problem.

"What do you mean? How long?" Nelly asked her. Dr. Mendelson offered only vague answers, but Nelly wouldn't let it go. "When we ask most people to write down their dreams, they write anything between half a page and a page and a half," the doctor said, and then tilted her head toward the notebook. "Shira, on the other hand, wrote eighty pages the first night, and almost a hundred last night." She said they tried finding a precedent in the professional literature but couldn't.

"I don't understand, how long does Shira feel every dream lasts?"

"It really wouldn't be professional to give you a precise number."

"Seven? Eight hours?"

"I would estimate more."

"A day?" Nelly asked, lowering her fist onto the table.

Dr. Mendelson reached for one of the notebooks, picked it up, and gazed at the words. Then she looked up at us. "There are no certainties, we're still very much in the dark here. But I believe it's highly probable that Shira feels as though every dream lasts years," she said, and quickly reiterated that it was merely an initial estimation.

"Days?" I asked, as if I had misheard. Dr. Mendelson turned the notebook in our direction and pointed at a series of numbers that appeared at the top of the page. "I don't know if you've noticed these markings," she said and began flipping through the pages, showing us that they appeared every few pages.

6/11/2019
7/16/2017
13/8/2020
7/4/2022
27/5/2020
13/9/2018

"We think these are dates." She said they had never come across a patient who was aware of the dates in her dreams. "The notebooks always begin in 2015, and then leap between dates. In the first notebook, the earliest date was 11/6/2019. In last night's notebook the date 7/4/2022 appeared."

Nelly and I looked at each other and couldn't understand. Didn't want to understand. Dr. Mendelson explained that the dates never appeared in chronological order. That it was possible every dream was another moment on the time line, and the girl was bouncing back and forth from one dream to another.

"And Shira is the only girl in the world who's experiencing this?" Nelly asked nervously.

Dr. Mendelson said it was unlikely. That in theory, a lot of people could be experiencing dreams that lasted years, the only difference being that Shira was the only person who remembered them all. "And also the only one whose functioning was severely impaired by this."

I considered the stack of notebooks again. The words took on new meanings, from a bunch of free associations to possibilities. Every word was a possibility of who Shira could be. The infinity of her private future was laid out on every page, and I was afraid. Afraid that Shira was galloping toward that infinity, getting lost inside it. Dr. Mendelson said they'd carry on with the tests and start her on medication. She promised they'd try everything, and added that there was always the chance that just as her dreams had appeared out of nowhere, they'd eventually disappear. Said there was a lot we didn't know about the brain, and any attempt to offer an accurate answer as to when and how her condition might change or improve—would be irresponsible.

Nelly reached out and grabbed my hand. She hung her head, mourning our child. Maybe mourning us. Dr. Mendelson said that while she knew it wasn't much consolation, she had to remind us it could be a lot worse.

"Obviously it's better than terminal cancer," Nelly said with frustration and raised her head, squinting as if to hide the redness of her eyes.

"What I meant," Dr. Mendelson carefully weighed her words, "is that there's no evidence that the child is suffering." She said there was almost no indication that she was even having nightmares, and no symptoms of emotional distress. "It may very well be that to a certain extent, she's happy," she said, and we remained silent, having forgotten that was even a possibility.

8.

WE RETURNED WITH Shira to the B&B. Nelly's dad called that evening. Nelly said he hadn't yelled at her like that in years. He had tried getting an update from Nabil, but the latter hung up on him, thinking it was a prank. "My dad said we had some nerve firing Nabil without even telling him. Got himself all worked up over having to deal with this mess while he was on a cruise."

Nelly tried telling him it had simply slipped her mind. That with everything that was going on with the girl, her head wasn't screwed on straight, but her dad replied that with all due respect, that was no reason to go do such a stupid thing. "He said Nabil was coming back to work. And that if we tried pulling another stunt like that we were welcome to rent an apartment in Mitzpe."

"Did you explain that something felt off? That we felt that—"

"That was just hysterical nonsense," she said, and lay on the bed. "You know we were dumping all our shit on him."

I told her she was wrong even though I knew she was right. Then I sat there silently. I got up to brush my teeth, and Nelly gave up. When I came back to bed she was lying with her back to me. I tried thinking about something else. Not about Shira. I broke my rule and read that day's newspaper, but it didn't help. Even an article about a space probe landing on Mars made me think about Shira. "It's crazy," I said. "Human beings can send a spaceship to Mars but they have no idea what's going on inside their own brains, it's just absurd."

Nelly didn't respond. I wanted so badly to hear her voice that I decided to keep talking until she said something. "Every dream is a few years for her, can you even imagine that? It's totally insane. She must be feeling so lonely inside that thing. Really, just thinking about her like that, shifting between dreams with no one beside her, she probably—"

"She's right," Nelly said.

"What?" I asked, just to keep her talking.

"Maybe she's right."

"Who? Who's right?"

"The doctor," Nelly said and turned onto her back. Her eyes were closed.

"Right about what? What are you talking about?"

"That maybe this whole shitty situation," she said and sighed, "actually isn't that bad."

Now I was quiet and Nelly was doing the talking. "It's not like she's having nightmares. She's dreaming. Dreaming all the time," she said and opened her eyes, looking at me. "I mean really, Ofer, wouldn't you jump at that opportunity if someone offered it to you?"

"What opportunity? What exactly are you talking about?"

"Think for a second," she said. "Someone comes and offers you the opportunity to live inside your dreams, without nightmares. To jump from dream to dream every night, to feel as if the whole thing lasts for years. You want to tell me you wouldn't go for it?"

"Not in a million years," I replied.

"Really, Ofer? You'd really pass on it? To me it sounds even better than a cruise to the Caribbean," she said, then hesitated for a moment. "You know what the first thing was that crossed my mind when that Mendelson said the girl wasn't suffering?"

"What?" I asked.

"That maybe," she said, and fell silent for a moment. "Maybe Shira chose this."

"Chose what?" I replied, irritated. "You're talking in code words, Nelly, I don't understand."

"Chose her dreams. Chose to live inside them," she said and sat up, looking at the door as if she was afraid Shira might be standing on the other side eavesdropping. "I know I sound completely crazy. I know, honestly. But maybe with all those fantasies of hers, she found a way to live inside her dreams. And maybe, just maybe, she's choosing to live there, make an exit from this world." She looked at me. "Think, Ofer. Years. Every night is years for her. No wonder she's barely responsive, doesn't even recognize us. What's one day with us compared to years inside her own head?"

"What . . . what are you talking about?!" I barked at her. "You think she's choosing to be like this? Completely unresponsive? You actually think anyone would want to live like that?"

I got angry at Nelly. There was no way our child would choose to leave us. "You would think we abused her or something, that she had to escape somewhere."

"Maybe we didn't truly see her," Nelly said, and I knew that when she said "we" she meant "you." "I don't know, I'm starting to think we weren't really there for her. That we were too busy with our own lives. You know what I'm saying?"

"What's with the guilty conscience bullshit?" I hissed, getting even more annoyed. I told her I hated when she got like that. That once every few months she had those pseudo-pensive moments reflecting on her life and the very next day worked twelve hours straight again. "If tomorrow they call saying they want to appoint you CEO, all these questions would disappear in a flash," I said, and added, just as a dig, "that's what separates us from everyone else, remember?"

"What are you talking about?" she asked.

I thought she was being coy, but studying her expression, I realized she wasn't. She honestly had no idea what I was talking about. I reminded her about that night in the Galilee. What she had said. That drive to push forward.

"You said that's what separates us from the rest," I said. "The unapologetic desire to succeed."

She considered me for a moment with a serious gaze, and slowly her features began to soften. She laughed.

"Sounds like something you heard on a reality show," she said. "There's no way I said that."

I argued with her, reminded her of the details, that the sentence was said after we had gotten out of the Jacuzzi and into bed. She remained unconvinced. She flat out denied it, and I couldn't understand why. Then she got annoyed with me. "Listen, I don't remember saying it," she said, "but even if I did," she added with a hesitant tone, "it's just the silly ramblings of a clueless twenty-three-year-old. Nothing more than that. And anyway, the whole CEO business is officially off the table," she announced. She told me Hakimi had gotten the job two weeks ago. She said it as if it were some inconsequential anecdote, not something she'd been dreaming about for the past seven years. She couldn't believe she'd been stupid enough to think the move south would give her extra points. Didn't understand at the time that they were exiling her. I asked her when this had happened, and if she'd spoken with Zuzovsky, but Nelly said she was too tired to talk about it. Which was the last thing I'd expected her to say. I tried coming up with some comforting reply but couldn't, so I stroked her back gently, tugging her body toward mine. "Enough, don't turn this into an issue," she said, but gave in to my touch all the same. "Why didn't you tell me until now?" I asked, and she said I had enough on my mind and she didn't want to saddle me with her failures too.

"Maybe you're right," she said tiredly, and admitted that maybe she was just upset about not getting the job and that everything she'd said just now about the girl and our lives was a bunch of nonsense. That in a day or two she'd get her act together and find her next goal. "And then I'll just have the Shira business to deal with," she added. "No biggie, right?"

I smiled. She placed her head on my knees, and I brushed my hand through her hair. She smiled too.

"I can't believe how we laughed in her face," she said. I told her that when Dr. Mendelson opened the notebook, I thought she was going to order us to write "We're bad parents" forty times or something like that. Nelly laughed again.

"You know," I said, "I can't believe that in the twenty-first century they're still asking people to write down their dreams to understand what's going on with them."

"Yup," Nelly replied. "It's a shame your guys at Lucid didn't come up with some technology that would allow people to share their dreams. Because you know, watching someone's dream is much more interesting than another cooking show on Channel 2."

"Yup. You're right. It is more interesting." I continued to stroke her head. I suddenly had the vague memory of the research department actually exploring that option and ruling it out. How I would have loved to meet her there. Meet Shira in her dreams. One minute there could have solved this whole thing. "It is a shame," I said.

Nelly turned onto her side, pressed her cheek against my chest, closed her eyes, and fell asleep.

9.

THE FOLLOWING MORNING I saw Nabil wandering outside the B&B, tending to the sheep as if he had never left. Nelly came out and approached him. I stood behind her as she told him she wanted to apologize for everything that had happened, that it was an unfortunate misunderstanding, but the most important thing was that he was back. Nabil didn't say a word.

"Have a cup of coffee with us?" she asked. He raised his thermos and shook his head. "I really am sorry," I said. "I should never have fired you."

"Stop bullshitting me," he said without looking at me, and went back to work.

Nabil's words weighed heavily on me, but I was glad he was back. It allowed me to spend more time with Shira. I felt that she needed me more than ever. The notebooks alone took hours out of my day. The doctors made it clear that Shira had to write down her dreams every morning, that it had to be the first order of business. Once I sat her down at the kitchen table, she started writing without my even having to ask. She sat there for two to three hours, until the notebook filled up with words. When she finished writing the last sentence she leaned back, dropped the pencil onto the table, and I put her back to bed, waking her up again in the afternoon.

Shira's dreams became longer and longer. Every morning the girl wrote more and more words, but the doctors couldn't explain it. The only thing they cautiously dared to suggest was that the tests indicated the possibility that Shira's brain could no longer differentiate between wakefulness and sleep. Her sight and hearing were deteriorating sharply, and her sense of smell, taste, and touch was even worse. Her senses were barely functioning, which is exactly what happens to people while dreaming. They explained that might be what was making her so inert.

"That makes no sense," I protested, telling the doctors it didn't add up, because there were moments of absolute clarity in which Shira was fully aware of her surroundings. They, on their part, explained that it was like when people experienced a lucid dream—the person knows he's dreaming. They said it was possible that every now and then Shira's brain reset itself and understood the difference between a dream and reality, but before she managed to process the situation in full, she would revert back to her hazy existence.

We continued to take Shira to the hospital and the sleep lab, but by that point I had begun to feel that we were doing it more for the doctors than for Shira. They treated her like a math riddle you knew didn't have an answer but kept trying to solve just for the challenge. I was already exhausted from tending to her 24-7. The revelation regarding Shira's long dreams should have encouraged us, but in fact did just the opposite. Nelly and I felt as though we had managed to scale the high wall built around the child, only to discover an even higher wall waiting behind it. I tried hinting to Nelly that maybe it was time to start thinking about some kind of treatment facility, just to look into the possibility, but she wouldn't hear of it. She said there would be nowhere to put her because not a single person in the whole world suffered from the same problem. Said she wouldn't let her child rot in some loony bin. I started to think maybe she was right. That maybe the girl actually was choosing to remain in her state, and we needed to let go. At least a bit. But I didn't have the guts to say it out loud, so I kept quiet. I kept quiet and continued to tend to her, but a little less. I gave up on the veggies at breakfast. And on the ten minutes I'd sit beside her after she fell asleep. Sometimes even on the daily stroll to the hilltop, even though I knew she liked it.

Nor was I up to dealing with the app. It wasn't going anywhere. I couldn't schedule any meetings in Tel Aviv, and even phone calls with potential business partners couldn't last more than ten minutes because I had to check on Shira.

I sat in the kitchen every night holding the yellow marker, sifting through the notebooks for clues. At a certain point I stopped trying to decipher the meaning of the words and started to gauge the quantity. I'd sit there with a calculator and try to work out how long every dream lasted. The numbers made no sense. If Shira dreamed every night the duration of approximately three years, that meant that since this all began Shira had dreamed a hundred and twenty years. At least.

One night, Nelly got back from work, approached me from behind, and placed her hand on my shoulder. She looked at the calculator in front of me and said there was no point trying to measure the time inside her dreams. That it was a different kind of time, one which we couldn't even begin to comprehend.

"What do you mean?" I asked her. She sat down beside me and took the pencil out of my hand.

"I've thought about this a lot," she said, sketching a delicate line on one of the blank pages. She tried to explain that if we likened time to a straight line that moves forward at a steady pace, Shira experienced time as something entirely different. "If anything, I'm starting to think that Shira's time looks like a bunch of dots," she said, filling the page with tiny circles. Her theory was that every dream was a dot, and Shira bounced from one dot to the next with no particular order or logic. "One moment she's at her wedding to that Robert, the next she's back at Edna's kindergarten, and then suddenly she's a goalkeeper in the middle of a soccer game." She said that explained the fragmented sentences and why the dates were never in chronological order.

"Did you get a master's in quantum physics and forget to tell me about it?"

"Use that as a pickup line and you can get any woman you want," she teased and placed her hand on mine.

I looked at the page again, picked up the calculator, and continued to punch in digits. "I'm not sure I agree with you," I said, and added that even if I did, I wouldn't quit the calculations. If there was one thing that gave me any kind of comfort in this whole situation with Shira, it was the thought that the girl might live forever in her dreams.

After Shira and Nelly fell asleep, I went out for a stroll by the farm. I walked up to the road and stood on the curb. It was cold. Not a single car drove by. I couldn't get over what Nelly had said. That the girl consciously chose to live inside her dreams. It made zero sense, but on the other hand, everything that had gone on with Shira in the past month and a half defied the rules of logic. So let's say, for a moment, that Nelly was right. That Shira actually did find a bug in the system; that she discovered a way to live inside her dreams. Why would she want something like that? That kind of escape? I couldn't understand it.

There was a time when Shira was little that she liked playing pranks on us. Nelly or I would put her to bed, and she'd pretend to be sleeping, and the moment we walked out of her room she'd burst into laughter. Nelly could play that game with her for maybe an hour, acting as if it was the funniest thing in the world, but I didn't always have the patience for it. After a few times, I told Shira to quit fooling around. And she really did quit it but only with me, and continued playing with Nelly. After two days I got jealous of Nelly for getting to spend another hour with the girl, who would barely talk to me. During that same period, I'd put her to bed and stand outside her door, waiting to hear her laugh again. But I didn't hear a thing. It was the first time I realized Shira and I were on different wavelengths. That I simply couldn't understand her, no matter how hard I tried. Much like today.

My phone rang.

I silenced the ringing but kept staring at the screen. It was Nicolai. For some reason I suddenly thought maybe he could help, and before I even managed to process that thought, I had already picked up.

"Hello? Ofer? Hello?"

"Yup."

"Wonderful, finally! I been trying to catch you."

"Yeah, sorry," I said. "I've been a little busy."

"Never mind, happen to best of us. What important is we're finally talking," he said, and embarked on a desperate monologue about all the problems at the office. Said the CEO wouldn't stop yelling at him. That his best employee had quit yesterday, and that in two weeks' time his team was supposed to deliver a project and they'd barely gotten half the work done. "Every week someone off sick or take vacation as if we're not on deadline," he grumbled. "Just yesterday one took off for Liechtenstein for three days. I didn't even know that was a country until I look it up on Wikipedia."

"Neither did I," I replied, and Nicolai said that it was probably only a matter of time until they fired him. He admitted he hadn't thought being a development manager was so complicated.

"It is," I said, hoping my voice didn't betray my satisfaction.

"But never mind about my problems," he said with a certain despair. "How are you doing? Already planning retirement?" he asked, and I didn't know whether it was a bad joke or if he was being serious. I didn't want to get into it with him, so I just said I was working on a new project.

"Really? What kind?" he asked.

"It's all very early stages so I can't really go into detail," I said. "By the way, Nicolai, if we're already talking, I wanted to ask something of you. I have a somewhat vague memory of Lucid trying at some point to check the possibility of dealing with the subject of dreams. I'm probably wrong, but is there any chance you could look into it with someone from research?"

Nicolai started laughing even before I was done talking. "Oh, I know what you're doing!" he said. "Ballsy. For real. Actually sounds like totally cool idea. Little similar, but cool." Similar to what, I wondered.

"I know there was something, but I can't really remember," he said. "I don't want to give you some off-the-cuff answer, I need looking into it."

"So there actually was such a project?" I asked, making sure he understood what I was talking about.

"Yes, yes and yes. I think there was even a meeting about it, just few days ago."

I heard Nicolai taking a deep breath. "Say, Ofer, I also have little favor to ask you. Would you be willing to meet sometime soon, just to shoot the breeze like they say, maybe give some career advice?" he asked with slight trepidation in his voice. "I know it's probably a lot to ask, but . . ."

"Yes," I answered instantly, without thinking. "Sure, no problem. I'd love to."

He wouldn't stop thanking me.

I hung up and gazed at the empty road for a few more minutes before heading back home, feeling a flutter of optimism.

10.

"I THINK YOU be happy to hear what I discover," Nicolai wrote me in a text the next day, and added an emoji of a smiling face with sunglasses.

"What did you discover??" I texted back, adding the second question mark for emphasis.

It was only hours later, after a nerve-racking wait, that he texted back that he'd tell me everything when we meet. From that moment on I couldn't stop thinking about what they had developed over there. All I remembered was that while working there, the topic of dreams had come up. I just wanted to know if it was possible, if there was a way of getting inside Shira's head. That maybe, somehow, we could still fix what was wrong with her. I tried imagining what her dreams looked like, but no matter how hard I tried, I simply couldn't.

That evening, after I tucked Shira into bed, I sat down at the table and went through the notebooks. Nelly had started packing for her conference. She always started getting ready for her trips days in advance, which only stressed her out more. After half an hour she couldn't take it anymore, grabbed a cigarette and went outside, coming back in two minutes later. She approached the kitchen cabinet and fished out a box of mint tea.

"We're out of the Mexican brand?" I asked.

"No, I prefer this one."

"Say," I asked her while she waited for the water to boil, "if someone told you you could see Shira's dreams, on TV for instance, would you watch them?"

"Of course," she said with her back to me.

"Yeah, me too, that's why lately I've been thinking—"

"Actually, maybe not."

"No?"

"Yeah, on second thought, I wouldn't want to," she announced and sat at the table, mixing a teaspoon of sugar into her tea.

"But why?"

She said worst-case scenario she'd watch a nightmare and agonize over how her girl was suffering. "And worse than worst-case scenario, I'd happen to catch a good dream."

"How is a good dream a bad thing?" I couldn't understand. "You said yourself it wasn't so terrible."

"Of course it's not terrible!" she exclaimed. "Living inside a dream? It's great. But that doesn't mean I want to see with my own eyes how happy she is without us," she concluded, basically saying it was easier to live with the ambiguity. I told her I couldn't understand her. That I'd jump at the opportunity without thinking twice; that I had the feeling it would solve everything; that I couldn't stop thinking about it since I started going through the notebooks; that if we understood what she was dreaming about, we could find a solution to the whole situation.

"How exactly? What good would it do?"

"I'm not sure yet," I said, "but I'll know once I see her dreams."

"You know you're just fooling yourself, right?" she said, and took a small sip of her tea. Then she said she didn't understand why I was getting so worked up about it; it wasn't as if it was actually an option. "Haven't you realized yet that we're not a factor in this? That this whole problem is between the girl and her own consciousness?"

"We're not a factor?" I asked, raising my voice. "Last time I checked, we were her parents."

She lowered her cup onto the table, putting her hand on mine. "You're better than me at this," she said, and after a few moments added, "luckily."

I don't know why I didn't just tell Nelly about the meeting. Why I didn't explain it might actually help. She might have said it sounded like a waste of time, but she would have understood. Maybe she would have even said it was worth my waiting until she returned from her conference and she'd make sure to take time off work and stay with the girl one morning so I could go to Tel Aviv. I had convinced myself it was the fear of letting her down that had made me hide the whole thing from her. But if I'm being honest with myself, I don't think there was any logical reason for me to be so surreptitious about it.

11.

TWO DAYS LATER, on a Wednesday morning, I dropped off Nelly at the bus stop. We made it there early, at 6:00 A.M., and I struggled to heave her suitcase from the trunk. Through the window I saw how Nelly caressed Shira's cheek before getting out to help me. It took a herculean effort and more than a few drops of sweat on my forehead to yank out the heavy suitcase and lower it carefully onto the sidewalk.

"Okay," I said to Nelly. "You're allowed one sarcastic remark, I deserve it."

She considered me for a moment, then hugged me tightly without saying a word.

We were the only ones at the bus stop. We held each other until the bus arrived. Nelly boarded the no. 660 to Tel Aviv, promising to return with a Toblerone from the central bus station, and I drove back to the farm with Shira. I sat her by the table and let her write in her notebook while I made her her favorite breakfast—an omelet with cheese and onion, a chopped vegetable salad, and a piece of toast with Nutella. I wanted to spoil her, to soothe my conscience over leaving her on her own.

"I have to go out for a bit," I told her while cutting her omelet. "I'll be back real soon, okay?"

She didn't answer. I gave her a shower, changed her clothes, tucked her in, and drew the curtains. Darkness fell over the room.

"Go to sleep for a bit, okay?" I told Shira, and kissed her forehead. Her gray eyes slowly drooped to a close, and I suddenly thought that maybe, somewhere inside her, Shira was giving me permission to go.

That maybe that very moment, she was the only one who understood me. The girl nestled her head deeper into the pillow. I couldn't tell whether she had fallen asleep, but I took it as a sign that I could leave.

I walked out of the B&B and locked the door behind me. I swept my gaze across the farm and didn't see Nabil anywhere. I rushed to the car, started the engine, and turned onto the northbound highway.

12.

WE AGREED TO meet on Yehuda ha-Levi Street. I couldn't find parking nearby so I settled for a side alley where I knew they didn't give parking tickets. It was my first time back in Tel Aviv since moving south, and I admit the mere thought of dodging parking officers made my heart flutter with joy, as if it attested to my return to a more advanced civilization. Nicolai insisted we sit at some new sandwich place, texting that they had the best roast beef in Tel Aviv. When I got there he was already sitting at the bar, holding a beer glass in his wide hands. I sat down beside him. I extended my hand, but he had other plans.

"A handshake, bro?" he said and lunged at me with a big hug. I wasn't exactly sure what to make of the gesture. Nicolai was taller than I had remembered, over six foot three. He had short blond hair and thick black-rimmed glasses. He wore a buttoned-up yellow shirt and purple plaid shorts. Fashion isn't my strong suit, but even I could tell it didn't look right.

The menu was handwritten on the wall, but I wasn't hungry so I just ordered a Coke and a glass of water.

Nicolai asked how long it took me to get there.

"Almost three hours," I said, and showed him on my phone where the farm was, but I saw he didn't really understand.

"I can't believe you drove whole way to see me," he said, and slapped me on the back. "You know that is my dream? To move to kibbutz when I'm your age? A quiet life, the outdoors. What more could a person want from life?" I nodded in hesitant agreement, preferring to spare us both from the dreary conversation about the differences between life on a kibbutz and a homestead out in the desert.

He began to vent his frustration about the company. I assumed it would only be a matter of minutes before we could move on to the subject that actually interested me, but it wasn't that simple. Nicolai wouldn't stop talking about his problems. I couldn't get a word in edgewise. He kept jumping from one subject to another, one moment talking about his difficulties as a development manager and the other about a new Vietnamese restaurant that opened in front of the office.

"Ever had pho?" he asked without waiting for an answer. "It will blow your mind. They put in ginger or something like that, this crazy punch that hits you out of nowhere. The only problem that one bowl of soup cost fifty-two shekels and it doesn't look like I'm getting raise anytime soon," he said despairingly, telling me that all his friends in the hi-tech industry were making fun of him and saying that twenty thousand a month was barely a military salary. He seemed to have forgotten that only a year ago, when I interviewed him for his position, his jaw almost dropped when I offered him a double-digit salary.

"Teachers would kill for a salary like yours," I said, to which he waved dismissively.

"No disrespect, but that's hardly the same," he said. "If tomorrow you give me thirty kids to teach, I can do it. Maybe I not be great, but I could do decent job. But if you tell school teacher to write something on Python, he don't know where to begin. Get it?"

I didn't tell him he had gotten the job because we didn't have the resources to recruit better people. I was so annoyed I thought I'd better not open my mouth. He started listing every occupation he could think of and explain why he could excel at any one of them. When he said that being a farmer was just watering plants, it struck me. That was exactly how I saw Nabil. Nicolai and I saw the world with the same eyes, convinced that people who didn't buy organic vegetables at the farmers' market were somehow inferior.

"I look after my kid," I said. "Trust me, it's a lot harder than programming."

"Sure, but you do that and work on app, you know?" he tried to explain.

"Not really," I replied. "I'm not working on the app. Most of the time I'm with the kid."

"What, that's all you do? Take care of her? Isn't that just giving her food or something?" he said and started laughing, realizing only after a few moments he was out of line.

"Sorry, I didn't mean it, it was stupid joke," he said and scratched his head with embarrassment. "So you're like stay-at-home dad?"

"That's exactly what I am," I said.

He took a sip of his beer, then slapped me on the back. "You da man, bro!" he said. "I wish I had dad like you. My dad used to come home every night at ten, half the time I thought he was burglar."

I didn't know what to do with his compliment. At first I thought he was just being ingratiating, but then I realized he wasn't. Nicolai just said what he thought, for better or for worse.

"Ah! I almost forgot," he said, gulped down the rest of his beer, and started rummaging through his bag. "I got what you wanted."

I shot up. "The dream project?"

"Yes."

"You smuggled documents out of the research department? I can't believe it," I mumbled.

"You didn't hire me back then for no reason," he said, and then yelled excitedly, "Here, found it!"

He pulled out of his bag a large, rolled-up blueprint—above and beyond what I had expected him to produce. He leaned toward me and, checking that no one was listening, whispered, "What I'm going to show you is top secret. They just finish working on it last week. You have to swear you won't tell anyone."

I swore.

Nicolai slipped off the rubber band and carefully unfurled the blueprint onto the table. A slogan in silver print appeared at the top of the page: "Yesterday's Memories Are Tomorrow's Dreams."

"It's the wrong side," I said and nearly snatched the paper out of Nicolai's hand, eager to see the blueprint on the other side of the page. But there was nothing there.

The page was empty, completely blank. Nothing but that stupid ad slogan. I studied the piece of paper for a few more minutes before looking up at Nicolai, who was staring at me with a big smile on his face.

"What's this?" I asked, baffled.

"You be happy to hear that after thorough investigation, this is all I came up with. This poster, printed a year ago. There is no project."

"How could that be?"

"There's not single project involving dreams. I thought there was, but turns out research ruled it out. They said dreams and memories are completely different areas, like oil and milk," Nicolai said. "I admit I was having a little fun with you with the slogan. Bet your heart missed a beat there."

I tried to explain that he must have misunderstood. There had to be some kind of mistake. There was no way I'd gotten this close just to find out there was nothing.

"I don't understand what you're saying."

"You said I'd be happy to hear what you found."

"Right, I found out there is no project. That's what you wanted to hear, no?" Nicolai said, at this point as confused as I was.

"Why would I be happy about that?" I asked and downed the glass of water in one big gulp.

"Because you want to build a start-up for dream sharing or something like that. That's why you wanted me to do corporate espionage," he said. "This is excellent news for you! Now you can build a competing start-up and make millions. My only advice is you take one of those neuroscientists or something because this isn't one of those piece-of-cake apps you build at home."

And once again he reminded me of myself, thinking everything in this world was a potential start-up. Actually believing the only thing that could drive a man to action was the desire to succeed. But I didn't want to make millions, I wanted to help my daughter.

"You're wrong," I told Nicolai. "There is a project. I remember. I know." He tried to tell me it made no sense. That he had asked around the research department and they all told him with complete certainty that there was no project. That today's technology just wasn't advanced enough to re-create dreams.

"But I need it," I mumbled more to myself than to him.

"Why do you need it? Explain to me, maybe that way I understand," Nicolai said in a worried tone.

"My little girl . . . ," I said, and started telling him about Shira. About her decline. About the hospitals and everything we'd gone through those past three months, letting it all out without coming up for air. Nicolai listened quietly, without saying a word. And only when I was done did I realize it was the first time I had talked about Shira without someone who wasn't Nelly. That actually, it was the first time since moving south that I'd really talked to anyone.

"It sounds awful," Nicolai said. He hesitated for a moment and then lifted his hand somewhat awkwardly and patted my back in a strange gesture of solidarity.

"I bet research warned you not to say anything, that's fine, don't tell me what it is, just tell me there's something," I said. "So I'll know I have something to count on."

"I wish there was, but really, there isn't," he said what I knew but refused to accept. "If you want, I can lie to you that there is," he said reluctantly.

I smiled. I told Nicolai how I'd been looking forward to going home and telling Nelly I had found a way to help Shira.

"Believe me, there's nothing worse than being helpless with your child," I said. "There really isn't."

"But maybe that's something a person has to know how to be," he said, and quickly qualified his statement, saying he didn't have kids so he didn't actually know.

We continued to talk for maybe twenty minutes, half an hour. By which I mean he talked and I nodded. I can't really remember what he went on about. I wasn't listening. I was trying to process the thought of having no way of helping Shira, and I didn't know how to do that. Finally I told him I needed to get back to her.

"Want me to buy you cup of coffee for road, so you won't fall asleep at wheel?" he suggested. I politely declined.

When I got back to my car I noticed I had a 100-shekel parking ticket and started laughing, vowing never to forget that life without parking officers had its advantages. I drove the whole way back with the radio cranked up high, trying to think as little as possible.

I parked by the B&B and stayed in the car for a few minutes, gazing out at the red hill. I felt I needed to scream, to vent all my frustration, but I didn't want Nabil or Shira to hear me so I settled for slamming my fists against the dashboard. Then I switched off the engine and entered the B&B.

13.

NOT LONG AGO I came across a study that might explain everything that happened to me that day with Nicolai. The study showed a few people photos from their childhood and asked them to think back and remember where each photo was taken. The thing is, one of those photos was doctored. The subjects were photoshopped into a hot-air balloon—a completely fabricated experience. The first time the subjects were asked about the photo, almost all of them replied they couldn't remember when it was taken. But when they were asked again a few days later, some had already concocted a whole story about that day in the hot-air balloon. They were so certain of their memory that even after they were told the photo was fabricated, some of them swore it was them in that balloon.

I guess I actually hadn't heard anything about dream-sharing technology at Lucid, but I was so desperate I needed something to cling to.

I think it happened to me twice that day. In hindsight, replaying the events in my mind, I can swear that when I sat in the car, I actually did see her, walking behind the sheep. That I was so busy beating myself up, I simply hadn't been paying enough attention. I'll never know whether that memory is true or not, but in any event, one thing I do know—when I walked into her room, Shira was no longer there.

It took me a moment to realize she wasn't there, and a few more moments to notice that the front door hadn't been locked. I started running hysterically from room to room, searching for her in every corner of the B&B; in her bedroom and ours, and the bathroom and the kitchen and inside and behind the closets, but the girl wasn't there. I kept at it for maybe five frenzied minutes before finally realizing that she simply wasn't in the B&B. I went outside, stood in the yard, and dialed Nelly's number, but hung up after one ring because what could Nelly possibly do about it? I ran around the B&B, but she wasn't there. I ran toward the sheep, the road, but Shira was nowhere to be found. And the only thought resonating clearly in all that insanity made absolutely no sense. That maybe the girl had finally given up her life here and found a way to dissipate into her dreams. That she had left reality behind and dove into her worlds, far beyond our reach, without a trace in the here and now. I was growing more and more convinced of it, until I saw Shira. In front of me. She was standing alone, a tiny dot on the hilltop, pretty close to the edge. Perched on top of the red hill, gazing into the abyss. Before I could process the sight, I was already running toward her as fast as my legs would carry me. My body took charge, racing in her direction. I roared out her name, over and over again, but she didn't turn to look at me. I was afraid I wasn't going to make it. But then I saw someone swooping up from behind her. Lunging at her. Nabil. He gathered my child in his arms, pulling her into his chest. Then he turned around and started walking down the hill with slow, heavy steps, kicking up a trail of red dust behind him. I saw Shira calmly falling asleep in his arms. Even my jealousy couldn't dampen my relief. I ran toward them, trying to rid myself of the sense of helplessness.

"Thank god you found her!" I shouted, and from twenty meters away already launched into a defensive monologue. That I had gone out for a meeting only because I had no other choice. And had locked the house. I was sure I had. And I couldn't understand how she had gotten out, I really couldn't. And that I know, I was an idiot for not telling him I had left the girl alone. Nabil nodded, and when I finally stood next to them, I fell silent. The whole world had been whittled down to her little body. Shira was the only thing I cared about. I hugged her as tightly as possible. Nabil let go, and I gathered her into me, shielding her.

Nabil opened the door to the B&B and we walked in, dirtying the floor with our dusty shoes. I put Shira into bed. Her eyes were closed. I covered her with the blanket. Nabil looked at me and then walked out of the room, leaving me alone with Shira. Her bed suddenly seemed too big for her body. As if the girl had suddenly shrunk into a bite-size version of herself. There was a mind-boggling dissonance between what had just happened and her small, delicate breaths. I studied her for a few more minutes, making sure she truly existed. Only then did I notice my phone vibrating. Nelly had called three times, but I was too tired to answer.

After making sure there was no way the girl could escape from the window, I left her room. Nabil was sitting at the kitchen table, his hands in the air. He didn't want to dirty the table. We sat together silently for what felt like forever. Finally Nabil put his hand on my back, giving it a gentle pat. He didn't say a word. He got up, went to Shira's room to check on her, and walked out of the B&B. I sat there alone for a few minutes, trying to make sense of what had happened, and failing. Then I dragged my chair into Shira's room, sitting not even an inch from her bed. I don't know when exactly I fell asleep, but when I woke up the next morning, Shira was standing in front of me.

She was smiling.

14.

MAYBE ONE DAY I'll tell Nelly what happened that day. I can't just yet. Nor do I think it would help. Nabil didn't say a word about it. When Nelly returned from the conference she asked him with a playful smile if I had done a good job taking care of the girl. "He's a schmuck," Nabil said, "but a decent father."

A few days later, Shira began showing signs of improvement. She jotted down fewer and fewer words in her notebook each morning, and at the same time, clear descriptions began to appear. She was also more responsive to Nelly and me, her empty gazes gradually replaced by long, intelligible sentences, by smiles and bright notes of laughter, alongside petulant glares and fits of prepubescent rage I'd never thought I'd be so happy to witness. Two and a half months after they had first emerged, Shira's dreams began to disappear. Dr. Mendelson thought perhaps Shira's mind had managed to fix itself. In her opinion, the girl had suffered from a disorder that made her remember every detail of her dreams. That it was very likely Shira was still dreaming as before—years every night—she simply didn't remember it anymore. But she added that it was equally likely that everything she was saying was "a bunch of hooey." That she could come up with a few other interpretations but had no way of proving any of them. She suggested we continue to bring Shira to the sleep lab so they could further explore the problem, but we refused. Nelly said the child's rehabilitation was more important right now than the sleep lab's chance of winning a Nobel Prize, and I agreed, although I wouldn't mind a family trip to Stockholm.

Even though Dr. Mendelson's theories sounded very convincing, I couldn't stop thinking that Nelly had been right all along. There was no medical mystery here; the whole story was actually pretty simple: One day Shira had decided to escape into her dream, and the next, she got tired of it and decided to come back to us. I shared my theory with Nelly but she ruled it out, saying that she never really believed the whole "escaping into her dreams," that it was just something she had said in a moment of despair. I think that if she knew what had happened there, with Nabil, she might have thought differently. It made no sense that one day the girl almost falls off a cliff and the next starts to get better. Maybe at that moment something had occurred to bring her back to reality. Anyway, I decided to leave well enough alone. To make peace with the fact that not all mysteries in life have a clear answer.

Yesterday, Shira came home from school for the first time since getting better. She burst through the door and announced, "The teacher said Mitzpe was the best place in the world to see stars!" She went on and on about it the whole afternoon, and Nelly and I suggested that all three of us go out that evening to the top of the red hill with head flashlights and the old telescope. Shira got all excited, took a detailed list of the constellations she wanted to see, and demanded we stay out until we found Orion and the Great Bear. Nelly and I couldn't spot anything so we made up the Blue Goose and the Little Lamp and the Anthill of the North. The whole way down we kept telling her it was really weird she didn't see them, and Nelly whispered in my ear that it would take the girl at least three more years to realize there wasn't actually a constellation called Aunt Leah's Hip.

When we got home Shira jumped up and down on her bed all fired up, until she exhausted herself and collapsed onto the mattress. Nelly went to take a shower and I stayed with Shira, watching her yawn nonstop.

"Shirush, are you sure you don't remember anything from your time at the hospital?" I asked her.

"I already said I don't!" she yelled, saying I had already asked her a hundred times.

"Yes, I know, it's just that your mom and I had a weird thought," I said, gently stroking her face.

"What thought?" she asked and closed her eyes, stretching her small arms. I told her that because she was such a special girl, we thought maybe she had found a way to live inside her dreams; to spend some time there, exploring all the different worlds inside her head. Shira opened one gray eye, looked at me and gave a small, mischievous smile. She didn't say anything, and I felt that maybe I had finally caught her. That maybe even now, she was still playing us. Before I managed to ask her anything else, Shira put her head on my shoulder, nestled against me for a few moments, and fell asleep.

The Jerusalem Beach

THEY WENT LOOKING FOR HER first memory, snow on the beach in Jerusalem. Tomorrow he would turn her in, but at that moment they were still riding the 480 bus together, second seat from the back. Lilian had fallen asleep, and Sammy was looking out the window, stroking his frayed leather satchel. There was only one thing he could say with absolute certainty—the world had changed since he last went out in it. She hadn't left their small apartment in Ramat Gan for years, and he wouldn't leave without her. He gazed at the forested hills along the way, remembered them more jagged, and told himself that time ate into everything.

"Remember the big fire?" he asked her, and her neck moved stiffly, clinching to her sleep.

Three boys in the back row burst into roaring laughter, interrupting his yearning thoughts. One of them was playing music from his cell phone, which gradually took over the rear of the bus. Sammy tried to parse the words but failed. He wasn't keen on confrontations, but fearing the noise would wake Lilian, he turned and shot them a look.

"How about being quiet?" he asked, hoping they didn't notice the slight tremor in his voice. The boy with the cell phone turned off the music, then broke into a defiant hum. Sammy went back to gazing out the window, but couldn't calm down.

The bus weaved into the city that used to be their home and passed by the white bridge. Sammy, who had prepared himself for this moment, took a yellow disposable camera out of his pocket and tried to capture the large structure in its lens. But only three days later, when the photos were finally developed, would he discover that the bridge had eluded him, and in its place appeared the congested intersection at the entrance of the city, and the reflection of a yawning man who sat in front of them.

The bus entered the central station; the passengers began to pile out, among them the teenagers who patted Sammy on the back and wished him a good day. The bustle of passengers woke Lilian and she opened her eyes slowly. Her eyes were a chestnut brown, and Sammy often wondered if they hadn't grown bigger over the years. Her hair and dark skin were also painted shades of brown, and he once told her that it was only because of her that he learned how much depth could be found in one color.

"Where are we, Sammy?" she asked; he didn't answer. She rose slowly, revealing a small bald patch in the middle of her scalp. Sammy quickly tousled her hair and hoped no one on the emptying bus had noticed.

Only when she asked again did he tell her they had reached Jerusalem, adding in an undertone that he couldn't keep reminding her over and over.

They hobbled off the bus. A young woman in a *Bnei Akiva* shirt offered assistance, but Sammy waved her away. Sammy and Lilian had shrunk over the years and were now nearly swallowed up by the masses. Pressed against each other they traversed the station, overcoming stairs, elevators, and slippery tiles until they reached the entrance to Jaffa Road. They inched toward the door and all at once the early August sun caught Lilian off guard.

"I'm cold, Sammy," she said, and sidled up against him. "The snow must be coming."

"It's summer now," he insisted, but Lilian wouldn't relent. She wrapped her arms around her body and started trembling. Even the hottest day couldn't stifle her snowy memory. Sammy let out a sigh and placed his satchel on the floor. He sluggishly reached into the satchel and took out the white coat he had once bought her. By now it was two sizes too big, but she insisted on wearing it with pride. She raised her hands like a girl waiting to be wrapped after a shower, and wouldn't move until Sammy also tied a scarf around her neck. Only then did she take her first step out of the station and followed him toward the light-rail.

Sammy grabbed Lilian's hand and demanded: "Don't let go," even though he wasn't sure whether she heard him over the clamor of the street. "Where are we?" she asked over and over; he didn't answer. He turned his gaze toward the steel-gray tracks, his ears anticipating the gravelly sound of the engine. For years he had been following the newspaper reports about the miraculous train that crosses the city streets, and was now eager to see it with his own eyes. Once again he pulled out his camera, but immediately placed it back in the satchel, deciding not to waste film.

Slow and heavy, the train pulled into the station. It was as big and silvery as Sammy had imagined, like the steel beast from Daniel's prophecy. He took a step forward to stand on the platform ledge. Lilian remained hidden behind him.

"Would you believe it, Lilian? A train in Jerusalem again," he said.

The doors opened. Sammy pulled Lilian forward. He wanted them to step into the car together, but he was assailed by an incessant stream of people. Sammy and Lilian's shriveled hands detached from each other, and for long moments the two elderly orphans ambled like a torn page, until they finally reunited and melded (became one). Only on their third attempt did they manage to board, pressing against each other and fighting for their place. A young man with a yarmulke whispered loudly to his wife, "Her coat alone takes up all the space." Sammy didn't say a word. He was too busy struggling to keep himself steady. Lilian didn't notice anything going on around her. The train set off and she stared at the city's buildings; Sammy thought to himself that she was looking at them as if at an old acquaintance she hadn't seen for many years—she knew they were familiar, but couldn't remember from where.

They stepped off the train at the Machane Yehuda Station.

"Are we at the beach yet?" Lilian asked. He didn't answer. The Jaffa Road he once knew had disappeared along with the train tracks, leaving him lost in time and space.

They wandered back and forth under the rays of the Jerusalem sun, which were hotter than those etched in his memory. How he wanted her to stop him as she had done so many times in the past. To tell him to quit fooling around, and then solve their predicament herself by asking a passerby for directions. But she didn't say anything, only wiped the sweat trickling down her forehead and struggled to keep up with him as he picked up his pace. They were utterly exhausted by the time Sammy noticed the flow of people coming in and out of one of the alleyways. He dragged Lilian after him, and they found themselves standing in front of stalls laden with vegetables, breads, and nuts. Sammy smiled contentedly and quickly looked at her with anticipation. After a few moments, as he had hoped, Lilian closed her eyes without knowing why.

When they were young, she had remarked that the market-goers let their senses deceive them. They think the experience boils down to a few colors and smells and don't know that it's all about finding a sense of quiet within the great noise. Afterward, to illustrate her point, she would take him to the most crowded spot in the market, next to the spice seller with the painted eyebrows, and make him close his eyes; to try to feel the motion of the people passing by, through, and over them like living water. Now he tried to close his eyes again, but just as back then, he was still too afraid.

He hadn't visited the market in over sixty years. On his twenty-third birthday, they left Jerusalem, and he hadn't been back since. He couldn't imagine himself wandering the market like a tourist, like a foreigner. As a child he had worked every summer at Dudu's bakery, and vividly remembered those florid, sweaty tourists who passed by the stalls with their wide straw hats and fancy Italian shirts, their anthropological gazes announcing the brevity of their visit. Sammy wondered whether they had made the long, winding journey to Jerusalem only to remind themselves who they were not. Lilian, on the other hand, had returned to the market several times as a teacher, chaperoning field trips. On those occasions, he would close the welding shop earlier than usual and dart home, eagerly awaiting her return by the wooden kitchen table. When she walked in, even before managing to put down her bag, he would bombard her with questions about the prices of tomatoes and eggplant and potatoes and cauliflower, and about Dudu's stall, although Dudu had long since passed away, and about the new goods that had appeared and those that were gone. She would answer slowly; words upon words upon words, knowing he needed to hear about the market like a man of faith hankering after a prayer's melody.

When did she tell him about the snow on the beach? He wasn't sure. But it happened here, during one of their first encounters, when she arrived to buy challah at the bakery and then slipped away with him into the nearby alley. That was where she told him about her very first memory. About children playing in the snow, digging with bare hands in search of the sand that had disappeared. About older men and elegant women sitting on green beach chairs in thick robes, trying to tan in the unbearable chill; about seashells that poked out from the white snowflakes, and about mothers shouting at their children not to go barefoot lest they catch a cold. She also told him about herself, the only one who dared to go into the freezing water. She described slowly walking into the sea while chunks of ice floated around her. She told him how she closed her eyes and went deep into the water; she opened them only for a second and saw before her the purest blue she had ever seen in her life.

To this day Sammy still regrets what he said to her back then. "It was probably just a dream," he determined, and then added with some certainty, "There hasn't been snow here in years, not to mention a beach." Since then, she no longer shared the chronicles of her first memory. At first he believed it was only a matter of time before he convinced her to talk about the beach again, but over the years he learned how stubborn she could be. It made no difference how many times he apologized and begged, she persevered in her silence. Even after they came to know each other's bodies, even after they married, and even decades later, when they moved into a retirement home on the other side of town, she claimed such a memory was too precious to place in the hands of another, even of a loved one.

Then came the Alzheimer's and ripped out her memories one by one. Their honeymoon in Rome; their evening at the Chinese restaurant; the traffic ticket she received on Highway 2; their son's death, the taste of pistachio ice cream; Abbott and Costello; the first cigarette they smoked together; the war and the one that followed; her father's voice; the dog they adopted for three days only to discover it belonged to the neighbors; the trip to David's Stream in Ein Gedi and the moment she slipped and fell; their two years in Boston; the run-down bathrooms in the Hebrew University dorms; her fear of death; the very specific way she liked her coffee; the opening line of *Anna Karenina*; the day she met Sammy.

All her memories were swallowed into the void. All but the memory of the snowy beach in Jerusalem. The only one she wouldn't let go of. She kept asking over and over when they would go back to visit, and hinted at its existence in muted ramblings that escaped her in her sleep. And still, whenever Sammy asked her to tell him again about her first memory or explain where exactly the beach was, she refused and withdrew into her silence. He reminded himself that it wasn't a real memory, but it did little to alleviate his frustration. How painful was her refusal to share with him the last testament to the woman she had once been. Even now, as they stood in the market. Even when he asked her to simply hint at the direction—she remained silent.

"Ask her," Lilian said, and pointed at a vendor behind one of the stalls. Sammy approached the woman, and with a slight stutter asked if she knew where the Jerusalem beach was. The vendor looked down at him from the stool she was standing on, a contemptuous gaze; she didn't even consider answering, merely continued to stack the sweet potatoes as if they were books on a shelf. "He asked you a question," Lilian's voice suddenly emerged from within her clouded soul to defend her husband's honor. "He asked you a question, why aren't you answering? He asked you, he asked." She approached the stall, and the vendor leaped in panic, hiding behind a wall of zucchini and admitting in a whisper: "I really don't know what to tell you."

Sammy rushed to apologize and dragged Lilian behind him. They stopped in one of the side alleys, and she continued to mumble for long moments, "Why didn't she answer you? Why didn't she answer?"

He stroked her hair patiently with his thick fingers, once again straightening it out. He bought her Turkish delight with almonds and reminded her that he used to bring her such sweets every Friday. She silently nibbled on a piece. Then they passed through the stalls and Lilian handed some of her candy to a beggar they stumbled across. They walked out from the other side of the market, stepped onto the faded crosswalk, and slipped into the Nachlaot neighborhood, leaving the noise behind them. The narrow streets felt spacious compared to the market's crowded alleyways. Sammy looked at the small houses. When he was young, he had felt they were perfectly suited to his size.

He grabbed Lilian's hand and guided her gently past a manhole and a gas tank, safeguarding her the way children protect their first pet. After a brief stroll, they stopped by their old synagogue. Four young Haredi men passed them by and entered the building. How he wished that someone would erect a monument in places like this. He would have even settled for a small wooden sign that said: "Here Lilian and Sammy passed notes during the *Maariv* service."

Lilian was tired. She bent her knees demonstratively, and Sammy quickly led her to the bench opposite the nearby playing field. Four large trees surrounded the field, serving as goalposts for a few boys and girls playing on the paved surface, padded with sand. Sammy sat Lilian on the bench; she gazed at the children and smiled, clapped her hands at them until they waved back. Removing an orange in a green plastic bag from his satchel, he sat down beside her, took the orange out of the bag, and peeled it with the kitchen knife he had brought. He then removed Lilian's coat and scarf to keep them from getting dirty, and served her small orange segments one by one. Juice dripped from his fingers. "Thank you," she said after receiving each piece. Perhaps with every bite she experienced the fruit's taste for the first time, he thought, and almost found comfort in it.

The football struck Lilian just as she was about to bite into the last piece. It collided with her face and knocked the orange segment to the ground. Lilian shrieked, closed her eyes, and rushed to shield her head with her frail hands. Sammy wrapped her in the coat, as if it possessed the power to protect her from all evils of the world. One of the girls, in a jean skirt and blue school shirt, approached them hesitantly, while the rest of the children formed a crooked line behind her. "Sorry, can I have the ball back?" she asked, and Sammy didn't know if the "sorry" was an apology or the only word she could think to address him with.

"Have you gone completely mad?" he yelled, and the girl retreated a few steps. "What's wrong with you? You're crazy, you almost murdered a person." The girl folded her hands behind her back and remained silent, which only vexed him more. "Don't you have eyes? Do you know how dangerous that was?" he lashed out at her, unleashing his rage.

"Sorry," the girl said again. "If we could just get the ball back."

The football was lodged between him and Lilian, a white and sooty patchwork of pentagons and hexagons. He picked up the ball in his trembling hands and intended to return it to the girl, but then looked at Lilian's face again, more fearful and frozen than he had ever seen it before. Without thinking twice, he took the knife and, with what little strength he had left in him, punctured the ball.

It slowly deflated, fell, and rolled on the ground, stopping at the girl's feet. She covered her eyes with her hands, but spread her fingers wide enough to peek at the disaster. She began sobbing and a few moments later, turned and ran along the path that surrounded the synagogue. One of the boys yelled, "He's a murderer!" and then ran away with the rest of the frightened children.

The playing field had emptied. Sammy looked at Lilian. The small bald patch was exposed again. Once more he tried to rearrange her hair, but Lilian refused to lower her hands from her head. She remained folded inside herself, and he no longer had the energy to fight her. They sat like that for some time, until the sun disappeared behind the synagogue. Hugging his satchel in both arms again, he tried to count the leaves on the tree and failed. He took out his camera, gently lifted Lilian's left hand, and photographed her tired face, telling himself that these moments should be documented too. He then slowly bent down, lifted the fallen orange segment from the ground, took a handkerchief out of his pocket, and started wiping off the grains of sand that clung to the fruit.

"Tomorrow they'll come take you," he said.

"To the beach?"

"There are people who can take care of you better than I can."

"Where's the snow, Sammy?"

"I'll come visit every day."

She leaned forward. Her eyes remained closed.

"I can smell the sea, can you?"

Sammy reached out to her with both hands, pressed his head against hers, and gently stroked the lines on her face. Then he whispered to her, "What's left for you there?" without expecting an answer. He closed his eyes, tried to imagine the two of them alone on her beach. Standing naked and wrinkled on the shoreline, she with her saggy brown breasts, he with his hunched back and pallid face. He imagined the horrible cold, and her convincing him to go into the water even though he wouldn't want to. Stepping in slowly and feeling the cold sand between his toes. And after they were already in up to their waist, he imagined Lilian turning to face the beach, resting on the waves. He would rush to grab her, while she floated on the cold water.

He opened his eyes, saw the synagogue in front of him, and looked at the small sandy field again. He quickly rose from the bench and helped Lilian up.

"Are we going home?" she asked; he didn't reply. He guided her slowly across the field, kicking the small pebbles out of their way.

"Where are we?" she wondered, and he stopped in the middle of the field, bent slightly, and kissed her left hand. Then he pulled away from her and heavily knelt on one knee. He remained in the same position for a few minutes, trying to catch his breath. With enormous effort, he bent his other knee and finally lay on his back on the thin sand. He remained still for several moments and then reached his hand up to her. She took it, placed her other hand on the ground, and leaned back. They lay side by side, panting. Only a small distance separated them. Sammy gazed at the darkening sky.

"It's the beach," he announced. "This is Jerusalem's beach."

She didn't say a word. Sammy stretched his arms and started moving them clumsily up and down.

"Soon the snow will be here," he said. "We need to practice."

She didn't understand, but immediately joined him, moving her arms back and forth.

“Now your legs too,” he said, once she caught the hang of it, and she complied. She spread her legs and immediately pulled them back together, over and over again, with wider and gentler strokes than Sammy’s.

Worshippers exiting the synagogue stared at them in confusion, but they kept at it—Lilian maintaining a steady rhythm with her arms and Sammy listening to her breaths. They didn’t smile or look at each other; they simply moved their arms and legs slowly across the sand, fashioning elderly angels on the snow of Jerusalem’s beach.

Neptune

1.

SHE ARRIVED A few days before the blood seeped into the sand. Three hundred, maybe four hundred meters stood between the outpost and the bus station with the white chalk graffiti announcing *You've reached the end of the world*, and by the time she had covered the distance, the rumor about the mysterious soldier was already whistling throughout the outpost like a bullet.

Cleaning duty was immediately suspended.

One after the other we let go of our brooms, garbage bags, and plastic bottles filled with sand and cigarette butts, and stared as she approached us in black boots, a camera hanging around her neck and white sunglasses that gleamed in the distance.

Even Yanai, who was on guard duty, rushed out of the security booth at the gate. He looked in the cracked mirror hanging outside the door, straightened his tactical vest, and ran his hand over his buzz cut. Then he winked at us and said, "This one. This one's going to be my wife."

By the time she made it to the security gate, half the platoon was waiting for her. We stood elbow to elbow while Yanai opened the iron gate that screeched nervously. She slid up her white sunglasses, wiped the sweat off her face, and revealed a strange pair of eyes. One blue, one brown.

"Finest girl who's ever stepped foot in the outpost," someone whispered, and we nodded.

"Welcome to Neptune," Yanai greeted her.

"Why Neptune?" she asked, as he was probably planning all along.

"Rumor has it that this outpost is as far from planet Earth as Neptune, if not farther," he replied, and she started laughing a split second before he completed the sentence, as if she was used to these kinds of jokes. Then she said that she served in the military newspaper unit, which we hadn't even known existed until that moment. She said her job was to travel to outposts all over the country and find soldiers with interesting stories.

"And why are you here, princess?" Yanai asked.

"For you, *prince*," she sneered, and said she had traveled here all the way from a kibbutz in the Golan Heights, which was covered in snow these days. She had heard there was a soldier in our platoon who graduated with a law degree from the most prestigious university in England and had left everything behind to enlist in the IDF. She explained that was a story people would want to hear, and then looked to her left, at us, and asked if anyone knew where she could find him. I noticed a ladybug tattoo on her neck.

We all knew who she was looking for, but no one was in a rush to answer; maybe because we feared that if we told her, she'd vanish as quickly as she had appeared.

"I'm not sure who you're talking about," Yanai eventually said, the very guy who took every opportunity to remind us that he scored a 96 on his Hebrew finals without ever learning the meaning of the expression "to give up." He shifted the sling of his gun behind his back and took a few steps closer to her. "You'll have to put out a bit more if you want help. More details, I mean. Name, rank, hobbies."

She smiled, embarrassed. I was hoping that someone braver than me would tell him to cut the crap, but other than someone's feeble "Come on, Yanai, stop it," none of us protested.

"Sit with us for a bit, we'll sort you out, don't worry." Yanai reached out to touch her hair. She jerked her head and took two steps back. Her black bag was pressed up against the fence. Her right sleeve caught on the wire, leaving a small tear. A single drop of blood dripped onto the sand. I think I was the only one who noticed.

"Don't get your panties all in a bunch, sweetheart," Yanai called out and drew closer to her, standing right in her face. "I don't bite."

Her face turned red. She looked away from him, at us, but we didn't say a word.

For years I blamed Yanai for everything that happened afterward, his vanity, his inability to restrain himself, the ridiculous thought that it was only a matter of seconds until she fell for his charms. But today I know that it wasn't Yanai, it was something about the outpost itself.

They say it was a soldier from the November '02 draft who started the whole thing. That he was the one who carved the question proudly displayed above the broken urinal in the grunts' latrines: "If a tree falls in Neptune, does it make a sound?"

This heralded other bursts of creativity: "If a soldier shouts 'No more!!' in Neptune, is he really shouting?"

"If a soldier goes batshit in Neptune, will he ever see the headshrinker?"

"If Waxman the CO shoots a camel in Neptune, does he finally get to join the recon battalion?"

Slowly but surely these jokes turned into serious philosophical debates that went on for hours. We found ourselves arguing heatedly about whether the "Neptune tree" phenomenon existed only within the confines of the outpost or also along the road that led to the bus station. Whether it had existed here since time immemorial or was born only when the outpost was built. And so, without expecting it, we started to get the creeping feeling that the things that happened in Neptune had eluded the space-time continuum. We had reached an unspoken agreement that it was okay to pull a cat's tail because they didn't really exist, or to cheat on your girlfriend, if you could just find someone to do it with.

2.

SAKAL WAS THE one who finally put a stop to it. He had been serving in the company longer than any of us, with only a month and a pre-discharge talk with the regiment commander standing between him and the beaches of Thailand. Sakal was the company sergeant major, a role that had turned him into a broken and tired soldier, but also a higher authority on all matters of seniority, rank promotion, and ETS. He had been two years ahead of me in high school. We were both music majors, but he studied classical and I jazz. And while he was strict about not speaking to us younger soldiers, I knew he was fond of me. Sometimes, when I was standing in line in the mess hall, he'd pat me on my back, and I'm also pretty sure he was the one who left the Pink Floyd CD under my bed, maybe as a reminder that there had been life before this wasteland and there would be life after it.

"What the fuck's going on here?" he yelled, approaching in field pants, holding a wet toothbrush. He shoved me and a few other soldiers out of his way, giving a blaring whistle. Before Yanai realized what was going on, Sakal was already standing in front of him, asking the female soldier what she was doing here. She stood up straight and explained, then took a step forward without missing the opportunity to step on Yanai's foot.

"You're looking for Korczak, sweetheart," Sakal said. He turned around, stood on his tiptoes, and swept his gaze across us until he spotted me standing behind the others.

"Go with him, the fatty with the curls will take you," he said, pointing at me.

I wasn't offended by Sakal's description. I was aware of the way I looked, but at that moment I felt that my large body stood in my way, rendering me incapable of hiding in a crowd. And I didn't want to accept the assignment of leading her to Korczak, to be marked by Yanai and the rest as the one who had taken away the only female soldier ever to arrive at Neptune of her own volition. I tried making myself smaller and lowered my gaze to the ground, recalling the first time I played hide-and-seek only to be instantly found.

"Show me where he is," she said, grabbing my left elbow and pulling me toward a row of buildings, letting go only when we were outside everyone's field of vision. She lowered her sunglasses and picked up her pace.

"Are you sure you're looking for Korczak?" I asked, just to make her say something. She slowed down, catching me panting, struggling to keep up.

"We'll find that out together," she said, smiling a comforting smile. Her words, alluding to a shared future, alleviated my fear of getting on everyone's wrong side.

"Yanai's just a jerk," I said when we started walking again.

"That's his name?"

I nodded.

"Unfortunately, or maybe fortunately, I've met worse." She asked how long we'd been serving in the outpost. I told her that the seniors were closing in on six months, but us juniors had only arrived from the training base three weeks ago.

"You don't look that young," she complimented me.

"Neither do you," I said, and immediately started apologizing profusely for how that came out. She laughed. It made me happy. She asked whether Korczak was a junior or a senior.

"Junior, but he's twenty-four, just immigrated here."

"No kidding. And his name is really Korczak?"

"Nickname." I told her that on our first night at Neptune the soldiers from the senior platoon woke us up in the middle of the night. They made us stand outside in the lineup square while Sakal presented the Ten Rookie Commandments, from the unconditional requirement to salute a senior soldier to the strict rule against eating chocolate pudding cups. After he read the commandments, Sakal pulled Korczak aside and told him he was aware he was three years his senior, and that he had no intention of pulling rank on a guy who could be his grandfather.

"But Korczak wouldn't have it, he demanded to be treated the same as everybody else. Which is why they started calling him Korczak, because he's like that guy from the Holocaust who went with the children."

"A righteous man," she said. Instantly regretting having portrayed him in such a good light, I mentioned that it was simply the logical thing to do, and that it was just surprising because Korczak was a loner.

"Don't take it personally if he's not too excited to see you. He's just that kind of person."

"Believe me, a display of excitement is the last thing I want from anyone around here," she replied and kept walking.

3.

KORCZAK WAS LYING on the top bunk of one of the many bunk beds in his room. A large piece of cardboard was perched against the windowpane, blocking the sunlight but not the heat. I wasn't sure we would find him there. When he wasn't on guard duty, Korczak would disappear for hours on end, and we'd try to guess where he'd pop up next. We usually got it wrong. On the second week of boot camp, the master sergeant of the training base caught him planting an herb garden behind the armory, and Yanai swore that only a week ago he had seen him walking out of the latrines after spending the entire morning there with an education corps guidebook. We were all familiar with Korczak's book obsession. His idea of combat-ready was having something to read on him, and this time was no exception; we found him with his face buried in words again, lying on the bunk with a flashlight strapped to his head and his eyes fixed on a small black book. Military bunks weren't designed for people as tall as him, and his large feet—one bare and the other in a gray sock—dangled over the bed.

"You have a visitor," I said. He didn't respond.

She approached the bed, tilted her head, and asked if he was reading *The Stranger.*

"I assume that if the IDF enlisted you, you're equipped with the cognitive ability to read," he replied. He looked up and blinded her with the flashlight before returning to his book. "On the other hand," he whispered, "I've been wrong about that before."

"What's the book about?" she asked, her casual tone trying to mask the insult.

He replied that it wasn't entirely clear. "Basically, about a guy who kills another guy because of the sun."

She thought for a moment and then said that there was a time when killing because of the sun would have made no sense to her, but since enlisting it didn't sound that far-fetched.

Korczak looked at her again. "Spend a few days here and you'll wonder why it doesn't happen on a daily basis."

Placing her hand on the bunk, she said it was impressive he was able to read such a complicated book.

"Actually, I'm just looking at the drawings, don't forget I'm a grunt."

She smiled and explained that she meant the language, because he had recently immigrated.

"I lived here for a few years in the past, so you could say I'm cheating."

"Really?" I asked, surprised.

"Yes," he replied without further comment. I think that if she had asked, he would have explained.

"You're from London?"

"Cheshire, if that means anything to you."

"Oh! You're the cat!"

Korczak lowered his book. "Have you still not realized that you've made it to Wonderland?" he asked, bursting into laughter. "He's the White Rabbit," he said and pointed at me. "And you, you're Alice."

"Why is she Alice?" I asked. Korczak didn't reply.

She told him she had come to the outpost just for him, that she heard he had enlisted in the paratroopers after earning a law degree from Oxford. She said she thought it was a great story. "People like to know what wonderful soldiers we have," she noted, and removed the cap of the camera lens. "It would make them happy to hear about you."

He was silent for a moment. "Then you're going to be just as disappointed as my mom was, since I don't have a degree."

She laughed before realizing he wasn't joking. "But your CO, he told me, I mean, I spoke to him a few times . . ."

"My CO is an idiot who doesn't know his soldiers," he interrupted her. "I'm willing to bet you he doesn't even know my name." Korczak explained that he had dropped out at the beginning of his third year in law school, and that he had spent the two years leading up to his conscription as a clerk in a dilapidated city hall building. "You can put that in, I'm sure it'll get you a Pulitzer."

I saw how the muscles in her face slackened; the realization that her whole trip was in vain was slowly seeping in. She sat on the lower bunk, held her head in her hands, and got up again.

"Okay, listen, I know what we'll do. We can say you went to law school without mentioning whether you graduated. A few white lies never killed anyone," she said, and placed her hand on his.

Korczak grimaced, shook off her hand, and returned to his book. "The nation will just have to make do without me," he announced.

She had yet to realize that she had already lost him. I think it wasn't the idea of lying that bothered him so much but the fact that the entire conversation had a clear agenda.

She tried to persuade him. At first he gave only monosyllabic answers, but eventually he stopped responding altogether. Finally she gave up and walked out of the room, with me in tow. She sat down on the curb and took out a cigarette. She asked me if I had a lighter. I said I didn't.

"What a shitty day," she mumbled under her breath, stepping on a piece of broken glass lying on the road. "I don't get it, do you have to be an asshole to serve here?" she wondered out loud, and quickly corrected herself. "I mean, not you. You're sweet, really."

I escorted her back to the security gate. A moment before we parted ways she gave me a hug and took a pen out of her pocket. She rolled up my right sleeve and wrote her number on my forearm.

"Try talking to Korczak," she asked. "If you get him to change his mind, give me a call."

She gave me another hug, and this time a kiss on the cheek too. I think she wanted the other soldiers to see. Then she turned around and walked back to the bus station, disappearing into the desert from which she had come.

I heard clapping behind me.

"Well, did you fuck her?" Yanai yelled out the window of the security booth, but I pretended not to hear. I quickly slunk off to my room, trying not to make eye contact. I kept turning it over in my mind, the prickly touch of her pen etching blue ink into my skin.

4.

I KEPT HER number in my cell phone under the name "Girl from the north." I also wrote it down in three different places, but still tried to preserve the traces of the digits she had scrawled on me. Most of them faded after two days, but during the weekend leave briefing on Thursday evening, I could still make out the four and the seven.

The briefing took place earlier than usual because Waxman and the other officers had to stay overnight at the training base for a regimental day seminar. Waxman glanced at his watch and announced that we had less than twelve hours before our weekend leave; that he wanted to believe a company of combat soldiers could get through one night without a babysitter. Then everyone scattered and I went up to the watchtower for guard duty.

I didn't like guarding at night. Most soldiers don't like pulling all-nighters in the tower. For me the reason wasn't tiredness or lack of sleep, but rather the elusive feeling that if I were ever to lose my mind, it would probably happen there. As if the soul's defense mechanisms were weaker at night. There was something about nights in the tower that magnified the feeling of detachment, the feeling that even if a missile were to destroy the entire outpost, no one would know. I would look at the dark sand for hours, wondering whether one day, in the distant future, Neptune would become the center of the world; that maybe a million years from now, right where I was standing, there would be a swimming pool, and dozens of kids diving into the water one after the other, not knowing a thing about the desperate soldier who had once stood there.

Around 2:00 A.M., shortly before my shift was over, I noticed a commotion starting down in the outpost, unusual for that time of night. Soldiers were crowding around the cabin showers. I peered through my binoculars, trying to see what the fuss was all about, but I couldn't make out a thing until one soldier burst through the crowd. It was Yanai. He was running toward his room in nothing but a towel and underwear, clearly agitated. Sakal emerged slightly after him, walking in the direction of the lineup square with slow and confident steps. Holding a plastic chair, he placed it in the middle of the square and stood on it. Another soldier, who couldn't stop laughing, handed him a megaphone, and Sakal tapped on it a few times.

"Hear ye, hear ye!" he called out, then waited for the rest of the soldiers to come out of their rooms with bleary-eyed confusion. Sakal raised his hand and announced that a severe crime had been committed in Neptune that night.

"The smart-ass will stand rookie trial!" he announced, and added that the defendant must report to the CO's office with an advocate, and that everyone was invited to come and witness for themselves the fate of rookies who broke the rules.

My replacement arrived twenty minutes before my shift ended, said that he thought a shitstorm was brewing and that he wanted to stay as far away from it as possible. I knew he was right, but my curiosity got the better of me.

5.

THE DOOR WAS OPEN. A few soldiers were huddled together on the bunks, listening to Yanai's shaky voice.

"Bejo started yelling at me to get out of the shower. He said that he and two other guys were sitting outside the canteen and saw me leaving the CO's room with a grilled cheese. I told them it couldn't have been me, that I was in the shower washing my hair like a little girl for an hour, but he wouldn't listen. Then Sakal showed up, got the entire story from him and now is putting me on trial." His left hand continued to shake even after he finished talking. His eyes were red. It was the first time I ever saw him like that. "They're going to fuck me over."

"Come on, bro, they only really beat the shit out of rookies in Golani, here it's just for kicks, they don't actually hurt you," someone said.

Yanai nodded.

"Yeah, you're right, bro." He got up and started pacing the room. "They better not piss me off even more, because if they do I'll beat the crap out of every last one of them." Maybe he felt better tossing around these empty threats.

"Okay. So I need an advocate to come to this shit with me. Any takers?"

No one said a word.

"What, am I the only real man around here?" he wondered in an irritated, unhinged tone. I think Yanai knew that wasn't the reason. The simple truth was that no one could stand him. He fixed his eyes on the uneven floor tiles.

"Did you do it?" A voice emerged from the corner of the room. It was Korczak, sitting in a crouching position. "Did you eat the grilled cheese?"

"No, they just want to teach me a lesson because I'm an asshole."

"Then I'll come."

"Really?"

"Really," Korczak replied.

Yanai bit his lip. "Thanks, bro. I appreciate it."

Korczak stood up and started scanning the room.

"Has anyone seen Kenan?" he asked. At first I thought I misheard. But after a moment he asked again if anyone had seen me.

"He's probably hiding somewhere stuffing his face with a pita," some soldier sitting next to Yanai said. Yanai immediately slapped him on the head. "You moron, he's here."

Someone else yelled in my direction that they were just joking around, but I was more concerned with Korczak's intentions.

"I want you to come with us."

"I just got off guard duty, I'm beat," I said, yawning, failing to understand how once again I was finding myself smack in the middle of everything. "Why me?"

"Because Sakal has a soft spot for you, that's why."

"He's right. So Sakal might just go easier on me," Yanai said.

"Can't do any harm, that's for sure. Don't worry, he won't do anything to you," Korczak added.

I tried weighing the pros and cons as quickly as I could, but before I could reach a definitive conclusion, Korczak turned around, placed his hand on Yanai's head, and moved it from side to side. "You cut your hair today?" he asked him. "Which number clipper did you use?"

"Three."

Korczak mumbled that he had a few things to take care of before the trial and left the room.

It was the first time he irritated me, getting me in this mess without thinking twice.

"That Korczak's an odd one," Yanai said, standing beside me.

"Annoying one," I replied.

"Yeah, right?" Yanai scratched his head. "You know, if this is too much for you, you don't have to come, we're cool."

A note of helplessness crept into his voice, and no matter how hard I tried, I couldn't help but feel some compassion toward him. "I'll come. I just hope it'll help."

"You're a real champ, bro," he said, giving me a gentle pat on the back.

Half an hour later the two of us were standing outside the CO's office. Korczak appeared only moments before the trial began, an inexplicable smile plastered on his face.

"Where were you?" I asked, already ticked off, but Korczak wouldn't say.

"Lower your head and keep your eyes on the floor," he told Yanai, and before he managed to explain, the door opened and Bejo was standing there.

"You have twenty seconds to put your berets on backward, take off your boot blousers, and enter the room silently," he said, and we quickly followed the orders.

6.

KORCZAK WAS THE first to enter, then Yanai and me.

"Salute your seniors," Bejo demanded, and told us to stand against the wall. We obeyed. Eight or nine seniors were sitting to our left on two frayed leather couches, looking at us with the solemn expressions of a grand jury. Sakal was standing in front of us, in the middle of the room, in a puffed fleece jacket and green baseball cap, the Israeli flag and company symbol hanging on the wall behind him. He was holding the seniors' stick—a thinly carved branch that granted its holder the authority to rule on matters of seniority, and served as an unconsoling consolation prize for those who were about to be discharged.

"Soldier, state your name, rank, and personal number," Sakal said.

Yanai replied. His beret fell on the floor, but he didn't notice.

"You're charged with breaking three rules," Sakal announced. "Entering the company commander's room without permission, eating cheese, and the unauthorized use of a toaster. Are you ready to be tried before the higher court of rookie affairs?"

Yanai nodded.

"Excellent. And do you plead guilty?"

"No," he stuttered, still staring at the floor as Korczak had told him to.

Sakal smiled.

"Then let's move on to the witnesses," he said as he turned to the seniors on the couches.

"Who here was near the canteen and saw a soldier leave this room with a grilled cheese?"

Three soldiers raised their hands.

"And can any of you point to the perpetrator?"

The three of them pointed at Yanai. Sakal, who seemed amused by the entire situation, shrugged.

"Three against one," he said, and waved the stick in the air. "Off with his head!" he yelled.

Yanai whimpered, recoiling as if a stray ball was heading in his direction. He tried to shield his face with his right hand.

The soldiers on the couches started laughing.

"We're just fooling around, cupcake," Sakal said with a smirk. "Don't worry, we'll knock you around for half a minute and call it a day."

"Sakal, you're fucking brutal, man, cut him some slack," one of the seniors called out. "He's about to piss his pants."

Sakal took two steps back. "You're right, twenty-nine seconds," he said, and grabbed Yanai's neck. "And remember it's only 'cause I got a soft heart, you know you deserve worse."

Yanai looked up.

"Wait!" Korczak roared. "I'm his advocate, right? Give me one minute and I'll prove to you he's innocent."

"It's the fatty who ate the grilled cheese!" Bejo parroted Korczak's British accent. Everybody started laughing again except Sakal, who seemed intrigued by the suggestion.

"A minute and you'll prove he didn't do it?"

"Korczak, knock it off," Yanai whispered to him. "It'll just make them angrier."

"Cut it out already," I said, backing Yanai.

"I don't want it!" Yanai yelled, but Sakal wasn't interested. "You should've thought about that before you chose him," he told Yanai and sat on the couch with the other seniors. He picked up the megaphone that lay on the floor beside him and announced: "One minute, advocate, give it to us."

"You're a fucking screwball," Yanai hissed at Korczak and looked at me helplessly.

With one hand behind his back, Korczak took a few steps toward the seniors.

"Who saw him leave this room?" he asked.

The three raised their hands again.

"And you were sitting outside the canteen, right? So what you saw was in fact his back?"

"Sweetheart, we may be old but our vision's still twenty-twenty," Bejo said.

Korczak took a step back.

"Okay." He stood next to Yanai without saying another word.

"That's it?" Sakal's voice blared through the megaphone.

"Yup, that was my only question."

"Wow, they got real geniuses at Oxford, huh?" Sakal said, and the rest of the soldiers behind him snickered like a well-rehearsed choir.

"Now if you could only open the door and turn off the light," Korczak added casually.

"What did you say?" Sakal asked.

"Turn off the light and open the door," Korczak repeated in a slow, clear tone. "It's really rather simple actions. I can do them myself if you'd like."

Bejo raised his hand in protest.

"Enough, he's turning this into a circus," he said. Sakal persisted in his silence, looking at Korczak with curiosity.

"Give me one more second, I'll prove it to you."

Sakal leaned his weight against the seniors' stick to pull himself up, then walked toward the advocate.

"I'm giving you one chance. But so help me God if either of you try to make a run for it," he said. It was only when their faces were inches from each other that I realized there was more than a show of kindness there; that maybe Sakal was seeking validation from Korczak. He wanted the company's intellectual to acknowledge his status.

Before any of the seniors managed to protest, Korczak had already turned off the light and opened the door. A streetlight from the other side of the outpost cast a faint glow on the two blurry figures that entered. Korczak closed the door, and the room was filled with complete darkness. I felt a pair of hands pulling me forward.

"Don't move," Korczak whispered, turning me around and positioning me somewhere in the room.

When Korczak switched the light back on, all I saw in front of me was the white wall nearly pressed against my face. There were people beside me, but I couldn't make them out.

"What is this shit?" one of the seniors cried out.

"You said you recognized Yanai from behind," Korczak replied. "So let's just make sure you're right." At that moment, with nothing to cling to but his voice, I realized the audacity of his tone, of his insistence not to grant even a shred of respect to those he deemed undeserving.

"I'm not going along with this shit," someone yelled. "In any other company they'd have had their asses whooped by now."

"Bejo, calm the fuck down," Sakal said. "You know what? The guy has a point. Tell him who you saw and we'll be done with this."

The room went quiet. I tilted my head forward so that my nose touched the cold wall. I heard the quiet, strained breathing of one of the guys standing beside me. It was Yanai, I was sure of it.

"So I'm acquitting him," Sakal announced.

"What did you say?"

"If you can't point out the person who stole the grilled cheese, I'm acquitting him," Sakal said, raising his voice.

"Fuck that," Bejo hissed and took two noisy steps in our direction. The figures around me tensed. I heard buzzed whispers, but I didn't know what they meant.

"That's him," Bejo finally said, and I froze.

"You're sure?" Sakal asked.

Another round of whispers followed. "Absolutely," Bejo replied. "It's the left one, I know it."

"Turn around," Sakal ordered us, and we instantly obeyed. Once again Yanai let out a yelp that echoed throughout the room. Only this time it wasn't a fearful whimper but a sigh of relief. He was standing in the middle of the row, next to the outpost's cook. On his left was an ordnance soldier who had been sent to the outpost for a two-week detention. Their faces bore no resemblance to each other, but Yanai and the ordnance soldier were more or less the same height and had the same skin tone. That's when I finally realized the whole stunt had been planned down to the last detail. Korczak had even managed to get the ordnance guy the same buzz cut.

Yanai and Korczak exchanged a brief glance, trying their best not to smile, but ultimately failing. The momentary solidarity made me a bit jealous. Stunned, the senior soldiers rose to their feet and stood in front of us, struggling to understand. Sounds of protest resumed, but Sakal soon silenced them with a shout.

"Okay. I have to admit it isn't too clear who did it," the judge said, and sat down on the couch. Yanai held his chest in disbelief, while Bejo shot him a murderous glare. Sakal picked up the megaphone again and turned up the volume.

"Due to these recent findings, I have no choice but to issue a new verdict," he announced, then paused for a moment. "The four of them will get their ass whooped, and we'll make it a full minute, so no one will feel left out."

"But you don't know who did it!" Korczak screamed.

"That's right," Sakal replied with a triumphant smile. "You may be some kind of genius but you still couldn't figure out that it never mattered."

Korczak's cry was swallowed up by the seniors' whistles and cheers. Before I managed to understand how I had turned into one of the defendants, Bejo and the other seniors were charging at us. Yanai pushed me back, trying to protect me. It didn't really help. I felt the first punch land above my stomach, in the lower rib. I tried raising my hands to shield my head, but I couldn't. The punches intensified.

I'm not sure how long it lasted. Probably not that long.

7.

I DIDN'T SEE him snatch the gun. But there was Korczak, standing with his back to me, holding a short-barrel M16 inches from Bejo's forehead. Two other soldiers drew their weapons at Korczak, and the room became as still as if we were all playing red light, green light.

At least four guys were yelling at Korczak to drop the weapon. He didn't respond.

"You wouldn't dare," Bejo said.

"I really don't know," he replied, and something about the uncertainty of his answer was more unnerving than an explicit threat.

Bejo closed his eyes. "You're fucking crazy," he said. His balding forehead gleamed with beads of sweat.

"I think you're overreacting a bit, don't you?" Sakal called out in a calm, almost cordial tone. He was sitting alone on the couch, seemingly indifferent to the situation. "It's a shame, we were having such a nice time."

Korczak kept aiming his weapon at Bejo, shifting his gaze toward the judge on the couch.

"Let them go."

Sakal got up and walked toward the door.

"No problem," he replied. "I'll let everyone out of here, just calm down and drop your weapon. It's all good."

Korczak must have felt that Sakal's instant surrender was suspicious, because he drew the barrel even closer to Bejo's head. Then he looked at the four of us and nodded toward the door, signaling us to get out.

None of us moved.

"It's all good, guys," Sakal said while opening the door. "Go, don't worry about it, it's all good."

The ordnance guy and the cook ran outside. I didn't move. Yanai walked toward Korczak and placed a hand on his shoulder.

"You took it too far, man," he said, making sure the whole room knew he had nothing to do with it.

"Come on, let's go," he said to me while moving toward the door, but I didn't budge.

"Hey, get the fuck out of here," Sakal grumbled and pushed me. I tried to stand firm, waved my hand in protest, I think I even shouted. But it was all for show. The truth is, all I wanted was to get out of there. I managed to look back one last time before the door shut. I saw Korczak cave, his hand slowly letting go of the weapon, which fell near his feet, and Bejo leaping at the tall Brit who collapsed onto the floor.

I waited for the door to be locked before trying to open it. So someone there would think I tried to help. Then I turned around. Yanai was no longer there. No one was there. I fled to my room, almost running. I lay on the bunk in my uniform, didn't even take off my shoes. I covered myself with the blanket, wrapping it as tightly around my body as I could, like my mom used to do when I was a kid. I looked up at the metal frame of the bunk above me. I tried counting sheep. I failed.

8.

I GOT OUT of bed at the break of dawn and started packing my weekend bag. Then I went to Korczak's room and stood by the half-open door. I pushed it an inch farther and peeked inside. The few rays penetrating the piece of cardboard against the window landed on Korczak's body. I heard him snoring. He had a big scratch on his cheek that sent shivers through my body. I didn't notice any other marks. I don't know how long I stood there staring at him. At some point he started coughing, and I flinched, taking two steps back.

When I left his room I called Waxman, without knowing what I was going to say. He didn't pick up. He didn't answer the second time either. I sent him a text saying that it was urgent and started wandering around the base, watching the sun take over the desert. I had to tell someone. I had to make sure the details made it out of Neptune and reached the real world, somewhere out there.

So I called her. I had the feeling she'd understand, but it didn't really matter to me anymore if she didn't. I wanted to talk to her. She picked up after the third ring, with a fresh morning voice. I pictured her waking up in her house up north, on a bed covered in snow. I told her everything. About the grilled cheese and the trial; Sakal and Korczak; the beating and the weapon. She asked me to slow down, to explain. She lingered on the details, led me inside my own words, and I gave into the softness of her speech.

She listened until I had nothing more to say, and then reassured me almost without words. With gentle breaths. She said she'd look into it, that she knew people who would do something about it, that they wouldn't let this kind of behavior just blow over.

"If I have to, I'll even call Carmela Menashe, the military reporter," she announced. "The fact that Yanai's an idiot doesn't mean he deserves this." She made it clear it might take her some time, but she promised to do whatever she could.

"Can you hang in there?" she asked, and I almost said that for her I could do anything.

"Yes," I replied.

"You're brave, that's good."

And despite all the horrible things that had happened the previous night, I found myself boarding the bus with a smile that couldn't be wiped off. I took a seat in one of the back rows and put in my earphones without listening to anything. I imagined her voice while falling in and out of sleep. About an hour before we reached Tel Aviv, Sakal appeared at the front of the bus and sat down beside me.

"That old woman won't stop talking."

I felt my blood coursing faster and faster through my veins. I tried to appear indifferent.

"What are you listening to?" he asked while shoving his bag beneath his seat. I pretended I didn't hear the question, and after a few moments he gave up. Sakal tilted his head to the right, looking at the old woman sitting in the opposite row. She was rummaging through two overflowing grocery bags, mumbling that she couldn't find her glasses. He bent forward, lit up the floor with his cell phone screen, and reemerged from the abyss with a pair of black-rimmed glasses, handing them to the woman.

"Bless you," she said. Sakal smiled and went back to staring at the seat in front of him.

"I'm not the giant asshole you think I am," he said.

"What?" I asked, feigning ignorance.

"I know what you think of me. I used to be like you once."

"Like me?"

"A kid. I didn't think these kinds of things happened."

I didn't respond. We made eye contact for a brief second.

"He's fine, just so you know. Got some bruises but nothing serious," he said. "Bejo checked him when it was over to make sure we didn't accidentally break any bones. Trust me, it's nothing compared to what the regiment commander would have done to him if he had found out he threatened another soldier with a weapon."

I felt like making a snide remark about the senior platoon's kindness, but I didn't dare.

"You'll turn out the same," he said, closing his eyes again.

"No, I won't," I quickly retorted, taken aback by his bizarre claim.

"You just wait," he said. "A few more months in Neptune or any other shithole outpost, and you'll get it. Believe me, you'll get it."

I wanted to argue with him. To explain how wrong he was, that I was nothing like him. But suddenly I was afraid that if I tried arguing, he'd somehow prove I was wrong. So I didn't say anything.

When we got off at the central bus station in Tel Aviv he told me he was going straight to an afternoon concert at a music club, and asked if I wanted to join him. I appreciated his attempt to appease me without making an official apology.

"This whole thing is going to blow up," I told him. I felt it was unfair not to warn him after all the times he'd been kind to me. I told him that I'd spoken to the soldier from the military newspaper. I said that she knew a reporter from Kol Yisrael. "I don't want to screw anyone over, Sakal, least of all you. But someone's got to take care of this."

Sakal smiled. It was that same mischievous smile he had when issuing his verdict.

"You really are a kid," he said, then paused as if considering whether or not to elaborate. "You think this was a coincidence? That Yanai hits on the CO's girlfriend and three days later we beat the shit out of him?"

I tried to grasp the full meaning of what he was saying, but I couldn't.

"Whose girlfriend? Waxman's? What are you talking about?" I asked him, but he didn't answer.

"What are you talking about, Sakal?" I shouted at him. He put his hand on my shoulder. "What are you talking about?"

Sakal wouldn't say a word. He turned around, cut in line, and entered the station. I stood still, trying not to think. I started to wander aimlessly outside the station. So many thoughts were racing through my head that I almost stepped on a kitten. I tripped. The kitten crossed the road, almost getting run over twice. I sat down on the curb and took my cell phone out of my pocket. I stared for a few moments at the name I'd given her in my contacts, "Girl from the north." Then I tried calling her again. She didn't answer.

9.

IT WASN'T UNTIL SUNDAY, when I returned to Neptune, that I had heard about Korczak's disappearance. The last person to have seen him was the ordnance guy who slept in the same room; he said that before he fell asleep he saw Korczak reading in his bunk. When he woke up, Korczak was gone. Six other soldiers heard the shot. They spent the entire Saturday looking for him. The only evidence they found was a cartridge near the canteen and a few feet away, a puddle of blood soaked into the sand.

They didn't find Korczak. Neither his body nor his weapon. Soldiers from the criminal investigation division arrived, investigated, and came up empty-handed; they declared him a missing person. I told them about the rookie trial, said it might have had something to do with that, but they didn't seem too interested. Rumors began to spread. A soldier who was on guard in the watchtower that night claimed he saw a tall figure hitchhiking from the bus station, and Bejo said that a friend of his from the adjutancy couldn't find Korczak's records on any computer. In a matter of days, a strange Neptunian thought started creeping in that maybe Korczak was simply a figment of our imaginations. An outpost apparition.

If it hadn't been for his mother, I would probably have filed these events under my long list of bizarre military experiences. But two weeks after he disappeared, his mother showed up—a shriveled woman wrapped in a scarf and red coat, who walked through the gate one morning dragging a suitcase almost as big as herself. She approached each and every soldier on the base, asking in her heavy British accent if anyone had seen her son. She spent the whole day under the blazing winter sun, moving frenziedly from room to room, locker to locker, searching with trembling hands for the precise point in time and space in which her child had disappeared.

The image of her searching for him behind the green dumpsters has been haunting me for years; resurfacing intermittently at random moments in my life. A few years ago I even hired a private investigator to try to find out what happened to him. I was hoping the attempt alone would grant me some peace of mind. The only revelation was a fine from a small library in one of the kibbutzim up north. Six overdue books, all by South American authors. I tried reading some of them in the hope of finding a clue—but there was none. And still, oddly enough, this discovery offered some kind of comfort. It reinforced my secret and irrational thought that maybe Korczak had existed as a kind of transcendental man, in the physical sense, and that the outburst of violence on that night had frightened him out of his lanky, awkward body and returned him to his original form—a consciousness that lived only between the lines of books that he read.

The Girl Who Lived Near the Sun

1.

IN THE MIDDLE of Neptune's central bus station, Grandma called me for the third time in a row. In a moment of weakness, I decided to answer, and within seconds a wrinkled and scowling six-foot-three hologram appeared before me. Before I could utter a single word and without any pleasantries to speak of, she got straight to the point. "What's the matter with you? Why aren't you coming back to Earth?" she scolded me. The people around me turned their gazes toward the small holographic woman. I quickly turned down the volume.

"Honey, this is no laughing matter," she proceeded. "It's been a year and a half now that you've been traveling all over the solar system, without popping by to visit your old grandma even once. You know I won't be around much longer."

"I promise this is the last planet. A few weeks and I'll be eating your matzo ball soup," I replied. She snickered.

"A few weeks? What's wrong with you? You're starting college in ten days for heaven's sake. Your friends are already into their third year and you don't even have a schoolbag yet," she said, and fell silent, knowing that one more sentence like that and I'd hang up.

"So how's the weather?" she asked, trying to change tactics. I replied that all in all it was fine. Gas storms every now and then, but nothing serious.

"And tell me, have you decided what you're going to study?"

"IR."

"What's that? Speak louder."

"IR. Intergalactic relations."

"Why would you choose that?"

"I met a few guys here who studied it. Sounds like an interesting field."

"Hmm. Interesting, I'm sure," she said. "That's not the problem."

"Then what is?" I asked, immediately regretting it.

"That until they send an Israeli ambassador to the Andromeda galaxy, it's a useless degree. Call your father, he's a smart man. He says you should study psychological engineering. That's where the world's heading. Soon people will start paying a fortune to reengineer their traumas."

"He never said that to me," I claimed, and she jumped at the opportunity. "Of course he didn't. He's afraid you'll think he's trying to influence you," she said, arms flailing. "Back in my day, parents still had a say in the matter, but today all I keep hearing is how they have to let you kids make your own mistakes. That it's the only way to get life experience. But you know what happens then? You kids get lost. You make so many mistakes that you find yourself on the other side of the solar system, alone."

I was quiet again, this time with a certain measure of guilt. Grandma leaned in, placing her virtual hands on my face, stroking it from billions of kilometers away. "What can I say, bubele, you can't keep putting your life on hold like this, it just doesn't work that way. You're not the only person in the world who has questions, believe me. The problem is that no one has the guts to tell you you're not going to find the answers. Not even on an abandoned asteroid."

The loudspeaker announced the bus's imminent departure, and I jumped at the opportunity and told her I had to get going. She folded her arms across her chest and gave me a worried look. I told her I'd call when I could and not to get worried if I didn't answer, because there might not be a good signal there.

"What am I going to do with you, my dear boy?" she said. "Just make it back in one piece. And take sunglasses, would you? The sun's awfully strong over there." I smiled. Her figure faded and disappeared among the dozens of passengers boarding the public space shuttle. I picked up my bag and followed them.

2.

I FOUND AN available seat in one of the back rows. A burly man with a Hawaiian shirt sat down beside me, taking up more than his share of seat room. Blue lights flickered on in the aisles of the space shuttle, which started cruising toward the center of the solar system. The driver turned on the radio to one of those nostalgic stations that liked starting every other program with Bowie's "Ziggy Stardust." I closed my eyes, nodding on and off. I'm not sure how much time had passed, but when I woke up again I saw the dark side of Venus out the window, and realized it was too late for a change of heart. I leaned back, closed my eyes again, and tried to conjure the face of the girl I was on my way to see.

I'd met her three months earlier, in one of those tacky space parties on the Rings of Saturn. I always hated parties, let alone the kind with a space suit dress code, but the two Australians I used to hang with back then managed to drag me along with them. I didn't even try dancing, just sat alone at the bar trying to sip their disgusting local beer through the straw attached to my helmet, getting more and more annoyed by the minute. I spotted her sitting two barstools away, flirting with the bartender, telling him she was from Israel. I mentioned that I was a fellow Israeli, and she said it was hard to miss. We got to talking about how even a 0.5 G-force turned the lamest dancer into a music video star. And how anyone who's never visited Titan didn't know what a crazy view meant, and how Israelis in space always insisted on walking around in sandals even when it was minus seven degrees outside.

I thought the conversation went well, because she laughed at least four times. I counted. I asked her when she was planning to return to Earth, and she said it wouldn't be anytime soon. She told me she'd been living on a small planet by the sun that she bought for a song from some old man who had built an underground condo there just to find out he couldn't live forty-nine million kilometers from the sun. She said she knew that sounded far, but it was actually as close as one could get. So she emptied her savings account and bought the planet off him. Also a private atmospheric system from the Space Depot, one of those advanced systems with a tropical weather feature; after three months of renovations she indeed lowered the temperature to 51°C, which isn't ideal, but the place was still cheaper than a two-bedroom apartment in Petah Tikva. I asked her whether Hebrew was the official language on her planet, and she laughed, saying she had invented a special language only the inhabitants of the planet could understand. I don't really remember the rest, because right after mentioning Petah Tikva, she tried to kiss me, our helmets bumping into each other.

She was heaving with laughter, said she probably had too much to drink, and put her head on my shoulder. I don't know how long we sat there like that, but at some point another girl appeared, announcing their ride was about to leave. Before I could wrap my head around the situation she was already up on her feet, saying she had to get going. I asked for her number, but she didn't own a holographic phone because there was no signal on her planet. She told me that if I ever happened to find myself in the area, I was more than welcome to pop by for coffee. It was only after she had already left that I realized I didn't even get her name.

It wasn't on the space shuttle's route, but apparently the driver was in a good mood because he agreed to make a little detour. I took my bag and got off at a deserted stop. The first thing I felt was an onslaught of sun rays, like the incessant flash of a camera clicking away. I quickly took my sunglasses out of my pocket. It provided only partial relief. I looked up at the sky, painted a bright purple just like she had described to me at the party. I didn't dare look directly at the sun, but a quick glance revealed it was much larger than it appeared from Earth. The bus pulled away, and I looked around me but there was no house in sight. There was nothing but blue sand dunes, and an indistinct smell reminiscent of caramel.

Before I could get my act together, I already felt the horrific heat on her planet. Sweat poured out of me, soaking my clothes. I started trudging along the small surface, no more than a few kilometers in diameter, so minuscule you could actually see the ground curving into itself. I continued on my wretched walk, quietly cursing myself for insisting on this visit. I lowered my backpack and took out a bottle of water. I was about to open the cap when I tripped on a large stone. The bottle fell and rolled into a crater.

"For fuck's sake," I hissed. It took me a moment to notice the staircase winding into the ground. I quickly descended the stairs. The heat abated with every step, until the temperature became almost bearable. At the bottom of the pit I found the bottle, and myself standing in front of a small dark door devoid of any sign. I was dripping onto the doormat and tried to wipe myself dry, without much success. I took a deep breath and knocked twice.

3.

IT TOOK HER about two minutes to come to the door. Her black hair was pulled into a high ponytail speckled with blue sand. She was wearing a faded white tank top and brown shorts. A thick sleep mask pulled up to her forehead was covering half her left eye. She let out a gaping yawn.

"Say, aren't you tired of trying?" she asked in English, her tone something between grumpy and desperate.

"What? No," I replied in English. "I mean, I . . ."

"What's that accent? You Israeli?" she asked in Hebrew.

"Yes."

"So why are you speaking English, dummy?"

"Because you did."

"You're not the sharpest pencil, huh?" she said and sighed. "At least you didn't come in a suit."

I had no idea what she was talking about, and couldn't snap out of the shock. "Wait, let's start over. Remember me?" I stuttered with a smile.

"Yes," she answered, and I'm fairly certain I felt a fleeting surge of optimism. "But I'm not selling the planet," she announced, and took a step toward me. "I've already told you and the others thirty times now, I'm not selling. Am I being clear?"

"What are—"

"Yes or no," she raised her voice. "Do you understand the sentence 'I'm not selling the planet'?"

"Wait, but . . ." I tried to explain.

"Listen, you're starting to get on my nerves. Do you understand or not?"

"No," I said.

"Too bad," she replied and slammed the door in my face. I knocked again, but she wouldn't open. I found myself explaining to the door that I didn't know who she thought I was, but my name was Golan. And that we had met at that lousy party six months earlier, on the Rings of Saturn. I heard her footsteps approaching.

"It's just that you said if I happened to find myself in the neighborhood, I should stop by. And, well, I was in the neighborhood," I lied. It took her a few more moments to open the door. "God, I can't believe it," she said, staring at me. Without a giggle to alleviate the tension, without an apology. I stood there, about to die of embarrassment.

"Okay," she finally said. "If you were stupid enough to come all this way, at least have something to drink before you hit the road again."

She waved me in, gesturing at a chair in her small kitchen, and started to fumble through her messy cabinets for glasses. The kitchen was open to the living room, or more accurately, a large couch by a hallway leading to the bedroom. The walls were made of blue rock and the living room ceiling was riddled with small holes, allowing the sun to filter through and light up the entire house. The bedroom was crammed with books and had only one hole in the ceiling. She explained reading was the only thing left to do on a planet with no signal. A large basket stood by the front door, filled to the rim with dozens of sunglasses and ski masks in different colors.

"Sorry," she said, handing me a glass of tepid water filled less than halfway. "The homeowner association is very strict around here about water usage."

I assumed that by homeowner association she meant herself, but I was afraid asking would bring on another insult. I downed the water in one gulp.

"Wouldn't you rather drink something cold in this heat?" I asked.

"I would," she said. "That's why I keep the water in the fridge for myself."

The rest of the conversation was nothing to write home about. Long stretches of silence and pointless questions that didn't interest either of us. After half an hour and a stingy water refill, I picked up my bag and headed toward the door. A brief goodbye was accompanied by an official, rather ridiculous handshake.

"Where did you park?" she asked as we stood in the doorway. I told her I had come by public transport. "You're joking, right?" She groaned, slapping her forehead. "Public space shuttles stop here twice a year."

I smiled and told her not to worry. That I'd been traveling for so long, I was used to waiting a few hours in the sun. She looked at me and sighed again. "I wasn't being funny. The next space shuttle will arrive in four months. And that's best-case scenario."

I hesitated and told her it wasn't a problem, I'd just make a holographic call to one of my buddies to come pick me up.

She sat down on the chair, biting her hand nervously. "There's no signal on this planet."

I didn't know whether to stay in the doorway or step outside. I started calculating how long I could live off the food and water in my backpack. A couple of days. Tops.

After a few minutes, she got up. "You can sleep here until we figure out a solution to this shitty situation," she said, pointing at the couch. Then she went to her room and came back two minutes later with a pair of square-rimmed sunglasses and jeans. I was left alone in her house, trying to understand how I had gotten myself into this mess. I lowered my backpack, slipped off my shoes, and lay on the couch. I tried to fall asleep, but the heat permeating through the walls kept me wide awake. I still hadn't worked up the nerve to ask her name.

4.

THE FOLLOWING PERIOD was marked by dire attempts to leave her planet. I spent hours on the sprawling dunes near her house, searching for a signal so I could text someone to come rescue me. I couldn't bear the thought of spending the next four months on her boiling planet. Four months of nothing but dodging the sun and her nervous glares.

We barely spoke. I slept on the couch and she'd slip in and out of her room with a grumpy pout, closing the bedroom door behind her and then storming back out. Every once in a while we'd sit together at her kitchen table, eating cans of peas and corn or crackers with jam, sometimes just an energy bar with too many raisins. We never ate anything nice. In each of these meals she'd put a single glass of water before me, advising me to drink slowly because that's all she had to offer. I brushed my teeth without water. Showers were obviously out of the question.

When I wasn't eating or sleeping, I spent my time outside. We had an unspoken agreement to avoid any interaction that would only exacerbate our frustration. I soon realized that unlike Earth, her planet didn't rotate on its own axis. The sun never set, but remained fixed in the same spot in the sky, distorting everything I thought I knew about the concept of day and night. The only refuge I found was under a boulder located by one of the dunes, which provided me a rare meter of shade. I spent hours on end leaning against the boulder, counting minutes that gradually lost their meaning. Every movement, every action was insufferable. The raging sun allowed for nothing but thoughts, and even they were a struggle to produce, flitting in disjointed fragments. Mostly as fears. Of returning home, to the same spot, going back to the rat race I'd spent a year and a half trying to outrun. I stayed for hours, maybe even days by that boulder, nodding on and off for unknown periods of time. I started feeling as if the shuttle would never come. That I was going to stay there, in the same spot, forever

One day, waking up abruptly, I found her lying beside me, sprawled out on the sand, this time with white sunglasses. She lay there silently, without a hint of shade or apology. I considered her for a moment, and then looked around me. The purple sky was painted green streaks, turning alternately blue and red, constantly changing colors.

"I think I might be losing my mind," I said.

She laughed. "I felt the same way at first," she admitted. She said she didn't really know what caused the colors to appear in her sky, but thought it probably had to do with the solar flares. "A little like the northern lights," she explained. "Only it isn't cold here, and like a million times more beautiful."

"It's amazing," I said, just to keep the momentum going. "I bet people would pay big bucks to see something like this. I mean, it could be one hell of a tourist attraction."

She considered me for a moment, then turned her gaze back to the sky. She said that on such a hot planet, you couldn't afford to waste words on chitchat. "Talking just makes you thirsty," she said. Then she was quiet again for a while, and I, out of sheer awkwardness, tried to be even quieter. We stayed like that, side by side, for some time. At a certain point, she got up, shook off the sand from her clothes, and extended her hand.

"You coming?" she asked, and I stood up as quickly as possible, without daring to ask where we were going.

On our way to wherever she was taking me on her little planet, she started to drill me. About my trip. About the studies I was trying to avoid. About my parents who didn't know what to make of me. She asked if I had a girlfriend. At first I said no, but then I told her about Sivan. Either because some part of me still missed my ex, or because I wanted her to know I wasn't the giant loser she thought I was. I told her we met three years ago. That I was sure we were going to get married at some point, but we ended up splitting six months ago via holographic call. She called me just as I had finished climbing the Olympus Mons on Mars, saying she couldn't take my roaming and roving anymore, that she was beginning to feel I wasn't so much trying to find myself as I was running away from her. I tried to tell her that wasn't it at all, but she didn't seem interested.

"So basically, you were too chicken to dump her so you waited for her to do it for you?"

"What? I just explained that she was the one who left me," I replied. "I didn't want to break up."

"So why didn't you go back to Earth?" she asked.

"Because I'm not done here."

"So you dumped her for a few more hikes?" she scoffed. "Because you haven't yet found the answers you're looking for?"

I didn't reply.

"It's okay, it's not like you owe *me* any excuses."

"What are you talking about?" I asked her, making sure she caught the severe tone.

"No one's willing to lose the girl he loves for a few shitty answers about life, it's just not how it works," she asserted. "It's simply a matter of priorities. She probably didn't mean enough to you."

"How would you know? You don't know me at all."

"You're right," she replied. "But there's one thing I do know. That you traveled all the way to the center of the solar system for some girl you met at a party, but haven't bothered to visit your girlfriend even once." Before I could reply, she quickly announced: "This is what I wanted to show you."

We were standing in front of a cluster of large green cactuses. She said she hadn't planned on growing them. What she had really wanted was mango or pineapple, but the trees couldn't survive on her planet. Eventually she settled for eleven cactuses, by special order. Two had withered and died, but the rest managed to pull through. She couldn't stand them at first, but she'd come to love them. A pair of worn-out gray gloves were lying next to one of the cactuses. She picked them up, put them on, and plucked a red prickly pear, splitting it open and offering me a piece.

"Isn't it thorny?" I asked.

"Only on the outside."

I warily accepted the piece. It was without a doubt the tastiest thing I had eaten in a long while. I said I was pretty sure it was the first time I'd had a prickly pear.

"Obviously," she said, then told me they had stopped growing them on Earth a long time ago. They just didn't have enough space over there.

The only place you could get prickly pears was on the black market in China, and even there they grew them under the ground, which made them completely bland, because it's the sun that gives them all their flavor. She said a few dozen prickly pears sets her up for a whole year. And people were willing to pay crazy money for them.

"Every once in a while some realtor shows up wanting to buy the planet," she said and laughed. "Weird guys in suits. At first I thought you were one of them." She told me she never actually listened to their pitch, but sometimes sold them a few prickly pears. Even gave them a discount if they promised to bring some to her family.

"Isn't your family flipping out about you being here?" I asked.

"Flipping out? They're the ones who encouraged me to move here," she said.

"What do you mean? Why would they encourage you?"

She didn't answer.

Once we were done she grabbed my hand and pulled us toward the nearest dune. I suggested we return to her apartment to get some rest, but she said that where there was no day and no night, time ceased to exist, so the concept of rest made little sense. Careful though I was, I still ended up with tiny thorns in my hands, but I didn't say anything. We started walking up the closest sandy hill. It was no more than thirty meters high, but scaling it in the insane heat required some real effort. Once we reached the top I collapsed with exhaustion, sure I was about to pass out, but she nimbly sat down beside me, folding her legs to her chest and hugging them. "I see you're quite the mountaineer," she said, winking through her sunglasses. I tried coming up with a witty comeback, but I was too busy trying to catch my breath.

"Right here, this is the closest a person can get to the sun," she announced. She pulled a pack of cigarettes from the pocket of her pants, fished one out, and held it up. The tip instantly lit up as it exited the atmosphere. She stubbed it out in the sand, saying she didn't smoke, that it was just a game she liked to play.

I lay down on the sand and told her about an experiment I had read about in which people were left in a lit room for an entire week. Almost all of them went completely bonkers. That was what scared me most on this planet, and I didn't get how it hadn't happened to her yet.

"Who said it hasn't?" she asked, and as if to prove her point, lowered her sunglasses and stared directly at the sun. Looked at it without even blinking.

"What, are you crazy?" I yelled at her and sat up, pressing my shoulder against hers. "You'll go blind!"

"You have no idea what you're talking about," she stated. "I've been doing this for three years and nothing's ever happened to me." She said it was only blinding for a moment, but then you could see perfectly fine. That only candy-ass scientists too scared to ever look up from their telescopes thought otherwise. "I honestly don't understand how people can spend an entire lifetime under it without looking at it even once," she said, and before I knew it, she had plucked the sunglasses off my face. "If you've ever wanted to find any meaning in life, this is a good place to start."

I couldn't stop blinking, could barely see a thing.

"Well, what are you waiting for?" she asked. I craned my neck, trying to open my eyes, but the light wouldn't let me. I barely blinked twice before fixing my gaze back on the slope. She sighed and lay down on the sand, still staring at the sun.

"Don't worry, it's okay. Most people don't even have the guts to try," she said, and closed her eyes. "You'll get there eventually. That is, if you don't pass out next time we climb the dune."

I didn't have anything witty to say, so I kissed her. She didn't smile or anything, just said it was a punk move kissing a girl whose name I didn't know.

5.

HER NAME WAS Ayala.

6.

HANDS REACHING OUT in the heavy heat. Gentle, tentative groping sticky with sweat and sand. The body operated differently in fifty degrees. Words dissolved, making way for long stretches of silence, inquisitive gazes, like children exploring their bodies for the first time.

After an indeterminable period of time, another real estate agent arrived on her planet. He was wearing a dark jacket and black trousers, dripping sweat along the sand. He found me and Ayala sitting by one of the craters and asked if he might steal a few moments of our time. Despite her limited patience, Ayala eventually agreed to listen on the condition that he bought a bag of prickly pears. He paid her and launched into his pitch, telling us this planet was worth a good few million. That it could be sold to a large research facility or to armies that wanted to train their soldiers under extreme conditions. He proceeded to explain that it was a once-in-a-lifetime opportunity, that she could take the money and live on an artificial island in Miami, which was exactly the same as here only twenty degrees cooler.

"So what do you say?" he finally asked, by now almost suffocating from the heat, barely breathing.

She lowered her sunglasses and gave him a quick once-over. "I'm not selling my planet to someone who'd wear that suit in this heat," she announced, flicked down her sunglasses and would say no more. He started throwing figures at her, unfathomable amounts of money that kept increasing. Three. Four. Five million dollars. But Ayala didn't even bother to answer. I looked at him with something of an apology. Eventually he gave up, picked up the bag, and started walking toward his Mercedes spacecraft.

"Wait," she called out when he was already a few meters from his vehicle. The guy tossed the bag of prickly pears onto the sand and came running back, asking if she had changed her mind.

"No, but this one here needs a ride," she said, pointing at me.

"Don't listen to her," I said. "She's crazy."

The man turned on his heels, and Ayala closed her eyes and smiled.

7.

THE SANDSTORM BLEW in a few hours later, maybe even a few days, I'm not sure. All I remember is us sitting in front of each other in the narrow shade of a cactus while she explained her theory about the fourth person. "Think how lonely it is to talk in first person. To admit it over and over again."

"Admit what?"

"That I'm alone."

"Of course you're alone. You're the only one on this planet."

"It's the other way around. Here I have no one to talk to, so I barely think about it. But back on Earth it drove me crazy. I felt like the whole language thing was keeping me stuck inside myself," she said, and started piling sand into a small mound.

"Come on, you're overreacting. It's just words. And besides, first-person plural pretty much solves your problem," I said. "We eat. We sleep. We. See? Not so lonely anymore."

"No, dummy. That's the worst. First-person plural just lumps you in with everyone else, erases you completely. Like it makes no difference whether you're a realtor or a Holocaust survivor. People get lost in that shit."

"You're the only one who gets lost."

"Fine, then I'm the only one," she snarled. "Then for me second- and third-person are even worse than worst. You say 'you' or 'she' and you completely take yourself out of the equation, as if you don't even exist."

"I don't understand why you're obsessing about it. It's just semantics."

"For you. For me it's more than that," she said. "That's why we need fourth-person."

"What's that? How would you even use fourth-person?"

"How should I know? I'm not a linguist," she protested. "I just know that when you use it you don't feel completely alone or completely lost."

"I don't understand what you're talking about."

"You know, like when you mix yellow and blue and they still haven't turned completely into green yet? That's what I'm talking about."

I told her the whole approach sounded a bit childish to me. That no disrespect, but I'm not sure first-person was the reason she felt lost or all alone in the world. That it was more complicated than that. A strong wind blew past us, crumbling the little mound she had built. Ayala got up and strapped on her ski goggles. At first I thought she was just having one of her *moments*. That I had somehow managed to offend her. But when I noticed she was gazing out at the horizon, I turned around. A wall of blue dust was sweeping up behind us. It was still a few hundred meters away, creeping toward us.

"What's that?" I asked Ayala.

"Come," she replied. "Now." She started to bolt.

"Wait," I yelled, but she wasn't listening. When I saw she wouldn't even look back, I realized she wasn't fooling around. She started running, and I tried to follow her but couldn't keep up.

"Hey, what's going on? Wait a minute!" I shouted, but she still wouldn't listen. Then the shade came. A large stain that gradually spread across the desert. The sandstorm bit into the sun, which instantly turned into a faded white dot in the sky. I ran as fast as I could, but all the dust made it hard to breathe. A wave of sand washed over me. I couldn't see. I had no idea where to turn. She didn't answer. I cursed myself for getting stuck there, in the middle of a goddamn sandstorm, when I could have been sitting in an air-conditioned college auditorium.

Her hand emerged from within the dust, pulling me toward her. I followed her, grabbing on for dear life.

"Careful," she said as I took another step and almost slipped down the staircase. She slowed down, leading me one stair at a time. "Slowly," she instructed, and I listened. I heard the door opening and she pushed me in. The door slammed shut behind me, and I kept my eyes closed.

"It's okay, hon, you can open your eyes," she said.

I waited a few more moments before opening them. The room was awash with a pale light, like the glow of a sunset. Sand was trickling in through the holes in the ceiling, forming small mounds on the floor. Ayala emerged from the bedroom with a few buckets. "Snap out of it already, it happens. Don't take it so hard." She handed me a bucket and told me to put it in the middle of the living room.

"Believe me, you were lucky I brought my ski goggles," she announced.

When we were done, I slumped down on the couch. The storm had made the apartment even hotter. There were three large holes in the ceiling above the couch, and the sand pouring through them was piling on top of me. I tried falling asleep but couldn't.

"You can come in here," she shouted from the bedroom. "And bring a glass of cold water." I quickly followed her orders, pouring water into a glass and placing it on her bedside table. Then I brought another glass for myself and lay down beside her. We stared at the ceiling in silence.

8.

THERE WAS ONLY one hole in the bedroom ceiling, which made it the only room in the house that wasn't sheeted with a thick layer of sand. While Ayala wouldn't come out of the room at all, I sometimes snuck into the living room for a change of scenery. I'd shift the buckets around, grab a bite to eat, but that's pretty much it. We spent most of our time in bed, side by side. The air got thicker, the room darker, leaving me and Ayala no choice but to get closer to each other. To burrow into one another until our sweat mingled. I told her I sometimes imagined our bodies as blocks of ice cooling each other off.

"That's a lovely way of thinking about it, but the reality of it is still super gross," she said and laughed. And she was right.

The crampedness edged out the romance, and neither of us was able to hide the particularities of the body. Wrinkles on her chin and hairs on my cheeks, calluses on the bottoms of her feet, a swollen scar on my back.

"Well, are you hopping on the next bus?" she'd ask every now and then, and I'd tell her I didn't know and hugged her tightly, hoping she wouldn't notice how tired I was getting of living in such a confined space. Of the heat and the sand. But she did.

One night, waking up drenched in sweat, I saw her reading *The Catcher in the Rye*. I told her I had read it in high school and kind of liked it. She stopped reading and looked at me suspiciously.

"Then what's the name of the girl who kept all her kings in the back row?" she asked. I had no idea what she was talking about. I told her I couldn't remember, that I had read it a long time ago. She sighed irritably and said I was just trying to sound smart.

I told her everything I remembered about Holden, about his journey through New York. She wasn't the least bit impressed. She snorted, said I probably hadn't even given any thought to what happened to Holden after the story ended.

"How am I supposed to know what happened to him?" I mumbled, and before I could say anything else, she cut me off. "He commits suicide," she said decisively.

"I don't think that was in the book," I replied hesitantly.

"Of course it wasn't." She said that because the author didn't have the heart to kill him off or admit him to some loony bin for the rest of his life, she was pretty sure that's what happened. "Someone like Holden doesn't grow up to be a psychological engineer or something like that," she teased.

I told her she could think whatever she liked, but it didn't make sense to get angry at every person who decided to grow up.

"It isn't growing up, it's giving up on your dreams. It's becoming a lame first-person plural, like everyone else."

"Oh come on, then what's the alternative?" I barked, sick of her patronizing me. The heat was driving me crazy. "What should I do instead?"

She fell silent.

"What, just quit? Go off the radar like you? That's the solution? Everyone should just find a hole to crawl into?"

"I don't know."

"How could you live here for three years and not know?"

A slight tremor passed over her lips. She considered me for a few moments before turning her back to me, lying on her side and gazing silently at the wall.

I started to understand how hard it was for her without the sun. Sometimes Ayala would slink into the living room and sit beneath one of the large holes, trying to catch the few rays that had managed to filter through the layers of dust, only to creep back into the bedroom even more frustrated.

"Fuck this. When will it end? It has to end already," she'd grumble to herself, stomping her feet on the floor. She'd get annoyed with me as well. All I had to do was snore or open a bag of crackers and she'd start yelling that I was unbearable, that I wouldn't let her breathe. She paced the room for hours, spitting out incoherent sentences.

Eventually the storm died down and the sun lit up the planet and house once more. It took us a good few hours to clear out all the sand. Once we were done cleaning in silence, we both knew we had to restore the previous order. I went back to the couch and Ayala went outside, leaving the door open.

9.

I CAN'T SAY exactly when I stumbled upon the pond, but it was without a doubt the most special spot on her planet. I marched all the way back to the house just to let her have it.

"How could you not tell me about the pond?"

"I have no idea what you're talking about," she replied, barely looking at me. At first I thought she was joking, but soon came to realize she truly didn't know. Eventually I persuaded her to come see. After walking a kilometer and a half in utter silence, we arrived at the shaded area, to a spot the sun couldn't reach. "I've never been here before," she said. The air was cool. The pond was hiding in the darkest spot—a reservoir of clear turquoise water that had pooled into a small crater, a few meters below the surface. We sat on the rim of the crater and gazed down at the water.

"It makes no sense," she said, studying her reflection in the water. I admitted I didn't understand it either. That maybe some frozen asteroid had once struck the planet. "And somehow, because of the atmosphere, the water . . ."

Before I could finish my sentence, she pushed me in.

My fear of crashing into the rocks was overtaken by the warm lull of the water. I held my breath for as long as possible before coming up for air, then sat on a large rock in the middle of the pond, my lower body still submerged. My clothes were completely drenched.

"I just wanted to make sure it wasn't toxic," she said, and smiled.

"Isn't this when you're supposed to dive in?" I asked her.

"You've seen too many movies, hon," she said, dipping her toes in the water. We were silent again, but it was a different kind of silence. Like when we had first met, and we each withdrew into ourselves. I tried guessing how much I'd already missed of my first year of studies, wondering whether there was even a chance of catching the tail end of the first semester.

"That's what I don't get about you," she said and paused as if contemplating her words. "You live your life as if you have no choice in the matter."

"But you're exactly the same," I replied.

She glanced at me before turning back to the water, brushing a hesitant hand through her hair. Then she got up and slowly made her way up the rocks, slipping back into the kingdom of the sun. I stayed in the pond for a while before climbing out of the crater, lying in the shade, and gazing at the purple sky.

On my way back to the apartment I saw her sitting on her favorite dune, staring at the sun with unshielded eyes. I stood beside her. She kept staring.

"So you were actually sent here?"

She nodded, then admitted that for the longest time she had tried getting her act together, but nothing worked. Tried all kinds of treatments that didn't help. "The only thing that helped a little was being in the sun." She said that whenever she called her parents on the phone, she could hear in their trembling voices how they were still hoping she'd tell them everything had worked out. "That all this craziness, it was just a phase," she said. "Like it is for you."

And then it dawned on me. "Wait, what phone?"

10.

THE ORANGE PAY phone was nestled not far from the cactuses. She had installed it there the very first day she arrived on the planet. I didn't ask why she hadn't told me about it. I don't think she would have answered anyway. I went there and called my parents, explaining that I had gotten stuck on the planet closest to the sun. They didn't sound especially concerned, said it had only been three weeks since I had last called. That school had started only a day ago.

Three days later they landed next to the bus stop, informing me there was one angry grandma waiting for me at home. I wanted to say goodbye to Ayala, but when I went back to the apartment to get my things, she wasn't there.

As we whizzed past Venus, I told my parents I was going to study psychological engineering. That I was going to make shitloads of money and finally start living. My mom said it was a terrific idea. Then she turned on the radio, saying there was a program about healthy cooking that she loved. I leaned my head against the window and tried to fall asleep, ignoring Ayala's voice telling me to stop kidding myself.

Debby's Dream House

1.

I FOUND THE job through a newspaper ad. I didn't even know there were people who built dreams. I was sure they were just created by themselves or something.

The first question Bruno asked me was if I was an artist or advertiser.

I said I wasn't.

"Very good. They're the worst. They think they're producing movies for the Cannes Film Festival," he said. "They work on a dream for two months and end up sticking a giraffe on a car roof in the middle of the desert."

I had no idea what he was talking about, so I nodded. Bruno said I got the job, and then announced that it was a shitty one. You work all night, bring your own food, and there were no holiday gift cards.

"Still interested?"

"What does it pay?"

"Fifty an hour. Seventy-five for overtime."

"I'm in."

Bruno shook my hand and made me sign an NDA. He asked if I was married. I told him Debby and I were going to tie the knot someday. He said congratulations, then warned me that even if I was taken prisoner and tortured, I couldn't tell her about my job. "Make up a cover story or something. I don't need people knowing who I am and start asking for a special dream for their wedding anniversary."

We left his office and went to the operations room. A small room; three screens set side by side. Looked a little like the control room of a shopping mall security guard.

"Every screen is a customer's dream. We pull twelve-hour shifts, 7:00 P.M. to 7:00 A.M., five nights a week."

He said that for now all I had to do was monitor the screens and call him if one of them became snowy.

After one shift I realized it was the easiest job I've ever had. That the only challenge it posed was keeping myself awake. I invented all sorts of games to pass the time. I tried to find out things about the customers' lives through the images that appeared on the screens. For instance, there was this one guy who had to be some kind of technician, because electronic devices appeared in all of his dreams, or this mother who dreamed only about her daughter. There was probably some story there. It was nice, looking at the screens, but what really kept me awake was thinking about Debby. About the breakfast I'd make her when I got home, or how I'd hug that big body of hers before she woke up.

Debby kept asking about my job, but I couldn't tell her anything.

"At least make something up, so I'll have something to imagine," she said, but I explained I didn't know how to lie. She smiled and stopped asking questions.

The lab was just a small room with a fax machine, a desk, and what looked like a big washing machine. Bruno explained that the daily customer reports were faxed in every evening at seven. Each report contained basic information about every customer, and a detailed description of his day. After reading the report, you'd come up with the idea for the dream, and then draw or write it down on a piece of paper. He said he kept everything in the big pile on his desk, and would choose a random page each morning.

"Aren't we supposed to build a new dream every day?"

"It's been years since anyone in the industry did that. Usually I recycle something from '85 or '91. They barely remember anything anyway."

Then Bruno showed me how to feed the page into the "washing machine," which was actually a big metal contraption that manufactures the dream. The paper spins inside the machine for two hours before spitting out the dream onto a little black disk. After a month, the work became more interesting, once Bruno started teaching me how dreams were built. He advised me not to put my heart into it since the business wouldn't be around much longer. It was a matter of a few years until the global dream companies took over the market. He said you couldn't compete with a Chinese factory that had thousands of workers and software that produces dreams in HD. I asked him how he even got customers, since people didn't know who produced their dreams.

"Most of the transactions are through the HMOs, but there are also a few labor unions that do it. Believe me, this whole industry's basically like the Wild West."

2.

RITA'S WAS THE first dream I'd ever built. She had just started working at a new law firm, liked classical music and evening jogs at the park near her house. According to her report, she had spent the entire day in the office and got into a fender bender on her way home. At home, she watched the news and fell asleep on the couch. That was it. I jotted down a few ideas on the page and came up with a pretty strange dream. I had her jogging in the hallway of her office; then a car crashed into the wall and a news anchor stepped out of it. Bruno said it was one of the lamest dreams he ever saw. That the whole bit with the car crashing into the wall was preposterous even for a dream. I asked him if he was going to scrap it for a new dream, but he sighed, switched on the washing machine, and said, “Fat chance.” A week later he used the same dream again.

I continued to build dreams even though I wasn't good at it. For every dream I got a thirty-shekel bonus, and Bruno was just happy he could go home an hour early. He asked me why I insisted on working so hard, and I told him that I needed the money to buy my Debby a house. That it was Debby's dream, that ever since she was a little girl, all she wanted was a place where she could scribble on the walls without looking over her shoulder. Bruno said she must be something special if I was willing to work so hard for her, and I told him he had no idea. It was around that time that Debby started interning for some interior designer, said he was a true artist and that she was learning a lot from him. I was happy for her, even though it was hard, barely seeing each other. She finished work every day at seven in the evening, so I only got to see her for an hour in the morning. I didn't bring it up, since it wasn't easy for her either. The problem was that even with us both working, we still weren't making ends meet. To have enough for a down payment on a mortgage, we would have to keep working like that for another decade.

I asked Bruno if there wasn't a way to move up.

“Nightmares are a hundred shekels a pop, but don't go there. You're a sensitive guy, it'll mess with your head.”

I told him to give me a chance, that I really needed the money. He hesitated but eventually agreed, giving me a report for the guy who always dreamed about electronic devices. He was thirty-four years old, a bachelor, and like I suspected, worked as a repairman at a small electronics shop. Two days ago he had fixed eleven devices, gotten off work at seven, and gone home for a shower.

I asked Bruno whether nightmares required a special technique.

"There isn't a technique, as such," he said, and admitted that even he found them difficult to build. He said he had once read a book that recommended going all out with the daemons and monsters routine, since it's had a good track record for thousands of years and was practically bulletproof. Or to try different Freudian theories, to choose something symbolic and work that angle. Bruno said that in either case it didn't always work, so I should just do what I felt like.

I didn't know how to produce monsters and didn't really understand enough about psychology. The only thing I could tell from all those hours monitoring his screen was that the electronics guy found it difficult communicating with people. So I built a pretty lame nightmare in which he's just walking down the street and everyone around him is speaking in a foreign language. And he tells them he can't understand, but no one answers him. Bruno said he didn't see what was scary about that nightmare, but he certainly wasn't going to pay me another hundred to build a new one.

The next day, after I punched in, Bruno told me he had just read the guy's latest report. It stated that he couldn't stop thinking about my nightmare after he woke up, he was so upset he barely left the house. Bruno gave me a pat on the back and said that good nightmares were great for business. That the Ministry of Health loved them, they were sure they helped people work through their issues, or something like that. He said that each dream manufacturer was required to deliver three quarterly nightmares per customer, so as far as he was concerned I could build nothing but nightmares. I asked him if he didn't think it was a bit much, since he himself had said that it messes with your head.

"There's nothing to worry about," he said, and added that he had only been trying to scare me because he didn't believe I would be good at it. I thought he might be lying, but I didn't ask more questions because I wanted the money.

That's how I got to building nightmares on a daily basis, and Bruno admitted that even he couldn't understand why they were so effective. I told him that while with dreams you had to be creative and craft elaborate fantasies for people, nightmares were a whole different ball game. Nightmares had to be simple, because what really scares people are the most basic things in life: that they won't have enough money to pay their bills, or that their wives will leave them. Those kinds of things.

"As long as the Ministry of Health keeps recommending us," he said. He told me he had already gotten phone calls from a few HMOs, referring several new clients that needed effective nightmares to work through their issues.

"One of them is even named Debby. Funny, huh?"

"Yup," I replied. I didn't tell him it was my Debby. That I had asked her HMO to transfer her to us. I figured that since we saw so little of each other, at least I'd get to read her daily reports and see her dreams every night. Bruno got a new screen for her. She was beautiful on it. I made sure to produce fresh dreams for her every day, mostly involving new homes. Some had large backyards and others swimming pools, and even a big Jacuzzi she could stretch out in. One morning when I came home from work, she told me she had had a really nice dream, but couldn't remember what it was about. It made me happy.

Toward the end of the quarter, Bruno told me not to put off Debby's nightmares any longer. It wasn't something I wanted to do, but a small one would be better than letting Bruno build her a big, scary one. I tried thinking about her phobias, like cockroaches and flying, tried doodling a few options, but I soon stopped. I felt physically ill at the thought of doing something bad to my Debby. Hurting her like that. So instead, I just built her another nice dream, that we were living together in the highest penthouse in the city, taking in the view every evening, and were really happy.

The next day was a Friday, and that night I looked up at the ceiling and told Debby I was on the verge of going crazy. She asked why. I wanted to tell her that dealing with her nightmares was agonizing. That it wasn't so much the nightmares themselves as the realization of how much damage I could cause her if I only chose to. But I didn't say a word. Not only because I wasn't allowed to talk about it, but because I didn't want her to be afraid of me. I thought it might be a good idea to quit my job. To tell Bruno I couldn't take it, and that I wasn't going to deal with anyone's nightmares anymore.

But Debby wanted a house, so I stayed.

3.

AS TIME PASSED I had more and more nightmares of my own, at least twice a week. But they didn't really work on me, because I already knew every trick in the book. I'd find myself getting bored by some man pointing a gun at me, and count the minutes until I woke up. Building all those nightmares had left me immune to my own, and that's exactly what troubled me. I had been sure that dealing with such dark material damaged the soul, but other than my fear of hurting Debby, it didn't seem to do anything. On the contrary, every time I met someone, I custom made them a nightmare in my mind. I'd buy milk at the supermarket and ask myself what would scare the cashier. Bruno observed I was enjoying it all just a little too much. Said that a few customer reports had mentioned sleeping pills, and he asked me to go easier on the clients. I said sure, but in truth I couldn't help myself. I was feeding off all those fears, and I didn't know how to rein them in.

The greatest source of comfort in those days were Debby's dreams. I could spend three hours building us a living room. I read her reports over and over again, thinking about what she was going through. The name of that designer she was working for started appearing more frequently. It was just the two of them at the office, and they had several meetings a day. It made me jealous. I asked her about him, and she said he was a nice guy. I told her the truth, that I was scared she'd leave me, and she hugged me tightly and said she'd never leave. Debby wanted us to talk more in the morning, but all I wanted was for us to lie together in bed with her arms around me.

"It's time we give up on the house," she said one day. She said it was too hard on her that we barely saw each other. That as far as she was concerned, we could live in a tiny rental our entire life as long as we spent more time together.

"I know how much you want that house."

"I don't." She pouted. "I've gotten along without it perfectly fine for thirty years." She said that she was starting to think I loved the house I wanted to buy her more than I loved her.

"Is this about that designer?"

"What are you talking about?"

"It's because of him that you're talking to me like this."

Debby said I was losing it. She wouldn't speak to me anymore that night, and I started to stress out. I began to think she really had fallen for him. That she was about to leave me. I started to suspect she had somehow found out about my job, knew I was getting daily reports on her, and had to find a way to hide their affair. She went out, and I lay in bed and couldn't fall asleep.

I decided to follow her. The bus pulled up in front of her office window, and I saw her sitting in front of her computer, and one window over, him sitting in the other room. I stood behind the bus stop and spent the entire day looking at them. I was waiting to catch them together, to find proof. But nothing happened. Every now and then Debby walked into his room for a few minutes, but it looked like they were just talking, nothing more. They didn't even have lunch together.

It calmed me down, made me realize I had been overreacting, and that Debby was great. And that I really loved her, and had to make up for everything I'd put her through this past year. So the next morning I asked Bruno for the day off. He didn't want to take my night shift, but eventually he agreed, said that nothing's more important than love. I spent the entire day shopping for Debby's favorite foods. Pasta and tomato sauce and salads and good cheeses. I bought only the best, so she'd know I'd always go all out for her. I got back to our apartment and spent the entire afternoon cooking. Then I set the most beautiful table I could, including a new IKEA tablecloth I had bought especially for the occasion and a bottle of wine we had been saving for a special moment. At seven in the evening I opened the door, sat down at the table, and waited for her.

But Debby didn't show.

At nine, I called her twice, but she didn't answer. I texted her a question mark. At ten thirty she texted back that she hadn't seen my message because she was in the shower. I wrote "ok" and went to bed. She called a few times, but I put my phone on silent. Trying to think as little as possible, I soon fell asleep. In the middle of the night she woke me up. Stroked me for a while. I couldn't look her in the eye. I didn't want to know.

"You want me to explain?"

I said no. She gave me a kiss on the back of my neck and lay down beside me. At that moment, the thought that Debby would no longer be mine started to creep in. I imagined myself waking up alone in the world, without her big body next to mine.

When I woke up in the morning, Debby had already left for work. I stayed in all day and went to the office only in the evening. Bruno asked how it had gone, and I told him it couldn't have gone better. Then I went to the lab, sat at the desk, and started building. It took me about half an hour to make her nightmare. I didn't do much. Just stood her in front of the mirror. Naked. With all her flabby skin and spots I love. I stood her in front of the mirror and just showed her the truth. That

I was the only one who'd love a big woman like her. That she wasn't worth much on her own, wouldn't actually be able to start a new life without me. I finished building the nightmare and swore to myself it was the last time. That after things settled down, and we went back to loving one another, everything would work itself out.

4.

THREE YEARS LATER, and Debby and I have a house. She designed it herself, including the sauna area, which was entirely her idea. Bruno sold me the business and retired. He calls every now and then, says he's on some jeep tour in Iceland or Greece, loving every moment. Since taking over the business we've gotten a lot of new clients, because no one does nightmares like us. I already have eight employees. They're not as good at building as I am, but good enough to keep our clients on board. I don't pull night shifts anymore, so Debby and I always go to bed together. She holds me tight and I kiss her on the cheek. Every now and then I plant a nightmare in her. Just to make sure she doesn't accidentally start thinking about leaving again. It's okay, it really is, because I'm fairly certain she doesn't even remember the nightmares anyway. My favorite part of the day is right before we fall asleep, when she hugs me so tight I can barely breathe. Sometimes I whisper in her ear that I can't believe we actually have the life we've always wanted, and she smiles, and says that neither can she.

101.3 FM

1.

SOME OLD MAN brought the radio set in a few days ago. Took him two minutes just to open the door. Benny went to help him out, carried the radio up to the counter. The old man slouched behind him, breathing heavily. Then he looked at Benny with his puffy eyes and said the radio had conked out.

"What make is it?" I yelled through the storage room window.

"Grundig 3059, wooden panel," Benny replied.

"Yowza, an antique. Need me to take a look?"

"Nope, it's a goner," he said, and advised the man against repairing it. Said the spare parts alone would cost more than three new Sonys.

"No, out of the question," the man said. "Nechama wouldn't stand for a new one."

I came out of the storage room and stood behind the counter.

Benny smiled, told him he could help convince her. That he'd give them a good price.

The man lowered his gaze.

"She passed away. Two years ago."

Benny apologized and turned to face me.

"Ever fix one of these?"

"No, but I think I can."

Benny hesitated for a moment, then told the old man we'd give it our best shot. The man nodded, rearranged his scarf and green cap and left the shop.

Benny shuffled into the storage room, placed the radio set on the table, and asked if I happened to catch last night's game.

"There was a soccer match?"

"It's like you're living under a rock. The basketball game! Maccabi made it to the finals."

"Oh, right. Yeah, it's awesome."

He smiled.

"We can watch the finals together," I said.

"I'd love to, believe me," he sighed. "But Yotam won't let me. It's his first finals."

"Of course, you're right. I wish I had a kid to watch it with."

"What's the rush to have kids? You have all the time in the world, you're barely thirty."

"I'm thirty-four."

"Even better, trust me," he said, and walked out of the room.

I stayed alone with the radio set. It was an early sixties model, old but in decent condition. It switched on but didn't pick up any stations. I spent a few hours fiddling with it but couldn't find the source of the malfunction. I changed the antenna and a few other parts, but nothing helped. It pissed me off because I hate wasting an entire shift on one device. Not that Benny would ever say anything. He really is a great boss. He knows talking to customers isn't my thing, and he's cool with me staying in the back room all day, fixing devices. He's always telling me to feel free to set my own pace, that as far as he's concerned, I can take all the time in the world, though, I'm not sure how sincere he's being. After all, it's not as if he has all that time to give me even if he wanted to. I know it sounds petty, but it bothers me when people say things they don't actually mean. Personally, I prefer being as precise as possible. I use iPhone notes to keep a daily record of my expenses and how much time I spend in front of my computer. That's how I know my daily repair average is eleven devices, and that it takes me fourteen minutes and seven seconds to get from my house to the old strip mall. If it wasn't for Nurit, it would take me thirteen and a half minutes. She works at the drugstore next to Benny's shop and stops me each morning at the entrance to the strip mall, always finding something to criticize. My slumped posture, for instance, or that I don't have enough hair to justify buying shampoo. I have the feeling she's like that with everyone, but I have no way of knowing. Maybe she just can't stand me.

2.

IT TOOK ME four days to fix the old man's radio. I mean, I thought I had fixed it, but I wasn't a hundred percent sure. It didn't pick up Galei Tzahal or Reshet Bet, only stations I never listen to, like 93.1 and 108 FM. The quality wasn't that great either; there was tons of static. I tinkered with it for two minutes and twenty seconds, until I finally stumbled on a station it picked up beautifully, 98.6 FM.

Four-hundred-and-thirty-plus-eighty-five-plus-six-hundred-and-fuck-wait-forgot-the-VAT-dammit-from-the-top-five-hundred-and-three-plus-one-hundred-no-no-it-makes-no-sense.

The volume kept going up even though I wasn't touching anything.

Benny walked into the room, asking if I remembered how much the woman from yesterday had paid to fix her microwave.

"Ninety-nine shekels and forty-five agorot." The broadcaster's words descended into a blaring garble.

"I told you to charge her two hundred."

"When?"

"Turn that off, turn it off a sec. Right before I went out for lunch. Don't you remember I told you to charge her two hundred?"

I tried to remember but couldn't.

Benny looked at the radio. "You were wrapped up with that, huh? Never mind, don't worry about it."

"I'm sorry, Benny, I can pay the difference if you . . ."

"It's all good. Keep working on the radio, take all the time you need."

I switched the radio back on. Picked up the same station. It was only after a few moments that I realized the voice was familiar.

Five-hundred-and-three-plus-one-hundred-idiot-three-hundred-and-sixty-five-shekels-fuck-what-on-god's-green-earth-okay-let's-see--that-comes-out-to-just-over-

I shot up in my chair, recoiling from the voice. I looked out the window into the shop. Benny was sitting at the cash register, counting receipts and scribbling in a notebook. He wasn't talking. The radio kept broadcasting. I stared at him and imagined him speaking.

One-hundred-and-fifty-plus-two-hundred-and-seventy-five-comes-out-to-why-is-this-not-adding-up?

I leaped up so fast the chair fell backward. Benny turned to me and smiled.

God-I-can't-take-him-anymore-what-does-that-pain-in-the-neck-want-now?

I turned down the radio and stepped out of the back room and into the shop.

"Haven't fixed it yet? Why don't you go out for a bite? You've been working all day."

"No, thanks, just looking for a screwdriver."

Benny yanked open the drawer and handed me one. I returned to the back room and closed the door.

Screwdriver-my-ass-he's-just-fucking-bored-wants-to-nag-okay-again-how-much-is-two-hundred-and-seventy-five-plus-

I turned off the radio, keeping my finger on the switch for another forty-six seconds. I didn't want to hear any more. I fixed ten other devices. At closing time, I told Benny good night and rushed out, avoiding his gaze. I went home and got straight into bed, feeling like my body was off-kilter. My hands were shaking and I couldn't steady them. Eventually I fell asleep. I woke up at seven in the morning and wrote down what I remembered of my dream. Or rather, my nightmare. I have about one per month, on average. I washed my face and left for work. When I arrived at the shop I immediately began running tests on the radio again. At nine forty the old man called, asking if we'd fixed it yet. I told him that we were still waiting for a spare part from Germany and it would take at least another week. He thanked me and hung up. Whenever a customer walked in, I began fiddling with the frequency. I couldn't catch the stations of the first seven customers, but at 10:53 a tall bearded man walked in. I started playing with the frequency until I heard a brittle voice coming out of the radio. I cranked up the volume.

And-shortbread-cookies-what-am-I-supposed-to-pick-up-now?-The-printer-and-Rachel's-meds-the-prescription-is-in-my-pocket-what-else?-Get-back-to-Yossi-about-the-apartment-tickets-to-Italy-yes-what-time-is-it-gosh-already-eleven-the-morning-flew-by.

I looked at all the devices I'd fixed. There was only one printer, small and black. I picked it up and approached the counter.

"Yes, that's the one," he said, pointing at the printer. "You guys are the best."

"*He's* the best," Benny said, slapping me on the back. I nodded and returned to the back room. I stared at the radio and decided it was enough. I wasn't going to turn it on again.

At around five o'clock, Benny said he had a wedding to attend and left me alone in the shop until closing time. I stared at the customers coming and going, telling myself I wasn't at all interested in what they thought. But at 6:23 an older woman walked in. She was looking for an iPhone case, standing there in a puffy down coat and red sunglasses, studying the case selection. I asked her if she needed any help. She lowered her sunglasses and gave me a once-over. It was clear she was looking at my receding hairline, probably thinking how ugly I was. I told her I was popping into the back room to fetch something. I walked in and tuned the radio to her station. I had to know.

The-black-case-isn't-that-bad-fucking-Amos-going-and-breaking-up-a-family-after-twenty-years-throwing-it-all-away-and-for-what-actually-the-silver-case-is-nicer.

She walked up to the cash register as I came out of the back room. I gave her a twenty percent discount without even telling her.

"Everything okay?" I asked softly.

"Perfect, hon. Why do you ask?"

"No reason."

"Honey, why did you ask?" She looked at my hairline again. It pissed me off.

"Because of Amo—" I wavered, falling silent.

"You a friend of Amos's?"

I didn't reply.

"He already told everyone, huh?" She put her hand on her neck, fondling a colorful necklace. I bagged the silver case. She snatched it from my hand.

"Tell your friend he's a fucking loser," she said and walked out of the shop. The noise from the radio gradually died down.

I stood rooted to the spot for a while. Then I called the old man to let him know the shipment from Germany had been delayed and it would take at least another month. He said a month was a long time, and I asked if he wanted me to cancel the order. He hesitated for a moment, and said no. That Nechama wouldn't have wanted that. He hung up. I'm not sure whether I was pleased or disappointed.

The following day I let Benny know about the delay as well. He didn't say a word, just thought he ought to replace me with his nephew who'd be out of trade school soon and willing to work for minimum wage. I went back to fixing other devices, but now I was averaging eight a day. I listened to the radio while working, keeping it low so Benny wouldn't hear. Apart from tuning in on the customers, I also liked following Albert, the building super, who mainly hummed Arik Lavie songs, and Nurit's station, 101.3 FM, which had the best signal. She had this funny quirk of reciting useless trivia about different countries. For example, in Canada there were more lakes than in all other countries combined, and the name "Spain" originally meant "land of the rabbits." And every day at noon on the dot, she thought of things she wanted to eat, like pasta with cream and sweet potatoes, or tuna salad with olive oil and feta. I also liked that while in person she was quick with the hurtful remarks, alone in her head she was much more hesitant—afraid that her boss thought she was too slow, or that her paycheck wouldn't stretch to the end of the month. One morning I popped into the drugstore to pick up toothpaste. Nurit was at the cash register. She looked up and said, "Always buying off-brand, huh? Cheap-ass." And I didn't say a word, just went back into the shop and turned on the radio.

Two-soaps-for-ten-is-a-great-bargain-I'll-buy-some-for-myself-too-bad-he's-always-rushing-off-it's-actually-nice-when-he-stops-by-oh-wait-last-month-it-was-three-for-ten.

My shoulders shot up. I made sure the door was closed and cranked up the radio. I listened to her station till the end of my shift; three more times she thought I was cute, and twice that it was a shame we didn't know each other better.

The following day, we met at the entrance to the strip mall.

"You're jumpy today," she said.

"Maybe," I replied, noticing the large beauty mark on her neck. I smiled. She smiled back. That day she had spent seven minutes and forty-six seconds thinking about me. Four times she had told herself that if I asked her out, she wouldn't turn me down. I thought about it, and about how it had been exactly three years and four months since my last date.

I walked into the drugstore to buy a pack of gum. Nurit was sitting at the cash register; she looked at the gum and said it tasted vile. I asked her if she wanted to go out with me. She considered me for a moment, and said no.

I said okay, dropped my gaze to the floor, and went back to the shop. Shaking, I sat down on my chair in the back room. The radio was still playing her station.

I-always-have-to-go-ruin-everything-such-an-idiot-I-can't-believe-it-fucking-moron-how-much-does-that-cost-twenty-six?-God-I-hope-he-comes-back.

I listened to her and smiled. After thinking about it for another hour, I decided to go back to the drugstore. I stood in front of the cash register. I said I forgot the receipt, to which she replied, "Nice to have you back."

We agreed to go out to a movie that evening. Six times she hoped we'd go to the new Angelina Jolie flick, and that I'd buy us a large popcorn with lots of butter.

We met by the box office. She was wearing a beautiful black dress. Straight off, I told her we were going to see the Angelina Jolie movie, and then I went to buy us a large popcorn like she wanted. Nurit said there was no need, and got truly annoyed when I told her I was going to buy it anyway. I was starting to freak out that maybe she had changed her mind and I was ruining everything, but I think I got it right because she ended up holding my hand the entire movie. As we walked out of the theater she told me she had a really great time, and I told her I did as well. I considered kissing her, but preferred not to before I knew for certain she was into it.

3.

THE FOLLOWING MORNING she thought it a shame I hadn't put my arm around her during the movie. Then she thought it was strange that a guy like me had never been in a serious relationship, which actually made me happy, because I admit I was starting to worry about it too. Nine times she thought yesterday was truly perfect, twice that my shirt was kind of ugly, and four times that she couldn't understand how she had gotten so lucky as to land someone like me. I found it slightly troubling that she had three negative thoughts, but mostly I was happy the date had been a success. Around noon she texted me to suggest meeting at a restaurant by her house, but I suggested we take a long lunch break and sit at the small café in the strip mall. I wanted to keep listening to the radio until the very last second. That way I was able to tell her "I get the feeling you just had a very annoying customer," and she said it was incredible how well I read her. We order cappuccinos, and sixteen minutes later I told her I had just remembered Benny needed something from me at the shop, and darted back to the storage room to listen to her. She thought it was a little odd, me disappearing on her in the middle of our lunch date, but also that she was having so much fun talking to me that she didn't really mind.

For our sixth date, I was the one who suggested we meet at the restaurant by her house, because I knew she wanted me to come up to her apartment afterward. It all happened just as she had hoped, including wine and dessert. And when we got into bed, I already knew what she liked. I gently nibbled her ear and pressed up against her once it was over. The following day she thought sex with me was probably the best she had ever had. Which was really nice to hear because I had always suspected I wasn't very good at it, but I admit the *probably* bummed me out. Not that I had time to obsess about it, because not a moment later she thought she loved me, like, for real. And I smiled, because it was the first time since the eighth grade that someone had said that to me. I was excited, but at the same time I had this niggling thought that maybe she was about to take it back. That she was overreacting and it wasn't actually love. But I told myself that as long as I had the radio, that would never happen. I'd make sure to do everything exactly as she wanted, and she'd never leave. Then I listened closely to every thought she had about me. Ninety-three percent were positive, and only seven percent were negative. It made me happy. Even Benny was happy for me, said he always thought we'd hit it off. That we'd probably have good-looking children. Which was another thing that made me happy, because it was something I enjoyed thinking about. But a few hours later, I picked up his station.

Fucking-slouch-doesn't-even-do-the-bare-minimum-anymore-takes-a-two-hour-lunch-break-every-day-and-for-someone-like-that-not-that-he-had-other-options-such-an-ugly-ass-couple-God-help-them.

Around noon that day, I told Nurit I could only take a thirty-minute lunch break. She said she had the feeling something was bothering me, and I told her about Benny. That I heard him talking about us with a customer. Nurit smiled, said she couldn't care less what people thought about us, and hugged me tightly. I felt like she was my anchor in this world, and really wanted to tell her about the radio. So I told her I read an article about some scientist in South Korea who was working on a device that could read minds. She was quiet for a while, then said it sounded a bit sad, everyone knowing what's going on in your head, not having a moment to yourself.

When I returned to the storage room, I didn't feel comfortable listening to Nurit's thoughts. I even tried going without for two and a half hours, but I couldn't take it. I had to know what she thought about the whole Benny thing. So I told myself I'd turn the radio on just for a moment. I heard her yelling to herself that it was a fucking catastrophe. That everyone was probably thinking the same thing. That we truly were an ugly couple. That she wished I wasn't so indifferent. That she really loved me, but the sex wasn't as great as she had first thought. And that she didn't understand why I always had to pop into the shop whenever we sat together. That maybe if she knew what I was doing in there, she'd understand me a bit better. I tried comforting myself that it was okay, that everyone had bad thoughts sometimes. But when I went over the data, I saw there was a 23 percent spike in her negative thoughts about me. It wasn't that there weren't any good ones. They were even the majority, 70 percent, but I couldn't focus on them considering all the bad stuff I heard. Among all her thoughts, one really stuck out—that if by the age of thirty-four I still hadn't been in a serious relationship, maybe there really was something wrong with me. And out of sheer frustration, I started thinking not-too-great things about her too. That she really was kind of ugly, and not that smart, and that sometimes I got the feeling that all the amazing facts she recounted in her mind about countries were less than accurate. And that very day, I found myself directing all these nasty remarks at her, like the ones she used to hurl at me. For instance, that her jokes weren't that funny, or that she looked older than her age. And these weren't just petty, frivolous comments, but verbal jabs aimed directly at her sore spots. I didn't even need the radio to know I was hurting her feelings. Eleven times she wondered why I was doing it to her, and the problem was I wasn't too sure myself.

A few days later we met during our lunch break, but didn't say a word to each other. We remained silent for seventeen minutes and forty-six seconds, until she asked, "What's going on?"

"What are you talking about?"

"Why are you being like this?"

I saw her body stiffen in pain in front of me. I'm not sure why, but it only pissed me off more.

"Because you're lying to me," I said. "You think there's something wrong with me."

"I never said anything of the sort."

"But you thought it, didn't you?"

She remained silent, frozen in her chair. I considered her for a few moments, then stood up, telling her I forgot something back in the shop and starting to walk away.

"Where are you going?" she yelled.

I didn't answer.

She started running after me, saying she didn't understand what was going on with me, and that I couldn't just drop a bomb on her and run away. I entered the shop without looking at her. I was sure she wouldn't dare make a scene in front of Benny, but before I noticed she ran right past me and into the storage room, locking the door behind her. The radio was turned on to her station. I started pounding on the door, but she wouldn't open. I peeked through the window. She was standing next to the radio, which broke into blaring static. She covered her ears.

"Turn off the radio," I yelled at her.

She reached out to the device, but instead of turning it off, she started fiddling with the stations. I felt as if she had stuck her hand inside my head. I shouted at her to stop. To quit it, now. But she carried on. Benny said we both had to get our acts together, but I just kept staring at her while she played with the stations.

She whipped her head up in my direction, but didn't look at me as much as through me. I felt entirely exposed. I tried listening to my own thoughts, to understand what she was picking up, but it was no use. I put my hands on my head like a shield, but knew it wouldn't help. I turned around and walked out of the shop. Soon enough, I broke into a run. Benny was yelling at me to come back, but I didn't care; all I wanted was to get out of her signal range. To get her out of me.

I made it home, took a quick shower, and got into bed. Benny called four times, texted too, but I didn't answer. I pulled the blanket over my head and tried my hardest to fall asleep.

I woke up late, arriving at the strip mall at 9:41. At the exact moment that I opened the door to the shop, the old man walked out with the radio.

"Wait, it's not ready," I said. "I'm not done fixing it."

"Liar," he replied, turning his back to me. I tried snatching the thing, explaining that the part from Germany hadn't arrived yet, but he wouldn't listen.

"Enough!" Benny yelled. I held onto the radio for another moment, before finally letting go. The old man let out a peeved sigh and shuffled off, eventually disappearing into the parking lot. Benny barked at me that I was crazy, that I couldn't treat a customer like that. I apologized, said I didn't know what had gotten into me.

I managed to avoid her the entire day, but the following morning at nine on the dot, there she was, standing at the shop entrance. I kept my eyes on the floor, trying to sidestep her, but she was blocking the door. Wouldn't let me avoid her. We stood there for a few minutes, until I lifted my gaze and looked at her. I had tons of feelings toward her, but I didn't know how to deal with not knowing what was going on in her head. There were so many things I wanted to tell her but I didn't know where to begin. I thought of giving her a peck on her left cheek, which I knew she liked, but I didn't know if it was still appropriate.

"You kind of suck at this, huh?" she said and smiled.

I smiled back.

4.

NOW I FIX an average of 15.6 devices per day. I'm still waiting for Benny to replace me with his nephew, but frankly his thoughts are a mystery to me. Nurit and I still meet every day, usually in the evening. Sometimes she comes over and I make us pasta with cream and sweet potatoes. She says it's delicious. I can't tell if that's what she honestly thinks, but I tend to believe her. She tells me Istanbul is the only capital in the world that stretches across two different continents, and I quietly think how lucky I am that she didn't dump me. And sometimes we don't talk at all, just sit silently side by side until we fall asleep. She won't tell me what she heard on the radio that day, and I decided it was best not to insist. Since that whole incident in the shop, she hasn't told me she loves me. I admit it worries me sometimes, but I try not to think about it. I'm not totally sure what we have between us, but maybe some things don't have to be spelled out.

The Meaning of Life Ltd.

1.

I WANT TO make it perfectly clear—at no point did I contemplate killing myself. Not at all. It wasn't as if I felt I didn't want to live anymore, it was nothing like that. It's just that suddenly, when I really thought about it, I couldn't find one good reason for getting out of bed in the morning. Why take for granted that I'd choose to get up, brush my teeth, and spend another day in this world?

Dad said he had felt the same way after high school. That living with structure was tough, but I had the feeling it went deeper than that. Because no matter how hard I tried, I couldn't ignore the strange insight that dawned on me—there are billions of people in the world, and most, if not all, of them have no idea what they're doing here. I didn't know where to start looking for answers. I wasn't into the whole recluse-on-an-African-mountaintop bit, so I gave it the greatest effort I was willing to make—I googled "the meaning of life." The results ranged from a meditation center in Rishon LeZion to the official website of Beitar Jerusalem F.C. A small ad at the bottom of the second page caught my eye:

"The Meaning of Life Ltd."

A personalized program for finding meaning in just thirty days!

I filled out my details.

The following day, a company representative showed up at my doorstep; a young woman dressed in a white blouse, asking me what I wanted to do with my life.

"I don't really know."

"Excellent, excellent," she exclaimed, and said she had the perfect program for me. "You have to join our search days," she asserted and sighed. "Seriously, it's the perfect fit for you."

"Search days? What's that?"

"You didn't see the piece they did on us for Channel 2?" she asked, genuinely surprised. "I don't want to give any spoilers. Come and see for yourself." She explained that if I signed up for the deluxe program, I'd also receive a weekly support group session, a personal mentor, and a voucher for a steakhouse uptown. She stressed that unlike all those amateurish programs springing up like mushrooms, theirs boasted a Ministry of Health approval and 82 percent success rates. We agreed on a trial period, and that very day I found myself at my first support group meeting.

2.

THE GROUP COUNSELOR was a guy called Yaron. Until six years ago, he had been a VP at a private investment firm; made shitloads of money, but was never truly happy.

"I remember that feeling of heaviness in your chest," he said, holding his left hand up to his heart and taking a deep breath. He said that thanks to the Meaning of Life Ltd., he discovered gardening was what gave his life meaning. That once he came to this realization, his life had transformed completely. "Who knew a single anemone could solve so many problems?"

Yaron set off a round of introductions, and very soon I felt that everyone else in the room had a better reason for being there than me. Yakov was searching for meaning because his kids had flown the coop; Miri had recently divorced her husband of twenty years, and since coming back from India in a stupor, Lian hadn't been able to find herself.

"Me? Well, I'm not sure, I don't really have a reason," I said.

"Sometimes not knowing is the hardest," Yaron replied softly, and the group nodded in agreement. At the end of the session Yaron handed me a questionnaire with all kinds of random questions, like what my hobbies were and whether I was more of a rural type or city boy. He said it would help them tailor the program to my specific needs. I asked him about the search days, but he just gave me a note with an address on it—26 HaBrosh Street, Petah Tikva. He told me that's where I needed to go and adamantly argued that any further information would just detract from the experience. He stressed that it wasn't a simple process, and because they didn't want me to give up midway, they had assigned Talia as my sponsor—a program alumna just a year older than me.

3.

"WHAT ARE YOU looking for?" she asked me during our first meeting, at a park opposite the Meaning of Life Ltd. offices, considering me with her big brown eyes.

"I don't really know," I said. "But it's not that I'm depressed or anything, my life is pretty much okay."

"I hate it when people think that."

"Think what?"

"That you have to be either a nutjob or a philosopher to want to find true meaning," she said, and brushed her hand over her neck. "Walking around this world without knowing why is basically living with a giant hole in your soul. The fact that everyone else ignores it doesn't mean you have to as well."

Talia told me how stuck she had felt until she arrived at the Meaning of Life Ltd., describing things I was certain existed only in my head until that moment.

"If it weren't for the company, I'd be spending the next seventy years without knowing my true calling in life is to find a cure for cancer." She told me that since coming to that realization, life had become much simpler. She had completed her GED and a biology research paper, and even received the Minister of Education's excellence award. Based on her research, she was invited to attend a young scientists conference in London, where she met her boyfriend, Christopher, a guy from Denmark, who had recently moved to Congo for a year of volunteer work. "We can't say anything for certain yet, but it looks like Chris and I have discovered the gene that causes skin cancer. If our assumptions are correct, it might pave the way for a new drug that could save tens of thousands of people a year."

"I can only imagine how that feels, walking around knowing you've saved so many lives," I said, without trying to hide my overwhelming jealousy. "That's exactly what I'm looking for."

"And you'll find it," she replied, sliding her soft hand down my shoulder. "It's all inside you, Eyal. Believe me. If you want it enough, you'll find it."

4.

THE FOLLOWING DAY I drove to HaBrosh Street. I couldn't find number 26. I walked up and down the street until a black jeep pulled up beside me. A bald man in a black suit stuck his head out the rear window.

"Those goddamn Frenchies are going to kill the deal," he yelled.

"What?"

The bald man opened the car door. "Hop in. Quick, there's no time. The meeting is in half an hour."

"I think you've got me mistaken for someone else," I tried explaining.

"Eyal Rubinstein? From the Meaning of Life Ltd.?" he asked, holding up his smartphone. There was a photo of me on his screen.

"What? Yes, but—"

"I spoke with Yaron, don't worry. Come on, get in, I have no intention of being late." He pulled me into the car and the driver set off.

"Motty, the company CEO," he introduced himself with a firm handshake. "I'll put it all on the table—we're running at a crazy deficit. If the French don't buy us out, it'll be a disaster. We're talking two hundred people out of a job, including yours truly."

"Wait a minute, listen. I honestly have no idea what you're talking about."

He pulled a newspaper out of the glove compartment and handed it to me. The headline on page four read: "French corporation Better Life reported to purchase a vitamin company from Be'er Tuvia in the next few days."

"I'm guessing that's your company? Great news."

"That's what I thought," Motty sighed. "Until a friend in Taiwan found out they also sent a representative to a Taiwanese vitamin company, the only difference being they had already made them an official offer. Those anti-Semites are only keeping us around as their plan B, in case something goes wrong." He leaned forward.

"Cut in front of him," he ordered the driver, then turned his gaze to me. "So what do you propose we do?"

"Me?"

"You see another strategic advisor in the car?"

"I'm not a strategic advisor."

"Crisis manager, negotiations expert, call yourself whatever you want. How do I get them to buy?"

"Listen, I'm really not the person to—"

"Yaron told me you're modest," he cut me off. "I don't like it. Hey, pull over, we're here," he instructed the driver, who ground to a halt at the entrance to an upscale restaurant. Motty got out of the car, opened the trunk, and returned with a smart jacket and pants on a hanger.

"Change. They'll be here any minute."

Two minutes later I was decked out in the fanciest clothes I'd ever worn.

"Custom made. Yaron sent me your measurements."

We got out of the car. A tall man with a mustache called out Motty's name. Judging by his accent, he was undoubtedly one of the Frenchies. Motty shook his hand before introducing me in his heavily Israeli-accented English as a company consultant. I didn't dare correct him. Motty opened the door and the three of us walked in and sat down at a round white table. The Frenchman immediately began to drill our waiter about the wine list, turning up his nose at every item until finally settling for a local merlot.

"Any news about the offer?" Motty asked.

The Frenchman apologized, saying their accountants were still going over the books. "We're a thorough company, hence the thorough due diligence," he explained, then suggested they go over the company's business goals again.

"Gladly," Motty said, scratched his cheek, and began to tiredly recite financial data I had no way of comprehending.

"How about we do it with the PowerPoint presentation, like last time?" the Frenchman asked while meticulously spreading a thick layer of butter on a piece of sourdough. Motty hesitated for a moment, then said it was no problem, we'd go fetch the laptop from the car.

"Say, what's up with you?" Motty asked once we made it to the car. "Your silence is some kind of strategy I'm not getting?"

I didn't know what to say. Having given up on getting an answer out of me, Motty lit a cigarette. A few moments later, my phone rang. It was Yaron, but I already knew it was too late to back out. I switched off the ringer.

"What brand is that?" Motty asked, pointing at my phone.

"Some sucky Chinese one. The battery lasts two hours."

"And they insist on calling them *smart*phones," he smirked. "They market them as if every single one of them is a Harvard graduate."

"I guess it makes people buy them."

"Yeah, huh? Too bad we don't have smart drugs. The French would have bought us on the spot."

"They don't know you don't have smart drugs," I mentioned, not entirely sure what I meant.

"Wait, what are you saying?" Motty asked. I told him I might have an idea, but I was pretty sure it wouldn't work.

"Just tell me, it's not like we have anything to lose."

I tried to explain. Unlike me, Motty seemed to understand what I was talking about.

"I'm really not sure it's a good idea," I stressed, but Motty was already walking back into the restaurant.

The Frenchman was chewing on a slice of smoked fish, and before we even took our seats, Motty announced: "I apologize, but we're pulling out of the deal."

The Frenchman looked up from his plate, staring at us with puzzlement, perhaps wondering if this was some kind of Israeli joke.

"We got an offer from a British company yesterday," Motty said. He explained that given their lack of good faith in the negotiations, we had decided to go with the Brits.

"What company? Good Life? Live Happy?"

"Unfortunately, I'm not at liberty to disclose that information, but I certainly thank you for your time," Motty said, and I added that we really were grateful. Motty's smartphone rang. He glanced at the screen and apologized, saying he had to take the call.

"No problem, we're coming over to sign," he spoke into the receiver. "Sure, the *New York Times* can write about the smart drug. But they need to make it clear that it's an entirely new kind of drug, something that's never been seen before."

"What smart drug?" the Frenchman asked me in an anxious whisper.

"I'm sorry but I honestly can't talk about it," I said, shook his hand and followed Motty to the car.

Two hours later, the Frenchman called with an official offer. Forty-five million. Motty nearly closed on the spot, but I told him to wait a day and demand another million. He nodded, unable to hide his smile.

"What will you do when they ask about the smart drugs?" I inquired, and Motty said it wasn't a problem—he'd ask the Meaning of Life Ltd. to send him a biotechie who could whip some up. I told him I wasn't sure it was that simple, but Motty just waved his hand dismissively.

"You did your job like an ace, and that's all that matters," he said and slapped me on the back; then he talked me into going to a bar for a celebratory drink.

5.

I FINISHED MY first search day at four in the morning, a little drunk from my first champagne. Ten minutes later, as I was brushing my teeth, I heard a knock on the door. For a moment I thought maybe I had forgotten something in the taxi, but when I opened the door I found a guy in a green jumpsuit glaring at me.

"What's the deal, Eyal? We've been waiting for you for half an hour."

"My parents are sleeping, could you come back some other time?"

"There is no other time, trust me."

Reluctantly, I followed him downstairs. The rattle of the engine coming from below was my first hint. A big garbage truck was standing at the entrance to the building. "Oh god," I muttered.

The guy hopped onto the back of the truck and waved me over.

At first I thought I'd hate every minute of it, but in truth, it wasn't too bad. There was something nice about experiencing the world before it woke up. Hanging out on the streets and not being stuck inside some office. Not that dealing with dumpsters was especially enjoyable, but it wasn't as bad as I had expected it to be.

That afternoon, people started showing up at my house for psychotherapy. One woman didn't utter a single word the entire session, while another burst into tears when she started talking about her fear of growing old alone. The following day, I found myself in a police officer's uniform, chasing down a drug dealer through the streets of Tel Aviv, and I finished off the week as a sweaty wedding singer in a small banquet hall. In the next group session I said I had never imagined life had so much to offer me, and Yaron assured me I didn't know the half of it yet.

6.

THREE WEEKS WENT by. More and more people in my group started to discover their meaning. Yakov realized he was born to be a medical clown, Miri enrolled in a yoga teacher training course in Rishikesh, and Lian opened a hummus joint in Haifa. I was the only one who still hadn't really gotten his act together.

"All these search days are really interesting, but at each one of them I feel like there's something missing," I explained to Talia. "Being a strategic advisor means working crazy hours, and being a psychologist seems too emotionally taxing. To tell you the truth, I'm not even sure I'm getting an answer as to why I should wake up every morning so much as I'm discovering a lot of good ways to evade the question."

Talia was quiet for a while, then told me she remembered those days well, when she didn't feel up to anything. "Before I signed up for the Meaning of Life Ltd., I'd go to the beach in Ga'ash every Tuesday afternoon." She told me how she used to sit on the cliff at the edge of the trail, with no one else around. She'd look at the waves until the sun sank into the sea, trying to understand how she still had the energy to wake up every morning.

"Do you still go to that beach?" I asked.

"No, the Meaning of Life Ltd. gave me the answers I was searching for," she said, "and I hope you'll find your answers too. I honestly do."

7.

TOWARD THE END of the summer, Yaron pulled me aside for a conversation. He said I was probably one of his toughest cases, and that the deluxe program didn't seem to be working for me.

"But here at the Meaning of Life Ltd. we can't afford to give up," he said, and explained they were about to launch the diamond program especially for people like me. A program designed for seasoned meaning-seekers, based on innovative methodologies devised in Austria, where this field was highly developed.

"Obviously I can't force you," Yaron said, "but I do think quitting now is like giving up a few meters before reaching the peak of Mount Everest."

I called Talia and told her I couldn't make up my mind. That on the one hand I was too tired to go on, but on the other hand I felt I'd come too far to quit now.

"Maybe the Meaning of Life Ltd. isn't for everyone," she replied hesitantly.

"What do you mean?"

"That maybe, maybe you really should give up. Even if it's just for the time being."

"Give up?"

"Yes. I don't think they'll be able to help you."

"But you said they helped you. You yourself said that if it wasn't for the Meaning of Life Ltd. you'd still be sitting on the beach in Ga'ash."

"But you're something else," she said, and I realized that sentence had been lingering in her head for some time. "I mean, I just think you're right. That in your case all these search days are just distracting you."

"Distracting me from what?" I asked, not sure how to respond to her sudden resolve. To the feeling that she had given up on me.

"I don't know. I honestly don't. But lately I've been thinking that maybe there isn't always one right answer, and that's also something one needs to learn how to live with," she said, and took a few deep breaths. "Maybe people should stop searching for one grandiose meaning and start living for the small, simple things, like a child's laughter, or green grass. I don't know, whatever makes them smile."

Now it was my turn to be quiet. After a few moments of silence, I asked, "You really think that'll be enough for me?"

"Maybe," she replied.

"Then apparently you don't understand."

"Apparently."

There was silence on both ends of the line, until I told her the MADA ambulance was already waiting for me outside.

"Good luck," she said.

I didn't answer.

8.

TALIA LEFT. YARON called me the following day, said she had been invited to continue her research in some Swiss institute and had to fly out without saying goodbye. "But don't worry, you'll meet your new sponsor tomorrow. A lovely guy named Amir who has just set up an Australian mongoose farm in the Arava. He can't wait to meet you."

And then it dawned on me.

I caught a northbound bus, got off at a stop on Highway 2, crossed the bridge, and kept going until I found myself standing in front of a fence sealing off the entrance to the beach. I slipped in through a small hole and started walking along the dirt trail leading to nowhere.

She was sitting right at the end of the trail, looking out at the sea. I sensed she wasn't surprised to see me there.

She said she was the last person who could talk about the meaning of life. "I'm hardly a whiz kid or some science prodigy, I've never even stepped foot in a lab. I also haven't been to any conferences in London, and I don't have a boyfriend from Denmark."

She explained she was just some girl who had been in the drama club in high school and was sick of working as a waitress while waiting for her draft date. The Meaning of Life Ltd. had paid her to play someone who had seen the light, to convince people that if they only upgraded to the diamond program they'd find all the answers.

"After a program or two, most people believe they've found the life they've always wanted, and that their problems have been solved. But in reality, only a very small percentage actually find meaning," she said. "Within a few months most of them realize the answers they were looking for aren't located on the tallest building in Hong Kong or a Druze village up north. But at that point they've stopped searching for the answers inside themselves."

She raised her arms as if about to hug me, then changed her mind and let them fall by her side. "I'm sorry," she said.

"I'm glad you don't have a boyfriend from Denmark," I replied.

She smiled.

9.

WE SAT SILENTLY on the beach for maybe an hour. She was a good person to be quiet with.

I think I'll keep on searching for meaning in life. But that day, sitting beside her by the sea, it was nice to live for a few moments without needing to know why.

Three Hours from Berlin

1.

TAMARA INSTANTLY RECOGNIZED HIM, despite the new round-rimmed glasses and black beard adorning his face. Unfortunately he recognized her as well, and she realized they were condemned to talk. She hoped the conversation would be brief, but knew the chances were slim: a preliminary update would take at least two minutes, reminiscing about their university days three minutes, and a general account of his life in Germany another five. And god help her if they accidently stumbled upon the subject of housing prices in Berlin.

Approaching him, she feigned a smile.

"Well well well," she affected surprise.

"I know, right?" he replied and hugged her. His red sweater was soft and thick. "What brings you to Hadera?"

"A three-day seminar."

"Wow, terrific. What's the topic?"

"Taxes in the digital age," she said, boring even herself. All she could remember was that his name was Michael Tsabari, that he had studied accounting with her in Jerusalem, and that one day, sometime after graduation, he had moved to Germany and become a video artist in a small town whose name she couldn't remember. "But never mind that, what's going on with you? What are you doing in Israel?"

He told her he was here on a short visit, something work-related, but she wasn't really listening. Sometimes, when engaging in such meaningless conversations, she felt like throwing in a random question like "Do you believe in god?" or "What did you dream of becoming as a kid?" But this time she couldn't even toy with the possibility, because he apologized and said he had to rush off, had a meeting with a famous curator who was interested in his art. "Too bad I don't have a few more minutes," he said and disappeared into the nearby alley. She found herself offended without knowing why.

2.

AT THE END of each day, she'd put the kettle on, study the white bits swimming at the bottom, and make herself a cup of black coffee with sweetener. Then she'd settle onto the living room couch, rest her tablet against her legs, and peek into the life of one of her hundreds of distant, virtual friends. That evening she checked out Micael's profile, devoting considerable time to the matter:

> *One year in Germany and still don't get Brecht ☺*
> *How do I break it to Grandpa that I've become a Bayern fan?*

#MilkyProtest: It is cheaper in Berlin—but I still don't like Milky pudding.

She thought about how there were three types of people in the world: those whose lives were worse than hers, those whose lives were just as boring as hers, and those whose lives she couldn't help but be jealous of. In Tsabari's case, one photo at a world heritage site and she succumbed without a fight. Tamara perused a few more photos. Michael was a good-looking guy. There was a childlike quality to his smile, especially against the sober black jacket he wore in many of the photos. Some of them featured a chubby German woman with a permanent smile on her face. Tamara wondered whether she was his girlfriend, thinking how she herself would never dare date a German man. She concluded that his life was better than hers, turned on the TV, and watched a trivia show in which the eliminated contestants plummeted through a trapdoor in the floor. Within less than an hour, Michael Tsabari had joined the dozens of people she was very jealous of and then completely forgot about. But later that night, he called.

He began by apologizing for running off in the middle of their conversation.

"Don't worry about it," she said, hoping her voice didn't give away how moved she was by this gesture.

"Maybe we could meet again?"

She didn't reply, but Michael was persistent—informing her that he would be in Hadera again tomorrow, and would love it if she could make time for him. He admitted he had a favor to ask, and that "it wouldn't be right asking over the phone."

She considered declining, but Michael's odd request provided her with the rare opportunity to forgo lunch with her boss, who always ordered the most expensive dishes on the menu and then insisted they split the bill. She told Michael she would have an hour-long break during the seminar, to which he replied that he wouldn't need more than that. He gave her the address of a café, asked her not to talk about their impending meeting, and once again ended their conversation abruptly. She tried to continue watching TV, but couldn't stop wondering what he wanted from her. Even if she wouldn't admit it, this sudden interest that crept into her life was not unsatisfying.

3.

THEY AGREED TO meet at one of those health cafés Tamara was sure existed only in Tel Aviv. It started to drizzle on her way there, and she wondered whether it was a good or bad sign. She sat at a window-side table. The walls were covered in light green wallpaper scribbled with tips for good living: "Switch to Soy, Go with the Flow, Communication Is Key." She had no intention of implementing any of them. In honor of the occasion, she wore a thin gold necklace with an antique coin pendant, which she now played with, sliding it from side to side.

He arrived wearing the black jacket from the photos, sat in front of her, and smiled.

"Pretty swanky for lunch in Hadera," she smirked. "Add a top hat and you'd look like a bona fide English gentleman."

He laughed and said he had left his pipe at home. He signaled to the waiter and ordered a spicy shakshouka with homemade bread. She felt like ordering the same thing but chose the lentil salad. The waiter cleared the menus, and the first thirty minutes of their conversation were dedicated to her impressive-but-entirely-made-up career aspirations and to his decision to move to Germany.

"I started toying with the idea the summer before I moved," he said, and told her he had spent the entire month of August on Rothschild Boulevard, two tents away from Daphni Leef. He had been hoping the protest would finally change things in the country, but once the tents had been taken down he realized that wasn't about to happen. Had she been in a more argumentative mood, she would have told him he sounded like a soccer fan who switches teams after one loss. But she wasn't.

"You want to explain why we're here?"

"It's kind of complicated," he replied.

"Hence the *explain*."

He silently dipped his fork into the tomato sauce and dragged it over some egg white. "I wasn't supposed to be here yesterday," he said, and looked up at her.

"No one's ever supposed to be in Hadera," she said, happy when she got a laugh out of him.

"I meant in Israel," he continued, his voice trembling. He said he was keeping his visit a secret, and asked her not to tell anyone she had seen him.

"Who would I tell?" she asked, trying to understand.

"I don't know, just don't," he replied and leaned into her. "I'm going to ask you a weird question, okay?"

"Try me."

"Let's say," he began slowly, weighing his words, "someone approaches you. He offers you a one-way ticket, and promises a life unlike anything you have known before. Would you go for it?"

"Someone with a jacket and a top hat?"

He smiled.

"What's the catch?"

"That you don't know where you're going," he said, his expression turning sober. "And you can't tell the people you love that you're leaving."

"I don't think so," she said hesitantly.

"Got it," he said, and without any warning raised his hand and signaled to the waiter for the bill. "I have to go."

"What?"

"I have to go."

"Would you explain what's going on here?" she asked, shocked that he'd asked her out for lunch just to ditch her halfway through.

"I'll tell everyone I saw you," she said, insisting on getting an answer.

"No, you won't," he determined, attempting a friendly tone.

"Watch me," she replied, and glanced at her phone on the table. The idea had just popped into her head. "I'll *share* us on Facebook," she announced.

She would look back at that moment for years to come; offer herself long, reasoned explanations about why she had insisted on not letting him go. In her heart of hearts she'd know that the real answer was simple—she was lonely and didn't want to say goodbye to the person who had accidentally knocked on the door to her life.

"Remind me of your last name again? Tsabari?" she asked as if she didn't already know.

He snuck a glance at her phone. "You mean *check-in*, not *share*," he corrected her, scratching his beard nervously. "You used to be nicer," he noted.

She knew he was right.

"When are you going back to Germany?" she asked, and when he didn't answer, started typing in his name to let him know she meant business. "When are you going back?"

"Never," he replied with sharp, uncontrollable resolve. She looked up from her screen and considered him, realizing he had divulged more than he had intended.

The waiter appeared with the bill, cleared their plates, and they both withdrew into themselves. Michael removed his glasses and rubbed his eyes until they turned red.

She thought she had taken it too far.

4.

"THE SUMMER AFTER the protest I was already in Berlin," he said with fixed sighs between sentences. He told her that three hours after landing in Berlin he had already rented an apartment with some hipster drummer. He spent the following two weeks like an overenthusiastic Japanese tourist, trying to capture the city through his camera lens and, for a few moments, even felt he had almost succeeded. He took a guided tour of the Reichstag and got drunk in six different pubs in Kreuzberg. He said the hipster drummer even hooked him up with a job at a record store in the neighborhood, and the Lebanese chick from the apartment upstairs had already hit on him twice.

"Sounds great," she said, to which he replied that indeed it was. "But after a month I realized there was no chance in hell I was staying there."

He explained that from the very first moment he couldn't stand the cold. All that fatty food. The German language and the ticket inspectors on the U-Bahn who had issued him two fines within less than a month. "I couldn't even stand the people who were genuinely nice to me." He described his period there like the first night of summer camp: feeling like you can't breathe, like someone's holding a staple gun to your neck. "The problem was I didn't want to stay in Germany, but I couldn't come home."

"Why not?"

He said people wouldn't understand. Not after he had told his boss he was leaving. Not after he had given up his sweet pad near the market. "Not after lecturing everyone about how no one in Israel had the guts to go after their dreams."

He told her how one night, in Berlin, standing in front of the bathroom mirror, he pictured himself as a wrinkly eighty-year-old who had lived an entire life he had never wanted.

A tremor shot through her. She felt as though he'd stolen a thought right out of her head and passed it off as his own. He proceeded to say that later that evening, he was browsing Facebook and for a moment, felt an overwhelming desire to take a selfie, lying in bed in his grubby wifebeater and with a dejected look on his face. To upload it onto the social network, "to show everyone how far a cry my Berlin life is from what they thought." He was about to take that photo but decided at the last moment there was no point. He clicked on his profile and studied the hundreds of pictures he had posted over the years, and felt they all portrayed someone else's life.

"So you realized Facebook was a giant lie? How perceptive of you."

He said she was right, but that's exactly what he found absurd about it. "Everyone knows their virtual persona is a big fat lie, and yet they insist on maintaining and even perfecting it."

The passion with which he spoke reminded her of herself at sixteen, when she had finished reading Che Guevara's biography and swore allegiance to the communist revolution, an oath she broke two weeks later when she started working at McDonald's. "So let me guess," she said skeptically. "Right then and there, you decided to delete your Facebook account, promised yourself you'd start living an authentic life, and since you were already in the mood, bought one of those self-help books."

"Quite the opposite," he replied. "It just made me realize how far I could stretch the lie."

She didn't understand. He turned his gaze to the wall. She couldn't be sure, but assumed he was looking at the poster that hung there: "Join a gym. Not tomorrow. Today."

"Are you living the life you wanted?" he asked.

"Yes," she lied.

"Then there's no point trying to explain."

Once again they sat in front of each other in utter silence. She glanced at the clock on her phone while he fished a hundred-shekel bill out of his pocket and put it on the table.

"Please, don't tell anyone we met," he said, got up, and walked out of the café. She didn't try to stop him. Instead, she went to the bathroom and stood in front of the mirror; her mascara had smudged under her left eye. She stuck out her tongue and laughed, then thought to herself that she had to start working out. Maybe volleyball.

She managed to make it to the final lecture, something about hi-tech corporations and regulation. She sat down in the back row and closed her eyes, recalling that when she was little, she used to close her eyes and feel as if the whole world disappeared along with her.

5.

IF IT WEREN'T for the photo, they probably never would have spoken again. Two hours later, when she logged into Facebook, she saw what he had posted. Michael stood there in a blue coat, smiling and pointing at a sign in German behind him. For a moment, she thought it was an old photo that had popped up in her feed, but then she noticed it had been posted twenty-seven minutes ago. The location—Germany—appeared below, along with a status that left little room for doubt: "If I spotted a spelling mistake, does that mean I'm finally a local?"

The facts didn't add up even when she tried her hardest to make them, but eventually she decided to let it go.

She went back to the office the following day. It was a busy period, like always, and she was looking for excuses to leave early. She made plans to go out with the head of human resources, a short, chipper girl, three years younger than her. She felt it was a great opportunity to prove to herself that she could make new friends. But after an hour, during which the head of human resources insisted they rank the five hottest men in the office, Tamara felt their relationship had run its course. When she got home, she shared on Facebook Ehud Banai's song about the thirty-year-old boy. She felt that the songs she shared offered the world some insight into her existential state. She never got a single like for the songs she shared, and perhaps that was the reason she shared them so often. Then she went over her WhatsApp contact list, hoping to find some forgotten loved one. When she reached the letter *M*, she saw Michael's face. She clicked on the photo and zoomed in. He was holding a beer bottle and staring into the camera with a serious expression, looking tougher than in real life. She thought to herself that maybe that's what he meant by stretching the lie.

The green dot appeared by his name. She forwarded him his Facebook photo with the German sign and added: "Funny status, I just don't understand how you made it to Germany so quickly . . ."

He called not a moment later. "I gather you saw the photo," he said.

She didn't reply.

"Listen, it's a funny story, but . . ." His voice was swallowed by the loud background noise.

"Where are you?"

Dodging the question, he carried on with his confused monologue. She focused on the background noise, picking up on a mechanical voice blaring over loudspeakers: "Special offer, three Cokes for ten shekels!"

"You're still in Israel," she determined, surprised by her own conclusion.

He was quiet for a few moments before asking, "What do you want?"

"An explanation."

"I can't give you one over the phone."

"Then let's meet," she replied. She thought she may have taken it a step too far, but decided to wait for his reaction.

"Hadera Stream?" he suggested.

She agreed, but not before feigning hesitation.

6.

THE FOLLOWING DAY at four, she excused herself from the office and drove to Hadera in the beat-up Subaru Leone she had bought two years ago from a redheaded fellow who lived on a settlement in the West Bank. The three chimneys from the power plant loomed large as she parked, then took the stairs down to the stream. Michael was already there, standing with his hands in the pockets of his gray wool coat. She quietly crept up behind him as he gazed out at the water. She put her hand on his shoulder, and he turned around.

"I'll explain everything," he said.

"Wait," she replied, wanting to take it slowly. She stood beside him, contemplating the stream. When she was little, she had promised herself that when she grew up she'd live outdoors. She took a deep breath and sat down on the bench. Michael remained standing. "You're welcome to sit," she said.

He sat beside her with a straight back. The sun was collapsing into the horizon. He told her about a poet who had once immortalized the stream, but he couldn't remember the poem's name.

"That's not exactly a line to make a woman fall for you."

"I'm supposed to make you fall for me?" he replied with utter seriousness.

She smiled, enjoying the fact that she couldn't fracture his innocence. "That's up to you." It was cold, and they both started exhaling trails of white steam.

"Remember I told you about that time I stood in front of the mirror and pictured myself as an eighty-year-old?" he asked, and said that was the moment he realized his social network identity could free him. A "get-out-of-reality-free card," he called it. A card that would enable him to do what he had never before thought possible: live the life he wanted to live, and at the same time, the life that was expected of him. He confessed that he had never been a video artist. After a month in Berlin he came home and had spent the past year here, in his room, in a tiny apartment with its back to the sea.

She listened to the note of excitement trilling through his voice, a note produced by someone divulging a big secret for the first time. She sidled up against him, placed her hand on his knee, felt it tremble.

"It's cold," she said.

Michael told her about his alternate biography. How he had chosen video art as a profession because it was a field no one around him knew anything about, and a town a three-hour's drive from Berlin, so that no Israeli would think to come looking for him. He said he spent a week driving up and down Germany in a rental, taking thousands of photos with a chubby German girl who wasn't even his girlfriend, but a failed actress he had hired for the shoot.

She told him that she had lied once too, when she posted a photo of her and a friend from the summit of Mount Kinneret, with a caption about having climbed their way up, when in reality they had taken the Subaru, which barely made it.

"Living on the edge, huh?" he said.

"'Cause moving to the burbs is really flirting with danger, right? You're quite the daredevil," she said, giving his ribs a gentle poke.

"I chose this city after careful consideration," he said, explaining that he went over his friend list on Facebook and made sure not one of them lived there. Then reasoned that it was far enough from his family and friends in Jerusalem, and not interesting enough for them to choose it for a spontaneous weekend vacation.

"And yet, here I am," she replied.

"A glitch, for sure," he replied, and placed his hand on her shoulder in an awkward gesture, pulling her closer to him.

She was moved.

"You know, it sounds a bit cowardly, running away like this," she said, and when noticing his expression felt that yet again she had ruined a good thing before it had even begun. She leaned into him and kissed his lips gently, as if to compensate. They drew their faces apart and smiled. He took her hands in his and warmed them up.

They met once every few days. At first his refusal to step outside the borders of Hadera upset her, but with time she came to love the city in which things happened and didn't happen simultaneously. She'd leave work early at least twice a week, reassuring herself that she'd make up the hours the following month. She enjoyed the whispers of her colleagues as they tried to guess where she was slipping off to. "I'm sorry, but I really can't say," she'd reply and consider their intrigued expressions, feeling as if she was holding in her hands something real they could only wish for.

They mostly met at the café, but every so often scheduled a date somewhere foreign to romance: the HMO cafeteria, a bench outside the Social Security offices. During these meetings—limited in time and space—she always divulged more than she intended. She told him about the scar on the back of her neck, about the first and only time she smoked weed, about that day she ran away from home at fourteen, took a bus to the beach and stayed there all night, only to come home in the morning and learn that her mother had been taken to the hospital for a panic attack. He always nodded understandingly, and she wasn't sure how to deal with his persistent refusal to be cynical toward anything she said.

7.

SHE WAS FIRED a month later. Her boss claimed they were forced to make painful cutbacks. She didn't believe him, but refrained from arguing. Being laid off helped her make up her mind. Michael's offer had come a week earlier. They were strolling through the Hadera Forest and he told her that until she was there with him, she wouldn't possibly be able to understand.

"But there is no getting closer than this," she said, sticking her hand out to measure the tiny distance between them.

"Closeness isn't a matter of geography," he asserted, then added that if she really wanted to understand, she'd join him.

"Where?"

"Germany," he said. "If you have the guts, that is."

A clipped laugh escaped her. He stopped in his tracks, and she gently brushed her hand over his beard.

"I'm listening. Explain to me how it's supposed to work," she said.

"There's no instruction manual, you just come," he replied.

She looked up, mumbled something about how it was going to rain, and he stroked the back of her neck and said he couldn't understand how she could give up a chance for true freedom. She grimaced. Got upset. There was something condescending in what he had said.

"You're right," she announced. Then she confessed that maybe she had chosen accounting only because her parents had convinced her to study something practical. And that most of her conversations with her friends were indeed shallow and meaningless, and that yes, she had gotten a nose job when she was eighteen. "But you don't get it, that's what holds me together." She explained that all those restrictions and tiny rules she had adhered to almost religiously were what kept her sane. Made her feel safe. And if watching *MasterChef* once a week was the price of a normal life, she was willing to pay it.

She wanted to win the argument, but he wouldn't reply. He withdrew into one of those silences of his.

They made their way back to the car in oppressive silence. A moment before parting, her car door already open, he took a yellow envelope out of his pocket and handed it to her.

"What's that?" she asked.

"A plane ticket to Berlin," he said and caressed her cheek. "Two weeks."

"Hadera or Germany?" she wondered in confusion, and he quickly replied, "Your choice." He told her she was welcome to use the plane ticket and spend two weeks alone in Berlin. "Or you can come here," he said, and promised he'd wait for her at the entrance to the train station, that she wouldn't even have to give him a heads-up. That he'd be there, waiting, in case she decided to show up.

She looked at him and asked if he was trying to make her fall for him.

"That's up to you," he replied.

She adjusted the rearview mirror, closed the door, and started the car. She stopped at Apollonia Beach to look at the waves. She had planned on staying there all night to mull over his offer, but the cold got to her after ten minutes. Once again she thought back to the time she ran away from home; today, no one would have a panic attack if she disappeared.

Friday night at her parents', she announced she was considering a trip to Germany. She rushed to explain that she needed to clear her head, and immediately felt that she had blown her cover. That everyone at the table now knew that for the past two months she'd been in a bizarre relationship with a guy from Hadera who wasn't even there, and that now she was considering whether to go on a vacation in Germany or to visit him. But her confession received only a nonchalant reaction. Her father recommended a hotel in central Berlin and her aunt patted her on the back and said it was important to have a bit of fun. Tamara smiled, slightly disappointed that once again she had been edged out of the center of attention.

8.

HER PARENTS INSISTED on driving her to the airport; they bid her farewell at the entrance to Ben Gurion, her father looking a little sad, her mother settling for a brief hug and rushing her off to the duty-free shops. Before they said goodbye, she took a selfie with her parents, thinking the ruse should start from the very first moment. She posted the photo along with the status *Then we take Berlin*, and told herself the tribute to Leonard Cohen made the lie a little less horrible.

She watched them walk away, already missing them terribly.

She entered the airport and slipped into the bathroom; squeezing herself into a stall along with her suitcase, she sidled up against the door, took her phone out of her left pocket, and called the airline. She had prepared an elaborate story for why she couldn't make the flight, but the customer service lady didn't even ask. Tamara opened her suitcase and fished out a long floral dress. She had gotten it from her mother a few years ago, and had since announced to anyone who would listen that she'd never wear it, hoping now that putting it on would make her harder to recognize.

Half an hour later, the cleaner having already knocked on the door twice asking if everything was okay, she came out of the stall. Taking the escalator downstairs, she passed by the arrivals hall and made it to the platform two minutes before the train's departure. She quickly bought a ticket and boarded the last car, plopping her bag onto the seat next to her. Fixing her gaze on the floor, she prayed she wouldn't run into anyone she knew. She was happy to discover that her selfie with her parents had been awarded eleven likes as well as a comment by some girl she didn't know, who wrote "couldn't be more jealous."

Tamara leaned her head against the window and tried to fall asleep.

9.

HE WAS WAITING for her at the entrance to the station. She didn't notice him at first, was busy studying her reflection in her cell phone screen. He let out a little cough and she jumped, startled and then embarrassed by the situation. They were silent for a few moments, and he kept staring at her.

"Nice dress," he said.

"I'm glad you like it," she replied. "It's the last time I'm wearing it."

He hesitated before reaching out and brushing his hand over her hair. There was a certain measure of awe in his touch. She liked it.

"You got a haircut," she said. His short hair made him look more serious. He wrapped his arms around her, pulling her into him. It had been years since someone had hugged her like that. Tightly. Not her exes, not her friends, not her family. They stood there for a few moments. When he let go of her, she wished he hadn't. He picked up her suitcase. "Heavy," he remarked as they descended the staircase.

They headed out of the station and started walking. Tamara was hoping his apartment was close by; she felt as if she had flown halfway across the world.

"We'll just take two photos for Facebook and then go grab a bite."

"Can't it wait till tomorrow?" she asked and let out a giant yawn, but he said that unfortunately there was no time to waste. He explained that the first few hours of the disappearance were critical, since no one had any reason to question it yet. He then told her there were a few places in Hadera that if you photograph them at the right angle and crop part of the background, looked exactly like Berlin.

"If only the people of Hadera knew," she said.

He smiled.

She considered whether to continue objecting, but curiosity got the better of her.

Not far from the train station there was a stone wall covered in oversized graffiti art.

"What, like the Berlin Wall?" she scoffed. "Listen, it looks nothing like it."

"Wait," he said, lowering the suitcase next to a big rock and waving her to follow. He stopped in front of a big drawing of Bob Marley with his eyes closed.

"You've thought of everything," she said, and he smiled contentedly, pointing at the word *Legende* that appeared next to the painting.

"Why is it misspelled?"

"It's in German," he explained. He asked her for her phone, then positioned her with her back to the wall, took a few steps back, and photographed her against the painting.

"Give us a real smile," he asked, and she said it was difficult to smile when she was afraid of stepping in dog poop.

"We have each other," he said, and when she looked at the photo she realized he was right. It was awfully easy to create the illusion of happiness.

They hiked up a narrow trail back to the street. He took her hand and blew warm air into it.

She looked at the people trudging along the sidewalk and then at him, thinking how much intimacy had sprung up between them since he had become the only person in the world who knew her exact location.

They went for a bite at a mediocre Italian restaurant. She ordered ravioli with mushrooms and he told her to take a photo of it, preferably from above. She protested, noting that it wasn't a German dish, but Michael insisted that when it came to photos of food, national indicators were irrelevant.

"Beer is the only telltale," he argued, and ordered them two bottles of Weihenstephaner. He said he preferred Goldstar, but the ends justified the means.

"So really, you live to impress others."

"Well, part of the time," he admitted. "The problem is that others do it all the time."

His apartment was on the second floor of a building not far from the train station. He said he believed it was a Jewish thing, the need to live next to an exit route. He opened the door and she fumbled her way to the bed before he even turned on the light—as if to say, no more photos. She closed her eyes and after a few moments felt him lying down beside her, his hand reaching out but not touching. She turned around, pressed her face against his, and kissed him. Then she opened her eyes and caressed his cheek. They both smiled mischievously, as if they had pulled one over on the world and lived to tell the tale.

10.

WHEN SHE WOKE up the following morning, a cup of coffee was waiting for her on the bedside table. She looked around curiously, surprised to find out his apartment wasn't the dim hideout she had imagined it would be. The floor was parquet, the walls a light cream. She recognized textbooks from their university days in the heavy bookcase, above which hung an acoustic guitar. Michael emerged from the kitchen with a tray laden with bread, an omelet, and chopped vegetable salad, saying it was a small, insufficient compensation for persuading her to spend two weeks in Hadera. She bit into the fresh bread, nibbled the salad, and considered asking if he was ideologically opposed to salt, but decided against it.

He had a folder on his laptop that contained dozens of photos of tourist sites in Berlin. "Time to create some lies," he told her. "I shot them all myself," he boasted, and asked her to choose three. He said they didn't have to be the prettiest photos, but of places she was likely to visit.

"And then you photoshop me in?" she wondered.

He grimaced, apparently finding the idea offensive. "Hell no," he protested. "You have to know how far you can stretch a lie. For instance, the photo with your parents isn't that great."

"Why?" she asked, insulted. He told her he had researched her Facebook user habits and concluded she wasn't the kind of person who posted selfies.

"I find it a little troubling that you'd know that," she said. "That's nothing," he said. "Nowadays you have algorithms that can determine whether a person has cancer or is about to divorce his wife just by his expression in a photo."

Michael said that if anything, it would have been much more like her to post the Leonard Cohen song without the photo, but reassured her it was a mistake that wouldn't actually raise any suspicions. He suggested she wait two days and post a photo of a tourist site with a funny status, like she had done during her trip to Athens, and that toward the end of the week she upload that German DJ's remix of the Asaf Avidan song. She couldn't bare how painfully accurate he was, or see the point of living in a world in which her every breath was so predictable.

She took a shower and called her father to let him know everything was okay. Michael thought it might not be such a good idea, and suggested she settle for a text message, but she made it clear it wasn't up for negotiation. She also knew there was no need to worry, because her parents never took much of an interest; the most she could expect of them was a perfunctory question like whether her hotel offered breakfast.

Her father's voice soothed her. She thought he'd probably feel sad if he discovered she'd been close by this entire time.

Afterward, Michael took her to the café that served as his office, a five-minute walk from his apartment. He told her he sat there with his laptop a few hours every day, doing the books for a Canadian online gambling company that operated via a Gibraltar-based server. When he first moved to Hadera, he promised himself he wouldn't go near accounting, but after his savings ran out he decided four hours a day was a sacrifice he could live with.

"I know it's not as romantic as a video artist in Germany," he said, "but I realized that—"

"Then where are you actually?"

"What?"

"Where are you really?" she asked, resting her hand on the table.

"What do you mean? I'm here."

"Yeah, now. But sometimes you're in Germany. And when you're working, you're in Canada or Gibraltar," she said, struggling to put her thoughts into words.

"I'm not the only digital nomad, you know."

"So," she said, putting her other hand on the table too. "It doesn't seem messed up to you? Living in a world in which the body has become, I don't know, meaningless?"

"On the contrary," he replied firmly. "It's liberating."

She didn't like his answer. He took his laptop out of his bag and placed it on the table.

"Maybe you should spend the rest of the day on your own," he proposed.

"What are you talking about?" she asked in a huff, and he quickly clarified that he wasn't trying to get rid of her, putting his hand on hers in a conciliatory gesture.

"You're welcome to stay here with me," he said. "I just thought you came for yourself too." He explained that these two weeks were a rare opportunity to do whatever she felt like doing. Without thinking about work or even him. "To really experience this freedom," he said.

She reached out and gently caressed his cheek. "I was hoping you'd say that," she lied, terrified of spending a single day in this world without a defined purpose.

She wandered the streets, feeling slightly relieved when she stumbled upon an old man playing the accordion. She dropped a twenty into his case, grateful for the opportunity to just stand there for a few moments. Then she walked into a nearby ice-cream parlor and bought a pistachio gelato. She ate it slowly, wishing to prolong the moment of defined action. She had left her phone in his apartment but didn't want to go back, didn't want him to think she was having a hard time being alone.

She decided to go to the beach. For the first time in years, she took the bus, and when she got there she discovered she was the only beachgoer on that winter morning.

On Saturdays during the summer months it was impossible to walk more than an inch of shore without stepping on some kid's head, and now she had the entire place to herself. She stood in front of the water, realizing that all the years she had spent traversing the world were without ambition. She didn't want to buy a house in Givatayim. Didn't want to climb up the company ladder. Didn't want to go on vacation in New York. She wasn't sure who she had borrowed these dreams from, but knew with absolute certainty they weren't really hers. She stretched out on the sand, her hair saturated with the tiny grains. The gray clouds sailed above her. The girl who ran away from home would have been proud of her.

On the way back, it started to rain. The two older women sitting in front of her on the bus kept exchanging glances, and she felt proud of herself.

"Where were you?" Michael shrieked when she walked into the apartment, quickly wrapping a blanket around her. "You got wet?"

He sat her at the kitchen table, served her corn soup, and told her how guilty he felt for sending her out into the world without an umbrella. She didn't like corn but gobbled it all up.

"How was it?"

"Good," she replied. "Really good."

He smiled with satisfaction. "I didn't think that after only a few hours I'd find myself like this," he said.

"Like what?"

He blushed. "Missing you."

She smiled. Spotting the Lonely Planet Germany travel guide on the table, she asked, "Researching ideas for new posts?" He said no. He sat down beside her and said he was starting to prepare, in the event that she decided to stay for more than two weeks. In that case, they really would have to go to Berlin together, to take more photos. "Otherwise people will start getting suspicious. And it doesn't hurt to stock up on photos."

"Maybe," she said, taking a few moments to savor the idea of the two of them in a four-star hotel, sitting on the balcony gazing out at some river. If they even had a river over there.

11.

SHE BEGAN TO realize that the upkeep of a fake life took quite an effort.

They spent hours each day drawing a detailed map of all the places she visited, the dishes she ate and the shopping she did, searching for post-worthy moments. The real satisfaction came when she finally let her imagination run wild. For instance, the post she wrote about sneaking into an event thrown for the Mayor of Berlin, or the photo she uploaded of a beer bottle she had spilled over a married German man who tried to pick her up. She was pleased by the likes and comments of people who didn't bother to conceal their jealousy, relished the thought that maybe someone was looking at her profile the way she used to look at other people's.

They spent a considerable part of their day together, but there were moments when Michael would withdraw into himself for no apparent reason. He'd disappear from the apartment for hours at a time, or spend all morning in bed, brooding, an indecipherable look on his face.

"This isn't easy for me," he admitted. "Being on my own for an entire year and then suddenly spending all this time together."

It wasn't easy to hear, but she understood. She tried to give him space, hoping to learn how to cope with his soul's unpredictable undercurrents. She told herself life wasn't black and white, and that she had to learn to live with the grays. She tried to ignore the niggling thoughts. Mostly one that kept popping into her head about the small yet essential difference between her and Michael. Because despite the fact that she was enjoying the whole experience, she simply couldn't understand how someone could live like that for an entire year. She was beginning to suspect that he wasn't really looking to live two lives simultaneously, but only one.

"After a month it kind of gets old, doesn't it?" she asked one evening, adding that her two weeks were almost up. He didn't reply, but his expression read loud and clear. She realized that for Michael, existing in the real world was merely a technical glitch that kept him from living where he really wanted to.

"Don't you understand that life is out there?" she asked. "The internet isn't an actual substitute."

He didn't deny it. "I think the same way sometimes," he said. "In the past few months I've been asking myself whether it's time to get out of it. On the other hand, there are so many possibilities I haven't even explored yet," he said, and a twinkle flashed in his eye. He started talking about the infinite potential of online living, about the possibility of preparing in advance thousands of posts that would continue to upload years after his death. To completely free himself of the limitations of time and place.

"But why do you keep running away from what's happening here?" she asked with frustration. "Why not live the life you want in the real world?"

He bit his lip and nodded, as if he had already asked himself the same question more than once. "Because this thing called life is made up of just two feelings," he said. "Missing someplace you've never been to, and longing for someplace you'll never be. The rest is routine. Drab routine that consumes even the most beautiful moments in life. After all, even people who build rooms in paradise have to pay income tax."

"So what is it that you want?" she asked, and he smiled.

"To create a single, flawless space. One in which every moment is pure happiness. Facebook lets you do that. Live only the peaks and chuck out the rest, you get it?"

She froze. "Wait. The people who build rooms in paradise. What?"

He smiled. "You don't remember?" he asked. "In the university cafeteria. A bunch of us were talking about what profession we'd choose if money was no object."

"I remember vaguely," she mumbled, hugging herself.

"You were the only one with a good answer. You said that when you were little, you realized not everyone wound up in the same heaven, because each person had a different notion of heaven. That as a child you imagined heaven as a big apartment building in which everyone had their own room where they realized their wildest fantasies." She looked at him and remembered how she had imagined a man whose room was an island with coconuts, and a woman whose room was a whole city underwater.

"And then you said if that was what heaven was like, you want to be the woman who builds the rooms."

Her heart started racing. "Strange that you'd remember," she said.

He put his hand on her arm and stroked it with a gentleness she didn't know he had in him. "I loved you even back then," he said. "The rest was just for protocol."

She didn't think he'd be the first to confess. She drew his face to hers until their foreheads touched. She closed her eyes, and instantly knew the one thing she truly wanted. "We'll go," she said. "We'll go to Berlin."

This time it was he who hesitated. "Let's wait a day or two, think it over," he said, and admitted that since their last conversation he had begun to wonder whether he was in fact taking it all a step too far.

She wouldn't let him back out. "You'll have an entire week with me in Berlin to think it over," she insisted.

An hour later they had already bought tickets and even booked the first night at a hotel. What few doubts he still had soon faded, and in the following days he didn't stop talking about the trip, where they'd visit and in which restaurants they'd eat. She settled for a laconic email to her parents announcing she was extending her trip. She didn't care about Berlin. Or about the vacation he went on and on about. She just wanted more time with him. She knew there were things between them that needed more time and closeness to grow. She just had to make sure they made it to Berlin in one piece.

One evening, while at the grocery store, she spotted from between the shelves a woman who had gone to college with them entering the shop with a stroller. She quickly pushed Michael's head into a cucumber display. They kept perfectly still for a few good minutes, hiding between the tomatoes and sweet potatoes, looking at each other with that secret smile of theirs. Once the woman and her baby left the store, she sighed with relief, thinking that maybe it actually was possible to live an entire life like this.

12.

HER MOTHER CALLED two days before the flight, in the middle of the night. She didn't hear the phone ring. When she woke up to go to the bathroom, she happened to see the text message.

"I took Dad to the hospital. Chest pain."

Tamara dialed her mother's number in a panic. She called again and again until her mother sent her another text saying they were in the examination room and she'd call her later.

"I'm coming," Tamara wrote her, to which her mother replied that it was a shame to cut her trip short especially for them, and promised to update her when they knew more. Without reading the rest of the message, Tamara started picking up the clothes scattered around the apartment. Michael woke up and found her sitting on the floor, trying to stuff another sweater into her bag.

"What are you doing?" he asked.

She pointed at her phone and he read the texts, sat down beside her, and wrapped his arms around her in a tight embrace.

"Just don't forget you're still in Germany," he said while stroking her hair. "I'll find you the earliest flight. You'll be there by tomorrow afternoon. Maybe even before."

Her body recoiled from him. She leaned back and considered him, certain he was joking.

"Did you really just say that?" she asked, furious at his tormented expression, as if he had hijacked her pain.

"How are you going to explain to your mother that it only took you an hour to get to Ichilov?" he said. "I know it's a tough situation, but we have to think straight."

She pushed him off her, then picked up the shirt he was sitting on.

"The last thing I care about right now is your fucking Germany," she yelled, and the more she thought about what he had said, the more absurd it seemed. "Never in my life have I thought a person could be so detached." She got up and started pacing the room.

"You knew what you were getting into," he mumbled. "It could burn me too, don't you get it?"

She wanted to kill him. "What's wrong with you?" she screamed at him. "Don't you understand my father is dying?"

He didn't answer, and she had nothing more to say. She looked at him again, saw him withdrawing into himself, fixing his eyes on the floor, and couldn't understand what she was still doing there.

"I'll call you a taxi," he said without looking at her. He tried to dial, but his hand was shaking badly.

"No need," she announced and started walking toward the door. Slowly.

"I hope you come back."

Once outside the apartment she called a taxi herself. Waiting for its arrival, she got another text from her mother: "Gallstones. He'll be fine. Sorry for making you worry. Good night, have fun."

She slunk back into the apartment. Michael was sitting on the couch, breathing heavily. She poured herself a glass of water and sat down beside him.

"He's fine," she said.

"Glad to hear," he replied quietly, without looking at her. "You're right. I've gone too far."

She patted his head gently. Said she was the one who'd gone too far.

He didn't reply.

"I hope you don't regret that we met," she said, revealing the fear that had been building up inside her those last few days.

He looked up, his eyes red. She gazed at him, at his hands that were shaking.

"Us meeting," he said. "It wasn't a coincidence."

He admitted he had stalked her on Facebook. Orchestrated a chance encounter the moment he saw she checked "attending" for that conference and realized she'd be in Hadera. He confessed he had no idea what would come of it, but decided he didn't want to let such an opportunity slip by.

She placed her glass on the table. "Surprising," she said.

"That I stalked you?"

"That I didn't figure it out myself." She looked him in the eye. "But why me?"

"Because of the rooms in heaven," he said.

She didn't buy it. "Why me?" she insisted.

"Because I was alone," he mumbled and added that she had been right from the start. That it had all gone too far. That he had completely lost himself this past year. "I have to get out of here," he said.

"Wait," she replied. "Let's fly to Berlin and decide there."

He didn't say a word.

13.

THE EVENING BEFORE the flight, she found him sitting by the bed, packing his clothes. Then he announced he was going to buy a book for the flight, kissed her on the cheek, and left the apartment. She lay on the bed and closed her eyes. She felt a heaviness settling inside her.

When she woke up it was already night. Tamara reached out for her phone, checked if there were any new WhatsApp messages, and logged into Facebook. She wanted to see how many likes she had received for the most recent photo she had uploaded. The fourth post that appeared in her feed was Michael's. He had uploaded it thirty minutes ago.

> *There's no place like home*
> *Back in Israel in a few hours.*

An airplane emoji appeared next to the text, and according to his check-in, he was "en route to Israel."

She got out of bed and went into the kitchen. As she had suspected, Michael was sitting at the table in his familiar black jacket, a small suitcase at his feet. He looked at her quietly, as if he had been waiting for her.

"An English gentleman about to board his carriage," she said.

He smiled. "I'm sorry. I can't stay here anymore."

"You couldn't wait a week?"

"I'm an impulsive guy."

"I hadn't noticed," she replied in a sarcastic tone, afraid she was going to burst into tears. She pulled up a chair and sat down in front of him. She kept looking at him, how different he was from the insecure guy who had sat across from her at the restaurant.

"The apartment's paid for till the end of the month," he said, and told her he thought she'd be better off going to Germany. "It'll make it easier to describe where you've been. It's not the same without being there in person."

She didn't see the point trying to convince him to stay. She had come to terms with it quicker than she had expected.

"Were you happy with me?" she asked.

He smiled again.

"Yes," he said. "Reality didn't have the chance to mess that up yet."

"Life isn't black and white. You have to learn to live with the grays too," she told him.

"True," he said and got up. For a moment he seemed to be considering whether to hug her, and eventually decided he should. She got up but didn't hug him back.

"But I can't," he said. "I'd rather have you without all the grays."

His words were physically painful.

He turned around and walked out. She sat down in his chair, listening to the sound of his suitcase being dragged down the stairs.

14.

THERE WAS NO river view. No balcony either. But the hotel room was comfortable and cozy, and the people were as nice as he had said they were. She hadn't actually planned on checking, but her phone automatically connected to the hotel Wi-Fi, and he had just uploaded a few photos from his homecoming party. She looked at the people surrounding him, didn't recognize any of them. A bespectacled girl sat next to him for the entire party. She clicked on her profile but couldn't find any information about her.

She lay on the bed. In a moment of desperation, she shared Amir Lev's song about Holden's ducks. She wasn't sure what she meant to say by it. But maybe that was why she felt it was the most real thing she had ever posted in the virtual world.

How to Remember a Desert

1.

AND THERE, IN the white waiting room, she suddenly cringes, realizing Amichai was right. Had been right all along. That two people actually could be in the very same spot, without so much as a molecule separating them. That nowadays, you could squeeze into another person's insides, hold on tightly without letting go.

"There will always be some space left," she'd protest whenever Amichai brought up the idea, and secretly thank whoever it was that made sure to put that space there. But Amichai was adamant. He sidled up and squashed and crushed, and she let him keep trying. And he really did try. In the bedroom, the bathroom, the car. He'd press up against her wherever he could. Before she left, she told him her skin was red from all his bizarre attempts. But he kept at it till the end.

A young woman in scrubs walks in, calls out the names of people in the waiting room. Ruthie considers her, thinks her eyebrows are nicely done. Then she turns her attention to the couples sitting around them, and realizes they're the oldest one in the room. She tries guessing by how much. At least twenty years. Maybe even thirty?

"Ilan and Ruthie Zamir?"

"He's Zamir, I'm Meiner," she rushes to correct her. "I mean, as of tomorrow we'll both be Zamir." She glances at Ilan, worrying he might have taken offense, but he seems unperturbed.

"It's fine, nowadays you can hyphenate after the wedding, be Zamir-Meiner," the woman says, and Ilan replies with a smile, saying, "Too late to fix us, we're old-fashioned."

A few people in the room start laughing.

"Welcome to Lucid Memo," the woman says, reminding the room that pre-wedding couples are entitled to a pampering spa treatment after the procedure. Then she explains the process. Goes over safety regulations. Hands them forms and points out that at the end of the procedure some might experience light-headedness, "especially patients of advanced years." Ruthie wonders whether that last comment was directed at them. Before leaving the room, the woman says the couples will be called one at a time. Two men sitting to their left are holding hands and whispering to each other. One of them turns to her.

"I have to ask, are you related to Meiner the founder?"

"You don't have to, you want to," she replies, and Ilan quickly adds, "He's her ex-husband. Very nice fellow."

"Did he at least give you a discount?" the guy asks, and someone else laughs and says, "Discount? They'll be lucky if he doesn't plant a false memory in them."

"He's a decent fellow," Ilan says, and she takes his hand and squeezes it hard, the way she always does when people talk about Amichai.

2.

THE WOMAN LEADS them into the procedure room. Two round and wide machines stand in the middle of the room. She explains they look and operate a little like MRI machines, then hands them green hospital gowns and asks them to change in the little nook behind the curtain. Ilan goes in first. She follows. The gown is a size too small, but she doesn't mention it.

"Excited?" the woman asks. Ilan says yes. Ruthie nods.

"So how many memories are you sharing today?"

"Two."

"They didn't explain when you signed up that you have to do at least five?"

"I'm not doing more than two," Ruthie announces, and Ilan adds, "We agreed with your people on two when we spoke on the phone."

"I apologize, we don't even have an option for two on our price list."

"Then we'll pay for five and do two," Ilan replies, and Ruthie smiles. She loves his resolve, how he doesn't play games. How he stands behind her.

The woman makes a quick call. Inquires. "I'm sorry, they should have updated me," she says. "Two it is." She reminds them it's important that the memory they share have a defined time and place, otherwise the machine will struggle to copy it, explaining they had yet to nail the abstract memories. "The whole procedure will take thirty minutes. If one of you needs to tinkle, now's the time."

"We went at home," Ilan says, and the woman smiles. Handing them each a glass of a clear liquid, she explains it's supposed to help the brain register the new memories. She stresses its blurring effect. Ilan drinks it slowly. Ruthie downs it in one gulp. It's terribly sweet.

"Let's begin."

Ilan kisses Ruthie on her cheek and moves toward his machine. Ruthie approaches hers and lies down on the table. The padding is cold. Typical of Amichai not to have thought about that.

She looks at Ilan who looks back at her and blows her a kiss. It embarrasses her, so she fixes her eyes on the ceiling, picking up a buzzing sound. The machine kicks into motion, sliding her into a white tunnel until it swallows her whole.

"Close your eyes," a soothing voice announces through the speakers. "Deep breaths."

She tries. Thinks about her and Amichai's son. How he told her that the day he entered that machine, he realized she was wrong. That people weren't meant to roam this world alone. Told her about the first time he and his wife, Naomi, exchanged memories. Said, "Where words fail, technology prevails." She looked at her lovestruck child and felt happy for him. Tried not to think about the unfortunate yet inevitable distance a child must travel away from his mother.

"Doesn't feel right to me," she confessed to him when they talked about the machine. Said it felt a little too close, all the memories and photos and messages people share with one another all day. He rolled his eyes at her. She thought he probably told Naomi his mother was no longer "with it," the way he spoke about other people. For a few years now—since her senior citizen card appeared in the mail—he's been looking at her differently. Testing her whenever she forgets where she has left her keys or struggles to remember the name of some old classmate.

"Ruthie, I can see by your pulse that you're a little stressed," the voice said. "Don't worry, everything's under control."

"I know."

"Good. Keep focusing on your breathing. Now I'm going to ask you two to think about the first memory you want to share."

She tries to remember. Only then does she realize she had no intention of sharing a single memory. That she had agreed to go through with this whole farce only because her son had been so adamant. For a moment, she considers backing out. Or maybe just evoking some trivial, insignificant memory. Lunch break at the office or something like that. Why not share it with Ilan? After all, it would make him so happy. Make both of them happy. She feels she's resisting the direction the world is heading in, but doesn't know why.

"Try to remember what was around you that moment, what you saw, what you smelled."

She feels every muscle in her body rebelling against her. Tensing one by one.

"Try to feel the temperature where you're at."

Her body vetoes the request; she sees nothing but black. They'll be onto her any moment now. They'll ask her why she isn't remembering, what the problem is.

"We'll continue the procedure in a sec," the voice says, and she knows she's been made.

The noises from the machine die down.

"We apologize, there's been a slight glitch. With your permission, we'll repeat this step. Take a deep breath and think about—"

"Wait," she says. "I need to go to the bathroom."

"Can't you hold it in for a bit?" the voice replies. "It won't take much longer."

"No, I have to go now."

"It's a little problematic interrupting the treatment in the middle. Could you wait another—"

"No, I can't. I'm about to pee myself. Hello? Can you hear me?"

After a moment's silence, the table starts sliding out, slowly. The young woman is standing to her right. "Come, we'll do it quickly, okay?" she says with that annoying smile of hers. "I'll walk you there."

"I don't need escorting."

"Better I go with you," she says, "it'll be a bit difficult to walk with the sedative we gave you."

"Everything okay, my Ruthie?"

"Yes, Ilan. Yes. Just popping into the bathroom."

"No problem, I'll be waiting here. Love you."

"Be back in a sec."

The woman helps her off the table. Ruthie approaches the changing nook, picks up her pants, and takes her phone out of the pocket. The woman tells her there's no need to take anything with her, but Ruthie ignores her. She feels a bit wobbly and holds on to the woman as they make their way down the hallway.

"You want me to go in with you?"

"No, no, I'm fine."

"Okay, I'll be waiting here. Just make sure you come out through the same door."

"No problem," Ruthie replies, and thinks about her son. Sometimes he gives her the same look the woman's giving her now, when he's not sure she has understood him.

She walks into the bathroom. There are only two stalls, both unoccupied. She chooses the left one, locks the door behind her, and carefully lines the seat with a few squares of toilet paper. She sits down, reaches out to put her phone somewhere but can't find a single flat surface. The phone bleeps with an incoming text message. She tries to open it but can't. She hates this smartphone, wanted to stay with her old dumb one but her son saddled her with a new iPhone. He had bought it for her as a gift and two months later discovered she'd been walking around with the battery switched off and the old dumb phone hidden in her pocket. He refused to talk to her for three days, until she surrendered the old phone to him and was left to battle the touch screen on her own.

She somehow finds herself on her contact list. When she tries to go back, it scrolls down the list instead. She stops at Amichai's name. Stares at the letters. She tries to return to the home screen, but accidentally dials him. She tries to press END, but nothing happens. The screen turns black, the phone still dialing.

"Damnit," she hisses when she hears Amichai's voice mail message.

"Hey there, you're welcome to leave a message."

A man of his stature with such a simple message? Nice. She doesn't utter a word, hoping the line will disconnect on its own. She knows him, after ten seconds of silence he'll hang up, she knows he will. And if he doesn't? He'll think she's stalking him. He won't understand why she's calling him a day before her wedding. Better she say something so there won't be any misunderstandings.

"Hi, it's me. You won't believe where I am," she says, hesitating whether to continue. "In your building. The company building. Sharing memories with Ilan. Can you believe it? Our son, that little devil, managed to talk me into it."

She hears the bathroom door open. "Everything okay?" the woman asks.

"Yes," she replies from inside the stall and covers the screen with her hand. "It'll take me a few more minutes."

"Okay, try to hurry. Give me a shout if you need any help."

"Thank you," she says, and wonders what help she could possibly need. She hears the door shutting and turns back to the unresponsive screen. "Well, anyway, I thought you might be here. But we're almost done, so never mind. See you tomorrow at the wedding. Okay, bye now."

She tries to hang up, but doesn't know if she succeeded. She gets up, sweeps the paper squares into the toilet bowl and flushes. Standing in front of the sink, she feels her legs slacken. Good thing the woman's waiting outside. She looks in the mirror, thinking Ilan must be getting worried. Sticking her hands under the hand dryer, she comforts herself with the hot air. Then she opens the door and it comes gushing down.

Cold water washes all over her. Cascades off her shoulders. Everything shrinks inside her; she tries to protect herself but doesn't know how. Where is it coming from? Her body feels different, stiff. Soaked and freezing. She looks at her hands, baffled. She's completely dry. There's no water. And as quickly as the sensation appeared, it subsides.

She pauses, then stretches, trying to get her bearings. But she can't shake off the confusion. "Say, what was in that sedative you gave me?" she asks the woman, but the woman isn't there. Neither is she herself there. It isn't the same hallway she came from. Black tiles, hazy daylight filters in through the dark windows. She tries to open the bathroom door. It's locked. She notices a silver digital door lock on the wall. Doesn't know the code. Wants to call someone but doesn't know who. She tries Ilan, but he doesn't pick up.

"Hello, I'm stuck," she yells. "Hello?"

Nothing. She starts staggering along the hallway, trusting herself less with each step.

"Anyone here?"

No answer. She reaches out with her left hand and supports herself against the wall, wandering through the hallways, stumbling in and out of rooms. She has no idea where she is. Or how to get back.

And for the second time, all at once, water pours over her without leaving a trace. This time a gentle drizzle. And it's no longer ice cold. It feels pleasant, almost caressing. The sensation is accompanied by a vague image. She sees her son in front of her, standing shirtless under a big waterfall, laughing and shivering in his gray underwear. It's been years since she saw him like this, exposed.

She understands.

This isn't her memory. It's Ilan's, the memory he had wanted to share with her, from the trip he and her son took two months ago. Only the two of them, to the Judaean Desert. She tries to fast-forward and rewind the image in her head, but can't. All she feels is Ilan's body emerging from within her, bent and stiff. She remembers what her son had told her about the day he entered Naomi's body. How he felt her like he'd never felt her before. "It was like we were both in the exact same spot."

And she feels it too. The stones needling Ilan's feet, the dull back pain he's been complaining about for the past year.

Her phone rings. Pulls her away from the body. The screen goes black again. She fights with the phone, pressing buttons until the ringing stops.

"Hello. Hello? Can you hear me? I got stuck. Can you hear?"

"Ruthie?"

She recoils.

"It's Amichai. Where are you stuck?"

She takes a deep breath. "Oh, no, I'm just, I was just talking to someone here, how—how are you?"

"Good. Heard your message. You and Ilan still in the building?"

"Yes, actually," she says and presses her head against the wall. It's cold, reminds her of the water.

"Good, happy to hear. They're treating you well?"

"Yup. Everyone's real nice."

"Wonderful. You want to pop into my office for coffee?"

She closes her eyes. Her son is standing in front of her, under the waterfall, drenched. The image slowly clears, she sees every part of his body becoming sharper.

"Actually we're still in the middle of the procedure."

"Got it. You're welcome to pop by afterward if you feel like it. My office is on the fourteenth floor."

She feels the oily moss beneath her feet.

"Okay, Ruthie?"

"Sure, okay. I'll see how it goes here, I can't promise."

"No pressure, we're seeing each other tomorrow," he says, and she tries to picture Amichai's face. Recalls the wrinkled white shirt he wore on their wedding day. The line disconnects. She drops the phone to the floor, stares at the tiles, sees the water swirling beneath her. Reaching her knees. She closes her eyes, feels the memory starting to stir inside her like a movie, the water rippling around her in a veil of mist. A slow breeze blows against the back of her neck. Out of the corner of her eye she sees children playing, but they're a blur. She can't zero in on them. She's focused entirely on her son. His laughing body. A healthy, deep laughter. He's yelling something. Shouting with a big smile. But she can't hear him. Can't read his lips either; the water is obscuring the image. She feels Ilan's body answering, telling him something, but she can't make out the words.

Ilan must have been thinking about her, she's sure of it. He knew how she longed for such moments with her son. How she wished for more of him. She realizes Ilan had only good intentions, but the more she thinks about those intentions, the angrier she gets. For showing her what's missing, letting her see it with her own eyes. She stays there a few more minutes, trying to delve deeper into the memory. Now she can smell the desert too, reminding her of the two years she worked in Mitzpe Ramon. Everything becomes sharper, more lucid. But she can't pick up a single sound. Her son is standing in front of her, still yelling words she can't hear.

She stares at the ceiling. Can't understand what she's doing here. She never even wanted the treatment. She holds her head in her hands, hoping to extract the foreign memory that's been planted inside her. It's no use. She looks both ways, making sure the hallway is clear, and lets out a feeble cry. She wants to scream, but doesn't want anyone to hear. Then she starts walking down the hallway, makes it to the elevator exhausted and presses the button, feeling the dizziness has slightly abated. The elevator door slides open and she walks in. Glancing at the buttons, she presses both the fourteenth and first floor, still undecided.

3.

SHE MAKES HER way up to Amichai's office on her own. When the door opens, she is standing before a beautiful parquet floor and marble walls. They don't notice her at first, but halfway to the receptionist's desk, she sees several of the employees already staring at her.

"Everything okay, ma'am?" the secretary asks. "You look a little pale."

"I'm absolutely fine," she says, making sure to smile, hoping the smile will make up for the green gown and the tired body. "I'm here to see Amichai. Where is his office?" she asks, and thinks about Ilan. About the sadness he'd feel if he found out they'd met. When he finds out they'd met. The receptionist peers at his computer screen.

"I'm sorry, I don't see any appointments in his schedule."

"I used to be his wife," she says.

The receptionist hesitates, signals to the girl sitting next to him, whispers something in her ear. She gets up and scurries toward one of the doors, knocks, and enters.

"Is that Amichai's office?"

"Just one moment, ma'am."

The girl walks out and whispers something to the receptionist.

"He's in the middle of an important meeting," they tell her. "It'll take at least half an hour."

"I just want to say hi, may I?"

"I apologize, we're being instructed not to disturb him."

"I see," Ruthie replies, and lets out a sigh. "No problem, some other time."

"I'm sure. Would you like us to escort you back to your treatment, Mrs. Zamir?" The receptionist smiles, and she knows they're onto her. They know.

"Yes," she replies submissively. "Perhaps if you could just tell me first where the bathroom is?"

"Of course. Here on your left."

Ruthie nods in gratitude and takes a left, then backtracks toward Amichai's door, opening it. The receptionist yells out something, but she ignores him. She enters in big strides, sits down on a soft white armchair, and fixes her gaze to the floor.

"Close the door, it's fine." She hears Amichai's decisive tone, followed by the sound of the door shutting. She looks up, meeting his eyes.

4.

HE LOOKS ALMOST OLD, and yet barely changed. Most of his hair has turned white, but his skin is still smooth and taut. She's never seen him in a suit before, but his posture is as steady and calm as she remembers. He looks at her and says into the receiver, "I have to take care of something here, I'll get back to you in a sec." He hangs up and stares at her.

"Been a while," he says.

"Indeed."

He asks how she's been doing. She says well.

"Tea or coffee?"

"Nothing," she replies.

"How was the treatment?"

"What can I say, all this technology of yours is very impressive," she says and wavers, biting her bottom lip.

"Everything all right, Ruthie?"

"I'm tired, Amichai," she sighs. "I can't."

"You can't what?" he asks, leaning forward and extending his hand to the middle of the table. She recalls that strange ability of his, to express empathy and aloofness at the same time.

"I don't know what I'm doing here," she says, turning her focus to a bookcase. Neat and tidy. She thinks about the house they shared in Haifa, in the early days of their relationship. How they slept on the floor for nearly a month because the mover disappeared along with their boxes.

"Ruthie, I'm not sure I'm following."

She thinks about the house they moved into afterward in Ramat Gan. And their trip to Jordan. Thinks about their son, who's still stuck in her head, under the waterfall. She tries to stop all these memories from resurfacing, and can't.

"Get it out of me," she says.

"Get what out?"

"The memory you planted inside me. Erase it."

"What memory, Ruthie? From the treatment just now?"

She nods.

"What's in it?"

"What difference does it make? I don't want anything in my head. Don't want anyone poking around there."

She sees he doesn't know what to make of her. That he's sure she's gone mad. She knows him too well. "It's not that simple, Ruthie. We can't just erase it, the technology still—"

"But I don't want it," she shouts. "Enough, I don't want it."

He scratches his head, takes a piece of paper out of the desk drawer, and starts scribbling on it. She knows that shtick of his. To appear busy until things work themselves out. She won't let him.

"I'll sue you," she says, gripping the armrests.

"What?" He looks up at her, baffled.

"You heard me, I'll sue. I'll hire the best lawyer I can find and sue you. The whole country will hear about it."

Amichai leans back, considers her with a stern expression. Slides a finger across his chin. Something has changed in him. Now she sees he's different. Not the Amichai she first stumbled upon in the Turkish market, but the serious, authoritative CEO everyone's talking about.

"Why are you here, Ruthie?"

"I don't know," she confesses, lowering her gaze. "I honestly don't."

"Money? Is that it?"

"Are you crazy?" she exclaims, stroking her arms.

"How much?" he asks.

"I don't want anything from you," she retorts, noticing his hand holding the pen is shaking. He notices it too, and hides it under the table. He glances at the computer screen, then back at her.

"It was all your idea."

"What?"

"This whole company."

Now he's the one who seems a little off.

"What on earth are you talking about? I was never into all those experiments of yours," she replies, and knows he understands what she means perfectly well.

"Right, and that's why you said what you said."

"Said what, Amichai? What are you talking about?"

She sees a tremor of hesitation shoot through him, as if he's holding back from telling her. He doesn't trust her anymore. "You said I have to find another way, because it won't work through the body alone."

She can't understand what he's talking about. She tries, but fails. But it's written all over his suddenly pale face—he's not lying. "I don't remember saying anything like that," she replies quietly.

"Memory is a strange thing," he replies, and starts elaborating on the technical process. Explains how a memory is imprinted into the brain, and how his machine works.

"What are you rambling on about? How do you remember a desert?" she cuts him off, and he says something about the neurons in the brain. Clarifies that a memory can't simply be erased. He explains all these things she has no interest in knowing. She's looking at him, but her entire being is underneath that waterfall.

Then, a knock at the door.

"Come in," he says, and she already knows.

5.

SHE HOLDS ILAN'S hand the entire ride home. Clasping it tightly. Waiting for him to say something.

"I don't know what I was looking for up there."

"I do," he replies in a soft, gentle tone despite himself. They turn off the highway and into the city.

"You know, one memory did transfer to me," she says, looking out the window.

"I know."

"The problem is—"

"It had no sound."

"How did you know?"

"They told me. Explained they didn't burn the memory well."

She glances at him through the rearview mirror, hoping he'll look back, but his eyes are fixed on the road.

"Is it from the trip you took two months ago?"

"Yup. In the desert."

"You were cold," she says, and laughs.

"Yup," he replies, trying to suppress a chuckle. She notices, and grasps his other hand in hers.

"Was there sound in the memory I shared with you?"

"You didn't share a single memory."

"What?"

"You didn't share anything with me."

Her legs tense. She presses them together.

"That's what they told you?"

"No. I know you."

She takes a deep breath and turns on the radio, hoping to find a song she likes. She doesn't.

"What did you talk about?"

"Who?"

"You and him. What did he say to you over there, under the waterfall?"

Ilan shoots her a quick glance before turning back to the road. They continue to ride in silence. Ten minutes. Maybe fifteen.

"He shouted that it was a shame you weren't there. That you could stand under the water for a whole hour," he finally says with a smile. "And I told him he was right."

Ruthie lets go of his hand.

"I don't get it, I thought you'd be happy."

She takes big gulps of air, feeling as if she's suffocating.

"Pull over," she demands.

"What?"

"Pull over. Now."

"There's nowhere to pull over, Ruthie. We'll be home in a minute, we'll talk it all over."

"You can pull over from the other lane," she asserts, pointing at it with her entire body.

"I can't switch lanes, it's a solid yellow line."

Ruthie leans in, making sure the road is clear, and jerks the wheel left.

"Ruthie, enough!" he shouts, pushing her off. The car swerves, almost crashing into a parked car. Ilan manages to brake in time. The front fender almost grazes the rear fender of the car in front of them. The alarm goes off.

"You've lost it completely," he says, shifting into reverse. He wants to get out of the middle lane but she won't let him. She raises her arms and throws herself over and into him, pressing up against him as closely as possible. At first he still tries to continue driving, but soon realizes he doesn't stand a chance. The car behind them keeps honking at them, but they don't move. She sidles up to him even closer, and he caves. Wraps his arms around her.

"I can't breathe," he says.

"You're doing fine," she replies.

He presses her against him with big, merciful arms, and she continues to squeeze herself into him. Clinging on as tightly as she can without letting go.

Anita Shabtai

YOU PROBABLY DON'T GET WHAT the big deal is about striking up a conversation with you guys. What's so difficult about talking to a taxi driver, you just put one word after another and toss them into the air, right? Probably seems like the easiest thing in the world to you. But I'll have you know that for some people it ain't that simple, coming up with something smart to say off the top of your head. I'm not talking about everyone, obviously. For some, it just pours out of them like water. My dad, bless his soul, was a real expert, I'll tell you. You've never seen anything like it. He hadn't even entered the taxi yet and was already talking, and wouldn't stop until he got out. And don't get me wrong, Dad wasn't normally much of a talker. He was actually the silent type. He'd return from the printing house every evening and barely say a word.

Any homework? Dinner? Shower?

That's how he'd talk, stingy with words. How do you explain it? That in taxis he'd talk when everywhere else he was so quiet? What can I tell you, when I was a little girl I thought maybe every person had only a limited number of words they were allowed to use a day, and that Dad preferred cashing them in all at once, getting it all out. Today I'm not so sure. All I know is that every conversation always started the same way. Dad would hand the driver a note with the address, and sigh. The driver would ask "Why the long face?" and Dad, with the few words he knew in Hebrew, would tell him about Mom. About the cancer.

But don't feel sorry for me, he'd say, it's the little girl here who got the short end of the stick. He'd explain that he was taking me to his aunt in Haifa who wasn't even really his aunt, but she was all he had left from Thessaloniki. He'd tell him that we made our way from Tel Aviv to Haifa every week, even though it cost him half his salary, because every kid needed a woman to hug them tight. And only after Dad let out a bit of his sadness would he start talking about the rest. He once told me that secrets were like money, and that if you shared a really good one, the person you were talking to felt indebted. So after he told them about Mom, they'd open up like artichokes, every last one of them. They'd start telling him things. My God, the things they'd tell him! Even the name of their mistress! And I always wanted to join in, but it's hard for me, you know? So I wouldn't say anything the entire ride, and once we got home I'd run to the mirror, stand there for hours, and try to imitate Dad's serious tone.

Did you see how they hanged Eli Cohen? Those Syrians don't answer to no one. Or—can you believe Dayan stole those artifacts? I'll never get how he pulled that off with only one eye.

During one of those rides we heard the song "Jerusalem of Gold" on the radio, and I suddenly got the courage to yell out one of Dad's old sayings.

"What a voice that Shuli Natan has, like an angel I tell you."

Dad and the driver laughed so hard that right then and there I swore I'd never utter another word again. You see, that's why I say that for some people talking isn't easy. No two ways about it. For some, this thing called *living* is just a bit too much. I, for instance, can tell you that I missed out on life by just a few feet. What can I say, it started out so fast that by the time I noticed, it was speeding ahead without me. You probably think this is just a bunch of hooey. That I didn't really make an effort. But trust me, I tried, I tried harder than anyone, it just didn't work. Nope, no two ways about it; there's always someone who misses the last bus, and in this lifetime it happens to be my turn.

When did I realize it? Good question. I can't really put my finger on it, but I think that when I was little, things were still okay. I won't lie and tell you I was some girl wonder, but not everyone has to be Einstein. But it's true I didn't really have friends. I mean, if kids talked to me, I'd answer, obviously. But if they didn't, I'd keep quiet. The problem is that things kind of got stuck at that point. You see, people think that all you need in order to exist in this world is to breathe, but it's a lot more complicated than that, just so you know. 'Cause you also need to brush your teeth, and eat, and take a shower every now and then. So many tasks, how are you supposed to remember them all? I think it was in eighth grade that my name somehow got left off the list. Who knows, maybe it was seventh grade. I guess some secretary made a mistake. I don't really know how it happened, but one day the math teacher took attendance, and never called my name. I was going to say something after a few days, but the kids in my class convinced me not to. They said that way I could skip classes whenever I wanted, and I thought to myself that I shouldn't ruin the one lucky break I finally got.

By the time I was in high school they'd stopped grading my papers. I mean, I still handed them in, but whenever the teacher waved the paper in the air and asked who wrote it, I wouldn't answer. At first I kept quiet because I really thought it was better that way, and later I just couldn't bring myself to answer.

I know what you're thinking. What's so difficult about raising your hand and calling out your name? What's the big deal? Today I would have sorted it out in no time; as you can see, talking isn't a problem for me today. But back then? Just to approach someone felt like climbing Kilimanjaro. That's why I'm telling you you shouldn't judge, you understand? Because when you meet a person, you only see part of his life, but never the whole movie. And who knows, maybe just a second ago a volcano erupted in his soul and you never even knew. That's why I also think God slipped up with the Ten Commandments, 'cause if he had put "don't judge" in there, maybe things would have looked different.

The army didn't even bother to send me a draft letter. I called them almost every day. They were always very nice and promised to take care of it, but let's just say it's been forty years and I'm still waiting. Eventually Dad had enough and he got me a job at Hedva's grocery store. He said that by the time I finished waiting for life to begin, it would already slip through my fingers. But from there it was all downhill. 'Cause you see, getting lost in a class of thirty kids still makes some sense, but getting lost in a tiny grocery store—that takes real talent.

After the grocery store Dad found me a job at the dry cleaner's, and then at the bakery near our house, in the Shapira neighborhood. He always tried to help as much as he could, but he admitted he was getting too tired. We'd sit at the kitchen table every evening, completely silent, and I could actually see how the years had made us more alike. Each with his own wrinkles. One evening he asked me how my day was, and I found myself yelling that I couldn't keep going on alone like this. That it wasn't healthy going through life without anyone. Dad was quiet for a few seconds, and then said that if God had wanted us to live in pairs, he would have created us that way to begin with. You probably think that was painful for me to hear, but to tell you the truth, it was reassuring. At that moment I finally realized that this is it, this is my life. And that's also when I started blabbing like there's no tomorrow, 'cause I knew no one was listening anyway. Believe me, it's not as bad as it sounds. I look at people passing me on the street, and it doesn't look much better. So what if people actually answer them when they say something, it doesn't make much of a difference. If anything, it's the feeling of being a bit stuck in place that bothers me, like I'm on a train that only stops where there are no stations, you know? But I think, maybe, others feel this way too, so why do I get to complain about it? That's what I told myself when Dad passed away. That if I'm hurting like everyone else, I should be thankful I feel anything at all.

Not many people turned up at the shivah. Just a few people from the neighborhood and some guys who worked with him at the printing house. They promised me everything would be fine, that life was just beginning, and then walked out the door and never came back. The only thing I have left from him are his Holocaust reparations that keep coming every month. I tried explaining to the Social Security people that Dad kicked the bucket and that they don't need to keep sending the payments, but they wouldn't listen. I don't mean they heard me and didn't do anything, I mean I went one by one and spoke right into their ears and they didn't even respond. As if I didn't exist. Finally I gave up and went to visit Dad in the cemetery. The bus took a lot of turns and by the time I got there I was already exhausted, so I just lay on the grave to rest a bit. I looked at the sky and couldn't understand how seven billion people got along just fine, and for me, just managing to wake up in the morning felt like a half a miracle. At some point I fell asleep there. I can't tell you how long I slept, but the noise woke me up. I turned my head and saw Egged bus drivers marching on the other side of the fence. They were all wearing blue shirts and ties, protesting against something. Don't ask me what, I don't remember. But they were screaming so loud, there was no point trying to go back to sleep. I remember looking at them and thinking to myself, Why don't you join them? Be around people for a bit, why not? No reason to be embarrassed. So I got up and approached them, and marched with them for about an hour, maybe more. At some point I also found myself shouting along with them. At first quietly, almost whispering, but then I remembered no one was listening and I shouted at the top of my lungs. Against the mayor and the minister of finance, and God and Dad and the prime minister and the aunt. Against whoever deserved it, because it felt good to let the anger out. And I kept going until someone put his hand on my shoulder. He asked if the union had sent me and said he'd never seen such a serious protester before.

I swear, that moment I was sure my heart had fallen out of my chest and rolled into the street. I couldn't understand how I was suddenly seen. It's true that I wanted someone to talk to me, but I always thought I'd have some time to get myself together before that happened. To do my hair, to put on something nice. That's why I started to panic, and before he even managed to say another word, I ran away as fast as I could. I got home, out of breath, and didn't leave the house for three days. Didn't even dare to look out the window. And all that time I tried to understand how it was possible that I had suddenly been seen. At first I told myself I had probably imagined it, but as time went by I started thinking that maybe it had to do with the shouting. Maybe when you shout, even a person like me can be heard. And the more I thought about it, the more sense it seemed to make, and I actually felt like someone had given me an opportunity to reenter the world through the back door.

Anyway, I started going to all kinds of protests. I'd take a bus to wherever I needed to go. To the Golan Heights, Kiryat Shmona, the Dead Sea, and the factories down south. I went wherever they wanted me to go, figured out who's against who and started shouting. Usually it was only a matter of minutes before people started looking admiringly, whispering to each other, *Look at her shouting, look*, and I'd blush and continue, wishing the whispers would never stop. At first I still made sure to check if I even agreed with the protesters, but very early on I realized I didn't need to. I mean, not that it's not important, obviously. It's just that I'd get there and listen and they all always seemed so miserable and so right, that at a certain point I decided that if someone is in enough pain to scream his heart out, who am I to tell him he's wrong?

But the bus rides were hard for me. 'Cause you need energy to ride every day to some kibbutz in the Golan Heights or some settlement near Nablus, and at my age I can barely handle a bus ride inside Tel Aviv, you know? Luckily, about two years ago the protests near my house began. Against all those people from Africa who sleep in Levinsky Park. One day I saw a flyer for a protest near the central bus station, and a few hours later I was already standing next to all these people I know from the neighborhood. I was so happy I almost thought someone had organized the protest just for me. Everyone was standing there trying to shout, but to tell you the truth, it looked like they didn't really know how to do it. Before I could even think it through I took someone's megaphone and started shouting *Bibi, go home!* And, *No to a police state!* You know, the usual stuff, nothing special. But right away everyone was looking at me as if I were Édith Piaf, no less. Some even clapped their hands, said they stood a real chance with me by their side, and to be honest, I felt the same way. So we started to protest every week, just us, from the neighborhood. But it wasn't enough for me, you know? I need a protest at least every two days, I just can't make it without one. I suggested we do something every day, even just something symbolic, that I'd even provide refreshments, but they said they didn't have time for it, 'cause they have work and families and kids. I was getting really angry at them, but then the protests in support of the Africans started, thank God. All these people I didn't know started protesting along with the Africans, saying we have to let those poor souls stay. At first I hesitated whether to join in, I admit. Protesting one day for and the next against seemed a bit much, but I told myself I had to. Not only for the soul, but also 'cause who am I to say which side is right?

I have to admit that during the first months I still had my doubts, but they disappeared the day I met Meir. He has a fruit and veggie shop in the neighborhood; he comes to all the demonstrations against the Africans, always in a pressed shirt. This Meir guy doesn't say much, you see, unlike me. He isn't big on talking, but when he does talk, he says beautiful things. He said his heart goes out to those poor souls from Africa. That he has no beef with them. That he isn't fighting against them, he's only fighting for his own life. That in a different world he'd be playing backgammon with each one of them, and would even let them win. He would come to each demonstration straight from his shop smelling like basil, and I'd stand behind him and sniff his shirt. One day he turned around, said he was sorry he stank, and I shouted that he didn't stink at all. Meir asked me why I was always shouting, and without even thinking I made up a story about how I could barely hear, that I have a problem with my ears, so he smiled and said that if I shout like that no wonder I have a problem. Apart from that conversation we didn't really talk much, but over time we started standing closer to each other, and in every demonstration I'd wait until we were all squished against one another to stand even closer to him. He wouldn't say anything and I wasn't sure if that was a good sign or a bad one, but I kept doing it because I thought that in this life I have nothing more to lose.

But it turned out I was wrong. I discovered this on the day of the big demonstration in support of those Africans. You probably heard about it, it was on every channel. While I was shouting into the camera that Israel is an apartheid state, the whole neighborhood showed up. Apparently they decided to take over the place and fight back. Once I realized this I tried to hide, but it was too late. Someone saw me and started yelling—*Look, it's Anita,* and soon enough everyone was yelling *traitor* and *leftist* and *enemy of Israel.* And the funny thing is that the pro-Africans also started yelling at me because they thought I was a mole. People were pushing me out of the demonstration and I found myself standing smack in the middle between those for and those against, shaking. And the worst part is that I suddenly saw Meir standing in front of me. He didn't say anything, only took a few steps closer and whispered in my ear, *Say, are you with us or against us?* And I instantly shouted as loud as I could, to make sure he heard me, *I'm with you, I'm with You.*

Meir grabbed my hand and pulled me out of there. Everyone kept shouting at us, but he told me I shouldn't listen to anyone. We got on a bus, and Meir said he was inviting me to a restaurant uptown, that he felt like pampering me. I yelled that I couldn't, since I didn't even have nice clothes on, but Meir said there was no point arguing because he'd drag me there if he had to. He also said I didn't need to shout anymore 'cause he could hear me perfectly fine now.

We got off on Ibn Gvirol Street and went into one of those really nice French restaurants, the kind I'd never been to before. He ordered for the both of us, appetizers and main courses and wine, said today we'd eat like kings. I yelled that he was the most romantic person I'd ever met, and he blushed. Then he asked me again to speak more quietly, 'cause it was a fancy restaurant and shouting isn't very appropriate.

I could tell that striking up a conversation wasn't easy for him, but he did his best. He asked me what I did for a living and I shouted *not much*. Then he asked whether I had kids, and I told him I didn't. Meir was quiet for a while and then said it was weird how loud I was at demonstrations while here I hardly had any words, and I told him he was right and felt that I was about to disappear again. At some point he told me I looked kind of pale, and that maybe I should wash my face, and I said it sounded like a good idea. I went to the bathroom and stood in front of the sink. I told myself that I had to calm down. That I couldn't let the one person who finally came into my life get away. But then I looked in the mirror and nearly screamed; my skin was so pale, almost see-through, that I could barely see myself.

I rushed out of the bathroom and started shouting across the restaurant at Meir that everyone in this country was corrupt and that you couldn't trust no one no more. That the minister of finance was a freaking joke. The diners all looked at me like I was some crackpot who had just escaped from the loony bin, and Meir whispered that this just wouldn't do and that I had to calm down. I knew from his expression that I was losing him, but I couldn't help it, because at that moment I realized that I'd do anything not to disappear again, even sell my Dad's grave. Meir gave up, lit a cigarette, and sat there quietly while I continued to shout about how everything's shit here and that you can't get a moment's peace and quiet in this country. He finally asked for the check and left a hundred-shekel tip to make up for the embarrassment I caused. When we stepped out into the street I shouted into his ear that it had been the best day of my life, and he said he was happy to hear that. Then he asked if I could make my way home on my own 'cause he had to run a few errands in the area, and I didn't say a word, since I knew I had caused him enough grief.

And that was it. I actually just came from the restaurant. You know, I think I'll stop going to the demonstrations in the neighborhood. There are enough poor souls in other cities, enough reasons to protest. So I'll have to take those long bus rides again, but I'll survive. Better than bumping into Meir again.

What, we're at the central bus station already? That went by in a flash! Can you turn here into Shapira? Oh, I see you're stopping here. No problem, I'll get off. I'm leaving a fifty-shekel bill here, okay? Do you hear me? I'm leaving it here next to the seat, okay? Well, never mind, I have to go. Worst-case scenario, you'll see it tomorrow morning, and think it fell out of your pocket.

Lennon at the Central Bus Station

1.

ON ALVIN'S TENTH BIRTHDAY, the tall-woman-with-the-chin-hair brought him a white rabbit with a black ear. The rabbit was crammed inside a plastic Tupperware box, lying on a half-eaten lettuce leaf. Her eyes were open and her front legs kept scratching the box. Alvin pressed his face against the lid and listened curiously to the screeching sound of her whistle.

"Mazel tov, sweetie. Happy?" the woman asked, patting Alvin's head.

He didn't reply. Her hands were coarse but her touch gentle. She took a creased fifty-shekel bill out of her purse and handed it to Alvin. "Buy her a carrot if she gets sad," she told him.

Alvin fondled the bill with both hands and shoved it into his left pocket.

The woman petted the rabbit on the back and she froze. Alvin looked at them both inquisitively.

"Pet her, sweetheart, pet, what are you so afraid of?"

Alvin reached out, touched, and recoiled. Dropped his hand to his side. Then he tried a few more times until he gave into the soft touch of the fur. "I always wanted a rabbit," he whispered.

"This ain't a rabbit, sweetheart," the woman announced with a smile. "What's this animal called? Uhm. I forget. Cova. Cava. Cavia. Oh, for fuck's sake. You know what I'm talking about, right?" Alvin grimaced. The tall-woman-with-the-chin-hair sighed. "You need to learn more words, honey," she said. "If it weren't for words, I'd still be thinking you people and the Thai are one and the same." She reached into her shirt pocket and fished out a lighter with a picture of a naked woman on it, and a poorly rolled cigarette. She was about to light the cigarette, but then looked at Alvin's face and put it back in her pocket. "Well, did you ask your mother why she isn't sending you to school?"

Alvin nodded.

"And . . . ?"

"She says she loves me," Alvin said, still stroking his possibly-rabbit and wondering if she liked it.

"What was that?" the woman asked, leaning into Alvin. "Explain, honey, so I'll understand."

Alvin filled his mouth with air and tried to hold his breath but gave in after a moment. "She said other parents don't actually love their kids," he said and tried again, this time taking in even more air.

"What do you mean?" she asked. This time Alvin managed to hold on a bit longer, until his cheeks deflated and shriveled. The tall-woman-with-the-chin-hair patted him on the head. "Tell me, sweetie, tell me."

"She said other parents let someone else look after their kids because they can't be bothered to do it themselves."

"And your mom keeps you close because she loves you? That's what she said?"

Alvin bobbed his head up and down in a dramatic nod.

"Holy crap," the woman mumbled. "And you're fine with it? Spending all day in this dump of a station? Not going to school?"

"Yes," Alvin replied, arching his thin eyebrows and curving his mouth into a crooked grin. "Yes, yes, yes," he repeated. He wanted her to stop asking about the outside world. The thought of things that happened outside the borders of the central bus station was unnerving. Sometimes he'd peek out the large windows, gazing curiously at the buildings in front of him. He could tolerate them, had come to terms with their existence, but not with whatever was behind them, everything he couldn't see. He had once tried to imagine that infinite black stain, and for the first time in his life felt the unsettling presence of nothingness.

"What are you doing?!" the tall-woman-with-the-chin-hair shrieked. His fingers were covered in white fur. "Why did you rip out her fur?" she grumbled, grabbing Alvin's small hand. There was a pink, exposed patch of skin on the possibly-rabbit's back. The woman pulled him forcefully and sat him down on the nearby bench. Alvin lowered his gaze, his eyes reddening. "It can't go on like this, Alvin. Do you understand what I'm saying?" the woman scolded. "You understand it can't go on like this?"

"Whatever," Alvin grumbled. "I don't even want her."

The tall-woman-with-the-chin-hair sat down silently beside Alvin. Then she suggested they name the possibly-rabbit, said Peter sounded nice to her, but Alvin just shrugged. They were both quiet for a while longer, Alvin gently stroking the possibly-rabbit, but only with one finger. The tall-woman-with-the-chin-hair gave him a kiss on the head. Said he was adorable. Alvin was focused on the tiny animal who was lying on her side, thinking how she was even smaller than the RC Cola can his mother used to treat him to once a week. When he looked up, the tall-woman-with-the-chin-hair was no longer there. She had left the lighter with the naked woman on it behind. Alvin looked at the picture, put the lighter in his pocket and went out for a little stroll, holding the plastic Tupperware box in both hands.

2.

ALVIN WANDERED AROUND the sixth floor, pausing by one of the doors to look at the passengers getting off the bus and going into the station. He eeny-meeny-miny-moed the passengers until his finger stopped on a man with a mustache. He started following him, but got tired of it after a few moments. He turned around and bounded down the stairs, arriving on the fourth floor panting, and stopped next to the McDonald's. He pressed his face against the window, ogling an elderly couple eating corn sticks and drawing the possibly-rabbit's box to the window thinking she wanted to see them too. A piece of corn stick dropped out of the woman's mouth, and her husband rushed to shoo Alvin away with menacing arm-flailing. He quickly retreated, leaped up a different staircase, and found himself smack in the middle of a small forest of Christmas trees. Amid the trees were a few tables laden with colorful Christmas decorations and chubby Santa figurines. He reached out to one of the trees and touched the pointed leaves. They were both prickly and soft. He wondered whether leaves felt pain. He plucked a leaf off one of the smaller trees, used his other hand to open the plastic box, and tossed it in. The leaf landed on the possibly-rabbit's head; she responded in utter indifference, wouldn't so much as raise her head.

"Yo, chopstick, whatcha doing over there?" the salesperson yelled. "Either buy something or get lost."

Alvin fled, fixing his eyes on the dirty tiles. It was only when he reached the pay phone that he felt he was finally out of danger. He leaned against the wall and held his left hand to his chest, making sure his heart was still beating. He lifted the box and peered at his possibly-rabbit, calming down only after he saw she was breathing. Then he resumed his stroll and popped into the record shop minutes before closing time.

"Do you have a Beables CD?" he asked the saleswoman, and pulled from his pocket the bill he had received from the tall-woman-with-the-chin-hair.

"There's no such band," the saleswoman replied, chewing a gray wad of bubblegum.

"Bearbes. Beaters. Bealbez," Alvin said. "Oh, for fuck's sake. You know what I'm talking about, right?"

"Watch your language," the saleswoman reprimanded him. Alvin shrunk into himself. She turned around, and then tossed a burned CD of *Abbey Road* onto the table.

"Beatles," she said and snatched the bill out of his hand, holding it up to the light.

The photo on the cover was faded. George Harrison's body was cropped in the middle. Struggling to hold both the box and the CD, he decided to chuck the CD into the box. The possibly-rabbit made no objection. She hopped onto the CD, put her head on McCartney's bare feet, and fell asleep.

The clock on the big electronic board flashed nine, and Alvin started skipping toward the jewelry stand where his mother, Prudence, worked. He paused by the entrance to the drugstore, spotting her faux-gold earrings from a distance. Her black hair was gathered into a tight bun, and a red sweater clung to her match-like frame. On the other side of the stand stood a young Eritrean couple studying the rings in the display. The dark-skinned woman was wearing a white embroidered dress, and had a faded cross-like tattoo on her forehead. She noticed Alvin staring at her and smiled. Alvin blushed, then dubbed her the woman-with-the-drawing-on her head. He always gave names to the people he liked, those he didn't want to get swallowed up by the throngs at the station.

When the couple left, Prudence began to cover the stand with a stretch of blue fabric. Alvin ran toward her. He emerged on the side of the stand, stood on his tiptoes, and tried to pull the heavy cloth with one hand, but somehow got entangled in it.

"Stop!" Prudence commanded. Alvin stopped in his tracks. He closed his eyes, felt two hands coming to free him. Then he felt a brief caress. Then nothing.

"What were you trying to do?" Prudence hissed and went back to tidying up the stand.

Alvin didn't dare look at her. He gazed at the possibly-rabbit who was still fast asleep. He jerked the box twice. Her head hit the plastic wall. She immediately woke up, trying to find something to support herself against. Alvin smiled.

"Come on, let's go," Prudence said. She left the stand holding two red bags and glanced at the possibly-rabbit.

"What's that, a hamster?" she asked and didn't wait for an answer. Alvin looked at his pet. He was confused.

"Maybe," he said.

They went to the food court on the sixth floor, stepping out through the metal door and finding themselves in front of some big green dumpsters. The loot piled in the corner of the room was relatively meager—five umbrellas, two kettles, a few computer keyboards, and a busted TV set. Prudence inspected the items carefully, finally picking up a black kettle and taking a closer look at it.

"We're taking it," she announced, and put it in one of her bags. "Come on," she said, "we're going home."

Next to the kiosk they took the staircase down, passed by the smelly bathrooms and then by the closed office that served as a makeshift church on Saturdays. Alvin liked going to church. He liked the songs, liked the cookies they handed out at the end of the sermon, liked ogling the girl-with-the-headband who always sat in the front row. He never talked to her but always stared, averting his gaze only when their eyes met. He and his mother stopped visiting the church after Prudence knocked over her chair and screamed at the priest that even God himself knew better than to tell her how to raise her child. He liked remembering how his mother picked him up in her arms and everyone stared at them. Even the girl-with-the-headband. Alvin couldn't hide his smile.

They reached the end of the third floor, which was empty. They stopped in front of the wide corridor leading downstairs.

"There's only homeless people and drugs down there," said a cleaner with a neon orange vest and black kippah who popped up behind them. He looked at Alvin's box and announced, "That needs a bigger cage, tzaddik."

Alvin wanted to ask the man whether she was a rabbit or a hamster, but his mother had already begun pulling him away. They started back toward the stall and waited for the cleaner to disappear before returning to the wide corridor. They rushed down the staircase, clutching the gray handrail. A pale fluorescent light illuminated the abandoned shops. The sour smell of urine became more pungent as they descended. When they passed by a poster of a bare-breasted woman, Prudence rushed to cover Alvin's eyes, although he continued to peek through the slits between her fingers. The large silhouettes of passengers from the floors above danced on the tiles. Alvin tried to dodge them, fearing that if he stepped on one of the silhouettes, he'd make someone upstairs trip.

They slipped into a side corridor and paused in front of three big windows boarded up with torn cardboard. Prudence started rummaging through her bags for her keys. Alvin sidled up against her legs. A bearded man in a military jacket and black Crocs staggered toward them, reaching out as if to pet his hamster-rabbit. Alvin clutched the plastic box and turned his back to him. Prudence noticed the man only after opening the door. She tried to scream but no sound came out. Alvin quickly pushed her into the dark room and shut the door behind them, barely managing to lock it. The red bags dropped from Prudence's hands. They stood perfectly still, making themselves smaller, making their breaths quieter in the pitch-black room. The hamster-rabbit started making noise. Alvin opened the lid and tried petting her, but the animal kept dodging him. After a few minutes, Prudence turned around and lifted one of the cardboard panels hanging over the window, then peeked out into the hallway. Only when she was confident the man had left did she turn on the light, painting the room in a yellow glow. Prudence leaned against the wall, put her hand on her head, and slid down to the floor. The kettle found its rightful place alongside the pile of items crowding the floor: pairs of shoes, a few wall clocks, broken chairs, and old newspapers. Hundreds of objects Prudence had gathered from across the station in the hope of someday finding a use for each one of them.

Alvin paved his way to the mattress in the corner of the room. He put down the box but wouldn't look at the hamster-rabbit, still holding a grudge.

"Jesus Christ," Prudence whispered, rubbing her chest in a vigorous circular motion. "Jesus Christ. They'll find us in the end. You understand how dangerous it is?"

Alvin nodded, even though he didn't actually understand. He didn't know who exactly was looking for them. In the past, Prudence had mentioned cops who wanted to kick them out of the country. She explained it was the only reason they were staying in the station, because it was the one place they wouldn't dare arrest them. But with time, the cops turned into the homeless and hookers and criminals, who turned into the baddies, who finally turned into vague, nameless, faceless figures. Alvin had already begun to doubt that anyone in the station was actually looking for them, or even knew of their existence; but he didn't dare ask Prudence, because more than anything else, he feared confronting his mother with a question she couldn't answer.

Prudence got up from the floor and let out a loud sigh. She crossed the room with small steps, made it to the corner where the toilet bowl stood with a green hose suspended above it. She pulled up a small chair, turned to face the wall, and started undressing, stacking her clothes in a pile on the chair.

"Don't look," she told Alvin, and turned on the cold water. Alvin quickly averted his gaze, lay down on the mattress, and stared at the ceiling. The lighter fell out of his pocket. Alvin stared at the naked woman for a few moments, and flicked the wheel a few times. It took him several attempts until a feeble flame appeared.

He lay on his side, drew the flame to the box. A smell of burned plastic took to the air. He snuck a quick peek at his mother, who was still showering with her back to him. Then he drew the flame to the box again. It burned a small hole into the plastic. The hamster-rabbit looked up at the spark and immediately scurried to the other side, pressing herself against the wall. Alvin gently turned the box around and drew the flame to the plastic wall again. Once more the hamster-rabbit fled to the opposite corner and froze.

"Idiot," Alvin said, drawing the flame to his pet. She tried to escape but he wouldn't let her. She started squealing in that annoying whistle of hers. Her tiny hairs got torched one by one, exposing her pink skin again. When the flame started singing her skin, she stopped fighting. She curled up into a ball in the corner of the box. Silently.

"What's that smell?" Prudence yelled and turned off the faucet. "Why does it stink in here?"

The lighter fell from Alvin's hand, hitting the CD cover. He didn't say a word. Prudence turned on the faucet again. He looked at the hamster-rabbit and felt regret. He started petting her, surprised by how quickly she gave into his touch again. She drew her tiny nostrils to his fingers. Alvin tore her a small piece of the lettuce she was standing on, and she nibbled it eagerly.

3.

PRUDENCE TURNED OFF the water, wrapped a towel around her body, and sat down next to Alvin. Tiny droplets slid off her black hair onto the mattress. She gazed at the three gilded Jesus paintings that hung on the wall, then asked Alvin if he thought she was pretty. He said yes, and she stroked his back and instructed him to open the fridge and eat the sambusak leftover from yesterday. He suggested they share it, but she didn't answer. She watched him slowly work through the cold pastry and collected the sesame seeds that scattered across the bed.

"I bought you a gift," he said between bites.

"What are we celebrating?" she asked, and he quickly pulled the CD out of the hamster-rabbit's box, his hands slightly shaking.

Prudence ran her hand over the cover, and for a moment Alvin thought he spotted a smile. A rare occurrence that usually presented itself when they went up to the seventh floor, stood by the big glass windows, and basked in the warm sun.

"Nice," she said.

"It's the Bealers," he replied. "Your name, it's because of them."

She didn't say a word, only blinked heavily. Alvin leaped out of bed, plucked from the junk pile a broken boombox they had collected a few months back. He placed it on top of the small fridge and plugged it into the socket.

Prudence reached out a long arm and grabbed Alvin's shoulder.

"No noise," she said. Alvin insisted they listen only for a few moments. Prudence said no. Eventually a compromise was reached.

"You can play it," she said, "but with no sound."

Alvin snatched it out of her hand, carefully opened the case, and inserted the CD into the stereo, making sure no sound came out, fearing his mother would change her mind. He went back to sit by his mother. They sat shoulder to shoulder, gazing at the blue digits changing on the display. The CD kept skipping. Alvin sat up straight while Prudence brushed her hand through his hair. Finally he got tired and lay down on the bed. He stared at the hamster-rabbit who lay next to him, until he closed his eyes and fell asleep.

When Alvin woke up she was no longer there. He tried falling back asleep. Unsuccessful, he opened his eyes again and noticed the hamster-rabbit's box perched on the boombox. He jumped out of bed and leaped toward the box. It was washed clean. Empty. The air halted at the tip of his nose, refusing to enter his body. He searched behind the fridge but there was nothing but broken glass and a piece of chocolate that had melted and congealed. Then he started canvassing the room, rummaging through the junk, tossing aside clothes and pans, exposing the dirty tiles. He stomped his feet on the floor, kicked a kettle. Then he turned around, and only then spotted his mother. She was sitting on a plastic chair by the door, pressing her face into the small slit between two cardboard squares, looking out. He walked up to her. "Where?" he asked.

Prudence didn't answer.

"Where?" he asked again, tugging on her pants, hard. "Why did you take her away?" he cried. She didn't even notice him.

Alvin walked out the door and stood in front of her. He saw her eyes staring at him, filling with fear, then her hand reaching out and pulling the cardboard squares together until they concealed her completely. He waited there for a few minutes and gave up.

4.

HE LOOKED EVERYWHERE; behind the pay phone on the first floor, under the bench by the number 5 bus stop, between the display racks of the phone shop on the fourth floor. He asked every person he knew, from the man-with-the-bags to the old-lady-with-the-orange-scarf. He felt the words dissolving on his tongue. No one understood what he was talking about. A hamster-rabbit? What's that? And he, the whole time, throughout the entire desperate search, didn't know if he wanted to find his hamster-rabbit because he was worried about her or because he wanted to punish her.

It had been hours, and the missing hamster-rabbit refused to be found. Alvin was slowly coming to terms with the loss of his first and only pet, promising himself that by evening he'd forget about her. Passing the supermarket for the third time, he spotted her. She was going up the escalator to the fourth floor, sniffing the rail. Alvin broke into a run. He cut past three people on the escalator even though his mother said he should always wait patiently. He turned left and saw the hamster-rabbit slinking underneath the tables of the pizza parlor, nipping between the legs of the security-man-whose-son-died-in-the-war and slipping through the door and out of the station.

It was the smell that made him realize he was outside, the acrid scent of petrol and diesel coming from the buses and taxis. Alvin coughed and looked around. The words he knew could describe and define only some of the things he saw. The people zipping past him. The honking of the vehicles and the tall buildings. The problem was the things that were similar to what he knew, but not exactly the same. The buses that seemed particularly small, each with a slightly different color and shape. The signs brightening up the street in red, yellow, and green. The trees, which were significantly bigger than any tree he had ever seen inside the station, sprouting and spiraling into the sky, which was also different. Something about its clarity. As if it was a cleaner blue than the one he saw through the windows of the station. But before he had time to contemplate all this, he felt fear lunging at him. He was staring into the unknown.

Amid the jumble of background noise he heard the hamster-rabbit's whistle and then saw her, not far from him, trying to flee the stampede of feet surrounding her. A fat soldier with a big duffel bag accidentally kicked her, knocking her to the curb. He bent down, tried to see that she was okay, but the hamster-rabbit had already crossed the road, and Alvin hurried after her.

"Stupid kid," a driver who almost ran him over yelled. Alvin kept running, pulling away from the bustle of the main street and arriving at a big, oddly shaped parking lot. He couldn't see the hamster-rabbit but her whistles still filled his ears. He lay down on the cold asphalt, scanned the objects around him. It took him a few moments before he spotted her again. She was standing in front of him, next to a pair of brown sandals sporting dry, cracked feet. Then a chubby hand reached out and scooped up the hamster-rabbit, carrying her out of Alvin's view. He got up from the floor, sidled up against a minibus, and peeked through the front windshield. Not far from him stood a short, dumpy woman in an oversized black shirt. She had dark curly hair, a double chin, and small round glasses perched on the tip of her nose. He came around the minibus and stood in front of her. He watched her gazing at the hamster-rabbit with a serious expression, holding her in her wide hands, petting her with big, circular motions. The woman whispered something to the animal. She was about his mother's height, but clearly older.

When she saw Alvin standing close to her she jolted and almost dropped the hamster-rabbit. Her face flushed. She started shouting and it took Alvin some time to understand what she was saying. "Is this yours? . . . I mean . . . I'm sorry . . . I just saw her and . . . sorry, really."

She handed him the hamster-rabbit but he didn't take her, just kept listening to the small animal's whistles. They were light and calm, nothing like the noises she made when he held her.

"She's not mine," he said. Then he asked, "What's your name?"

"Shabtai. I mean, Anita," she replied. "Sorry, my head isn't screwed on straight today," she said and withdrew into her silence.

"Maybe you know what animal that is?"

The woman pushed her glasses up the bridge of her nose and stared at the animal, studying it up close. "It's a guinea pig, I think," she told Alvin with a loud, clear voice.

He thought it was a funny name. Guinea pig. "You take her home?" he asked.

Shabtai-I-mean-Anita hesitated and started to giggle. "I think so. I mean, why not? I have room for it. A little company could be nice," she mumbled and immediately backtracked. "Unless you want her, of course."

Alvin lifted his hand to pet the hamster-rabbit, but changed his mind. "No," he replied, then turned around and ran back toward the station. He thought he heard Shabtai-I-mean-Anita yelling something, but he wasn't sure.

Having crossed the road, he slowed down his pace and stopped by the big dumpster at the entrance. He wondered whether the trees inside the station would eventually grow as tall as the trees outside it. Then he looked at the people in the station. He decided he wouldn't move from his spot until he counted ten wearing a green shirt. He stood there for nearly an hour. After spotting the eighth person in a green shirt, he noticed his mother passing by. She was holding her bags, moving swiftly, and bumped into the cleaner with the orange vest who was pushing a big metal cart. A collection of computer keyboards and umbrellas scattered across the floor. Prudence bent down, tried to gather the loot while swarms of people surrounded her from every direction. Alvin entered the station and ran toward her.

Flies and Porcupines

SINCE THE DAY YOU ENLISTED, Yonatan, I've been trying to catch time. Literally catch it. I reach out with both hands, wait for a few moments to pass between my fingers, and quickly close my fists, trying to grab as many chunks of it as I can. At first I didn't catch anything, because catching time is truly tricky. After all, flies are a lot clumsier and I've never managed to catch a single one.

I remember the day I told you about it. It was a Friday. You came home exhausted after two weeks of guard duty. We were all sitting at the table, and Mom and Dad wouldn't even look at their plates until you finished wolfing down two whole servings. After dinner we sat in the living room and you started telling us stories. About how Itai spent his entire shift talking on the phone, and about Rozner the commander, and how you and Roee played tricks on him all day. And you went on and on about how nothing happened on that base, truly nothing, and that it was even safer than it was here at home, up north.

Later that evening you milled around the house and I followed you like a shadow. You shaved for a night out with the guys, but really you did it for Meital, who didn't like feeling she was petting a porcupine. And then, when we heard a switch go off in their bedroom, you drew closer to me and whispered that now you could tell me. Someone had almost infiltrated the outpost while Itai was on guard duty, and it was pure luck that Rozner happened to be on patrol and caught him. And that in two weeks you might be sent off to Gaza because there was a shitstorm going on over there. And you told me not to tell them a thing, because Mom was stressed out enough as is, and it wasn't good for Dad's blood pressure. But that I needed to hear it, because in a few years it might be me.

And I tried to commit everything to memory. Every piece of advice and warning, and every word out of your new military lingo. I even remember the tricks you played on Rozner. Finally, when you were about to go out, you asked me if I was making any progress with the girl I had told you about, and I explained I'd been busy. And when you asked what I had been busy with, I stood in front of you and mumbled awkwardly that I was trying to catch time.

"The last thing a ten-year-old needs is time," you said. "What could you possibly do with it?"

And since I honestly didn't know, I said I'd been meaning to stop anyway, which only ticked you off even more. You immediately demanded I show you how I tried to catch it, so I reached out, fingers spread wide, and you examined the distance between my hands, the speed of my catch, and strength of my grip.

"Well, no wonder you can't catch any, you've got no patience," you announced, and even though you were supposed to have headed out long ago, you demonstrated with your big hands how you have to wait for time to settle between your fingers. And the moment you caught a chunk of it, you shouted at me to bring a bottle, and I ran to the kitchen while you continued to wrestle with the chunk that almost slipped from your fingers, and only at the very last minute we managed to push it into the bottle. Panting and sweating, we looked at the bottle and saw the chunk swirling inside it like a guppy in a fishbowl. Then you told me you had to get going and that I shouldn't worry. "I've got plenty of time on my hands with all those guard duty shifts; I'll save some for you."

And then there was that day, when Mom wouldn't stop watching the news, and Dad just sat silently in the living room. And I, who was kind of bored, fooled around with time, trying to do what you taught me. And after a few moments, I felt it. It almost slipped between my fingers, nearly invisible, but I knew right away I was holding a chunk of time in my hands. I pulled it closer to me so it wouldn't escape, and Dad, who couldn't figure out what I was doing, started yelling at me to stop behaving like a child. Then Mom approached me and said he didn't mean it, but I knew he did.

From that moment on, I wouldn't stop catching time, tearing off bigger and bigger chunks of it. I think time didn't like my stealing from him. I tried explaining to him that he was infinite, and that all I needed was a few small pieces, but he wouldn't listen. He fought me over every tiny particle. At night the chunks would start acting up, trying to escape from the bottle, but I'd hold the cap down hard, wouldn't let them get out. I kept filling up the bottle throughout your entire shivah. Everyone was there. Your whole gang came with Roee. Rozner stopped by too, even cried a little. Meital couldn't make it, but don't worry, I'm sure she'll visit eventually, because despite what you may think, I know she always loved you, even when she felt like she was petting a porcupine.

Everyone came to pay their condolences, and I tried to appear mature and serious, but I didn't actually pay them any attention, I just kept trying to catch time. Even after the shivah. And when I stuffed that last piece in the bottle, I went to your room. The room no one had gone into in over a month. I passed by your guitar, the pile of Pink Floyd records on the floor and the copy of *The Lord of the Rings* lying on your nightstand, with the bookmark a few pages from the end. I walked up to the board Mom made you for your birthday. I looked at it real close, studying every photo a thousand times. I touched the board, dragged my finger across every photo, comparing them to one another, searching for the right one. Finally I chose the one we took on the beach on your birthday. Everyone was in it. Mom and Dad in the middle, you hugging Meital with one arm, and with your other, slapping me on the back. And we were all doubled over with laughter, because the American with the baseball cap who took the photo didn't quite understand which button to press.

I carefully removed the photo from the board and placed it on the bed. Gently, I opened the bottle and very slowly poured every last bit of the time onto the photo. And for three seconds, I was back there.

To tell you the truth, I hadn't remembered the slap being so hard.

I have since improved my technique and fill up three bottles a day (flies I can already catch with one hand, but I always let them go). And I've also been working on a new plan. Yes, it's brought my grades down, and I don't have much time for friends either, and everyone around here thinks it's foolish, dragging all these bottles and boxes into your room. If they had the energy they'd tell me as much, but they don't. But you, if you'd pop by for a moment, you'd understand right away. I want to fill this whole house with time. So much that it would last my whole life. And not only mine, but Dad's too, because his blood pressure isn't that great, and Mom's, because she's too tired to do anything. And with all that time we'd have with you, maybe we'd finally start living, instead of staying stuck forever in one still moment.

Acknowledgments

This book was published thanks to many good people.

Deborah Harris, my agent, who believed from the first moment, and is always there to give good advice (even when I call after midnight). Hadar Makov, who gave this book a real chance before it was published. Alma Cohen Vardi, who taught me that stories have a temperature, and other important lessons. Daniella Zamir, who translated the stories beautifully to English, and yet managed to keep their original Hebrew spirit. Noa Manheim and Kinneret Zmora Bitan Dvir, who opened the first door. Ben Schrank, Olivia Dontsov, and all the people at Astra, that helped the stories cross the Atlantic Ocean, and gave them a warm home.

Dr. Gal Raz and the others at the Immersive Media & Cognition Group, that helped me better understand narratives, and how they affect the human brain. Friends and family who read and commented on things I wrote, before I realized I was writing stories. My parents, sisters, and my grandfathers and grandmothers, who taught me to love good stories and Jerusalem. Neria, who was there since our first meeting in Havana.

And last, thank you, the reader, for visiting Jerusalem Beach.

Photo by Goni Riskin

ABOUT THE AUTHOR

Iddo Gefen was born in 1992 in Israel and currently resides in Tel Aviv. He works in neurocognitive research at the The Immersive Media & Cognition Group in Sagol Brain Institute, Sourasky Medical Center, and Tel Aviv University, exploring how storytelling can improve our understanding of the human mind. Iddo leads an innovative study to diagnose aspects of Parkinson's disease using storytelling and augmented reality. *Jerusalem Beach* is his debut collection, and recipient of the Israeli Minister of Culture Award (2017); Iddo won the National Library of Israel "Pardes" Scholarship for young writers (2019). His debut novel, *Mrs. Lilienblum's Cloud* Factory, will be published by Astra House.

iddogefen.jerusalembeach@gmail.com

ABOUT THE TRANSLATOR

Born in Israel in 1983, **Daniella Zamir** is a literary translator of contemporary Israeli fiction. She obtained her bachelor's degree in literature from Tel Aviv University, and her master's degree in creative writing from City University in London. She currently lives in Tel Aviv.